A Dress the Color of the Moon

JENNIFER IRWIN

GLASSSPIDERPUBLISHING

Edited by Vince Font
Cover design by Jane Dunnet
www.jane-dunnet.com
Published by Glass Spider Publishing
www.glassspiderpublishing.com

For Chase, Campbell, and Bailey.

Acknowledgments

Special thanks to my agent, Trodayne Northern, who guided me through the writing of this book. Trodayne and Leslie Varney at Prentis Literary did their very best to get *A Dress the Color of the Moon* picked up by a publisher while fighting an uphill battle. I am deeply grateful for their efforts. Their faith in me as a writer and dedication to helping me along the way has been a wonderful blessing.

To my tried and true beta readers, I'd be completely lost without your encouragement, detailed feedback, and the gift of your time while reading my pages. My words feel too small. I name them in no particular order: Jan Hargraves, Jim Caldwell, Chris Drum, Cary Fuller, Silvia Capistrano, Leonard Tillerman, Charlie Hargraves, Patricia Fairweather Romero, and Isabel Timerman.

To Carolyn Kavanagh, who gave me hours of her time on the phone so I could learn more about various subjects in the story of which I didn't have enough knowledge to make them sound real.

To my wonderful developmental editor, Andrew Wooddell. You kept me on track while recognizing that there was something special happening when I moved from first person to third person, and back and forth in time rather than telling me it was too complicated.

Heartfelt thanks to Tracy Christall, Michael Benedetto, and Silvia Capistrano, who spent many hours helping me flesh out the story and the characters. Every long weekend, poolside, game-watching, dinner, lunch, cocktail-hour, puzzle-solving chat gave me the seeds I needed to bring the characters to life.

To my amazing publisher, editor, and all-around great human, Vince Font at Glass Spider Publishing. Thank you for taking me under your wing. I'm honored to be a part of your team.

To Cary Fuller and Isabel Timerman, who were there for me during the final push. Cary nailed the nitty-gritty details, the grammar, tense, and timeline issues, which made all the difference. And to Isabel, who took out any unnecessary bad language and gratuitous smut because she felt I was too fine of a writer to fall into that trap.

To the passionate readers of *A Dress the Color of the Sky*, who encouraged me to write the sequel. My heart is full over the love that you have for Prudence Aldrich and your desire to know how she fares in the world after rehab.

To my inner circle, my family, my loves. Without you, I wouldn't be chasing the writing dream.

Finally, thank you to the readers and book bloggers on social media who give their undying support to the indie author community. You make everything worthwhile. Thank you for reading, reviewing, re-tweeting, reposting, taking gorgeous photos, and for spreading the word about the books you read that are published off the main grid. You epitomize the meaning of grassroots marketing.

The most common way people give up their power is by thinking they don't have any.
—Alice Walker

Chapter One: Prue Present

I chose to believe I was better. Five weeks earlier, I had checked myself into Serenity Hills for the most humiliating addiction. My hope was that I had left my pre-rehab sexcapades on the fabric-covered chair in Room 103. Within those four walls, the members of the Purple Group spilled their guts under therapist Mike's watchful eye. My raw, vulnerable insides had been wiped clean. It was time to face the trail of destruction I'd left behind in Los Angeles. I clung to the faint hope that rehab had provided me with the tools to finally make better choices.

The further I stepped from the sanctuary, the more I worried about the possibility of the old Prue making an unwanted appearance. One concerning thought plagued me: that the peaceful sensation I carried inside was nothing more than a façade. My life was a complete shitstorm. The anxiety checklist ran amok—getting a divorce from Nick, ruining my boy Christian's life, my friends finding out I was a phony, an eviction notice taped to the front door.

When the plane touched down, I powered up my cell for the first time in over a month. An onslaught of notifications dinged and chimed. I'd last seen my phone when I dropped it in the bin at the nursing station during check-in. Some texts probably had gone undelivered, but there were still more than I could bear.

I typed out a message to Christian, letting him know I'd landed safely. His visit during Family Week and everything he said was my reality check. Our chairs facing each other, Christian's trembling hands as he held a sheet of paper. My only instructions were to not speak but to acknowledge.

"I need a mother, not a friend," he said. "Spend time with me doing the things I like to do." The pause before he dropped the bomb. "Please don't leave me alone so much, especially not all night." A fire blazing through the house, Christian trapped. An intruder trying to break in or him getting violently ill with no one there to help. In rehab, the panic attacks often hit me at night, sweating, barely able to breathe, sick to my stomach.

I scrolled through messages from various men I'd kept in the rotation prior to checking into Serenity Hills. The abrupt detachment from technical devices had removed my ability to text so many guys, as previously was part of my daily routine. At rehab, I replaced sexting with healthy outer-circle activities like prayer and meditation. The interior designer in me caused distraction while visualizing my peaceful space—the colorful throw pillows, a tinkering fountain, and a Buddha figurine. A sense of permanence took me back to the time my landlord handed me an eviction notice while I was loading Christian in the car for school.

"Are we going to have to move?" Christian squirmed in the back seat. A barrage of questions rolled off his tongue. "Is that lady gonna kick us out? Will we have to live in our car?"

The cramped, overheated cabin closed in around me. I pressed my arms to my side to stop the rolling sweat. A little girl stood on the seat in front of me and smiled with her matching dimpled cheeks. I returned the smile while wondering how fifteen years later, the memory of holding my tiny, lifeless daughter in a dimly lit hospital room still haunted me. The nurse allowed me a few minutes alone before tearing her away from me. I took in my baby's face and swore there was a hint of dimples on her tiny cheeks. The pregnancy belly shrunk over time, but the grief remained like a bad friend I couldn't get rid of no matter how hard I tried.

An announcement blared over the intercom. I turned my attention back to my phone as I deleted texts from anyone I'd either flirted with or engaged in any sort of sexual relations with. I also removed them from my contacts. *Poof. Gone. As though they never existed.* Then Christian responded to my text.

Yay! I'll score a ride from the beach to the new place. A Snapchat popped up of him and a friend. The ocean sparkled in the distance.

I sent a Snapchat back, our preferred form of communication. A selfie giving the thumbs-up, figuring the new place he mentioned was the old house but not the place I'd been for the past five weeks.

The next message was from a woman I hadn't heard from in over a year.

Hey, it's Frankie we met at that wine thingy in Jackson Hole last year. I hope you remember me! We were with those assholes lol I just wanted to say hi & hope we can hang out soon ☺

Frankie and I had taken a break from our *dates* to visit the ladies' room. We shared lip glosses and secrets. She confessed to being a paid escort; I admitted to the same. I tallied up my new sober life's checks and balances list. A fine-tuned skill learned at Serenity Hills. Frankie might represent my pre-rehab life and be a potential bad influence, but I didn't want to judge her for how she lived her life just because I was changing mine.

Hey Frankie, sorry it took me so long to get back to you, been super busy.

15

I'd love to get together. Let's make a plan!

On my way to baggage claim, my phone buzzed. It took a minute to dislodge the device from my skintight jeans, and I criticized my fat ass for overeating and cursed the son-of-a-bitch in-house psychiatrist for refusing to let me use the gym. The truth came out in the designated smoking veranda at rehab—no one checked out with just one addiction. We were all cross-addicted. My addictions were stated out loud in group like a horn blast when a boat crossed the finish line in a regatta: sex addict, body dysmorphic, and love avoidant. I stopped walking. A man bumped my shoulder.

"Sorry," he said. He paused. His gaze moved from my face, down my torso, and back up again. The attention covered me with a coating of validation.

"Take a picture, it lasts longer," I said.

"I was going to ask you for your number, but never mind."

"Exactly," I said. He started walking then turned one more time while shaking his head. My phone chimed again.

Welcome home, Chickie Prue! I'm in baggage claim waiting for you.

I shot back the Spanish dancer emoji and stepped into the ladies' room. With my carry-on wedged between my feet, I gazed at my reflection. Five weeks without access to any beauty products had taken a toll. My once vibrant auburn hair had turned dark at the roots and brassy on the ends. The Chanel lipstick I'd checked in with was at the underground level. I dug into the tube with my fingernail and swiped some on my lips, then rubbed the rest on my cheeks. Still, my face looked different—calmer—perhaps even fewer worry lines, a reminder to keep up the daily meditations.

I glanced at my ass. *Dammit, I look like the national spokesperson for IHOP.*

Part of me wanted to head back in the direction of the plane, but I continued on my forward journey toward baggage claim. Within moments I spotted my best friend, Lily, through the bustling crowd.

A ticker tape in my mind—both of us getting stung by a swarm of bees, losing our parents within years of each other, making cocktails in our dorm room, skinny-dipping at the sandspit, my brother peeing on our heads from a tree. Lily brightened the baggage area with her smile, the years she'd spent in braces and nighttime headgear clearly worth it. She wore distressed jeans, espadrilles, and a celadon linen button-down knotted at the waist.

The quintessential California girl from Long Island.

"There you are." Lily opened her arms to me.

The simple act of hugging was our lifeline at Serenity Hills. Even Lily had been on the receiving end of countless embraces when she visited me during Family Week. She'd been a real trooper about it. Normally, she tended to be standoffish with strangers.

"I have a surprise for you." She lifted her heels off the ground as we did in our barre classes. "You and Christian have a new rental house."

"Now I know what Christian meant when he said *the new place.*" I bit a piece of cheek. "I figured that bitch landlord would end up evicting me." I inched myself closer to the moving carousel.

"Not evicted, moved." *Strategizing, negotiating, wheeler-dealer Lily.* "I thought you and Christian could use a fresh start and wouldn't mind Nick moving into your old place." She took the carry-on from my hand. "He ditched his wannabe bachelor pad and took over your lease. I moved your stuff out so he could bring his crap in. The whole process only took one day."

I gave her the stink eye at the mention of Nick, my soon-to-be ex-husband. A pit of rage boiled inside of me. "How does Nick get to swoop in and rent my house?" The bags began to drop at a high speed. "Where is he getting that kind of money when he claims to be broke?"

Could it be possible to love and hate someone at the same time? The situation made me want to scream and throw a tantrum on the airport floor like Christian when he was two. My foot tapped while I pictured my murder weapon. *I should have listened to Mike and committed to an extended three-month aftercare program.* I inhaled through my nose, counted to three, and exhaled. A 1960s woman released from the looney bin.

"Here's the thing, why not let Nick look like the hero?" Lily spoke with purpose, thought, and conviction, something I admired about her. "The upside is that Christian doesn't have to move twice, and his parents are living close together. Who cares where he's getting the money from as long as you're off the lease? That landlord was a complete nightmare." The tone of her voice rose.

"I'm scared." I gnawed on a fingernail. "I don't exactly have rent covered until I start back to work at the design firm. How much is it a month, anyway?"

Lily took the finger from my mouth. I tugged my earlobe with the other hand.

"I'm your landlord. You'll be renting from me." The same smile as when we were kids—sweet, self-assured, confident.

"The last thing I want is to be a burden." A man helped me lug my oversized suitcase from the conveyor belt—the bag filled with nothing but over-revealing rehab-inappropriate clothes.

"You've never been afraid of hard work. Find that inner grit you used to have back in NYC when you started in the design business.

You blew me away the way you lugged those massive fabric sample books all over town, working overtime and weekends to get the job done. You'll be back on your financial feet in no time." Lily slung my carry-on over her shoulder and headed to the car.

As I followed her through the maze of LAX, I prayed she was right. The car noticeably sank under the weight of my bags. I reached for my purse to offer to pay for parking then remembered loser girl spent her last few bucks on a pack of Twizzlers to eat on the plane.

"Hand me my wallet," she said.

A little kid who is dependent on everyone. My phone dinged with another message from Frankie.

Working evening shifts at Bare Elegance, so mornings r better. We could go for a walk or grab a coffee. I'm easy.

*   *   *

What impressed me about Lily was her talent for compartmentalizing her life. I would have been far better off if I'd managed to garner the same life-coping skills. Lily lost her father on 9/11 and remained in New York to care for her mother until she passed, even though she desperately wanted to leave.

Between Lily's family business and her husband, Binky, inventing an app that alerted people that something had fallen in their pool, they were financially set. A year before I checked into rehab, Lily and Binky had permanently moved to Los Angeles with their two children, Charlie and Madi. They purchased a contemporary-style house on the Strand in Manhattan Beach, which I decorated for them. They sold their home in Goose Neck Harbor furnished. Lily left it all behind without a passing thought.

As we drove down the Pacific Coast Highway, I wondered if this latest rental house purchase—hell, even her original move to LA—was her way of monitoring my disastrous life.

I'm good with that. I need watching.

"I'm beyond excited to show you the house. But first, I thought we could make a pit stop at our favorite spot."

I closed my eyes and could almost smell the ocean. "I dreamed about that rock in rehab."

We wound our way down the coastline to the sleepy neighborhood of Palos Verdes, which resembled the Italian Riviera with a hillside of barrel-tile roofs overlooking the sea. The sun sparkled on the water. When we found our spot, she grabbed a shopping bag from the back. We walked across scruffy grass to a narrow dirt path that edged along the cliff to sit on a flat boulder shaded by a tree.

"I came here a ton over the past five weeks since you've been gone," she said.

A surfer paddled for a wave and missed. My eyes welled up, and a tear rolled down my cheek. To be away from Serenity Hills felt both surreal and dangerous. No longer would I be monitored, and no longer could I find solace in any mistakes.

Lily clutched my hand with hers. "You're going to be fine. We both are because we have each other."

She unzipped a soft-sided cooler and pulled out two cans of champagne. She cracked one open, handed it to me, then opened hers.

"Must be weird to drink after so long, especially knowing that most of your rehab friends can't drink," she said.

I nodded, grateful that alcohol wasn't my addiction.

"Remember when Henry and I visited you at Edith Woodson and we popped that bottle Dom Perignon on the hood of my pickup?" she said. "I still can't believe I stole that from my dad and didn't get caught."

The bubbles tickled my nose. "How could I forget?" I laughed. "Back when we played that Grateful Dead cassette to death."

Lily flicked a bug from her thigh. "We were so full of hope back then. That's how I feel right now, like we're both getting a fresh start." The sun turned a soft tangerine, sinking and breathing against the horizon. We clinked cans. "Cheers to lifelong friendships and new beginnings."

"I'm not cured, you know." Not at all trying to be morose. "With all I've been through, I can't be fixed in five weeks. I'm terrified of letting everyone down."

A surfer turned his board to face the shore and vigorously paddled. The wave lifted him up, and he soared down the face. I assumed he was void of any consuming thoughts over the possibility of drowning.

"I know," Lily said. "All you can do is your best."

*   *   *

The cottage rested on a side street a few blocks from the beach. It was a ten-minute drive from my new home to Lily and Binky's strand house. Her daughter Madi was going into fourth grade. Charlie would be starting eighth with Christian.

The Spanish-style home had a green patch of grass and a bright-orange front door. A post-and-rail fence created a buffer between the house and the street. White rosebushes and bougainvillea dotted the entrance. The air was filled with the scent of fresh wood chips.

I followed Lily inside. Each piece of furniture was positioned exactly where I would have put it. I peeked into the master bedroom, where everything I owned was neatly arranged, including linens on the bed.

Lily squealed from behind me. "Your vibrator is in the drawer. I figured you must be dying to use it."

A rush of heat wound through my pelvis. "Thank God," I replied with a grin, but the harsh reality of life hushed the excitement over the vibrator.

Things to do: Talk to Nick about custody, call Sam at Patrick Dunn Interiors, find a females-only Sex Addicts Anonymous meeting, and make an appointment with Dr. Sheryl O'Brien.

"I'm thrilled you approve of where I put everything. It's not easy being best friends with an interior designer." A soft apricot light filtered through the window, casting a glow over Lily's complexion. I wondered if I would have done the same selfless things for her.

"I feel guilty that you did all this for me."

"Are you kidding? I loved every second of it. I didn't unpack all the kitchen boxes or hang artwork since I figured you'd want to do that yourself." Lily admired her handiwork. "I almost forgot, your car is in the garage, keys to the house and car are on a hook by the back door." She pointed toward the general location. "Binky has been surfing a lot with the boys."

Binky in boardshorts, wet hair, toned abs, walking up the beach with a surfboard lodged under his arm. The unwanted addict crept in, invading my mind like a worm burrowing a hole in my brain. A cunning worm who will try to squeeze its way into any crack in my armor.

"Awesome." Her husband was like a father to Christian, filling the void Nick left behind with the one thing a kid needs most—time. "Thanks." I stood there with nothing to offer. "I'm going to start working so I can pull my financial weight."

My phone buzzed. I hesitated to check it but remembered I had a child who might need me. Nick's name loomed in the notification.

Welcome home. I would love to see you and drop off your four-legged furry friend, Lou. He missed you and I'm free tonight.

"Nick just texted me. Reality."

"Well, that didn't take long." Lily's hands were set firmly on her hips. Had I ever known Lily to fear, the look on her face would have been it, but Lily never got scared.

"I made my decision. The whole thing between us has run its course. I have to tell him." A light breeze from the open window blew my hair around my face. "I'm dying to pick up Lou but not ready to face Nick."

We lingered in the driveway, and Lily gave a friendly wave to a car passing by while my arms remained glued to my side.

"I was wondering about my piano," I said.

An hour of tinkering on the keys would be a healthy outer-circle activity.

I have to call Mrs. Sutton, my childhood landlord, and tell her how she helped me to survive my childhood. It was more than her gift of my education and a baby grand piano. She filled the half my mother left empty.

"Ugh, I was avoiding that one." Lily tucked the front tail of her shirt into her jeans. "Nick apparently sold it."

"What a tool."

Lily stepped into the car and pulled the seatbelt across her chest. "Text me if you want to hang out later."

I grabbed my phone to message Nick back. *I can't tonight, I just got home and need to settle in. Can I swing by now for Lou?*

The response bubbles appeared in an instant. *Wow, let me know when you can squeeze me in your schedule. I'm not home. You still have a key so let yourself in.*

I double-clicked on the message to add a thumbs-up symbol. At least that way he knew I received his passive-aggressive text with no intention of responding.

The window between Christian coming home from surfing and Nick catching me at his house was small. I drove over to my old rental to pick up my dog. It proved more than difficult not to snoop. The once warm and inviting home appeared chaotic and unkept. Dents in the wall-to-wall carpet where my furniture had once rested like ghosts from my past. A familiar breeze blew in the kitchen window. I gazed out the patio where my old life played out. Christian skateboarding in the driveway, and me pulling weeds in the garden with no clue where Nick was or when he would be home.

When Lou spotted me, his tail moved so forcefully that the whole lower half of his body wagged too. I searched for his leash and finally found it under a pile of mail. When I turned to grab Lou and leave, I glanced in the sink—two wine glasses, one of them rimmed in hot-pink lipstick. An unexpected sense of relief wound its way through me.

Lou licked my arm the entire drive home. When I opened the door, he ran straight to Christian's room and jumped onto his bed.

With crossed legs, I settled on the floor of my room. I opened the meditation app and set the timer for ten minutes. My legs were crossed underneath me and both palms faced toward Heaven, I closed my eyes and cleared all thoughts from my mind.

Planet Earth was beating like a heart. I zoomed in closer and closer to find myself, sitting in my new room. *I'm as small as the pin tip, but there is room for me. My heart moves in rhythm with the Earth. With every beat, the hardened edges of my heart soften and smooth.*

After meditation, I sat at the kitchen table to put together a to-do list, but I was interrupted by the sound of a car pulling up the driveway. My child bounded out of the back seat and unleashed his surfboard from the roof rack. I hopped up to greet him.

"Hey, Christian." There was a reassuring glimmer in his eyes. *My Christian.*

He dropped his board on the grass. I mouthed *thank you* and waved as the carpool driver mom drove away. Perhaps this woman considered me an absent mother—or worse, a bad one. I wondered what Christian told his friends at school when they asked where I had been the past five weeks. *My mom's in rehab for sex addiction.* I reenacted the possible explanations, almost wishing that for his sake I had been an alcoholic or drug addict instead. Any leak of such comprising information could be used to bully him. I resorted to the Serenity Hills feelings chart—*I feel pain, guilt, and shame.* The sickening thought of my son's sheer embarrassment over others finding out such awful things about his mom.

Christian's salty hair had turned two shades blonder than when I last saw him during Family Week. The sun-bleached hair showed well with his tan skin and a dotting of freckles across the bridge of his nose. An inch of the beach clung to his ankles.

"I'm glad you're home." Christian wrapped his arms around me. I savored the moment, knowing he was soon entering the fiercely independent teen years.

"Me too." I didn't want to ride him over the sand the minute he got home but felt as though I had no choice. I announced, "Please wipe off your feet so we don't bring the beach in the house."

I held the door while he brushed off his lower extremities with a towel. Not the time to pick a fight over something so small. Grains crunched as I moved across the kitchen. I jotted the number *one* on a sheet of paper: *Buy a hose.*

I wanted to enjoy the last few days of summer with Christian. He would be starting eighth grade next week, and with it came the added parental responsibilities. My life was about to become crazy busy — shopping for clothes, school supplies, all the driving, helping with homework, and the burden of extracurricular activities.

Christian draped himself in a chair with a hungry look on his face, and I realized I'd forgotten to buy groceries. Out of instinct, I checked the fridge. There was a fresh container of guacamole and a bag of tortilla chips resting inside. Lily had stocked the house with all the basics. I set the chips and guac on the table in front of him with a glass of water.

"What do you think of the new house?" I pulled up a chair across from him.

"I haven't stayed here yet." He chugged the water.

"I love this house," I said.

I vowed to keep the lines of communication open with a balance between being his parent and not invading his personal space.

"Your dad and I decided that you will keep living with me and visit with him when he has time."

Christian dipped a chip in the guacamole. "Please don't get back with Dad." His expression told me he wasn't messing around. "Dad doesn't love you. He doesn't know how to love." He wiped the crumbs from his mouth with the back of his hand. "You both seem happier when you're not together, and I'm happier too."

"I appreciate you expressing how you feel," I said. "I'm not planning on getting back together with him. We will always be your parents, and we both love you very much."

"I'm so relieved." The worry lifted from his face.

"My focus is to make our lives better, work hard at my career, and continue to heal."

"Cool."

He pushed the tortilla chips to the middle of the table. I had no clue where Lily put the chip clips. Before rehab, something minor like that would have stressed me out. It was refreshing to be able to leave the bag and not concern myself with perfection.

"I came over here with Lily and Charlie to organize my room." Christian headed down the hallway, and I followed. "Ta-da!" He raised his arms for the big reveal. There was a built-in desk with a computer station along the wall, a tall bookcase, and a shelf to display his Dungeons and Dragons figurines. An electric drum set was tucked in the corner. "Isn't this awesome?" He lay down on his bed.

"It looks exactly like your old room, only in a new house."

Christian nodded. "I know."

We exchanged a few stories, doing our best to fill in the blanks of the weeks apart. It was endearing to listen to my son's voice, to hear the openness of it. It gave me hope that I might not have messed him up too badly and that what they say about children's elasticity might be true.

After dinner and a bit of television, Christian put himself to bed. I kissed him goodnight and left his door ajar. Then I went to each room, seeing what remained of the unpacking.

There were things I missed while in rehab. One of them was my mother's mahogany jewelry box. I picked up the box from my bureau and sat it next to me on the floor. The dark wooden container symbolized so many moments in my life. I knew it was the right place to keep my baby's ashes.

The lid squeaked as I lifted it open. Like a Russian nesting doll, inside the box was a smaller one which held my daughter. I brought the urn to my mouth and kissed it and told her I loved her.

There were times when I had drowned in her ashes. I gave myself permission to wallow. The mourning process never ended. There were ups and downs, but the ache in my heart became a reminder of the childhood abuse I had survived, and the indelible mark it had left on me.

I set the smaller box aside and looked at the few baubles that belonged to my mother. I pulled them out, pressing each piece up to my nose, searching for the familiar scent of her perfume which was long gone.

I ran the tub and hunted for the best bath bomb or bubble bath I could find in my haphazard collection of products. As I eased into the scented baptismal waters, a flash of goosebumps covered my body. I sank in deep and turned off the faucet with my toes. With closed eyes, I prayed to God for the strength to go on and begged His forgiveness. There were days when I wondered why I'd been chosen to endure so much hardship, but I believed there was a reason for my suffering. God had a plan for me. I trusted Him and the journey He had laid out for me. When my fingertips were thoroughly wrinkled, I stepped out of the bath to savor my first evening alone in five weeks.

Chapter Two: Prue Past

Everyone referred to Mike as *The Great Oz*. When Alistair was strug-gling with the idea of never drinking again because it would lead di-rectly to using cocaine, I convinced him to schedule a private therapy session with Mike. Anyone who committed to checking into a five-week rehab program was fully acknowledging their life needed fix-ing. Alistair couldn't be delusional enough to believe Mike held the magic bullet to keep him off cocaine forever. He happened to be a therapist, a great one too, but he was not a superhero with superpow-ers. When I stepped out of my evening appointment with Mike, Alistair was outside the door leaning against the railing.

"Hey," I said. Mike stood behind me in the doorway of his small office. "I'm glad you decided to take my advice."

His eyes were purple and swollen. "Almost a full moon." He glanced at Mike. "You ready for me?"

"Yup," Mike said.

Alistair gave me an easy wave as he passed. When the door closed I looked up, searching for answers. The moon kept its secrets, but I remained hopeful.

I strolled across the grass separating the work buildings from the patient residences. No better time than now to do an emotional recap of my session with Mike. There were days when the private therapy sessions seemed hard and left me hopeless, and this was one of those sessions. A stressful phone conversation with Nick earlier had jangled my nerves. He unraveled me like a knitter undoing bad stitches. After the call, no one could calm me down. I lay down on the lawn and gazed at the sky. The brightness of the moon washed out the stars, but I still managed to find one to wish on. Time moved to a different rhythm in rehab. Some days blew by while others dragged out with no end in sight. There was not much alone time, and I cherished this moment of peace. I tended to be one of those people who lacked focus with any sort of distractions around.

As Mike prescribed, I pictured my life with Nick and without him. I could feel the tears surfacing, the answers to the tough decisions not coming as easily as I had hoped and imagined they would.

I dragged the back of my hand across my nose and looked off in the distance. A figure approached but I couldn't tell whether it was a resident or an employee. It didn't take long for the shimmering light of the moon to reveal Alistair. Time, once again, playing it fast and loose.

He bent down to pick up a stick and began peeling the bark. I felt like a creepy voyeur and turned away. When I glanced up, his shoulders had slumped forward in defeat. My curiosity dug at me over what had unfolded in his private therapy session. Especially the shared secrets.

Alistair glanced in my direction. Squinting through the moonlight, he spotted me. As he approached, he quickened his pace with that smooth, confident gait of his. I stood and waited for him to come closer before speaking.

"Hey," he said. He seemed distracted in thought but pleased to see me. "I'm having a rough night."

"Me too," I said, avoiding his gaze while peeling a jagged cuticle.

An awkward silence was exchanged between us.

Alistair tossed the stick. "Sorry to hear that," he said.

I kicked off my sandals, signaling that I wanted to stay and talk things out. The game of pretend came easily, as it helped me survive my childhood—a stringed quartet playing music, me in a colorful dress, Alistair thinking I was the most beautiful woman in the world.

We drew closer together. My heart pounded. He extended his hand, a vulnerable gesture yet one I was hesitant to accept.

I craved human contact, to be touched, to be wanted. After some resistance, I relaxed beside him, my legs crossed beneath me. I raked through the blades until my hand paused next to his, grazing skin to skin. An electric current coursed through me. His eyes met mine, our faces illuminated by the moonlight.

"Let's pretend we're anywhere but here." Alistair picked at the grass and laid the random blades in a pile next to him. "Perhaps a concert in the park."

He caught me staring. My cheeks burned. He inched closer until the warmth of his breath was on my lips. We closed the space between us. Our mouths began searching for answers. All of my problems disappeared, sealed with a kiss.

"I'm sorry." I pulled away from his grasp. "This is wrong for both of us."

"Please stay. I need to talk to someone." His eyes begged. I ignored the fire in my pelvis, the part of my body I could not control.

"I'll stay."

"I'm trying to figure out how my childhood experiences may have led to my coke addiction." I took in his stunning profile as he rubbed his thumb and index finger across his trimmed beard. "Mike said I might have to go backward to move ahead."

"I agree," I said, working on my listening skills and fighting my strong desire to interject, feel important, give advice—nothing more than another way to fill the void from when I was a kid.

"Tell me about your mom." I crossed my legs beneath me.

"Are you sure?" Alistair pursed his lips. I nodded. "My mother raised me on her own—she worked nights. I find it difficult to discuss her, but I know I must."

I admired the lines of his face, the aquiline nose, dimpled chin, and chiseled jaw. "Go on. Tell me everything."

The moon rose over our heads as Alistair shared the painful parts of his childhood with me. Rather than focus on my physical attraction and his magnificent face, I dug into his pain and listened. That was the best thing I could do for him as a friend. We all needed someone to listen, we all wanted our voices heard.

I glanced at my mother's watch. "It's getting late. I better head back to the room."

"Thank you," Alistair said. "For everything."

"That's what friends are for." I opted against bringing up the kiss. "Would you mind waiting a moment so we aren't walking together?" Reality setting in; my life was a disaster, and I was a rule-breaking train wreck.

"Goodnight, sweet Prudence."

I turned and walked toward my room. A giddy yet nervous energy swirled in my stomach, and I hoped he would keep what happened between us a secret.

*　　*　　*

Since the shared kiss with Alistair and confessing my indiscretion to Mike, I moved slower than normal that morning. I spent a little too long choosing an outfit and was officially late. My thoughts about Alistair, our conversation, and kissing him were close to obsessive, which concerned me. When I hit the main walkway, I kicked it up to a light jog. Gloria, my rehab bestie, was a few steps ahead. My pace picked up enough to catch her, which resulted in arriving at the meeting all sweaty. If you barely moved in Arizona, you dripped with sweat. "Hey."

"Yay. I love it when we're both late." Gloria's flip-flops snapped with every step. I glanced at her peachy butt cheeks lifting and lowering. She was in her uniform of leggings and a Vegas resort logo tee. She turned the most basic attire into a barrage of sensuality overload completely by accident. *I would die for that ass.* "So hard to wake up today, like I have bricks on my head," she said.

Her bricks, I figured, might be from weaning off Xanax and a combo platter of antidepressants.

"You look cute," she said. Her pillowy lips made me want to take a long nap.

"Thanks." I took the compliment with a smile. Next step: believe the words.

"No time to brush my hair, but I did brush my teeth." Gloria flashed her pearly whites. I cherished the camaraderie we had built. She lived two doors from mine. We hated our roommates and loved "girly" activities like painting our nails and wondering why our eyebrows were more like evil stepsisters and less like twins. Some friendships felt forced. With her, it was effortless.

I let Gloria enter Room 103 first. She tended to be anxious if she didn't sit in the same seat every day, which had to be next to me. Then I felt pressure to make sure I sat next to her. A vicious cycle.

Mike leaned against his desk, patiently expecting two stragglers to walk in at any moment. He never came across as irritated or upset. Since checking into Serenity Hills, I realized that when Nick expected me to do something wrong, I lived up to his expectations. When Nick grew suspicious, it made me want to cheat. My rehab counselor had the opposite effect because he saw the best in me. Mike saw the best in everyone.

As I beelined for my seat, I noticed Mike's new haircut. In rehab, any sort of change from my daily routine became accentuated and somewhat disconcerting. I breathed easier after discovering my favorite spot remained unoccupied. The moment my butt hit the chair, Mike pressed play on the boombox. The lulling sound of meditation music filled the air. Time to quiet the mind using the processes we learned through trial and error. Some days it seemed easier than others.

I struggled to focus, knowing that any second Alistair would come barreling in. The seconds ticked in my head. *One one-thousand, two one-thousand, three one-thousand.* I strove to fake the inner peace expected of us. When the door blew open, I looked up. His chest heaved. A layer of sweat glistened on his sublime face.

Alistair grabbed the last available chair and grunted when his lanyard hooked around the rolled-up paper tucked under his arm. It took everything in my power to not burst out laughing. I found humor in the worst scenarios. Mike informed me that finding humor in difficult situations meant I was avoiding my emotions. I figured he was probably right, like when my stepfather beat me with a belt and I couldn't stop laughing because I didn't want him to know it got to me. With my eyes squeezed shut, I suppressed the laugh that wanted to spill out until the music stopped.

Alistair had transferred to my group after a misunderstanding with his other leader. He had bravely boycotted an assignment when the original therapist asked him to drag around a bright-red vinyl block dangling from a long, clanging chain for the rest of his time in rehab. The foam monolith symbolized that if Alistair continued drinking alcohol, he would end up using cocaine. One vice preceded the other. Alistair had chopped up the vinyl-covered foam block and left the misshapen blobs piled outside the counselor's office.

I could appreciate it on some level. As someone who tended to overreact to even healthy bits of anger after so many years with my evil stepfather, Raging Richard, I fought my overeager fight-or-flight that screamed for me to run and hide. Since Alistair checked in a week behind me, he thankfully missed hearing my timeline and "meeting" Raging Richard. I had learned that it was far more relaxing to be in a meeting and not in the spotlight. I kicked back and waited for the show to begin.

"Alright," Mike said. "We have a lot to do today. I'm going to need everyone's complete and total attention." His eyes bounced around the room. I assumed he was talking directly to me, but he focused on one of the other "inmates" so I rested easy.

Mike tapped his fingertips together. He dressed in a conservative manner but wore his clothes well. His muscles filled every inch of the sensible no-iron khakis. His button-down stretched from his expanding bicep when he took Alistair's rolled-up paper. "Are you ready to present your timeline?"

Not sure why he asks when the answer is always yes.

"I'm not having the best day," Alistair said. "Between switching groups and vanquishing the demons of my past, I'm quite drained." He kept his eyes on the timeline. Ever since the kiss, I avoided him and tried to squelch my brewing sexual desire. I saw zero benefits to starting a romance in rehab, but I couldn't help but fantasize about what it might be like to have him inside of me, his smooth skin pressed against my breasts.

Dammit, Prue, get your head back in the game.

"Let's start with introductions." Mike signaled for Alistair to begin. He had an undeniable power over us. At times I wondered what would happen if everyone started to boycott the assignments or hurl a chair through the window. *A rehab coup.*

To me, Mike's presence was synonymous with safety. He conveyed more than physical strength. The way he spoke and carried himself, I couldn't imagine Mike being anything other than skilled at negotiating with an out-of-control addict. His kind blue eyes softened the dangerous edge his defined angular muscles gave off. A classic Hollywood jawline, but it bore a noticeable hook scar. Its twin resided above his left eyebrow. The whole picture screamed *I am sensitive and evolved—a nice enough guy, but don't fuck with me.*

Per the norm, Alistair's outfit proved to be the highlight of my day. He wore dark jeans, fresh white sneakers, and a faded green tee. I assumed he paid dearly for the fade. Alistair didn't appear to be the type to keep worn-out things. I parked my gaze on his movie-star looks for a little too long. When I turned away, Mike stared at me with a *you've been warned* expression.

Alistair sipped from his water bottle, the classic stall tactic we all used to avoid the inevitable. "Right, I'm Alistair, coke addict, sex addict, and love avoidant."

"Thank you," Mike said. "Continue around the room and introduce yourselves before Alistair begins his timeline."

He instructed Gloria to go first. I didn't hear a word of what anyone said. Whenever I said my crap out loud, my heart pounded so hard my shirt moved across my chest like an alien was trying to burst through. After we all spoke, Alistair crawled to the middle of the room and stretched his paper out on the floor—two sheets taped together to make one, which I hadn't seen before.

It's going to be a long day.

*   *   *

Alistair confessed to a tinge of relief after his mother died from breast cancer—a lump that had spread through her body like a drop of ink in water. His self-diagnosed survival mechanism was to suppress his anger. According to Alistair, anger was pointless and didn't change a thing.

"Did you cry when your mother passed?" Mike's voice drilled a hole in the thickness Alistair had created with his account. I knew most of us empathized with him all too well. We hung on Alistair's words like clouds in a deep-blue sky.

Alistair crossed his legs as a well-behaved kindergartener should. "No."

"Continue." Mike's pen bobbed across the pad with a life of its own.

"My mother arranged for me to live with the landlord until I turned eighteen so I wouldn't be deemed an orphan." Alistair took a tattered photo from his breast pocket. "This is the only picture I have of me and my mum."

"Would you like to share it with the group?" When Mike asked, we knew Alistair had to say yes.

Alistair nodded.

When the picture landed in my hands, I took an imprint with my mind camera. She was a natural beauty. A coat of envy wove its way through me. *His mom was prettier than me.*

"On my mom's deathbed, I found out my birth father was an American ambassador."

I braced myself for the gory part of his timeline, the part that had landed him in rehab.

"As an adult, I see how weird it is that my mum paid a coworker of hers to take my virginity." He coughed. I shifted in my chair. *This is finally getting interesting.* "My mother wanted me to understand a woman's body and be an experienced lover." His cheeks turned mottled and red. I pictured them doing it. It was both sick and intriguing. *I bet he is a champ in bed.* With Mike breathing down my neck, I feigned disinterest.

"What else?" Mike redirected the conversation, I guessed, to avoid triggering us.

"Right, sorry." Alistair glanced in my direction. "My birth father happened to be married, so there was to be no evidence of their affair." He ran his hands along the edge of the paper. "He told her to handle it when she found out she was pregnant with me." He rolled up his shirtsleeves.

"How did you feel knowing that your mother had kept this secret of who your father was from you for all those years?" Mike could wait all day for the reply.

Alistair stared at the ceiling as though the answers lay within the soundproof tiles. "I'm sure she had her reasons."

"But how did you feel?" Our leader held the bone and rarely let go.

"Angry, I suppose." Alistair ignored our guide better than anyone

I had seen. It wasn't easy to avoid Mike's persistence. It was clear he was not going to let this one go.

"Go on." Mike dug into us to find the source of what drove us to rehab. The story ran far deeper than the actual addiction. It all flowed from our past.

"Many therapists told me I have obsessive-compulsive disorder although I resist the diagnosis. Since checking in here, they said it yet again, so I believe it might be the truth."

"Elaborate," Mike said.

Alistair rubbed his nose. "When I was a kid, I kept a flashlight next to my bed and an extra set of batteries in the bedside drawer."

I imagined his survival mechanisms left him feeling small and meaningless, just as mine did for me.

"Were you afraid your mother might forget to pay the electric bill?" I asked, forgetting to follow the hand-raising protocol.

Mike nodded. He acknowledged that I had more to say. One of the positive things about sharing was that we were less like freaks and weirdos when someone else had similar things happen to them.

"I have anxiety when my gas tank gets below a quarter because my mother used to run out all the time," I said.

Mom telling Henry and me to push the car while she steered to the side of the road. She left us alone while she walked to the gas station, with no clue if or when she would return.

"Solid stuff," Mike said. "As children, we have experiences that can instill fear and cause us pain. As adults, we overcompensate to ensure these things won't happen again."

We let his words sink in. The semicircle of heads bobbed. We knew what he was saying. We had compensated.

"What I'm trying to do here is to help you understand that you aren't children anymore. You have control over your tank and whether your home is light or dark."

No matter what he says, I'm never letting my gas tank past the quarter mark. Not ever.

Gloria wiggled in her chair. My stomach rumbled. Mike glanced at the clock. "Alright, let's take a break for lunch. Be back here in one hour."

Chapter Three: Prue Present

With a towel wrapped around my body and dripping wet hair, I faced my closet head-on. The old me plotted outfits while in the shower. Beauty routines came right back; fashion, not so much.

The frantic pace of my old life had become a distant memory. I accomplished only a fraction of the things I used to squeeze into a day. There were unwritten expectations of those who worked as decorators to represent the industry in chic, updated fashion that resonated with our design style. The weather was unseasonably warm because August was usually touted as one of the most temperate months. On my first day back to work, I wouldn't be climbing any ladders, so I chose a silk dress with an easy drape in a moss-green print.

Nothing else in my closet fit due to the extra ten pounds I'd gained from being a sloth in rehab. After hurling a few dresses to the floor, I coached myself. *I will lose weight, it will just take some time.*

I had no idea if anyone at work knew my whereabouts for the past five weeks—a thought that made me nauseous. If I worried about what everyone thought about me, I wouldn't be able to walk out the door.

The parking lot at Patrick Dunn Interiors was filled with a variety of SUVs, the essential accessory for those privy to what the job was really about. The backs of the vehicles piled with fabric sample books, shopping bags, a toolbox, oversized pillows, Schumacher,

Brunschwig and Fils, chintz, silks, mohair, the list went on.

Sam King and I had jockeyed for the head position under Patrick before he moved into semi-retirement. Sam won.

I parked, reapplied lipstick in the fluorescent car mirror, and took a moment to gather myself. While I stared at the entrance, I came to the realization that my competitive spirit was nonexistent.

As I opened the car door, Sam's assistant pulled up beside me.

Nothing bad happened, it will all work out.

We exchanged niceties. She hoped I had a lovely vacation, a clue about what Sam told everyone.

The first meeting on Sam's schedule showed my name. His assistant confirmed I still owned my old office, a bonus, so I dropped my tote bag beside the desk and headed to my meeting with Sam.

Entering Sam's workspace was stimulation overload. A variety of inspiration boards were scattered about the room. Eclectic art decorated the walls. A human bust draped with scarves, beads, and talismans collected from around the world. Zebra skin partially covered the custom-stained, hand-honed French plank floors. His glass-topped desk was full of notes, fabric swatches, and sheets of paper with loosely sketched ideas. The organized chaos soothed both the left and right sides of my brain. Every single item created a glorious canvas of imagery. I stood in the presence of a creative genius. Nothing in Sam's office happened by accident. Two elaborate design boards rested against the wall, his ready position for presenting to clients. The desk stirred a memory of me kneeling beside it, Sam's pants around his ankles.

"She's alive!" Sam's small, round glasses gave his face a chic but inviting appearance. "My darling, I missed you." I loathed his hugs. His eye pattern moved from my shoes to my hair and back down again. "You look healthy." I took the hit with a smile.

"I'm glad to be back. I obviously need the work."

"I bet you do after all that world travel." His tone was mocking and curt. "We are busy, busy." We were an awkward couple who had engaged in mutually agreed-upon extracurricular sexual activities but knew better than to discuss the past. He sat on an Eames chair and I chose the loveseat covered in the hot new lavender shade making its way into everyone's homes. "Tell me. How are you?"

"Great." I fussed with my dress. He leaned over the Lucite coffee table and touched my knee. I glanced at his hand. He removed it. "What projects do you want the most help with?" The boss gave instructions once. I beat myself up for forgetting to bring a pen and pad. Sam noticed my lack of preparedness, strolled to his desk, grabbed a few things, and dropped them on my lap. "Thanks." I took copious notes while he bombarded me with details.

Teddy knocked lightly as he walked in. Another designer who started the month before my breakdown. His wardrobe consisted of an impressive array of over-the-top colors and a mix of patterns. I'm not sure he owned socks, he wore them so rarely. Today was no different sporting bare ankles and fitted floodwater pants. His shoes ranged from Italian loafers to trendy name-brand sneakers. The biggest shocker was that he claimed to be straight. *I am waiting for that shoe to drop.* His girlfriend, a clueless blonde whom I loathed, had been my client and exemplified everything I hated about the design business. I passed the project over to Teddy because she was an uppity, over-demanding bitch who wanted everything yesterday. Teddy thanked me for passing the hottie off to him and how easily she made decisions. The two of them fell in love at first sight. I didn't believe a word he said. Numerous people in the office told me that he talked shit about me behind my back.

"Prudence, what a nice surprise." Teddy dropped a bag of samples on the desk then sat beside me on the loveseat. "Are you staying awhile?" He swooped in for a kiss. I moved the wrong way and he smacked one right on my lips.

"I'm planning to." The pad slid from my lap and dropped to the floor with a thud. When I bent over to pick it up, Teddy's eyes bore through my back. I prayed no fat rolls billowed over my bra strap.

"This girl has been with me since the beginning. I can't live without her," Sam said with the same half-smile as when he wanted me to suck his dick in the parking lots of restaurants. He would lure me there under the pretense that we needed to talk.

"I'm going to get to work." My lard ass could barely lift off the sofa.

"Let's have lunch," Sam said.

"Fine," I replied.

"Great to have you back," Teddy said as though he was my boss. He remained on the sofa, and I was sure they would gossip about me after I left.

"There's a new seafood restaurant on Manhattan Avenue. I'll have my assistant send you the address. Meet me there at one," Sam added just before I made my grand exit. My dress stuck to my armpits. *Shit, I forgot to put on deodorant.* I stepped into my office and closed the door, grateful to make it through the first meeting. The battle wasn't over, but I had faced the tiger. *I have fabulous new skills.*

My office became a sacred space. I refused to engage in illicit activities in my personal space with Sam. It was my sanctuary, where I sought respite from the pressures of work. At Serenity Hills, I wracked my brain over how Sam and I had crossed the line from business friends to friends-with-benefits. The task of blowing him moved from exciting to a chore to downright disgusting in the span of three weeks. His insatiable sex drive unnerved me, and his constant begging became a source of contention. I should have talked more about Sam in my sessions with Mike.

I scanned my office. My favorite pink roses sat in a vase on my desk. A small card rested next to the flowers. I dug under the envelope and tore across the paper.

P-

I have missed you. This office is dull, dull, dull without you.

Love,

Sam

I unpinned a photo from my bulletin board and stared at it. A woman beginning to spiral but unwilling to see her behavior as a problem. Sam's arm draped around my shoulder, his eyes locked on me while I laughed and looked at the camera. I tucked it in the drawer, not wanting to be reminded of the affair, but unable to completely discard the past.

My MacBook had a light coating of dust that I swiped off with my hand. I powered it up and told myself to take things one step at a time. An old screensaver of a young Christian popped up, which lifted my spirits a bit. I jotted a to-do list, fabrics to be pulled, and which showrooms to visit. Most of the important emails came from Sam as he prepared for my return. I could tell by the tone that he missed me and my work ethic. One email in particular caught my eye.

We've landed a huge new client who specifically requested to work with a woman. Congrats. What a way to start back! I'm not going to lie, I've never seen anyone request a gender. This guy must have checked out our website and laid eyes on you, or maybe someone from your past? Either way, don't fuck it up. His budget is a million for a loft. Not sure the location yet but he's coming into town and wants to set up a meeting xx Sam

It irritated me that Sam ended emails with two kisses. My mind wandered back to how it had begun and what I could do to stop it. It baffled me why I had chemistry with men who I would never consider as life partners. Sam had confessed his undying love for me, but I never pictured him as someone I would want to be with long-term. I didn't want him, and he secretly resented me for it.

*   *   *

I survived sitting through a pleasant yet uneventful lunch with Sam. He did, however, insinuate that he would enjoy reconnecting in the ways we had in the past. Rather than be blunt in turning him down, I found grace in redirecting the conversation back to decorating.

After work, I drove straight to Culver City for a females-only SAA meeting. There were moments when I would try to assert that I might not be an addict, that perhaps it was all in my head. This was not one of those times. Despite the lunch having gone harmlessly, I was glad to be there, but after the first full day of work, my mind craved silence.

Still, I pulled into the church parking lot. A few recovering addicts clutching their Sex Addicts Anonymous books meandered toward the building. I opened my glove box and slid out the book.

My goal for SAA meetings was to not compare myself to others or judge anyone. Every addict professed to different rock bottoms. We all needed help from an issue that had caused our lives to lose control. Sign-in and volunteer sheets rested on a table by the entrance. I signed in and put the pen down when I saw the year-long commitment required for volunteering. It was more important to me that I meet my obligation to attend thirty meetings in thirty days. After a month, I'd regroup to evaluate my progress.

I moseyed over to the refreshment area and prepared a cup of ginger tea. The tables were arranged in a horseshoe for easier conversation. I preferred the middle so I could see the door and anyone who was speaking. The meeting began with a prayer, and then the leader read from the book. After announcements, they opened up for sharing. I made a pact to share at every meeting over the course of thirty days. Other addicts' stories reminded me about the parts of myself I needed to improve. The gnarly ones were rough to hear, constantly triggering memories of just how bad things had gotten for me pre-rehab. Maintenance of personal boundaries was one of those goals. After the third woman finished speaking, I raised my hand.

"My name is Prue. I'm a sex addict." The group welcomed me in unison. "I'm doing well, but I live in constant fear that the bad habits will creep back in." I fought the urge to tug my ear or twirl my hair. "My focus is to be there for my son, but after he goes to sleep, I worry about being alone. When I get lonely, I fight off temptations to text someone just to fill the void. I'm weakest in the evenings when the silence starts to get to me."

The women in the room listened and nodded. I imagine many sighed with relief that I was the one talking, hoping I might share something worse than what they'd planned on sharing. Chalk it up to human nature. At least I hoped it was.

"There have been a few minor slip-ups, mostly things with my phone. I still get elated when a random guy texts. I try and delete them right away. I even removed their names from my contacts."

The eyes in the room said what I needed to do.

"I guess I should block every person who sends me an illicit message. I still get a thrill from negative attention. My boss, he and I used to have an inappropriate relationship. Today was my first day back. When he started staring at me the way he does, I was angry, but also thankful. Grateful, even. Baby steps." A laugh unwittingly spilled out. "Thanks for letting me share."

When I brewed over the stories that had been shared during the drive home, my mind pictured the scenarios, obsessing over every detail. The SAA meetings were nothing like in rehab. There was a distance between me and the other attendees that allowed me to box myself into a separate category. Most of the female sex addicts hadn't attended a five-week inpatient program. The twelve steps worked well for alcoholics and drug addicts, but it was difficult to apply to sex addiction. I would need to engage in physical intimacy to have healthy relationships in the future. Sex is what differentiates friends from lovers.

Once I got on the 405 freeway, I turned on a mix of old rap music. Dr. Dre on full volume was the best medicine for mind-clearing. One thing that repeated in my head as surely as Dre's reprise was the prospect of abstinence for a year. This, I believed, would prove to be impossible.

Chapter Four: Prue Past

Mitch and I headed to the smoking area. Mike requested that I refrain from speaking to any men, including one of my closest rehab friends, Mitch. I rationalized talking to him because he was gay. Most of our private conversations happened while sitting together in the smoking veranda. Even though I had quit smoking many years ago, I didn't want to miss the unsupervised conversations.

"Apparently, there are only two people who know that Alistair has never driven a car: his secretary, and his business partner," Mitch said. "I found out by accident when I overheard him on the phone." He blew a stream of smoke toward the peak of the veranda.

"And now there are four people," I said, picking a small scab on my elbow.

"Touché."

"How does he manage to travel around?" Figuring Mitch wouldn't have a clue. I found it impossible to picture crisp, put-together Alistair taking the tube or hopping on a bus with droves of common-ers pressed up against him.

"A private driver." Mitch draped a smooth, dark arm across the back of the bench.

"Damn." *I'm wearing couture from head to toe, Alistair holds my hand as we exit a London hot spot, the driver is waiting out front. He ushers us into the car. Once the door closes, Alistair kisses me tenderly on the lips.*

"From what I gather, he can afford to do whatever he wants." Mitch showed utter delight to be reporting such solid information. He understood the poverty mentality plaguing me since childhood, and that I would be impressed by something like a full-time chauffeur.

After I confessed the Alistair kiss to Mike, he requested that I not speak to Alistair for a while. But enforcing personal boundaries proved to not be easy. When I spotted him through the bookstore window after leaving the smoking veranda, I beelined for the door, pretending to be on a mission to find a certain book.

He glanced up when the door opened and waved me over. The space between the shelves provided shelter for us to talk on the down-low.

My adult rule-breaking ways went against who I was as a kid, the ultimate rule follower who feared even the thought of disobeying the rules. Somewhere, a hundred-and-eighty degree shift happened. Now I got high off the idea of breaking a small one, sneaking a banana from the dining hall to eat in my room, or staying in Gloria's room well past lights-out. This amounted to nothing compared to the blatant way in which I continued to communicate with Alistair. These conversations left me giddy in a high-school crush kind of way.

"Mitch said you've never driven a car and have a private driver," I said, a book in my hand in case a shop worker wandered over.

"Did he, now?" Alistair kept his eyes on the literature with a seductive smile. His face appeared smoother than normal, clean-shaven rather than his usual perfectly trimmed stubble. He said he saw no point in getting his license because, at the time, he couldn't afford a car. The full-time driver he ended up hiring also happened to be his dear friend from high school who was now depending on him for income.

There were twenty minutes left until the afternoon session would begin, so I barraged him with questions, the childish side of me refusing to relent. *Impulsivity*. The cause of endless adult-life problems. *Wait a few moments before moving your mouth.*

"Can I help you find something?" The store clerk stood at the end of two rows of books, her blue apron cinched around her waist.

"No, thank you." My sweetest tone. "We're discussing an assignment for one of our lectures."

"Very well," she said. It didn't matter whether or not she believed me. When I wanted something, I got it. And right then, I had a deep curiosity about Alistair's life story.

He told me he had seen an ad in the paper for a training program at an investment firm shortly after his eighteenth birthday. "Back then, the stock market was like the wild, wild west."

And he would make one hell of a sexy cowboy.

"When I started trading, money flowed like the drink refills at a fast-food restaurant." He painted with his words while understanding that I craved details. Inside me lived an interior designer who could take in the style, color palette, furniture, lighting, and every nuance of a room in a matter of seconds. I needed specifics, and he provided them in great abundance.

Alistair told me that he reported to an Indian man named Dipesh who slicked his hair back with a thick coating of pomade and wore ill-fitting suits on his scrawny frame. He cheated and churned the accounts he managed, which made him a hefty two percent on every trade.

"At that time, a college degree had no value to my success. The only thing that mattered was passing the Series 17 securities exam."

I shelved a book when the cover curled under the heat of my palm.

I slid my hand along the stack and took another without disturbing the clean lines.

"The firm insisted the trainees pass the first time." He stepped to the next self-help reading section. I kept in sync with him, as though we were dancing. The trading desks buzzed with the kind of energy that excited Alistair. "I love the competition. Best of all, no one cared that I was born and raised in the East End as long as I succeeded."

There was never a statement I could relate to more. *Cover up the tracks of an impoverished childhood, and never let anyone find out about your past.*

"I was paid ten percent on all future commissions the first year."

Like two halves of a coin. One of us is heads; the other tails. Together, we make a whole.

I convinced myself that we had what it took to be a great couple, but something gnawed at me.

Am I just fascinated by his wealth?

He glanced at the Ferrari wrapped around his wrist. We had ten more minutes. "Whenever I made a sale, I marched over to the bell outside the boss's office and rang it."

"I bet the clang of victory created a seriously competitive sales floor," I said, thrilled I could follow what he was saying.

Alistair said he grew accustomed to the roadblocks he received from potential customers. "Selling is simple. You can't overthink it." It was the way he lured his prey, and thus far it had worked for him every time.

"I'm the woman who overthinks about overthinking." I laughed at the sad truth.

"I passed the securities exam the first try with a perfect score." His eyes sparkled with excitement. "A month later, the senior partner at a competing firm invited me to lunch, and I knew things were about to change. The guy took me to a swanky restaurant."

Olives piled in an icy martini glass, young Alistair wild-eyed and full of hope. His energy matched mine. I could see him playing me, and I didn't care.

"He said I was a powerhouse and wanted me on his team. I never looked back."

By then, he moved out of the East End and into the city and splurged on a few bespoke suits. The aching hunger he had once known became a distant memory. Alistair couldn't shake the thought that at any moment, everything might be taken from him.

"There's a saying in London," he said. "If you can hear the Bow church bells when you're born, you're a Cockney. It's hard to rid yourself of that label."

I could relate to that more than I cared to admit. Out of fear, he'd lived below his means, saving huge amounts of money in case something happened. With practice, he covered up the Brummie accent.

My New York accent, a distant memory, yet another thing we had in common.

There was a subtle art to sharing enough to appear open while letting others do the talking. It was more about the questions a person asked than the answers. As long as he was on top, no one messed with him. The more money he made, the more women flocked towards him.

The fatter the wallet, the hotter the chicks.

"We better head back, I'll go first." Ten steps down the sidewalk, Alistair opened the bookstore door.

Mitch acted as though he was privy to the fact I had been talking with Alistair.

53

The perpetual matchmaker.

I avoided eye contact in fear of tipping off Mike. Once everyone was in their seats, the meditation music started. I was not a natural at meditating. The entire process resembled torture. They said it was more about accepting your thoughts than clearing your mind. All I could think about was hearing the rest of the story about how Alistair had built his empire. I also berated myself for never being successful. The fool who gave every penny to Nick, who, in turn, lost it all.

"Hope everyone is ready to be present and focused this afternoon." Flecks of tinsel in Mike's sandy hair. *Distinguished.* The sleeves of his shirt neatly rolled up.

He raised a hand to gain our attention. I spotted a hint of ink. My therapist, drunk and shirtless, his arm being branded in a tattoo parlor. Mike moved his chair closer to the group. He never wanted to be larger than us, careful to stay at our level.

"Alistair will continue to move through his timeline," Mike said, focusing on the man of the hour. "A gentle reminder to refrain from sexually explicit stories, details of drug use, or anything that may trigger someone in the room. Please keep things as bland as possible while sharing."

Even Alistair became enthralled by the inexplicable strength of our leader. Mike passed him the rolled-up paper. He moved to the carpet and stretched out the paper along the floor. It began at a set of shoes on one side of the room and touched my sandals on the other.

"The guys at my firm partied hard, which on many occasions would require a pick-me-up," he said. "Steve was from New York and had fallen for a British girl while on an exchange program in London. He was a regular coke user and offered bumps off his house key in the bathroom before the trading floor opened."

A chain of fidgeting rolled through the room. Most of it came in the form of nose-rubbing.

Alistair had failed to find the glaring moment when he realized he might have a problem with cocaine. Sure, he confessed to loving the high. It helped ease a brutal hangover for a big day at work. He had been quite stealthy about hiding the habit from his girlfriend, Eleanor.

I don't know Eleanor, but I hate Eleanor with a fiery passion.

They met when she was the receptionist where he did his training program. He had vowed not to mix business with pleasure.

"Eleanor is extremely attractive," he said.

My stomach turned. I wanted to leave the room. The problem was that I didn't have the guts to ask Mike to be excused to use the restroom. The thought of listening to Alistair prattle on about Eleanor was beyond annoying.

"Every guy at the firm was after this woman, but it became clear her interest was in me."

Not one person in the Purple Group moved. They each lived vicariously through Alistair. We had led boring lives in comparison, especially me.

"Things came to a head at the holiday party." Literally to a head because she blew him in the bathroom. Alistair had been drinking and was more outgoing than usual. He claimed to lack the same level of attraction for Eleanor as the other men in his office.

This whole story is killing me. I squirmed, crossed my legs, and chewed my cuticles. Mike glanced over. I rested my hand back in my lap. My water bottle rested underneath the chair. I grabbed it and took a swig. The sip was less than satisfying.

"Before Eleanor, I tended to date a different set of women."

"I'm going to ask you to move along with the story," Mike said.

"Please only use details as it pertains to your addiction." He took an inventory of the group. A hen checking on the baby chicks.

"Right. Sorry. I just felt caught in two worlds. One in which I had made money but didn't belong, and the world in which I was most accustomed to, with women who were rougher around the edges, less educated, and perhaps less demanding." Alistair stretched his arms in front of him and rolled his head from side to side.

"This is an interesting phenomenon often seen with patients." Mike walked over to the flip pad resting on an easel. I took it upon myself to try and guess which color marker he would choose, a game I played in my head to prove I understood him. Most of the time, I chose wrong. He picked up the orange one and drew a line straight down the page. On either side of the line, he sketched boxes; at the top, a dollar sign. "The success comes too fast, there isn't time to emotionally catch up. A limbo land in which you have a foot in two worlds." Mike checked the clock. I prayed for the time to move faster. The fun meetings blew by and the dig-deep ones dragged on forever.

"I believe you are right," Alistair said. "I was edgy when I started to acquire wealth. Guilty of success and yet riddled with feelings of inferiority because I never fit in with the others who had grown up with wealth."

"Bingo," Mike said. "The guilt became a springboard to your addiction. That combined with a desperate need to feel as though you belonged in your new life while not abandoning your old one."

"Quite right. I had an attraction to women from my neighborhood. The ones who weren't so caught up in society and concerned with their looks, preoccupied with what everyone else thought about them."

I sighed with a bit too much enthusiasm due to our similar lives. I also felt forced to fit into both worlds. The poor kid in the rental cottage with one measly bathroom on the palatial estate.

"I preferred to be seen out in public with a woman like Eleanor and to have intimate relations with the working-class women I grew up with."

"We get the idea," Mike said.

"Sorry." Alistair slumped like a scolded boy and gazed at his timeline. "The point I'm trying to make is that I learned the rich girls liked me because I had money, which I found odd because they'd grown up wealthy themselves. The poor women didn't care how much I had in my bank account."

Every one of the women in the group crossed and uncrossed their legs like synchronized swimmers.

"Would you say you felt more like yourself around the ladies from your hometown? You could be more authentic?" Our leader was the Border Collie, we were the sheep.

"I preferred rough girls with solid street smarts." When Mitch eyed me, I almost fell off my chair. He mouthed "that's you." I prayed Mike didn't see.

Gloria leaned in closer to my ear. "Sounds like someone I know."

"Gloria, please share with the group what you just said. We can't have secrets." Mike was losing control and pulled out the lasso.

"Uhm, I was just telling Prue I had to pee."

"You can excuse yourself to use the facility."

I flew my arm in the air. "May I go too?"

"When Gloria returns."

Dammit.

According to Alistair, Eleanor was descended from the royal family. Her skin resembled porcelain with strawberry-blonde hair. "I wondered if she ever went outside," he said.

I wonder if her bush was the same color as her hair.

"Most nights, the guys met for drinks after work. I had begun using blow every day." He scratched his nose. "Any time I tried to stop, I became depressed."

"One of the side-effects of chronic cocaine use," Mike interjected. "Continue."

Alistair blamed his lack of discretion at the annual holiday party on being under the influence. "Everyone saw us shag and leave together." I might have been wrong, but I was pretty sure he blushed.

"We can see the correlation between Alistair's behavior when he was not using and when he was. It changes who we are down to the core." Mike signaled for Alistair to continue.

"Once we started formally dating, I thought it would be best for Eleanor to leave the company. I found her a position at another investment firm, which also meant she couldn't keep track of me the way she had before."

"What was your breaking point?" Mike pushed us to discover the root of our troubles.

"I visited my mother's grave every year on her birthday." He sipped from the water bottle issued to us at check-in. "When I bent down to put flowers on her headstone, my nose started bleeding—blood dripped all over the granite. The more I tried to wipe it off, the more it smeared. I also suffered from chronic sinus infections, which in turn created unpleasant inquisitions from my doctor. I did some research, told my partner I would be taking a five-week leave of absence, and checked myself into Serenity Hills."

"Alright," Mike said. "Break down the barriers and engage in relationships based on rigorous honesty." He addressed the group. "I've said this before. The secrets make us sick. Tell the truth to everyone, including yourself. Comments, questions?"

I raised my hand. "I heard a rumor in the smoking area and I wanted to get it out in the open." I fiddled with my pencil then turned toward Alistair. "Does Eleanor know where you are?"

The question had been rolling around in my head and I wasn't sure if Mike would shut me down, but he didn't. Alistair gave me a lingering look and as he spoke, his gaze remained on me.

"The rumor you heard is true. I told her I needed time off from the relationship to do some personal work." His eyes pleaded for forgiveness.

Mike released a deep sigh. "The twelve-step program includes making amends to family and friends affected by our addiction," he said. "I'm not singling out Alistair, this is for the entire group." I had been holding my breath and dramatically exhaled. "It will be important for your recovery to have rigorous honesty with Eleanor while you're here. We can meet in private to discuss your options."

The disappointment showed on Alistair's face. I slumped in my chair, the snitch who outed a friend, the momentary high long gone.

"This is for everyone in the room. It's impossible to move forward with a healthy relationship with anyone after rehab when the relationship is based on lies." Mike stood. No one moved. Perhaps they were consumed with thoughts about who they needed to come clean with between now and checkout day. He raised his arms for us to gather for prayer. As the group formed a circle, Alistair took one of my hands and Gloria held the other.

"I'm sorry," I said.

A prickly sensation moved across my scalp. He gave my hand a squeeze. The room filled with the Serenity Prayer. Never had the words captured more meaning than they did at that moment.

God grant me the serenity to accept the things I cannot change, change the things I can, the wisdom to know the difference, and the willingness to take action.

When the prayer ended, time stopped in its tracks. The room bustled with people gathering their bags and water bottles. Alistair released my grasp.

"I'm going to email Eleanor tonight," he said.

A wave of relief passed through me followed by an electric shock of nerves. The last thing I needed was all his attention focused on me.

Be careful what you wish for, Prudence.

Chapter Five: Alistair Present

Alistair lugged his Vuitton roller bag through the aftercare lobby. The Serenity Hills driver, some guy named Jimmy, followed with the other two. Even though he'd only been there a week, he couldn't wait to leave.

Time stood still since he'd checked out of Serenity Hills. The days moved slowly in rehab and even slower in aftercare. When he laid it all out in his head, only two weeks had passed since he last saw Prue.

He parked himself in the back seat of the SUV while Jimmy loaded the trunk. A brutally long haul. His eyes glazed over as he said goodbye to the saguaro cactus and horrific deciduous climate. He couldn't remember ever being this burned out.

Jimmy put the car in drive and adjusted the rearview mirror. "You decided to check out a few weeks early." He passed the car phone charger to Alistair and he plugged in.

"I have a pressing personal matter to deal with in Los Angeles. Time to go." He scratched his elbow, wondering why the fucking driver would care how long he stayed, and frankly, it was none of his business.

"As long as you feel ready. It's your journey." The rhythmic turn signal clicked.

"I'm ready."

Jimmy pulled out while Alistair powered up his phone. The air filled with chimes and dings of downloading messages. He tipped his head to the towering saguaro, the arid, repulsive climate, and to the geckos that swarmed the paths. On his next glance out the window, the car was pulling up at the airport. Alistair stood on the sidewalk until the car disappeared.

The flight attendant pulled up the drink cart. He figured to her, he was nothing but a pompous-looking adult. All of the illnesses he had been diagnosed with in rehab were slowly beginning to detach from his personal life. He believed he wasn't an alcoholic but rather a man who enjoyed the sweet taste of liquor, and all the scars it masked, a little too much.

"I'll have a vodka soda. Make it a double." Alistair put on his headphones and scrolled through his playlist, the ache over missing music still quite raw. When the chosen song began to play, he cracked open the two nips of Titos and poured them over the cup of ice, then topped it off with a splash of soda. The first sip went down easy. Before Alistair could take a breath, the cup was empty.

"Another drink?" The stewardess held her hand over the cans in anticipation of his order. Her voice was raspy and her shiny black hair had been pulled back neatly in a bun. Alistair admired the way her red lipstick didn't wander outside the perimeter of her lips.

"Yes, another vodka soda, please."

She smiled, and her hazel eyes sparkled as she poured the liquid into a fresh cup. Alistair chugged his second round as he read through his texts. The alcohol kicked in fast with a light, breezy buzz. A fresh sensation coursed through his body. He could feel the warmth travel from his feet to his head. He stood on a thin tightrope; the fall would be worse the second time around.

Alistair believed that for him, complete sobriety was as unrealistic as sexual abstinence. A drink could suppress his dire craving for cocaine. The most important thing was never touching the euphoric white powder again.

He received a pile of messages from Mitch regarding Gloria's memorial service. He added everything to his calendar. Back to getting reacquainted with the organized man he was before the proverbial wheels came off his bus. He reread every text he had sent to Prue. As much as he tried to deny it, she held an uncharted power over him. It was a power foreign to Alistair, which compelled him to experience and understand his emotions—ones he found to be real, unmuted, and unfiltered.

He closed the messages and scanned his emails. His shoulders rose up at the sheer quantity dumping in his inbox. Far too many to scroll through. Alistair typed a name into the search function. Everything else could wait. Nothing new from the detective, which meant everything remained status quo. He had never mentioned a word of this to anyone in rehab. Not to Mike, not to his comrades in the smoking area. It was too important. He feared any outside involvement might jinx his dream of finding Susie.

This was the third investigator he had hired. Detective Yang professed to be an expert when it came to women who worked in adult entertainment.

"Strippers? Strippers change names about as frequently as eighty-year-olds change diapers," the detective had said. "What else you got for me to go on?"

Regardless of his skepticism, Alistair had sensed a confidence in the detective's voice and an underlying empathy that drew him in. And damn, this guy charged a fortune.

Detective Yang located Susie a few weeks before Alistair checked himself into Serenity Hills. *Everything happens for a reason.* What kind of impression would he have made had he been all jacked up on blow?

Alistair hadn't worked out, had been eating too much, and felt like a bloated pig. Food had replaced other cravings. He took another sip. His fingers slipped and the ice dumped into his face, vodka splashing everywhere from his pants to the tray table in front of him.

"Fuck," he mumbled under his breath. He dabbed a napkin on the wet spots, more upset about the lost liquor than his damp seat or the stain on his pants. He closed his eyes and leaned back.

A tightness radiated across his chest. Over the years, Alistair had tried to picture what she might look like now. It seemed futile trying to keep his emotions in check. He stretched his arms overhead, in disbelief that he was finally close to finding Susie.

Chapter Six: Prue Present

Nick texted me saying he wanted to discuss our "situation." It irked me that he used the word *situation* to describe our fifteen-year marriage. The time had come for me to stop avoiding the inevitable. We needed to part ways, and it wasn't going to be easy. The limbo land we had been living in only confused me and damaged our son. I offered to meet him at Starbucks—neutral territory, as my therapist advised. Unbiased spaces were essential when discussing difficult topics like child custody, alimony, and divorce. When we didn't meet somewhere neutral, we ended up in the sack with zero issues resolved and me walking away with a crippling feeling of regret mixed with unwanted nostalgia.

Fine, he texted. *Starbucks in Riviera Village at five thirty.*

See you then. I added a smiley face to maintain a friendly vibe and because it made me feel better. I went straight from work to meet Nick. Just after I parked, my phone buzzed.

I'm not going to make it, sorry. A meeting ran late.

Nick and his perpetual issues with sticking to the plan. Some idiot leaned on his horn while I pounded out a text.

Unexpectedly, he showed up at my front door with pizza and flowers. Dark circles rested underneath his eyes, a reminder of the insomnia that somehow always managed to be my fault. His suspicions about my cheating and overspending etched prominently into his face. *The holes in my heart stuffed with all the wrong things for all the wrong reasons.* An awkward silence engulfed the space between us.

"These are for you." Nick passed me the haphazard bouquet. His expression turned serious. My posture stiffened.

"The peonies represent the past, from our wedding. The daisies are for the present. May our days be fresh as a daisy. The roses are our future, which I hope will be rosy."

His sentiment caught me off guard. He released a condescending smirk as if he knew I could see straight through him. *What a phony.* I lifted an eyebrow, pressed my lips together, and forced a fake smile. I clutched the flowers in my hand. Each stem prickled against my palm. The petals felt tainted and cursed—just like our marriage.

"That's sweet," I replied. The memories of our life together were bleary with layers of toxic waste. "Nick, where's my piano?" My tone went from coy to assertive.

"I'm sure Lily already told you." He bit his lip. "Classic move for you to dig and make me say it." His gaze trailed to the side. Each word fortified all the bad parts of our relationship. I stared at him with my arms crossed, determined to not let him off the hook this time.

"I sold it, alright." His monotonous voice reopened deep wounds tucked away for safekeeping. He was blithely unaware of my attachment to the piano, and the worst part was he probably would have sold it regardless.

"It was not yours to sell." *My newfound strength since attending rehab.* "That was a gift from Mrs. Sutton, the woman who owned the estate I grew up on." A fire ignited inside my chest. "You had no business selling my possession." Nick took a dramatic breath and shot me a "here we go again" look before exhaling.

"I needed money to pay your Serenity Hills bill."

Nick with the perfect comeback.

We ate at the kitchen table. Nick tried to mend the broken pieces of our life together with mediocre pizza and Chianti while our son entertained us with his most recent obsession, Mario Kart on GameCube.

Lou licked my toes and curled up with his muzzle on my foot.

"Lou is pretty stoked to see you," Nick said. "He never liked me that much."

Poor Nick, no one loves him, not even the dog.

We both went to Christian's room. Despite myself, I savored watching Nick make goofy jokes while Christian laughed. The part of Nick I fell in love with. Self-deprecating humor that entertained but contained a sharp bite when pushed to the edge. I kissed my son's cheek. "I love you."

Nick followed me to the kitchen and watched while I took inventory of my things. The cruel way he'd treated me during Family Week left me guarded.

"I'm sorry about everything. I acted like an ass." Nick began stacking the leftover pizza slices to be put into the fridge. He regarded me closely, his sanctimonious eyes digging for any sign of a reaction.

"I want a divorce." I paused my movements and stared at him coldly, hoping my expression of contempt would yield some sort of unexpected reaction. "Too much has happened. I was thinking we could use a mediator to make things easier." I resumed unloading the dishwasher, unsure of what to do with my hands.

"Is this what you want?" His tone was sharp.

I loathed hurting him but had no choice. There was no turning back. A panic attack revved its engine. The fear of never finding love, the reality that I had failed at the most important commitment of my life, caused my chest to tighten and sink. I faced it down now. Fear got the best of me before, but clarity stared me right in the face. I needed to be my authentic self. In truth, the majority of my anxiety was financially based. I kept telling myself I could do it on my own.

"My decision is made." I sat at the kitchen table, defeated. He remained standing. The power struggle was over. Not a drop of fight left inside of me. "I have a few names of mediators. Do your own research and throw in suggestions. We don't have any assets. From what I gather, this is a numbers game when it comes to child support and alimony."

I couldn't catch my breath. The apprehension that Nick may hide his income, cheat his way out of paying. *Why stay with someone I don't trust?*

"In the meantime, I could use some help with Christian. I won't get paid until the end of the month. He's growing like a weed and needs clothes, school supplies, all the registration fees. I simply don't have the money."

I propped my head in my hands. All I wanted to do was sleep until it was over. The final painful chapter, my old, unhealthy life—all the indecision, the weeks in rehab not knowing what to do, his split tongue, the eggshell walk. The realization he could never love me back.

"I will always care about you." It all came crashing down. "This is so hard. I need closure. The whole situation is killing me. We gave it our best shot." My voice cracked.

Nick dropped a paper towel in front of me. "I'll look into a lawyer. I don't know what else to say other than I'll give you money when I can."

All of his empty promises had left a gaping wound, but every time he made a concerted effort, I wanted to believe he would follow through.

He stood over me as though he might touch my back. The heat of his hand radiated through me. The man I hoped he would become throughout the course of our marriage was simply an illusion. Nick would never change. "I'm . . . Prue, I'm shocked." He let out a nervous chuckle and redirected his gaze in my direction.

"You're shocked? The last time we spoke, you told me you were going to fight me for custody. You said you were in love with Naomi." The ups and downs, the way he jerked me around with his indecisiveness over whether he wanted me or Naomi, was driving me to insanity.

"She's too demanding. I changed my mind, and for the record, I also said I loved you, back at Serenity."

I would not let his empty words make even the slightest dent in my decisions. The lies were painfully obvious. Had they always been?

Nick opened the wine cooler and pulled out a bottle. "This is mine." In swirly, silver metallic letters, *Happy Birthday Nick*, scrolled across the label.

"Take whatever you want."

"I will." Nick stood behind me, his breath hot on my neck. "If I find out you're having a revolving door of men through this house, I will take Christian so fast your head will spin." He smacked the table. I jumped in my seat.

With the wine in hand, he walked out the door. Deep in my heart, I believed he would never come back. The line had been drawn. Nick wasn't one to grovel, especially if he believed he couldn't win.

I remained seated. It was hard to tell how long. The sun had set and soon enough, the kitchen strapped itself in black. I craved wine but worried drinking alone would drive me down a bad path.

I will be solo from this moment forward. You have to live your life, to be in the moment.

A text came through from Alistair, which I barely had the energy to read. *Hey, I've been thinking about you nonstop. I decided to stay for aftercare and just got my phone back. Call me when you can. I've been dying to talk to you!*

I poured myself a glass of chardonnay. It was warm. I threw in a cube of ice and toasted to my strength, resilience, and a new chapter.

Chapter Seven: Prue Past

The music came to a sudden halt. When I opened my eyes, I caught Mike staring. I smiled, and without hesitation he dodged my gaze. It was hard not to obsess over what that meant, but I did my best to respect him as a professional.

A punchy sensation tickled my throat and whirled through my belly. Whether I should or shouldn't, I reveled in sitting in a room with Mike and Alistair. A dream come true. Multiple dreams, actually. Mike kept me grounded with his firm yet kind demeanor and the way he saw the best in me. The Brit, my eye candy, the sexy hunk with impeccable style. I suppressed a squeal before snapping myself back into reality.

"Morning, everyone." The sun beamed through the window. Mike's thick lashes shadowed his eyes. I looked at the smooth skin above his beard and yearned to kiss him there. I adored the contrast between the prickly and soft textures. He moved to the blinds and turned the pole. "If you did not put your assignment in the box, please do on your way out so I can read them during lunch. We will discuss them in the afternoon."

He leaned over his desk to glance at a notebook while I admired his high and tight ass in the khakis he often wore to work. His scent was always fresh and clean with a hint of citrus. I avoided asking him what cologne he used, fearful I would be crossing a line. Or worse—

make him uncomfortable.

"Remember, homework is not graded. The assignment gives me a pulse check on your emotional well-being and the progress of your recovery. Let's start with introductions, beginning with Mitch. Then, Alistair—you need to complete your timelines to finish. Are you ready?"

"Yes." The unforgiving overhead lights cast bold shadows across his face.

Mitch had small pouches under his eyes which either meant too much salt yesterday or not enough sleep last night. Other than that, he looked put together, with fresh white sneakers, olive-green khakis, and a white logo-less polo shirt.

"Mitch, alcoholic, bulimic, body dysmorphic, love avoidant." He tapped his fingers as he listed his own addictions. "I think that's it, unless I can add my favorite one: freak."

I let out a laugh before realizing I was the only one. *Classic Prue, always finding humor in the disturbed.*

"Mitch," Mike interjected, "refrain from name-calling out loud and in your head."

When introductions were over, we moved our attention to Alistair, who had crawled to the floor and laid out his timeline. His cheeks had turned blotchy. I figured the mottled skin symbolized shame and embarrassment. My mood shifted from hopeful to anxious. I couldn't stand watching anyone suffer, especially not Alistair.

"Around seven," Alistair began, "I figured out my mum worked as a high-class call girl."

Our eyes met. I didn't flinch—I was no better. *I partook in the same career choice.* The paper was written in his neat penmanship. *The duck floats serenely along the surface, but we can't see the feet frenetically moving under the water.*

As his story continued, a young Alistair stood before me in his navy-blue uniform of shorts, knee socks, and a matching jacket. "My mum said she would be happy if I did well academically."

The similarities of our childhoods became more and more apparent with each story he told. Parallel lives. *Both* of us academic overachievers, not because we were smarter than anyone else but for the sole purpose of pleasing our mothers.

"I got a thrill from sharing how well I was doing in school with her." He smiled in the sweetest way. It was the smile I imagined little Alistair would give to his mother. His desire to please her was obvious even now.

The more I learned and listened, the more I felt a kinship between his pain and my own. I was introduced to a brand-new perspective. Our similar pasts and an insane attraction for him were equally competing with one another.

"When I maintained straight A's, my mum would tell me I was a clever boy." Alistair's posture lifted. "When I smiled, she'd smile back. But there was always something unspoken behind it, as though my face reminded her of something sad." Alistair redirected his attention to Mike. "She told me not to count on my looks."

Gloria touched my knee. I turned toward her and smiled. The expression she returned worried me. "Are you alright?"

Mike and his keen ears tuned in, which was subliminally my goal. "Gloria, would you like to share something? You are all welcome to add your input. These timelines are heavy. This is a safe haven to let out your feelings."

"I don't know," she said. "I'm a little sad. Not sure why."

I reached for Gloria's hand and pulled it onto my lap. With her, the walls were always down, nonexistent. I ached when she shared the horrors of her life and yearned to save her. Saving her meant I could save myself. It wasn't too late for her to rise above what had happened. She was still young and malleable; I believed there was a silver lining. In the short time we'd been together at Serenity Hills, I opened my heart to her. I couldn't help but have deep empathy for everything she had endured, to understand the pain beneath her smiles.

"These shares can be triggering, especially when the wounds are still raw. Alistair's pain is his. We don't need to take on his pain as ours, nor should we."

Mike continued, his wisdom enticing nearly everyone in the room.

"Empathy, like most things, can be used in positive and negative ways." He took inventory of the group. "If you are needing a break for self-care then please take one. This is a no-judgment zone. Put your happiness first."

Gloria shook her head. She would white-knuckle through. A few moments went by in uncertain silence.

I raised my hand. "There are similarities between my childhood and Alistair's." A breeze outside coated the window in a layer of Arizona dust. "An 'A' became my golden ticket."

"Finding common ground is a wonderful way to learn that we aren't alone, our stories are universal." Mike signaled for Alistair to continue.

"Around five, my mum stopped having a sitter stay with me. She said that I was old enough to reach the bolt, so I was old enough to be alone."

Gloria asked to be excused. I waited for her to walk out before raising my hand while wondering what it was about Alistair's story that triggered her so much. The harrowing memories were too much for her to bear.

"I was five when I started being left alone too," I said. A stray curl dangled over my eye. I self-consciously tucked it behind my ear. "It's weird how things sound worse when they're someone else's story." I had an overwhelming desire to crawl to the floor and wrap an arm around Alistair. It occurred to me the person I truly wanted to hug was little Prue.

Gloria came back with a cup of tea. The color had returned to her beautiful face. I silently praised her for taking care of herself, for knowing exactly when she needed to take a break.

More momentary silence. Each of us in the group navigating the bog of our thoughts noiselessly, shuffling through the survival techniques we used to get through our childhoods.

The little Alistair I'd imagined beaming minutes ago now stood alone in their flat while his mother was out turning tricks with Johns somewhere. I sat in the chair filling up with self-loathing. *I did the same thing to Christian.*

Mike coughed. I shifted my attention back to the room. "As adults, we have choices to make with regard to our past. Can anyone tell me what those might be?" He waited for us to engage. He would have waited all day for an answer. Mitch raised his hand. Mike tipped his head.

"I made the choice to forgive my dad," Mitch said. "There was no point in confronting someone like him. I have the power to unwind the damage he caused me, but I can't change him."

"What are we doing to ourselves when we harbor resentment?" Mike wrapped his hands around one knee. A painful silence surrounded the space. Mike was the teacher and we were just a bunch of high schoolers who hadn't done their homework.

"Anyone?"

"Poisoning yourself?" Rhoda blurted out. "Sorry, I forgot to raise my hand."

"What else?" Mike probed.

Bo's cowboy-boot-clad feet tapped the carpet. "The way I figure it," he said with his smooth Southern drawl, "my mom had her reasons for never saying she loved me." The pearl snaps on his western-style shirt sparkled under the overhead lights. He paused, and I imagined him untangling the words he was about to speak. "I can break the chain."

"Yes," Mike said. He pushed up his sleeves. "Anyone else?" He checked the time. The room became restless.

"I haven't been able to halt the trail of abuse," I said. "Some of the things my mother did to me, I have done to Christian." An overwhelming sadness grew inside of me. "I want to do better. I'm trying to do better, but it creeps in and I can't stop it." I pushed back the tears. Gloria brushed her hand across my back.

"We aren't perfect." Mike softened his tone. "All we can do is our best. Acknowledge your mistakes to Christian. When we admit our misgivings, we take steps in the right direction." Mike's eyes bore into me. I raised my gaze to meet his. "Your son will forgive you. He is blessed to have you for his mom."

Was Mike flirting with me? Or was that simply what my twisted mind hoped?

A tear rolled down my left cheek. I praised the way Mike always made me feel sane, how his words had the power to reverse my guilt.

"Thank you." A box of tissues landed in front of me. I pulled one out and blew my nose.

"Alright, let's break." The listlessness of the group was as thick as the fog over the Golden Gate Bridge. "I'll see everyone back here after lunch." Mike stood, our signal to form a circle. I went out of my way to stand between Alistair and Gloria. Both clasped my hands with theirs.

"I love you, Prudence." Gloria gave my hand a gentle squeeze. Grateful for the positive, uplifting energy, I chose to pass it along.

"I enjoyed your share," I murmured to Alistair.

We broke up the circle. Mike watched us gather our things and walk out the door. As I passed, he told me I was going to be okay.

Chapter Eight: Prue Present

The last few days of summer meant letting my son sleep in while I took the morning to organize myself. It wouldn't be long before Christian was back at school. The days felt counterproductive post-Serenity Hills. Life's conveyor belt either sent me flying or reluctantly dragged me along. Between my job and getting Christian prepared for school, I had zero time to cause trouble. *Not yet, at least.*

With just me and Christian around, the house felt empty and quiet. I often wondered if he resented me for not giving him siblings, or if he enjoyed the attention he got from being an only child. The morning moved efficiently enough that I found some extra time to make pancakes. It was a thank-you for all my son had endured while I was away—an apology for having to leave at all.

I put them on a plate covered in plastic wrap. Carefully, I jotted the symbols I always used: a smiley face, a heart, and a peace sign with a note letting him know I was at work and would be home in time to take him to lacrosse practice. I grabbed a travel mug, took one last look around the house, and headed out the door.

*   *   *

The chintz fabric had been made into drapes and dropped at the office. Each measured panel, cut, sewn, and trimmed with a luxurious

silk fringe, would soon be hung from a nickel-plated rod with matching rings. One of the interns helped me load them in my car. *The glamorous life of a designer.* After thirty minutes of driving, I pulled up to an
iron gate and pressed the call button.

"Hello?" a man's voice came through the speaker.

"This is Prudence Aldrich from Patrick Dunn Interiors."

The gate began to open. I drove into the turnaround. A tall, lean
man stepped out of the front door to direct me where to park. He
wore wrinkled khaki-colored shorts, Vans, and a t-shirt with a surf
logo emblazoned across the chest. A mop of dirty-blond curls
plopped on his head, which contrasted his sharp ferret-like features.

"Need any help?" He stood behind me as I shimmied the curtain
rod from the back of the car. I slid a hand over my rear to ensure my
dress hadn't ridden up beyond an acceptable range. He grasped one
end of the rod as I guided it out. "My wife mentioned someone was
coming to install curtains." *Executive turned surfer dude.* "I expected a
handyman, not, you know, a beautiful woman." He smiled before
rubbing his chin.

While the old me would have probably soaked in this kind of negative attention, the new me saw being alone with another woman's
husband as a nightmare come true. The dude hovered close as I
stepped on a small ladder to reach the brackets. I perched on tiptoes
to wind the new finial around the end of the rod. The more I reached,
the higher my dress rose.

"Those are some long legs," the man said.

A bead of sweat dripped down my spine.

"Thanks," I replied as blandly as possible. He offered a hand as I
climbed down. I accepted but avoided eye contact, fearful of the spell
he might cast. I moved a safe distance from him and took in my work.

"Looks great," I said.

He helped me gather my things. His muscular arm brushed across my shoulder. "I'm going to have to approve more design projects so you'll come by again." A crooked-toothed smile with a piece of lettuce dangling from his snaggletooth.

I arranged a variety of throw pillows on the sectional in different sizes and complementing fabrics then punched a crease in the top of each one.

"You sure have a special touch." Ferret man—lurking awkwardly in the doorway.

"That's it for today." I glanced at my watch, a half hour until my lunch with Lily. "When the family room drapes come in, I will contact your wife to have them installed." I stepped up from the sunken room to where he was standing.

"I'm sorry to see you go." He ran ahead to open the front door. I hesitated a moment too long. He leaned in. I caved and let his arms wrap around me and his chest press into my breasts.

Is there a sign that says "down to fuck" on my forehead, or am I simply an attractive woman?

A few miles from the house, I pulled over to the side of the road. *Nothing happened, it was just a hug.* I replayed our interaction in my head, wondering if I had said or done something to come off as flirtatious. Perhaps I shouldn't have worn a dress. I jotted down a note in my head: *Dress professional, not sexual.*

I reached into my bag and grabbed my cellphone. The number to Serenity Hills was listed in favorites, but I had yet to call for help. I thought just knowing it was there would have been enough. A lifeline for a drowning soul. But today, I needed more.

"Serenity Hills." A voice I had heard time and time again during my stint in rehab.

Please refer to the chart and identify your feelings. Fear, pain, guilt, and shame.

"This is Prudence Aldrich. I'm wondering if Mike Sullivan is available."

"Hello, Prue," the woman I referred to as Nurse Ratched replied. I imagined her perky grin through the phone. "Unfortunately, Mike is on a leave of absence." She gave me time to absorb her words. "Carla Barnard is handling his recent discharges."

I gazed at my reflection in the lighted car vanity mirror. "Is there a number where I can reach him?"

"I'm sorry, no, we cannot give out his personal information." Nurse Ratched taking notes on her clipboard. *Ex-patient verging on a breakdown.*

Without responding, I hung up the phone. I curled my hands into fists and slammed them against the dashboard. "Fuck!" I yelled.

Strands of loose hair blocked my vision. I counted down from one hundred in an attempt to stop the panic in its tracks. *You aren't having a heart attack, just breathe.*

Mike represented everything positive in my life. The five stages of grief—denial, anger, bargaining, depression, and acceptance. Each overwhelmed me all at once, my private emotional word jumble within.

As I put the car in gear, I received a text from Alistair. I felt like a real shit not responding to three in a row and tapped out a reply.

Congrats on making it through. Stay in aftercare as long as you can, reality isn't that fun . . . been thinking about you lots . . . -P

The old Prue was fighting her way out of the spackled and sealed cracks. A reminder I needed to follow up with Frankie.

Aside from Lily, Frankie was one of the only people from my old life I truly cared to stay in touch with.

After a few back-and-forth texts with Frankie, we agreed to meet for coffee in the morning.

*   *   *

My "boss" Sam had requested my presence at an afternoon meeting. I drove straight back to the office after lunch with Lily. My workspace was beginning to look like *Jumanji* with bags of fabric samples, tile, marble, wood squares, and some backsplash mosaics in piles on my desk. I moved things into more organized chaos and jotted post-it notes to mark the piles. Sam threw me right into the fire, which left me feeling a bit overwhelmed.

I checked my makeup in a mirror I kept in the drawer. The liner I had applied in the morning was resting right under both eyes. I swiped a finger along my lower eyelid and added some under-eye cover-up, blush, and a fresh coating of mascara.

As I gazed at my reflection, I wondered why I cared and who I was getting dolled up for. I decided that looking good was more about how I felt than what others thought. I closed my desk drawer and strolled over to Sam's office.

"Hello, Darling, already got wind from the client that she is enamored with everything you did. She is in L-O-V-E with the throw pillows." Sam took a breath, a scowl hidden beneath his smile. "Well, tell me, how are you?"

He rested his chin on his hands. I glanced under his desk, always curious about what shoes he would have on. Navy Belgian loafers with striped socks. *Classic.*

"Me and Isaac Mizrahi are the last people on earth still wearing them," he said.

I loathed it when he caught me checking him out. "And you wear them so well."

I did my best to fake a sweet and grateful smile. I took a seat on the lavender sofa, wondering how many different colors it had turned since our first days together. "I'm thrilled she was so happy." My eyes met his for reassurance. "So what did you want to chat about?"

"I want to talk to you about this amazing new account and the project you will be working on." He slid a file from beside his laptop and moved over to sit next to me. "The gentleman is single and wants an elegant design that exudes the LA lifestyle. He's from the UK, apparently. Only spoken to him once, but he's very sophisticated and, well, rich."

"Wow, the UK? As in England?" My mouth went dry at the possibility it could be Alistair. The thought came as fast as it went. He was still in aftercare. It was impossible. "What kind of house does he have?" I tapped my index finger against my thigh.

"The whole project is quite mysterious and peculiar. He hasn't closed on the property yet but is certain he will. It's apparently the entire floor of that new building Ten Thousand. The units were renting for forty-five grand a month, so I can only imagine the price to purchase one." The expression Sam made when he was about to gouge the shit out of a client. "Needless to say, money is no object and I will be taking you off all of your projects so you can focus every bit of your creative energy on this whale. I want you to work that Prudence magic." His hands flew through the air like Mickey in *Fantasia*.

I had no clue who the client was, what the unit looked like, or when he would close on his property.

"What if he hates me? You know, it's happened, and it could happen again. Not everyone likes working with me."

"Rubbish. He is going to love you." Sam grabbed his checkbook. "Here is an advance so you can go get yourself some new clothes. You've been looking a bit dowdy." He scribbled out a check, tore it out, and dropped it on my lap.

"Jesus, Sam." I stared at the paper. "Three grand will buy me a lot of outfits."

"Not the kind you'll need to be around this client. Here." He jotted a name and number on a sheet of paper. "Isabel is a stylist who has worked with a few of my better-dressed clients. Don't purchase anything until you meet with her." An expression I had seen before—the yearning and desire burning beneath the surface. "In other news, I miss you. I've been lonely without you." His failed attempt at puppy-dog eyes gave me second-hand embarrassment.

"Sam . . . I—"

He cut me off, his elbows lifting from his knees. "Alright, alright . . . I'm sorry," he said. His tone was squeaky and high-pitched.

"So when am I meeting this mystery client?" I asked.

"Soon. There are still some moving parts."

I dodged his hug and instead gave him a shoulder. While I was in with Sam, Frankie texted asking for confirmation as to which Starbucks we were meeting for coffee in the morning. I dropped her a pin with the location and confirmed I'd be there at eight thirty the next morning. I then collected my things and headed out to drive Christian to lacrosse practice.

It proved difficult not to obsess over all the mothers who I hadn't seen since my scandalous divorce and stint in rehab. In the rearview mirror, I studied my fine lines and wrinkles and admired how naturally I had aged.

You're better than them, and they know it, I told myself, wanting to believe it. After six seconds of breath-holding, I exhaled.

Chapter Nine: Alistair Present

While waiting to de-board, Alistair updated his credit card in the Uber app. He then drafted a quick email to his friend, who also happened to be his trusted driver.

Hello George,

I'm back on terra firma. Looks like I'll be in LA for a while. Any chance you're willing to relocate? I'll cover all expenses. Don't make me use Uber. I hate switching up drivers. If you can't then I will continue with our agreement for the remainder of the year, but you may want to begin looking for work in London.

Alistair

The buzz from two cocktails began to wear off. He searched for ground transportation signs or a designated Uber pickup area. With his bags clutched tightly in his possession, he ordered an Uber and headed out toward the street. The line for people waiting for cars was long. He anticipated a debacle, but things went smoothly. As he made contact with his driver, his phone rang. There was a swift transition between the guy grabbing his luggage and Alistair sliding in the back seat.

"Hello?"

"Alistair, Mark Weston." Before Alistair could respond, he continued. "I'm calling regarding the German bonds. The updates say they're close to a payout but not giving specific dates. My clients are hounding me for answers." His voice was sharp and self-assured.

"A deal of this scope is unprecedented. The information that Henkle Global is providing is coming directly from the Chinese government. They wouldn't forward anything they haven't received themselves," Alistair said. "This will happen. I just don't know when." Alistair checked the driver's map to ensure they were headed to the Peninsula Hotel in Beverly Hills.

"What the hell do I tell my clients?" Mark inquired. "Some of these people put everything on the line."

"Well, that is never a solid strategy, is it?" Alistair itched his nose and squinted to check out something on the floor of the car. "For their sakes, I hope this plan pans out as expected. Listen, send any irate people over to me. I'll defuse them. That way they're off your back."

"That would be great," Mark replied. An air of relief wafted through the phone.

"Give them my cell," Alistair said. "We're all going to win on this one. As I mentioned before, a historic deal of this magnitude . . . well, it takes time to move funds around."

"Alright," Mark said. "Update me if you hear any news worth repeating."

"Will do."

Still groggy from the plane cocktails, Alistair was filled with regret. He hoped he sounded clear and succinct on the phone. He was no longer on his A-game. His once quick-thinking brain had turned rusty. Blood ran from his nose—something he had gotten used to ever since quitting cocaine. He pulled a tissue from his bag and pinched the bridge until it stopped.

The thought of staying in a hotel made every hair on his arm stand on end. In the past, a lot of shit had gone down on business trips like this. Every fun night started with a cocktail from the minibar and ended with a few empty bags of blow. This was a more serious situation than he'd experienced before. He dialed the Peninsula to remove the liquor from his room. If he wanted a drink, he would go buy one. Alcohol at his beck and call in the room was an all-around bad idea. His phone buzzed. Alistair glanced at the screen.

Welcome back to reality. I can be there whenever you want. I'm sickened by the thought of you using Uber.

George

PS: Do you have a car?

His mouth turned up at the corners as he typed out a reply.

Excellent news, old chap. See if you can move me to the top of the list at Tesla. I have no doubt you can work your magic. Call Helen at the office and have her book you a flight. Copy me on all the correspondence so I'm kept in the loop.

-A

The Uber pulled up to the glamorous Peninsula hotel. Alistair sighed with relief. A bellman opened the car door and greeted him. The air was warm and dry. A gentle breeze moved the palm fronds flanking the entrance.

"Are you checking in, sir?" the bellman asked and reached for his luggage.

Alistair nodded and passed him a twenty-dollar bill. He accepted a glass of champagne from a woman near the check-in area and took a hefty sip while he stepped up to the front desk.

"Welcome to Los Angeles, Mr. Prescott, we're happy you're staying with us." The uniformed blonde at the front desk moved her eyes back and forth from Alistair to the screen in front of her. "We have you in the presidential suite for an unlimited number of days." She smiled. "May I have a credit card for incidentals?"

Alistair passed her his black American Express card and she swiped it through the reader. She handed him the room keys, explained the whereabouts of the gym and spa, then asked if he would be needing dinner reservations.

"I'm going to eat here in the hotel tonight," he said.

"Very well, sir," she said. "Enjoy your stay. Your bags will be delivered to your room momentarily."

The lobby bustled with chic, attractive women, and Alistair's insides lit up. He was back in the game and full of hope. The grandiose suite wrapped around the hotel with a fabulous view of the Hollywood sign and the Hollywood Hills.

After his bags were delivered to his room, he stretched out across the bed with his phone in his hand.

"Jeff, Alistair calling you back."

"Welcome to LA," he said. "Bad news . . ." Alistair cleared his throat and sat upright on the California king bed. Jeff sighed before continuing. "There's been a snag in the deal."

"Dammit." Alistair raked his fingers through his hair. His tone had transitioned from composed to neurotic. He kicked off his shoes and paced around the dimly lit room. "Look, Jeff, you've got to make this happen. I mean, it's the best space for my office. I'm in a time crunch. This can't be delayed any longer."

He peeled off his blazer and adjusted the thermostat.

"Give me four days," Jeff replied. "Are you willing to bump up your price range? They're playing hardball."

"For Christ's sake. I'm already paying top dollar per square foot. Hold out on them. I have a feeling they'll cave. The market is soft. I'm not going to let them push me around." Alistair's stomach rumbled.

"Whatever you do, do not let this deal fall through."

He hung up and wandered to the minibar. Nothing but snacks, sodas, and fruit juice. A mix of disappointment and relief washed over him. He grabbed a Snickers bar from the tray, his blazer from the sofa arm, and headed out the door. In the lobby, he punched in a destination on his Uber app and called a car.

When the car pulled into the turnaround, Alistair hopped in and barked out the address, "4824 West Imperial Highway, Inglewood."

"Got it." The driver hit the gas. "You put the address in when you ordered the car."

Alistair had been in rehab so long he couldn't think straight. "Right." He checked his phone. One unread message.

Prue: *Checking in to say hi. I hope aftercare is going well.*

Alistair smiled at his phone. The thought of Prudence made him feel calm and excited at the same time.

Can I call you later? X

Sure!

He lay back to rest his eyes. It had been a long, stressful day. When he opened them, the car was pulling up to the gentlemen's club Bare Elegance. Plastered to the building's front was a lit neon sign that read Bare Elegance Gentleman's Club in big script letters. A red Maserati was prominently parked out front, and the palm trees were illuminated by the LED lights that lined the black awning. A woman wearing fishnets, a hot-pink strapless dress, and sky-high heels was smoking a cigarette out front and talking on the phone. Alistair thanked his driver and stepped out. He could hear the vibrating electronic music from the entrance.

Chapter Ten: Prue Present

When I returned home from work, I began reorganizing the kitchen so the layout would match my frenetic cooking style.

"Mom," Christian yelled from his bedroom. "Can you edit this paper for me? I need an A."

After only the first week, we were back in full-blown school mode. The teachers piled on the homework. In the past, Christian had done his work without much issue. Not a genius but diligent, careful, and he understood the repercussions of a missed assignment.

I sighed at the thought of doing anything that wasn't changing into sweatpants, pouring myself a glass of rosé, and waiting for Alistair's call.

Stop daydreaming about Alistair and embrace parenting.

I tugged an ear as I headed to Christian's room.

"Take my chair." Christian slid a piece of paper in front of me. "These are the instructions. Follow the directions exactly or the teacher takes off points."

I reviewed the assignment, wondering if the old brain still functioned right. "Get me a glass of water, please. You're breathing down my neck." I smiled and rubbed his back. Knowing my fourteen-year-old son cared about homework was a relief. I prayed it would last.

"Fine." Christian took a few running steps down the hallway then slid the rest of the way in his socks. He barreled back with the water and started to tell me about his day. I threw a hand up and kept reading his paper.

"I made a few minor corrections. Read it out loud three times. That's the best way to catch anything that sounds off."

"Did you check to see if I did everything on the checklist?" *Give a man a fish, he eats one meal; teach a man to fish, he eats for a lifetime.* "I only checked it for fluidity and grammar. Go over the instructions to make sure you hit all the topics."

Christian moaned as I gave him back his chair. "It's a solid paper."

"Leave the door open in case I need you," he said.

Life moved along while I waited to tuck in the covers and call Alistair. Thinking of that plummy voice of his coming through the line soothed and excited me. Not being distracted required focus. I whipped up dinner: turkey meat sliders on Hawaiian rolls with a side of brown rice and steamed broccoli. Forcing vegetables down my son's throat made me feel like a better mom.

Instead of sitting at the table, we ate in the family room and watched a few episodes of our favorite show. When I returned from taking our plates to the kitchen, Christian laid his feet on my lap. His way of telling me he wanted a massage. While I rubbed his size-thirteen paddles, we laughed at the same scenes and anticipated what might happen in the next episode.

"There's a ton of recorded shows," I said. "You didn't see any without me?"

"Nope," he said. "I didn't want to watch any without you."

"That's sweet." I passed him the remote. "Pick the next one."

A poignant silence was exchanged. Christian glanced at me. His glassy, turquoise eyes radiated hope. I thought about how innocent he still was, about everything I had not yet told him about my life. I wondered if I ever would. This was probably the last year I would enjoy him being a mama's boy. Before the drugs, before the sex, before the partying—when hanging with your mom on Friday nights wasn't social suicide.

"Mom?" He redirected his gaze down toward the shag carpet.

"Yes, honey?" I replied.

He looked back up at me, his complexion warm from the sunset glow coming through the window.

"I'm really glad you're home."

"Me too," I replied. He pulled his Labrador Retriever feet from my lap.

He stretched his arms. "I'm going to bed."

I waited for him to get ready before dipping into his room. "Sweet dreams." I turned off the light. "I'm super proud of you." I was careful with every word. "You have a wonderful balance of intellect, sensitivity, and wit. Those qualities will take you very far in life."

"Thanks, Mom."

I clicked the door closed and made my way down the hall to my room. My bed resembled a nest. A sanctuary from the harshness of the outside world; the smooth cotton sheets, the puffy goose down duvet covered in butter-yellow linen. Fine bedding was an obsession. It was something I had grown to appreciate while working for Patrick Dunn. He was a master at finding luxury items in off brands that were less pricey.

I lit the scented candle Lily had left on the bureau and slipped under the covers, wearing nothing but lace underwear. The sheets were cool against my skin. I propped myself against a large square lotus flower pillow. With everything feeling comfortable, I dialed Alistair. He picked up on the first ring.

"Prudence, it's wonderful to hear your voice."

"Sorry I didn't respond sooner." I twisted a chunk of hair around my index finger. "I tend to be a bit lame about keeping in touch."

"No worries." He soothed like the Xanax I avoided out of fear I carried my father's addictive gene. The momentary tranquility was replaced with a coursing wave of nervous energy.

If a girl doesn't feel edgy while chatting with a guy she likes, then he isn't worth pursuing.

"I got a new home. I'm renting from Lily, who literally moved everything while I was in rehab."

Something else bugged me, but I kept it to myself. The decision to move was not mine. Lily had changed my residence without asking. Guilt screamed at me from the Serenity Hills feelings chart. *I am an ungrateful brat.*

"A fresh start. You had expressed worry about where you would end up living. Must be such a relief."

"It is," I replied. "Christian started school, the homework situation is grim, and an overload of design work." I tore at a few split ends. "No complaints though."

"No doubt you are fabulous at your job and in high demand. Are you doing the thirty meetings program?"

"Missed one but then attended two the same day. Not perfect, but close." A prickle at the thought of whether he was policing me or curious. The old paranoid feelings Nick dumped on me resurfaced.

"I went to a client's house to hang some drapes. The husband was there alone. Super handsy guy, but I handled it pretty well." I instantly regretted my words, fearful Alistair would think I was trying too hard to come off as desirable.

"Oh, Lord. You're getting put to the test already." He laughed.

Phew. "I'm proud of you for holding your ground. That can't be easy."

"And I made a decision about my marriage. I had a moment of clarity. The one that failed to come in rehab." These words I had not yet spoken aloud. "I asked Nick for a divorce."

An awkward pause commenced.

"Jeez," he said. I bit the inside of my cheek. "How did all that go?"

"I don't know . . . trying out this new thing where I don't talk shit about my son's dad."

Alistair let out a chuckle. I fantasized about his soft smile. "Excellent strategy." He paused to speak to someone. "How did Nick handle it?"

"He acted surprised and hurt. Rehab taught me about how I ended up in such a complete train wreck. I don't want to repeat history."

Rambling, my greatest talent.

So much had happened since I'd last seen Alistair the day I checked out. It seemed as though a year or two had passed in the span of only a few weeks. This was our first official unmonitored conversation. "It helped sway my decision when I saw evidence of Naomi at Nick's house."

"That sounds in line with everything you shared about Nick in group." He took a sip of something. "I have crazy news."

"Do tell." We were playing ping-pong, and I was winning. His turn to share.

"Mike left Serenity Hills two days into Survivor's Week. No one is saying anything. Believe me, I tried to get the scoop."

"I actually found out today when I called Serenity. Nurse Ratched wouldn't give me his number."

"The Great Oz is gone."

I worried that I had Mike on a pedestal. But we all had. He held a magical balance of strength and vulnerability that made us believe we could trust him. Alistair's voice on the line wrested me from my thoughts.

"On a high note, I'll be heading straight to LA when I get out of aftercare." Alistair stopped speaking; I held my breath. "I hope to see you. You are always at the top of my mind."

I bit my lip and smiled to myself while twirling a ringlet around my finger. "I'm surprised and thrilled." My forced enthusiasm was coming through loud and clear. "Why LA?"

The idea of seeing him was almost too much for me to handle. I began to tremble. My teeth wanted to chatter. The farther I inched under the covers, the more vulnerable I became. When I was young, after my stepfather Richard had moved in with us, I grew accustomed to sleeping in layers of clothes regardless of the temperature. While the extra garments never stopped him from molesting me, they provided an emotional barrier. *My coat of armor.* I asked Alistair to hold on so I could throw on a t-shirt and sweatpants.

"I have some business in LA which may keep me there for a while," he said. "Oh, and of course, I'll be at Gloria's memorial service."

"Wait, there's a memorial for Gloria?" *Who planned this without me?* "Who invited you?" I prayed I didn't sound too snippy.

"Mitch organized it at the request of Gloria's boyfriend. The married guy she talked so much about, Tom. It surely was an oversight." He exhaled. "I hope I haven't screwed up somehow by mentioning it to you."

"No, you're probably right." I smoothed the edge of the sheet.

"I've got to go. They only let me talk for so long. Big Brother is still watching me. I'm hopeful for us and I miss you madly."

"You're sweet to say that. It will be amazing to see you." Gloppy, tapioca pudding words. It was too soon to be talking about the future and hope. All I could do was live one day at a time. The rules had been clearly laid out. No one should engage in a relationship until both people have been sober for at least a year.

"How are you handling aftercare?"

"I'm pretty down," he said. "The harsh reality of leaving rehab and fear of the unknown. I should be celebrating. My life is about to change for the better."

"It's normal."

"Goodnight, sweet Prudence."

"Night."

I hung up the phone a bit disappointed by the long-anticipated call. Most of the sweetness I'd intended to reciprocate I'd muted. Beyond that disappointment was me, seething over not being invited to Gloria's memorial service.

Chapter Eleven: Prue Past

Gloria and I sat on my bed playing cards. She found a deck in the break room and justified taking them with the claim that they were left unsupervised.

"Ya snooze, you lose," she said. Her nimble fingers cut the deck in half then tucked the edges of the two halves into each other. In one motion, they arched and flipped.

"How'd you learn to do that?" I asked. Gloria never failed to impress me, even with something as silly as shuffling cards.

"Vegas, baby," she replied with a wink. She split the deck, told me to cut it again, then put all the piles back together. "Do you know how to play gin rummy?"

"I've played it before but don't remember anything." I struggled with flexibility, and my knees popped up on the sides when I tried to sit like Gloria. Instead of worrying about my lack of yoga skills, I fixated on her tan shoulders and perky breasts. She exuded an enviable glow; a naturally confident, sexy aura.

"I can teach you." She sounded excited. After Gloria gave me a brief review of the game, my memory started to return. "Aces are low."

I obsessed over the easy way she moved. Her pink flamingo pajama pants slung just below her hips, the string of her panties peeking over her prominent hip bones.

"Face cards are worth ten points each, numbers are worth their face value, and an Ace is worth one point."

While she gave instructions, she rolled on lip balm as sensually as Lolita. No wonder Gloria made men's knees buckle.

"The goal is to collect sets like three or four of a kind, or consecutive ones with the same suit." Her thick-knuckled fingers dealt the cards. I shrugged. The competitive spirit within was lackluster at best. I didn't care about winning. I cared more about being in the company of someone I cared about, someone I admired. Gloria did that for me. She was an intriguing woman with an addictive presence.

"Let's start with an open round."

I made myself a mental note to buy new pajamas when I got home. My oversized boxers and worn-out pilled nightgowns from Target needed to be tossed. The frumpy sleepwear collection screamed for an overhaul.

"What did you think of the session today?" I asked, showing her my hand. She rearranged what I had arranged, which made me laugh.

"I felt bad for Alistair. He had a rough childhood." She reorganized my cards as she spoke. A noisy group passed by her window. "Alistair is so handsome, you almost can't feel sorry for someone that hot. I always imagine attractive people have it easier than the rest of us."

"As though you don't fit in that category. Jesus, you're sexy AF." No point in feigning disbelief.

"Well, Alistair never looked twice at me. He only has eyes for Prue." She flashed me a dramatic wink. "Get it? Instead of saying 'for you,' I said, 'for Prue!'"

This side of Gloria warmed me down to the core; her pure-hearted innocence. She had remained soft and kind regardless of what happened in her past, while I hardened like a cold slab of marble with a pulse.

"I'm sure he looks at you, but with the age discrepancy between you, he might think you're too young, so he doesn't bother." I gazed at my hand with no clue what to do. A therapist once told me some advice about talking with boys. She said they opened up more if you gave them something to do while you chatted—Legos, shoot a basketball, play a video game. I figured Gloria needed to be doing something to open up, and so I played along.

"Well," she said. "Tom is way older than Alistair, and he thinks I'm hot." Her shoulder strap dropped and revealed the edge of her areola. Every move she made dripped with sensuality. I stretched my arms in front of me; the thick-strapped top stayed put.

"Ugh," Gloria grunted. "I wish I had your boobs."

"Really?" I replied. I knew she didn't actually want my boobs. Regardless, the compliment felt nice coming from her.

"I think they make me look fat," I said, staring down at my blubber mounds.

"No, they don't! Men adore boobies, and I've seen Alistair check yours out quite a few times. For that matter, I'm pretty sure I caught Mike checking out your boobs too." Gloria laid her cards out on the bed. "I think I won."

I opted not to gaslight her Mike comment. "Yup," I said. "You won."

She began to shuffle. "So what was it like to make out with Alistair?"

"Fabulous, but the guilt is killing me. I mean, I'm a married sex addict, in treatment." *And I want to avoid the subject altogether.*

"Whatever," she said. "Don't avoid my question." Her root-beer eyes dug into mine.

"One of the most sensual kisses I've ever had. The guy has got mad skills. He didn't come at me with all kinds of sloppy tongue action or like some guys who latch on you like a remora." I laughed and Gloria acted more than perplexed. "Let's put it this way . . . I try not to obsess over where else his talents lie."

Someone knocked. One of the attendants opened the door enough to pop her head in. "Past curfew. Prue, time to head back to your room."

"See ya tomorrow." I slipped into my flip-flops.

"Come get me for breakfast." She paused for the attendant to leave. When I leaned in to give her a hug, she stood and took my shoulders in her hands. Her gaze moved from my eyes to my lips. Electric currents flew down my arms and blasted to my stomach. Instead of pulling away, I waited to see what was going to happen—to experience whatever she had planned for me. The thought of getting caught by the attendant added an extra layer of excitement.

In one smooth motion, she pressed her warm, puffy lips on mine. I relaxed into the moment and accepted what she was offering. Her tongue gently eased its way through my closed lips. My body softened under her grasp. I inhaled her familiar sweet candy scent. My tongue met hers then flicked it away. While we played cat and mouse, my pelvis filled with a rush of warmth. Gloria closed the kiss and pulled away to see my eyes, which I could barely open.

"I love you," she said.

My entire being was hers, and I would have done whatever she wanted in that moment. We passionately made out for a few more moments until I was hit with reality and pulled away. My cheeks flushed with embarrassment or perhaps shame that I was so turned on by my friend, so easily taken by her sensuality and mystique.

"Good night," I said, creating a bit of distance between us.

Gloria's hands moved from my shoulders to my fingertips. I smiled before stepping out into the Arizona night. Before closing her door, I turned to wave and she gave me a tender smile.

Dierdre, my roomie, was sleeping and the lights were out. I slammed my pinky toe on the corner of the desk and swore under my breath. The now reawakened sexual tension released in my quick temper. After brushing my teeth and washing my face, I kneeled by my bed.

Dear God, please protect me and guide me. I'm ready for You to help me. I'm ready to be saved.

I crawled into bed. The pillow was too hard, the sheets too scratchy. All I wanted to do was masturbate. If I could pleasure myself then I would fall asleep, but I didn't. I'd broken far too many rules already.

Chapter Twelve: Prue Present

The days moved along without the catastrophes I had created pre-rehab. I was behaving more like a grownup and less like a broken child. It wasn't easy, however. Christian had become harder to rouse from bed than in previous years. He had become more forgetful, too. I found myself constantly walking a line between nagging him and letting him fail to learn the associated life lessons the hard way. I wasn't entirely sure I'd struck the balance correctly.

The things I had struggled with before checking into rehab were still at the forefront. Most of the changes came in the way I viewed them.

I began every day with a prayer in which I stated my purpose. An innate desire to be perfect was replaced with the goal of being engaged. Perfect, I had discovered, was the enemy of good. I wanted life to be less about the plan and more purpose-driven. Mostly, I wanted to remain flexible when things didn't go exactly as I had hoped, or when the to-do list wasn't ticked off by day's end.

"You might need your books," I said as Christian strolled out the door empty-handed.

"Dammit." He threw his phone on the kitchen counter. "I still have to print my paper, too." He ran to his room while I poured myself more coffee. A message flashed on his screen.

I had always respected his privacy, but as he was embarking into his untrustworthy teens, I opted to read the message from some girl named Ashley.

I have the stuff.

I fought the urge to ask who Ashley was and what she had meant by "stuff." Better to find a way to bring up the subject when the opportunity arose. The last thing I needed was a battle when I was in the midst of regaining his trust.

With Christian out the door, I headed out to meet Frankie. I brought Lou with me since I harbored guilt over leaving him for so many weeks. I checked out my ass in my kitchen window, relieved it wasn't the tractor-trailer I'd envisioned. When I rounded the corner by the Starbucks, I spotted her.

"So great to see you," I said as I drew closer. Her pink-tipped hair gave off a youthful vibe. The cropped top exposed her trim waist and sweatpants that somehow went perfectly up her butt. "You look gorgeous."

"So do you." Frankie scratched Lou's back. "Who might this guy be?" she said in a baby voice.

"My needy child, Lou," I said. "I've been away for a while and he's been glued to me ever since I got home."

I hooked his leash to a bike rack while we ordered coffee. My new budget eliminated Starbucks, but I justified having coffee with a friend as "appropriate outer-circle behavior" and worthy of the cost. Frankie got a venti coffee and a chocolate croissant. I remembered being young and eating whatever the hell I wanted.

"Aren't you hungry?" Frankie asked. "You can't make me eat alone."

I added an order of oatmeal with my coffee. We sat at a table in the sun. Frankie put on dark, oversized sunglasses, which looked exceptionally chic compared to my ten-year-old Ray-Ban aviators.

"So where were you for so long? Some exotic vacation?" She licked the chocolate from her fingertips.

"I wish." I dumped every single packet that came with the oatmeal into the small paper cup. "I was in rehab." I gave her a moment to take it all in.

"I would die to spend time focusing on myself," she replied. "Rehab actually seems fun—yoga, therapy, healthy eating."

I smiled at her blasé attitude. She put down her croissant, perhaps worried she may have offended me.

"I mean, I don't know, it was definitely an interesting experience. You're probably thinking of glam rehabs like Passages in Malibu," I said with a chuckle.

Her eyes widened. "Where Lohan went, right?" She chewed as we spoke, which somehow looked sexy.

"Yes!" I said.

We shared a few laughs as she continued eating her croissant. She brushed the crumbs off her swollen lips while I stared. I hadn't remembered how beautiful she was, perhaps because I had been in a bad spot when we first met.

"What did you go in for?" she asked.

"Sex addiction," I said. "I mean, I don't tell everyone that, so yeah, I guess keep it between us. Obviously."

She responded with a reassuring nod. "I'm probably a sex addict." Frankie didn't miss a beat. "So have you seen Roger? That guy is such a tool." She took off her sunglasses. "I'm still hanging with his brother. He's got a bunch of girls he pays, but I'm his number-one ho sitting at the top of the food chain."

"No interest in ever seeing Roger again." I took a sip. "We never fucked, I only blew him. So weird. I used to fantasize that he would save me."

"I know, I fell into their trap too. I keep a few clients, but I'm in the midst of building a huge following on social media." She smiled with more enthusiasm than I would over Instagram followers.

"Damn, girl, loving your entrepreneurial spirit."

"I landed myself two sponsors—a lingerie company and this startup that makes CBD lubricants. You should try them. They really stimulate. Wait, I'll give you a sample." She hunted inside her giant tote. "Let me know what you think."

I swiped them off the table and tossed them in my bag. "Will do. So, are you dating anyone?"

"Nope," she said. "Given up on that. How about you?"

"I'm supposed to wait a year, but I doubt I'm going to succeed," I said, deciding then and there to confess about Alistair. "I met someone in treatment. Not the most favorable way to begin a relationship."

"Truth," she said. "I've seen those romances implode, but then again, a few have lasted. Who's the guy? Is he in LA?"

"He's from London but coming here for business and some other stuff. He's the dream package—loaded, sexy, and oh, an ex-coke addict."

"Blow is gnarly. I stopped, made me mad depressed."

"I'm not a drug person," I said. "I mean unless you consider rosé and chardonnay a drug."

"You crack me up, Prudence." Frankie laughed with her whole body. "I'm so glad to see you." She slung her bag over her shoulder. "I gotta hit the gym. Let's get together again soon." We hugged goodbye.

"For sure," I said.

"Bye, Lou." Frankie bent down to give him a pat on the head. "Text me."

Like a row of falling dominoes, every head turned when she walked across the street. A few cars even slowed down. I glanced at the blubber roll billowing from my tee. I made a mental note to lay off the dark chocolate before bed.

*   *   *

As I passed by Christian's room with a load of dirty clothes, I overheard him on the phone. The anxiety in his tone stopped me in my tracks. The level of his voice increased after each pause in the conversation and then, as though acutely aware of itself, dropped right off.

"This is not my fucking fault," he said.

I paused outside his door, my breath quiet and slow to hear what he was saying. Christian moaned. I wanted to interrupt, but my better judgment warned me not to.

"What was he thinking bringing that shit to school?" he asked. "Complete and total idiot."

I stood in the ready position. Saliva pooled in my mouth, fearful even the swallowing sound might give me away. I noticed the bipolar beat of my heart, the way it raced and stopped.

He went quiet. I assumed he was listening to the person on the other end of the line.

"My mom is going to kill me. I have to tell her before she finds out." His backpack fell to the floor with a thud. "Ashley, your parents are not going to kick you out." His chair squeaked when he twisted on its pedestal. "I gotta go. See you tomorrow."

I bolted to the laundry room. His door flew open.

Christian stuck his head around the corner. "I need to tell you something." His face was whiter than lambskin soaked in bleach.

I put down the laundry. "Sure." I followed him to his room, keeping some space between us while he sat on the bed.

"Well, one of my friends got caught with a pipe at school. There wasn't any weed, though." He fiddled with the pop socket on his phone.

"Was he suspended?" I asked, wondering what this had to do with my son.

"Yeah, for a week."

"Which friend?" My patience grew thin. "I'm annoyed you found it so important to tell me there was no marijuana. When a kid has a pipe, all evidence points to smoking." I made direct eye contact. "The district has rules for bringing drug paraphernalia on school property. This is a major offense. Plus, you're like the best lacrosse goalie in the area. Coach won't tolerate this sort of bullshit on his team."

He avoided my piercing gaze. "Oliver," he said, ignoring the rant that followed my initial question.

I wanted to blast out of the room and call Oliver's mom. "Who was on the phone? Oliver?" I asked, figuring it had been Ashley but desperate to know more.

"Ashley," he said. "She transferred this year."

A bombardment of questions rested on my tongue. I needed more explanation, but if I attacked him, he might shut down.

"The Principal asked Oliver to name the kids he had smoked with." He averted my eyes.

My stomach flipped then flopped. I leaned against the edge of the desk. "And?"

"My name got mentioned." His head turned down and his shoulders slumped over. "I'm sorry." His palms covered his face. "They might call you. I didn't want you to be blindsided." His voice cracked. I pressed my lips together to avoid spiraling into a rage.

"What does Ashley have to do with this?" I asked, eager to know more about this mystery girl.

"Oliver borrowed Ashley's pipe. The pipe fell out of his backpack right when a teacher walked by. Ashley was one of the people that Oliver mentioned when they asked him who smoked weed with him." He spoke quick and choppy.

"Thank you for telling me before the school calls." I set my voice to a reasonable tone. I was a hot tangle of constricting nerves. Everything I had done pre-rehab had led my son to this. Was it my fault? "You may be suspended, but at this point, it's hearsay. They will be watching you." I chose each word carefully. Inside, a volcano erupted from within my chest.

I cursed Nick for being an absent father. I cursed myself for being half-present before rehab and then leaving my son at such a pivotal time in his life, even if I left to treat my own addiction. The shadow of addiction loomed above, raining all manner of parental fears down on me. Christian could end up like Nick, a functioning alcoholic devoid of real emotion. The addict is cunning, each high convincing the body it needs more. I pictured my child addicted to meth. I imagined myself five years from now racing down different LA neighborhoods in a desperate search for my son. My pride and joy. My beautiful Christian. I watched the light in his eyes, the way it bounced and escaped.

"The school has zero tolerance for this sort of thing. So do I, for that matter."

I hadn't quite started yelling. I took a mental breath and looked him directly in the eyes.

"You will need to exhibit good behavior."

There were no upsides for me to me going into a rage. He was freaking out enough.

"I'm deeply disappointed," I said, recalling the day my mother had said the same words to me. "When did you start? How often?"

"While you were in rehab." A knife to my heart. "Oliver found some in his garage. We smoked out of an apple behind the mall one day when we were skating."

The deep disappointment displayed on my face and body—arms interlocked, legs crossed, brow furrowed. "How many times since then?"

He pretended to be thinking. I figured I would double whatever number he gave me. "Five or so."

So ten.

"I need time to think about how we are going to proceed. I've shared with you the pain my father's addiction caused me. I'm not sure what upsets me more, the fact that you're smoking pot or your nonchalant attitude." I took a breath, unsure of how to knock some sense into him. "I'm considering grounding you."

His eye roll threw me off. "For the record, I'm not a stoner. I don't like drinking, and all my friends who smoke are good students." He raised his left arm and slapped a hand against his thigh. "I mean, Mom, they are nice kids."

I clenched my jaw. "The point is, you are too young to smoke, or drink alcohol, for that matter." Fight-or-flight mode. "I don't care what everyone else is doing, you're my kid, I care about what you do."

While I spoke, I fought the urge to rearrange everything in his room—my way of calming down and gaining control.

"Okayyy." His tone was sassy and careless. "Whatever. I'm sorry for disappointing you. I don't think marijuana is that bad, but Oliver for sure shouldn't bring drug paraphernalia to school. Not that stupid." A high-and-mighty all-knowing teenager had taken over my child's body. "I practically make straight A's. It's legal in California."

A scream brewed while I fought the temptation to smack him across the face like Richard would have done to me. That would be repeating history, allowing my stepfather to change the course of my life more than he already had. I knew better and battled the learned behavior with all my might. This was my story. I would choose how it would unfold.

"I do not appreciate the way you're speaking to me. I need you to screw your head on and listen." My anger grew, but I kept myself in check. I crossed my arms over my chest and blew a hair off my face. "Your brain is not fully developed. Marijuana is a gateway drug. You know, I'm not against recreational or medical marijuana when a person is of a legal age, which is eighteen. You are not eighteen, not allowed to smoke, and that's final. I'm pissed beyond words. I need to search your bag."

"What? Why?"

"Give me your backpack now, please," I said.

"No, Mom. No," he replied, a condescending smirk wiped across his face. He crossed his arms.

"I said give me your fucking bag!" He jumped as I yelled. A flood of guilt engulfed my insides.

At least I didn't hit him.

He passed me his red, filthy, and torn backpack. I unzipped the front pocket and immediately found what he had more than likely purchased from a girl named Ashley.

I held up the Rasta-colored pipe and took a deep, disappointed sigh.

I watched a tear roll down his freckly, pale cheek.

"I'm sorry," he said.

*   *   *

While I stared mindlessly inside the fridge for something to make for dinner, Lily appeared at the back door.

"I brought food."

Her golden-streaked hair was wrapped in a tidy knot at the nape of her neck, the sleeves of her pink shirt rolled up. She dropped two enormous takeout bags on the counter.

"I discovered a new Chinese restaurant. I'll be right back, one more thing in the car."

She emerged with a bouquet that spanned the width of her chest, smelling like a flower shop. A memory came unbidden. The beater car parked under a copse of cherry plum trees in my childhood yard. Nicknamed the Dodge Fart. Lily and I would climb in the back and touch ourselves amongst the fallen flowers until we climaxed. Lily's hand would vigorously move in her shorts, her breath becoming heavy until her body shuddered. Watching her come would help me to reach a climax as well.

"What are the flowers for?" I asked, embarrassed by my intrusive thoughts.

Lily put the arrangement on a table. "I thought they might be from Nick, but they're from Alistair. I had to look to make sure they weren't for me. I was also curious who on earth would be sending such an elaborate arrangement."

She swiped a drop of water off the table with her sleeve. "Remember," she added, "you gave everyone at Serenity my address because you weren't sure where you'd be living." She took a letter from her back pocket. "This came for you too."

"I knew there was no way those could be from Nick because, I forgot to tell you, I asked him for a divorce." I let out an exaggerated grimace.

I watched her eyes widen and light up. I could tell she was trying hard not to smile. Was she happy about the divorce because it was toxic, or because it meant spending more time attached to her leash?

"Kind of major news to forget to tell me." I shrugged. She lightly rubbed my back. "But then again, you've had a lot on your mind." Her body language told the whole story—relief with a dose of mild concern. "I'm overjoyed for you. A door closes, a window opens."

"Sorry I didn't keep you in the loop." My shoulders lifted to my ears then dropped back down. "Feels empowering to finally make a decision." I opened the envelope that was wedged in the plastic fork-like holder. "To not be immobilized by my old indecisiveness."

Lily read over my shoulder and smacked her lips. "Not trying to sound judgy, but don't you think it's a little too soon to start dating?" She inhaled and walked around the kitchen table before pulling out a chair and taking a seat.

I admired the flowers for a moment then sat across from her. "Oh—he's just trying to be nice," I replied. "We got pretty close." A giddy schoolgirl laugh spilled out. "I mean, we all did, not just me and Alistair."

The card, written in classic cursive flower-shop handwriting: *I can't wait to see you xo Alistair.*

"So, you've been talking to him?" she asked.

Guilt wound through my chest. "We talked last night. He just started aftercare." A moment after reading the letter I'd taken from Lily's pocket, I looked at her and smiled. "I *was* invited to Gloria's service," I said. "The puzzle pieces are coming together."

"How sweet of Mitch to organize a celebration of life for Gloria," Lily said while aligning the salt and pepper shakers to be perfectly side by side.

"Alistair told me about the memorial, and I couldn't figure out why I hadn't been included." I headed to the takeout bags to dig into the food.

"Maybe I'll go too. You know, keep you company and what not." Lily was close on my heels.

"You don't have to do that," I said.

"Do you not want me to go?" she asked, a prevalent layer of anger just underneath her smile.

"No, of course I do," I said.

"I keep forgetting to ask you, how's work going?" Lily, stealthily changing the subject.

I set the table while she unlatched the containers. "Sam is up to his usual tricks, but we had a long chat and I'm sure the incessant flirting won't happen anymore." I tasted the garlic noodles from the container and moaned in ecstasy.

"I'm proud of you." Lily put a pile of rice on the plates. "When is Christian coming home?"

"He'll be home from practice in about a half hour." I slid two glasses from the cabinet and grabbed the bottle I kept in the fridge. We sat across from each other. I studied Lily's face. "You alright?"

Lily was not one to respond in an instant. Her mind moved in a more methodical and purposeful manner. "I'm fine."

Her husband, Binky, seemed a bit irritable lately. Not his normal jovial self. I wondered if they had been in a spat. She didn't hang out the dirty laundry and dealt with issues in her relationship privately.

"Actually, I lied. I found weed in Charlie's room." She put down her fork. "He told me Christian smokes too."

"I found out yesterday." I twirled noodles around my fork. "Our lives are a parallel universe. So bizarre." The tension from this latest turn stabbed me between the shoulder blades. "I overheard Christian talking with someone, and I eavesdropped." Lily clung to every word I said. "A text popped up from Ashley saying she had the stuff." I made air quotation marks. "Apparently that kid Oliver got caught with a pipe belonging to Ashley, and he told the principal who was smoking weed."

"You have a ton more information than me." She pushed the food around. "I met Ashley this summer. Her family moved from Santa Monica, and she is way more mature than our boys, both physically and emotionally."

I remembered when the mother of a boy in my middle-school class had referred to me as a "negative influence."

"I'm sure the school will call soon," I said, adjusting my ponytail. "I need to stay on it or this whole thing could take a bad turn."

"They're so young. I feel like I'm doing something wrong. Like I've failed at parenting." Lily breathed with frustration.

"You haven't failed, and I feel the exact same way," I said, wishing I could make everything better.

"Other than school, sports, and volunteering, Charlie is grounded."

"I'll follow your lead."

"This is going to be a long year."

She handed me a few drug tests, and I put one next to Christian's plate. "I wouldn't have had the guts to do this."

"Ya know, I'm kind of irritated at Binky." Lily helped herself to another glass. "He's turned into a stoner since we moved here, and now our kid is smoking. I pray Charlie hasn't figured out Binky is partaking in the ganja."

"Your husband is well within the legal age for the state of California," I said. "He's also quite pleased when he hits the kush, perma-grin and all. He never gets the telltale red eyes and cottonmouth. The only way I can tell he's smoked is that smile." I gave my best rendition of a Binky stoner smile.

"You're killing me, Smalls," she busted out. "I personally don't get the whole weed thing. All I do is get paranoid."

"Remember the first time we smoked the summer after ninth grade when Henry scored some ragweed at boarding school?" I smiled, remembering the scene like a movie. "I kept saying I thought I was Sylvia Plath in *The Bell Jar* while you stared at the door like the Feds were going to bust in." The irony of the situation hit me. "Just about how old our kids are right now."

Lily smacked the table. "You're absolutely right."

"We're in this together," I said. "Super sisters."

We locked pinkies like we did when we were kids.

"A funny thing happened on Saturday." Lily blew a laughing gasket before she could finish the story. "Madi spent the night at a friend's house." I braced myself for what was coming next. "I picked her up at the kid's house, and the mom said the girls were in the family room. I followed her to find Madi and her friend spinning around a stripper pole. I nearly died."

"I've got some of my own signature moves." I played the Spotify rap mix I blasted when I drove to work then started gyrating my hips.

Lily twerked her tiny rear. Meanwhile, we both blurted out nonsensical lines like, "Oh, yeah, hittin' that dance floor, werk that ass, gurl."

She performed a straight-legged bend-over with a head snap combo. "I'm like, welcome to LA bitch. You'd never see anything like that in Goose Neck Harbor."

We had consumed just enough wine to create the delusion we were sexy as hell. I was performing some kind of one-legged shoulder shimmy when Christian blew through the door with that judgmental yet appreciative expression only a teen can make. We couldn't halt our hip-hop moves fast enough.

"Am I interrupting something?"

The fun police. I straightened up to not embarrass him any more than I already had.

"We were just reenacting something from one of Madi's sleepovers." I was out of breath from all the gyrating. "How was practice?"

He grunted and dumped his stinky lacrosse bag on the floor. "Are those flowers from Dad?"

"Well." I stalled for an answer, or rather, the right answer. "They're from the guy you met during Family Week, Alistair." *And your mom is already getting bouquets from him.* "Aren't they beautiful?"

"I guess, but also kind of weird," he said. It wasn't my dance moves that embarrassed him, it was the constant attention I got from random men. I recalled Nick's comment about men going in and out of my home like a revolving door. My heart dropped to my stomach.

"Well, I can see how you could think that." I stared at the delivery as though a hidden message was hidden in the elongated plumes.

"I'm starving." He began opening the takeout containers and froze when he spotted the drug test.

I sighed. *Dodged the Alistair-inquisition bullet.*

Chapter Thirteen: Prue Past

All efforts to avoid Alistair proved to be absolutely futile. It was as though the campus kept getting smaller and smaller. I asked Mike if he might be available for a chat. Part of me hated asking him for time because of how much he already gave me, but Mike had some uncanny way of helping me figure out what I was doing wrong without actually giving me the answers. After the group broke apart from the Serenity Prayer, I slowly put everything in my bag to stall walking out the door. Gloria waited, so I had to tell her I was staying after group to speak with Mike.

"Is everything alright?" she asked with deep concern in her tone. I hated when she worried about me.

"Just dealing with some stuff. Nothing life-threatening. I'll meet you at lunch. Hold a seat for me."

"Of course," Gloria said.

She headed out with Rhoda and Deirdre, which made me feel better. Once the last straggler had moseyed out the door, I approached Mike.

"Can you spare a few minutes to talk?" I asked.

"Sure." He took a chair from the semicircle and put it beside his desk. "What's going on?" His thick brow furrowed, a sure sign that he had given me his full attention.

I dropped my tote on the floor and took a deep breath. "I'm having obsessive thoughts about Alistair. That fantasy world I visited a lot as a kid when I wanted someone to save me from my living hell. Have you read the fairy tale called *Donkeyskin*?"

Mike shook his head. "No, never even heard of it." He began copious note-taking while I admired his hands, a nice balance between strong and gentle. They were big but not oddly so, with neatly trimmed nails and zero jagged cuticles. His fluffed arm hair meant he definitely had some on his chest, and the thought gave me a guilty tingle inside.

"A sick, twisted, and sad tale," I said.

"Now I'm dying to read," he said, turning to his computer. "Would you mind if I looked it up?"

"Not like I've got anywhere pressing to be."

Mike inputted a long, arduous password so he could access Google. He read while I watched intently. It took every bit of strength not to tell him he was handsome, that I loved his eyes and wanted the story of how he got his scars. Mine couldn't be seen with the naked eye, but they were there.

Mike's gaze moved across the large screen. About halfway through reading the tale, he paused and looked over at me. "Doesn't it have a happy ending since it's a fairy tale?"

"Keep reading," I replied.

I believed that I was the princess in the fairy tale trying to escape the evil father, or in my case, stepfather.

The pony Mrs. Sutton let me ride, Balaam, hadn't littered gold, but he gave me the intangible gift of unconditional love. Mrs. Sutton played the role of the fairy godmother, saving me from the evil one by shipping me off to boarding school. When she read the story to me so many years ago, and after all the trauma I had endured, I believed I would somehow find my happy ending.

Mike relocked the computer and pushed himself away from the desk. "A fascinating story. Thank you for sharing it with me," he said.

I welled up until a tear rolled down my cheek. Mike clenched his jaw as he grabbed the box of tissues.

"Thanks," I said to him. I put my emotions back in their proper resting place. "I remember after Mrs. Sutton read it to me, I became hopeful for the first time since my mother left my father. If the princess could free herself from the king and find her prince, then I could too." My immature iterations mocked me. I shook my head and pushed a loose strand of hair behind my ear. "So dumb."

"That's where you're wrong. If something gives you hope, then it has provided you with a huge blessing. Hope helps us endure hardships and reminds us there is a rainbow waiting for us after the storm." His kindness almost made me start crying again. The smile Mister Rogers gave when he wanted the audience to believe everything would be better soon.

"The problem is that my life isn't a fairy tale, and no one is going to save me. Especially not some hot, rich prince." I fought a nervous laugh. The laugh won.

"You never know," Mike said. He smiled in a sweet, unassuming way.

"So I'm not a train wreck to think my life mirrors a fairy tale?" I asked.

Jesus, I sound like the main character in a cliché coming-of-age film.

"Why do you think fairy tales stand the test of time?" he asked. He stared at me and chewed his lip for a second. It seemed as though he was searching for an answer from within my eyes. "Because everyone wants a happy ending, even me."

I fought the urge to crawl into his lap and bury my face in his chest. The same way I got comfort from my mother when I was a child.

"You hold the power to create your own story. Like Dorothy in *The Wizard of Oz*," he said. His expressive hands added emotion while he spoke. "She held the power to return home all along, but she had to wait until she was ready." He looked at me thoughtfully.

With the ruby-red slippers on my feet, I clicked the heels together three times. "I have no clue what to wish for." My brow moved with a mind of its own due to worn-off Botox.

"It will come to you in time. Be patient."

Chapter Fourteen: Prue Present

It took five miles of running for my body to move into the relaxed zone. I stood at the sink chugging a glass of water. The high I used to get when I ran had eluded me since checking out of rehab. The frustration ate away at me, like not reaching climax but coming super close. I opened the fridge and pulled out a stick of butter and a few eggs. The run only eased a fraction of the angst inside, but this was the first Saturday where I had absolutely nothing to do. The boredom was killing me.

Rehab was regimented, scheduled down to the minute except when we socialized in the smoking veranda. Mike had never let me get away with anything. I couldn't manipulate him the way I could other men or past therapists. His advice echoed inside my head as though he was watching over me: "Just one step, but always a step ahead of your recovery."

I kept myself busy with positive activities, but the brain engine never stopped revving, thinking endlessly. As each footfall of my sneakers hit the pavement, I recited every damned healthy activity I could think of. It had been a homework assignment I completed at Serenity Hills.

Now I understood why we had to partake in the elaborate art project in rehab. We painted the rings on a large sheet, letting them dry overnight. Each ring was ready for us to fill with words that represented everything from forbidden activities to the healthy ones that would guide us through our new sober life. They were preparing us to deal with one of these boring kinds of days, the kind where I wanted to screw some idiot to avoid reality. Problems were always louder in the silence.

So this is what healthy looks like?

My life had become a complete bore. I presented the finished assignment to Mike, who chastised me over some things I put in the outer circle.

"But sexting doesn't always lead to sex," I'd argued when he challenged where I had decided to put some of my activities.

"Move it to the middle ring. No sexting after you check out." Mike spoke firmly but was never autocratic. "Activities like running, reading, baking, and spending time with friends belong in the outer circle. We went over this." He shot me a look of warning which resembled the ones my mother used to give me when I was on the verge of defiance.

The thought of never sexting again scared the crap out of me. It was a sure-shot way to get me out of a funk. I wasn't clear about how I could live without that small thrill.

I poked the butter. It was soft but still held its structural integrity. I flipped the stick over and peeled off the waxy paper. Cooking became part of a conscious effort to improve my relationship with food in association with a positive body image. *I'm fine with not being rail thin.* If I said this enough, I would eventually believe it.

I grabbed the bag of semi-sweet chocolate chips I kept in the freezer. I had to sync my phone up to the shitty speaker Nick had given me. *For being married to a guy in the audio business, you'd think I would own a decent sound system.* I switched to the mellow playlist. The first song annoyed me. Stop. I began deleting all the ones that provoked bad memories. My shame roiled deep inside of me. Something as small as music could trigger a downward spiral.

After getting rid of half of my playlist, I remembered to preheat the oven. I stared at the worn-out cookie sheet. It had been a wedding gift from a college classmate, another symbol of life with Nick. I prepared the family Christmas cookies on the same sheet every year. After frosting three reindeer, Nick inevitably lost interest. We exchanged laughs over our mutual lack of decorating talent. The cookie-cutter edges were never fully cleared of dough, which made the subsequent cookies progressively more mutated. I would mound sloppy piles of white creamy icing into separate bowls and add the food coloring. No matter how much I mixed in, it was far too pastel to represent Christmas. The mismatched tins were haphazardly filled and shipped to family and friends. I liked knowing they were enjoyed regardless of their flawed appearance. When Christian could stand, he joined in on the icing festival. A layer of colored sugar crunched under our feet. Green lips from licking the icing spoon.

I pulled the relic of a hand mixer from the drawer and beat together the eggs, sugar, butter, and vanilla. I refused to check the back of the chip bag. *What difference does it make if I mess it up?* I dug a spoon in the sugary batter with its pops of happy chips then resisted doing it again.

While the cookies baked, I lay on the sofa with a book. Everything distracted me: the ticking of the clock, a branch scraping the window, the cushion improperly wedged behind my back. My whole body itched. I ripped out a few strands of hair from my scalp. Self-sabotage.

I put in the last batch before I had to pick up Christian from lacrosse practice. The simple act of baking never failed to lift my spirits.

I said a prayer of gratitude to Mike for leading me toward healing and finding . . . no, *creating* some measure of comfort within my skin.

*   *   *

The next afternoon while doing dishes, a car pulled into the driveway. While I dried my hands, Binky waited at the back door.

"Handyman sent by Lily." He carried a small toolbox and was wearing a light-green t-shirt, board shorts, and a smirk that made him look like a thirteen-year-old. Binky and I had dated for a nanosecond in eighth grade—a subject we rarely acknowledged and never discussed. He was Lily's, and Lily was his.

"Hey, Binks," I said with a smile. He had maintained defined muscles and still had a full head of sandy hair from his youth. I ushered him to the master bath.

"How's everything going?" He unscrewed the showerhead while I opened the package containing the new one. It was a handheld with a long cord, one that would soon make me blissfully happy. He applied plumber's tape around the pipe to stop the incessant dripping. I took the old one from Binky and passed him the shiny one.

"Going well," I replied. We stood face-to-face between the sink and the tub.

"Take it as it comes. Don't be too hard on yourself." I leered at his outstretched arm. His toned, tan muscles moved with each sentence.

The caring words dredged up emotions sunken deep inside of me. We hadn't been alone like this since the eighth grade. My mind teleported back to that time when we sat on his parents' front porch one summer night smoking Marlboro Lights and listening to Elvis Costello.

"Oh, I know—Binks. I'm working on it." My words were scratchy and rough, only barely keeping some semblance of shape. I dropped my head in my palms. I deplored being weak and fragile. Binky gathered his arms around me. I let him pull me in, burying my tear-stained face in his shoulder. I inhaled his scent—a mix of salt water and Old Spice.

"You're doing great," he murmured. His hand brushed up and down my back the way a parent soothed a child. "Lots of change. It's no surprise you feel like crying." His voice in my ear blasted goosebumps down my spine. I pulled away, moving my gaze from his eyes to his mouth. The curve of his upper lip—so naturally sensual.

The space between us grew smaller. The light from outside had coated the interior space with a marmalade glow. I bit my lip and inched closer. His gaze unapologetically landed on my exposed bra. Strapped into silence, his uneven breath was the only detectable sound. I leaned in and pressed my desperate lips against his. I felt his twitch and shake. He took a step back in resistance. My mouth softly opened, searching for the unanswered questions of our past. We floated together. I lifted off the ground and landed with a thud.

"Mom," Christian said from down the hallway. Binky and I jerked away from each other. He stood at the entrance to the bathroom. "Oh, hi, Uncle Binky. What are you guys doing?"

I adjusted my posture and perked up. "He fixed my leaky showerhead."

Binky turned the water on then off.

If Christian knew, he would be ashamed to call me his mother.

"Oh, wow, much better pressure."

"Cool." Christian trotted off to his room.

"I'm sorry." I followed Binky out of the cramped bathroom. A twisting knot formed in my belly.

His cheeks turned red before they whitened. A long silence flowed through the open space between us.

"This is bad," he said after a minute. He waited until we were in the kitchen to talk about what had just occurred.

With a hand on his head, he paced around for a few seconds. I recalled the horrible feeling of rejection and guilt I had after sleeping with a married man. Sticky bedsheet, khaki pants zipped up, a glance at his fancy watch—"Keep this between us, please."

"Do you think Christian saw anything?"

"No, don't worry," I replied. He dragged the back of his hand across his mouth then reached for his toolbox. *A filthy whore.* "I'll walk you out." I moved along with him to his truck. He disregarded my obvious presence, almond eyes cast straight down.

"This is all my fault. I take one hundred percent ownership." I said. The reality of my actions began to set in.

Binky got in his car and put the passenger window down. "I'm telling Lily. You should too." His tone was stiff and uninviting. "She deserves to know."

A surge of nausea hit me hard. He rolled up the window and drove away.

I headed to the patio and eased into a lawn chair. A thick layer of fog lingered above me as I contemplated the seriousness of my behavior. I fought the urge to pull my hair, to rip the skin off my body, to hurt myself physically so I could draw focus from the pain inside. My thoughts raced as I struggled with what to say. Should I text her? Call her? The chickenshit pounded out a message, knowing full well I should confess to her face.

I did something supremely wrong. Something snapped and I kissed Binky.

He didn't kiss me back. I'm sorry seems too small and I'm scared to call you. I must be jealous of you and Binky. Clearly, I'm still a super fucked-up person and sick over what I've done.

The response bubbles appeared. My mouth went dry.

Call me now.

After a ring, she answered. I could hear her breaths through the phone.

"Look, I understand if you never want to talk to me again. Binky is on his way home to tell you." I gave her no space to speak. "I did it, not him—I don't know what else to say."

"What the fuck is wrong with you?" There was silence. "I can't remember ever being this angry at you." Her breath came quick and hard. Her voice started with a whisper then changed to a high-pitched shrill. "Wait, I'm not pissed. I'm *beyyyyyyond* pissed. This is so fucked up. This is such a betrayal."

I had only witnessed Lily display this kind of anger a few times since we had become friends.

Lily gasped as though she was pushing a sob deep into her gut. She exhaled.

"You are acting like a fucking whore, Prudence." A cold shiver traveled across my skin. Her tone was sharp. She stressed every word, very nearly every syllable. Her only goal in that moment was to hurt me like I had hurt her.

Success.

A long silence. "Oh, and you breached the hugest trust boundary in the history of our friendship and told me in a text message?" She hung up. I didn't bother calling her back. Binky would be arriving home soon.

I scratched my arm until it burned then ran to the kitchen and grabbed my keys from the hook near the door. "I'm going out to run errands," I yelled down to Christian's room. "Text me if you need anything."

In the car, I screamed. At the first red light, I dialed Alistair. No answer.

*   *   *

The month before my mother died on the hood of her boyfriend's cherry-red Porsche, I listened in on a phone session she had with her psychic. The psychic had told my mother that some tragedy brewed on the horizon. To the world, my mom appeared mainstream, but she often sought out the unconventional for answers. For a while, she found respite in the works of J. Krishnamurti. When his voice stopped speaking to her, she turned to a psychic healer.

It had been two days since the kiss and argument. I hadn't heard a word from Lily. It was the longest we had ever gone without talking to each other excluding the five weeks in rehab. The tightness in my throat battled a headache as bad as an exploding pressure cooker.

With Alistair about to arrive in LA, Mike's disappearance, the kiss, and Gloria's celebration of life coming up, it was time for a consultation. Thankfully, the psychic to the stars lived in Los Angeles. I remembered taking the psychic's card from my mother's jewelry box after she passed away. I don't know why. It was an odd sort of keepsake, but I'd kept it with me. Always there, nestled in the back of my wallet, pressed like a prom flower between the pages of a book.

She answered on the third ring. I begged, and she agreed to squeeze me in. My nerves kicked in. I was about to meet the woman who had predicted my mother's death.

Gram mocked my mother when she mentioned having her tarot cards read.

"It's a crock. Don't waste money paying someone when your instinct will tell you the truth."

Would Gram have said the same about me now?

I stared at my wrist—naked since giving Mom's watch to Alistair on the last day of rehab.

It was too soon to dive into a relationship. Too soon to be considering one. The kiss with Binky, a sledgehammer of evidence. And where was Mike? *I need Mike.* He'd know what to say. Hell, if he were around, maybe I wouldn't have been sitting on this ugly sofa.

The door to Madame Beatriz's office opened. A portly woman stood there, framed by the doorway. "Prudence, come in. Sorry to hear about your mother."

An icy chill shot through me. "Thank you," I said.

Madame Beatriz closed the door behind us. She wore dark slacks and a cobalt blouse—not the turban and beads I'd imagined. Just a regular woman in regular clothes. Except for one difference: she could predict a person's future. A roadmap of wrinkles adorned her face, the battle scars of a life well-lived.

"I remember your mother well," she said. "Please take a seat." She allowed me time to settle into one of the leather chairs before sitting down herself.

I took in every inch of the room. Two floral watercolors in matching frames sat on the wall above some shelves with books and various decorative items, three figurines, and a copper tray. A potted tree draped with twinkling lights illuminated the corner.

"I prefer to handle the fees before we begin," she said.

I took the money from the purse side pocket and tried not to grimace. The guilt over spending paled against my desire for answers. She tucked the cash in a box behind her where a Himalayan salt lamp glowed. Surrounding it were crystals and geodes in various sizes. Behind her hung a photo of a lotus flower bursting with sparks of light before a deep purple background.

"Can I get you some tea or water?" she asked.

"No, thank you," I said, anxious to get started.

"You mentioned an urgent matter."

"Well." I sat at the edge of the chair like a parakeet on a swing. "I'm at a turning point in my life and not sure what direction to take, who to trust, and who has my best interest in mind."

I thought she might interject.

"I recently learned that someone I care about and relied on moved with no forwarding information." The gravity of the situation proved difficult to communicate. "I'm a bit lost without being able to speak to him."

"Give me your right hand," she said, reaching across the table.

I wished I had a fresh manicure. She turned my palm to face up. "Listen to your breath," she commanded.

I obeyed. Fear rattled around my insides. I could practically see my demise and the faces of those I loved looming behind her next words. She would tell me to get my affairs in order. That I was not long for this world. The Grim Reaper waited with her scythe in the ready position.

"Is it alright if I invite you to visualize some things?" An energy force rolled across my chest. "Please refrain from responding until I finish speaking. I will ask you to conjure up an image. Accept the first thing you see. Do not question it."

"I'm ready."

The psychic let go of my hand. I laid them on my lap, palms up.

"Picture a body of water. You could be anywhere in the world."

I wanted to be on the beach at the Sound Club with Lily and Henry picking up horseshoe crabs and inspecting their undersides, but instead, I conjured up a serene lake.

"A vessel approaches. You understand it is for you. Someone could be driving, or you could make the journey alone. Go with the first picture that comes to your mind."

I tipped my head, the first images stacked and ready to be shared, the chaos telling me to think of something else. I remained steadfast to each original thought.

"Once you board the vessel, you will see an island in the distance. Go there. There is a house of some kind. You will leave the boat and walk there. Please observe whether the door is unlocked."

The designer in me became preoccupied with decorating the imaginary home, choosing colors, fabrics, the wood floors, the drapes, and the light coming through the windows.

"Inside the home, a deity awaits you with a gift."

Madame Beatriz sipped her tea. The cup clinked in the saucer.

The room fell silent.

"The first image that comes to your mind is the one you must say out loud. Do not manipulate your truths."

"I stood at the edge of a lake." The pictures came to life. "A canoe was there on the shore. I paddled alone. I came to an island with jagged cliffs and clusters of trees. I pulled my canoe up to a dock and walked along a trail covered with pine needles. Through a clearing, I saw a cottage. I stepped on the porch. The door was ajar."

Her expression remained unchanged. "Did you see the deity?" she asked.

"Yes." I became unmoored. "A woman cloaked in white with long, wavy hair was there. A halo of light surrounded her body."

"Did she have something for you?" Her ring-clad fingers intrigued me.

"Yes. She held a crystal sphere. Suspended inside the glass was a single dandelion right at the point where a gust of wind could blow the seeds from the stem."

Madame Beatriz showed nothing in her expression.

"The smooth water signifies calm seas ahead. Your journey will not be easy because you must paddle alone."

I cursed myself for not picturing a yacht with a sexy captain at the helm, champagne chilling on ice. A contemporary home on Saint Barth's overlooking Saline beach.

"The cliffs are future hurdles to be overcome. The pleasant cottage says you will find peace with an easy, simple life."

I would like to start over and retake the test. This time, I'll give the right responses.

"An open door means you will lead a joyful and fulfilling life. You are headed in a positive direction, but you are easily broken. Be careful of being tricked, of trusting the wrong people. Listen to your gut." She studied the tarot cards. "The gift you envisioned tells me you are fragile, delicate, kind."

She spread them out then tapped each card with her finger. I squeezed my knees together as though gripping a hundred-dollar bill.

"There are three men vying for your attention." She hovered a hand over a card: The Magician, The Three of Swords, and The Ace of Cups. "You must choose one. I cannot advise who. You, and only you, know the answer."

"Can you at least give me a hint?"

"Your heart knows the truth." She swept up the cards. "That's all we have time for today."

I peeled myself from the chair, totally confused. "Thank you."

Gram was right. This is all a crock of shit.

Chapter Fifteen: Alistair Present

After the Uber pulled away, Alistair was hit with a wave of instant regret. With no proper plan, he kicked a rock and watched it roll along the blacktop. Bare Elegance lit up the whole other side of the parking lot. Two men stood guard at the door. A woman in skinny jeans and a hoodie strode past him with a purposeful stride, a maroon snakeskin bag slung over her shoulder and headphones jammed in her ears. At the entrance, she removed her headphones to speak to one of the men. Alistair edged over to the satin ropes.

"You're here early." The doorman might as well have drooled on her chest.

"My spray tan is streaked to shit. I need to slather on leg makeup."

"Real-world problems." He performed a visual check of the area.

"Still looking for my big break." The woman dug around in her purse. "How's the crowd?" She flipped her bright-pink dip-dyed hair off her shoulders and popped a fresh piece of gum in her mouth.

"The usual," he replied. "Now that you're here, things will pick up."

"Yeah, right." She passed him a jewel case. "Play one, four, and five. 'Back Stabbers,' 'A-Go-Go,' and some song by The Black Keys."

Alistair savored his newfound anonymity. No one in Los Angeles knew him, which he found to be quite appealing.

"You're the only stripper on earth who dances to John Scofield."

The man put the CD in his coat pocket.

"I do my own thing," she said, tucking the pink tips behind her ear.

"The audio is giving me some issues," the doorman said.

"Awesome," she said. "Super fun dancing to static and screeching speakers."

He sized up her ass as she passed by. When he turned around, he spotted Alistair, who continued toward the entrance even though he wasn't entirely sure he wanted to go in. The bouncer asked for an ID. Alistair was certain he looked well over twenty-one. The guy examined his British passport and looked him up and down.

"You're from England?" Alistair wasn't sure if he was asking or telling, so he nodded. The man handed him back his passport. "Enjoy yourself."

Alistair's arm hair stood on end while a floodgate of bad memories crashed down on him. Memories of the things his mother had done to pay rent. On his tumble toward rock bottom, he had frequented similar places in London. The correlation between strip clubs and how much blow he snorted was easy to figure out.

He analyzed the room before taking a seat. After a moment, he spotted the woman who had walked in a moment ago as she disappeared backstage.

Nothing noteworthy played over the speakers, and the stage was unoccupied. Clusters of men sat around the poorly lit room. Some in suits, others in golf attire, and the usual lone wolves. The ones sitting alone depressed Alistair. He likely looked exactly like them. He wished his mate was with him, but this was something he needed to handle on his own.

Alistair chose a barstool. The doorman walked in and tended to the sound system. It went from flavorless and unmemorable to blaring the top 100s. After some auditory adjustments, the music leveled out.

"Entering the center stage is Brandy! On the side stage, let's give it up for Amber!"

A woman strutted to the pole in Lucite stilettos. Another ambled around the moon-shaped side stage, appearing rather bored. Alistair found the whole display to be stimulation overload, and he immediately began second-guessing his chosen seat. It would be important to sit somewhere with a vantage point that allowed him to keep an eye on both dance areas. He didn't want to accidentally forget the reason he had come.

"What'll it be?"

These establishments always hid a room or two for the elaborate lap dances and more intimate indulgences. Alistair, intent on finding such a room, didn't even hear the guy in front of him.

"What'll it be?" the bartender repeated with more sandpaper in the voice.

"Coke," Alistair replied. The guy dug a scoop in the ice bin, dumped it in the glass, and filled it with the dark, bubbling liquid.

"Five dollars."

Alistair wondered how the guy maintained a straight face when asking five bucks for a thimble of soda. He pulled out a ten-dollar bill.

"Was there just a shift change?" He may as well try to get some information from the guy while he commanded his attention.

"Yeah, coming and going. This is when most of the dudes start heading in after work."

"Right." He nodded, taking a long glance around the now-crowded space.

The bartender gave Alistair a curious look. "What's that accent?

Australia?"

"No, England. So, I'm wondering if there's a girl named Susie who might be working here this evening."

"Susie . . ." the bartender repeated as though he hadn't heard correctly. "Oh . . . you mean Frankie? Strawberry-blonde, about yay tall." He handed Alistair his drink. "This one's on me."

"Is she working this evening?" Alistair laid a twenty on the bar.

"What are you, a cop or something?" the bartender asked with a heavy Long Island accent.

"An old friend," Alistair replied.

He took the money. Everyone had a price. Alistair absently rubbed his nose. This whole situation turned out to be more stressful than he had anticipated, especially for a bloke fresh out of recovery. He bet that if he wanted to score some blow, the bartender would be the one to ask. He was always the one to ask. Alistair cycled through reflecting on his past and realized how much alcohol may have been a contributing cause to his extensive use of cocaine. All those nights out on the town in London, ending up at the strip clubs after the late client dinners, made him crave the drug even more.

"Only one girl answers to that name at the supermarket. She's backstage changing." He tapped the bar.

Alistair buried his face in his phone. He needed the distraction. The whole scenario was beginning to ride on his nerves, and the girls at home were far more personable. What was the name of the girl who had always danced for him? The tall, dark brunette with legs up to her neck. *Mona. Her name was Mona.*

A waitress leisurely lingered at the service counter. She was all business. She didn't even glance in his direction. Alistair wasn't accustomed to not receiving attention, which only made everything worse. It should have been a relief. He was here with a purpose. But it troubled him. He wondered if he had lost his mojo.

Her black mesh tank with nothing underneath left very little to the imagination. She handed the bartender a piece of paper. Alistair picked up his cell then put it back down, hoping he might catch her attention. The waitress smiled. He turned away. He was rough and awkward. Being sober had been so easy at Serenity Hills. He hadn't taken into consideration how much he'd underestimated the harsh reality of everyday life. The endless triggers would bombard him at every turn.

"She must not be that good of a friend," the bartender said to him, "or maybe you've got the wrong girl. The chick who was just standing here, that was Susie."

Alistair whipped around to see if he could find her in the growing crowd. He blotted his forehead with the cocktail napkin.

"I haven't seen her in many years." He felt himself crumbling under the pressure. "Is she dancing tonight?"

The guy laughed. "Yeah, she's got to waitress for the first hour, and then she strips. Settle in, buddy, it's going to be a long night. A little advice—you don't want to mess with Susie." He leaned across the bar. "She's been around here for a while. Girls like her can spot a snake a mile away."

Alistair ignored the insinuation that he was some kind of bad guy.

"I got mad respect for Susie," the bartender continued. "Everyone here has her back . . . if you know what I mean." He smacked the bar with his hand. Alistair flinched. "Watch yourself." He wiped a rag over his palm print.

"I'll do that." Alistair thought for a moment before stepping away. Trouble was the last thing he needed or wanted, or worse, to be kicked out. He saw no issue with kissing ass when it benefited him. "Thanks for the input."

He took a seat with a view of both stages. A considerably different scene from the nudie pubs in the East End, where the girls paraded around topless, collecting money and chugging beers before they danced. The fully nude spots in London's Soho went as far as encouraging audience participation, yet they were constantly being patrolled and shut down by the cops.

Alistair settled into his new seat and scanned the room. Two men a few feet away gave each other fist bumps when their dancer performed a straight-legged bend-over with a head snap in front of them. Both of them threw bills on the stage. The woman moved to the edge, and one of the men slapped a bill on her rear. She yelled, and the men began arguing before the bouncer showed them the exit.

Alistair blocked out the chaos and rolled through the latest dump of emails. One in particular caught his eye. After reading it, he texted Prue.

Bored but I'm exercising my newfound phone privileges from aftercare. I've landed a couple of VIP tickets to a Rams game next Sunday afternoon the day after my release and would love you to join me. We'll be seated in a box but could tailgate beforehand if you're interested. A driver will pick you up.

The pressing matter about the Chinese dragging their feet with finalizing the bond deal was weighing him down. There were days when he questioned whether the whole thing could turn out to be a complete sham while his clients grew impatient. He scrolled through his inbox and all the messages from investors inquiring about the payout. It was his job to appease them. Every single investor had signed a gag order. No one could discuss the bonds. Alistair tapped out an updated recap to send out to the investors.

Dear Client,

Before we discuss what we can on this update, let's start by making one point clear. This gag order is not a delay tactic on our part. We cannot share the timing until we are authorized to do so. This is final and applies to every client, group leader, and lead buyer rep. There are no exceptions. The people working at the office don't even know. By next Friday's update, we will have some news of great substance. The deal can only occur when the Quantum system has successfully been synched to all the prime banks in every country, and the process is still not completed.

Thank you for your patience,

Alistair Prescott

After Alistair sent the email, he reread the text he sent to Prue. He looked down at his phone in disgust—he couldn't remember ever hating himself more. The blatant lying about still being in aftercare to a woman he cared about resembled his pre-rehab life. The unsavory behavior, the way he had degraded so many women. He had been a complete and total pig. And now he found himself at a strip club again. Well, at least this time he was alone and sober.

He couldn't help but periodically glance at the exit door. Part of him thought about quietly slipping through it and never coming back. He pulled Prue's watch from his pocket and smelled the band. A hint of her perfume lingered in the rich, brown leather. He smiled and felt a modicum of calm. He turned the ruby-capped winder and put it back for safekeeping.

His phone buzzed. Prue accepted his offer. Despite his uneasiness with his current environment, he was filled with elation. Alistair folded over his knees and raked his fingers through his thick, dark hair. He sensed someone was standing over him. It was a woman with a gold ring dangling from a chain around her neck. His heart skipped a beat. He knew that ring and the bearer who wore it—his beloved Susie.

"Rumor has it you know me." A tray hung from her fingertips. "I don't know you, so whatever trouble you're looking for, look some-place else."

Before she got too far, Alistair spoke. "You wouldn't remember me." It took immense willpower for him not to scream and grab her and tell her everything. "Maybe you aren't the person I think you are, but I'd appreciate the chance to talk to you." His eyes were desperate yet controlled.

"I get off in three hours." She checked her bare wrist as though there was a timepiece wrapped around it. "If you feel like hanging, I might give you some time. Other than that, I'm here to make money, so either start throwing bills at me or get the hell out." She had a bruise on her collarbone, which she had clearly attempted to conceal with caked-on foundation.

"Sounds fair." He gave her a hundred-dollar bill. "For you." She took the cash and stashed it in her sky-high gold lamè shoe.

Alistair pulled the watch from his pocket. "This is so you know what time it is," he said, passing her Prue's watch.

She examined it. "Cartier. Not bad." She held the tray under her arm and buckled the band around her wrist. "See ya around."

Alistair couldn't recall when he had last eaten. His stomach rum-bled. A small buffet was laid out on the far wall. With time to kill, he headed over to check it out. Everyone in the food line avoided eye contact like in rehab. No one exchanged niceties—every man for himself. He loaded a plastic plate with wings, chips, and three cheese wedges then went back for another five-dollar Coke.

"I see you met Susie." The bartender moved the glass in front of Alistair. "For something stronger, you gotta go to the back room."

"I'm staying put for now. But thank you—I'll keep that in mind."

Alistair perused his email while he ate. All positive responses. That fire had been doused for now. He revisited the food table for seconds. Definitely not the worst he had ever tasted, and it hit the spot. By the time he got back to the bar, Susie was approaching the stage. He averted his eyes from the creeps watching her every move. A nervous sort of rage vibrated inside of him.

Aside from the one girl dancing on the small stage by the swivel chairs, most of the attention was on Susie. She coiled her way around the pole slowly before bending over to reveal her sparkly thong. The speakers blasted out a bizarre sound for this environment—a jazzy standard that Alistair recognized. Soon enough, Susie ditched the pole and crawled toward the patrons, allowing them to tuck money under the string of her bikini. Everyone cheered for her to remove her top.

Alistair looked away. He searched for a corner where he could wait until Susie got off her shift. A woman appeared beside him.

"Are you looking for someone? Or waiting for me?" When she laughed, her shoulders moved but her breasts stayed put. "I can sweeten up your drink for you if you'd like." Bright-orange lipstick adorned her gummy smile.

Alistair slipped her a twenty-dollar bill. "I'm going to sit over there. Please add vodka to my Coke." She parked her eyes on the money with disdain. He pulled a fifty from his wallet and dropped it on her tray.

The cocktail helped him relax. He began writing a follow-up email to the buyers. It was slow going with so much on his mind, but he managed to write something and saved it in his drafts. A ton of information had piled up in his brain since checking out of rehab. He had made lists of things he needed to do to unwind his life in London: women who had to go, male counterparts with whom he'd partied, an overall reevaluation of his friend circle. The hostess from earlier periodically came back to refill his drink. Save for that, no one bothered him.

The once-sleepy room was quickly picking up pace. The initial group of patrons was long gone. True to the first bartender's prediction, the room began to fill with men. Women strutted out from the back area, requested by name.

Every few minutes, he made sure Susie was in his line of sight. She moved to some guy's lap, where she gyrated her hips in a hula-hoop motion. A few other men flanked the surrounding chairs with women grinding on their laps. He went back to his phone until he heard a familiar voice. His ears keenly tuned through the noise and to the conversation happening with Susie.

The man who had been talking to her edged his way over toward Alistair. The closer he got, the more certain Alistair became that his worst nightmare was coming true. Approaching Alistair's direction was Mitch from Serenity Hills. The strut was familiar, and the same round glasses sat atop the ridge of his nose. Alistair contemplated darting out the side door, but they had already made eye contact.

"Alistair?" Mitch squinted his eyes, and Alistair repositioned himself to face Mitch.

"Mitch, good to see you, mate," Alistair replied. He took a long sip of his vodka-coke.

"Does Prue know you're in town?"

"I didn't know how long, I, uh—would be in LA," he said, stammering for words. "There is a good explanation, although I understand this isn't the greatest look."

"I'm here with a business associate," Mitch said, pointing in the direction of Susie. "A stripper just offered to sell me her Cartier watch. I thought to myself this looks a lot like Prue's." He motioned to the door. "I'm heading to the men's room."

"I'll tell you everything when you get back," Alistair said, but the music drowned out his voice.

Without another word, Mitch turned and walked away. Alistair waited for a reasonable amount of time for someone to use the restroom. He made a note of the time. Susie's shift would end in thirty minutes. Alistair dreaded leaving the room to find Mitch, but he also couldn't bear not explaining the situation and having it get back to Prue.

He entered an empty bathroom. Mitch must have left through the side door. Alistair cursed his bad luck while equally cursing the realization he had to pee. He stood at the urinal, panicking over how close those two had been in rehab. No way in hell Mitch wouldn't mention this to Prue.

After he dried his hands, he tossed the towel in the trash, where he noticed two used condoms. "Jesus." He returned to his seat in the corner and refocused. He dragged his phone from his pocket. There was nothing he could do to fix what had happened. Susie headed over to him. Alistair's palms began to sweat.

"I'm going back to change. Meet me out front in ten," she said.

Alistair regretted the second drink while also wishing he was holding a third.

Chapter Sixteen: Prue Present

My commitment to go to thirty meetings in thirty days fell short. I called my therapist, Dr. Sheryl O'Brien, to schedule a private. Not surprisingly, Dr. O'Brien insisted I go to females-only Sex Addicts Anonymous groups, which were inconveniently located in Venice at equally inconvenient times. Once I drove to the meeting and mustered up the guts to enter a room full of freaks, I would then feel bad for calling them freaks, even if only in my head. I became riddled with self-hatred in the form of a blinking sign lighting up my mind—I might not be getting better.

The women who attended SAA appeared normal. Once they started sharing their stories, I wanted to run. By my estimation, the majority of them had endured horrific childhoods. They had lived their own version of my dark closet. Some experienced multiple date rapes; others were molested by family members or friends. So many dark closets, each of us similarly acting out some sort of revenge against men. Even now, it still wasn't clear how sex equaled revenge. I figured it must be every guy's dream. *Sex with no strings attached, yes, please.* According to Doc O'Brien, I needed to associate intimacy with love.

The sound machine outside her door was at full volume, a sign that she was in the middle of a session. The longer I sat in Sheryl's waiting area, the more I fantasized about the weirdo currently in her office. Perhaps confessing about all the porn they'd been watching, the rub-and-tug massage parlor visits, or better yet, the plethora of people they'd banged in the past week. The other consuming thought—whether or not I was still a sex addict after a five-week stint in rehab.

Her door opened. I buried myself in a magazine as a man passed by. Sheryl stood silently by her office until the door closed behind him.

"Sorry, I'm running a little late today, had to squeeze in an emergency appointment."

"No problem." I followed her in.

Sheryl snapped her pad from the table beside her chair. I was thrown off guard by her updated glasses but relieved she was still wearing the same frumpy clothes. The new frames gave her a chic and trendy vibe. I ran through the reasons why she might have a new pair: a hot new lover, a promotion at the sex-addiction center, an important speaking engagement, or maybe she got in a scuffle with a patient who broke her old ones.

"Tell me how you've been doing."

I took a tissue from the box resting next to me and twisted it into a snake. This allowed me time to stall—should I tell her exactly what happened, or paint the rosy picture I preferred?

It's a miracle—I'm all better now!

How easy it was to lie to a therapist. When I recapped the times Nick and I lied in couples therapy yet believed we weren't, well, I could either laugh or cry. The whole thing became a comedy of errors. Rigorous honesty was supposed to be crucial within the four crème-colored walls. Unless, of course, the real reason for the appointments was to inventory last year's contemporary paintings and beige HomeGoods oddities on display in doctor's offices. I wondered who dusted the crocheted plant holder and groovy dream catcher hanging above the gently flowing water fountain. A hippie through and through. In my experience, hippies tended to be the least judgmental people around.

"I'm considering a candy-coated version of the truth." A fake, guttural laugh escaped from my throat without warning.

"Get the worst part out first." A calm, therapeutic tone combined with a head bob. "We can work forward from there."

I focused on her sun socks and stopped before inquiring if she owned some with stars and moons on them too. *Focus, Prudence.*

"I kissed my closest friend's husband." *There I said it.* Far better when I ripped off the Band-Aid.

Sheryl's pen wobbled. Her note-taking came to a halt. She looked up through the fishbowl lenses with her cartoon-like hazel eyes. What I would have given to read all the notes she had taken during our sessions. *Prudence is a freak and needs to stop fucking everything that moves.*

"Well," Sheryl said. "You answered that one all on your own." A long silence infiltrated the square room. Her gaze met mine, perhaps searching for more confessions she knew were there.

I took a deep, dramatic sigh.

"I might have been envious, or in some way wished I had chosen Binky back when he wanted me in eighth grade." My foot pretended to be a bucking bronco at the end of my leg. "Everything always pans out for Lily. Nothing ever works out for me."

"And is that Lily's fault?" Sheryl gave me her authentic soft smile. "You're taking this lighter than I would expect. This is your dearest friend. You kissed her husband. Could there be more here than you're admitting to?"

I stared out the window. *Dammit.* The reality of my actions hit me like the crack of a baseball bat landing a home run.

"There has been a small amount of anger building over Lily moving my home without my consent. I've been a bit bored, trying to follow the rules, don't text anyone I shouldn't be texting, keep my A-game going at home and at work." My foot quieted. "I guess I just wanted to stir things up in my life. The lack of drama is killing me."

"Have you confessed your indiscretion to Lily?" Sheryl put the notepad down. Things were turning serious.

"Yes. I texted her like a chickenshit, scared shitless to tell her to her face," I said, instantly regretting the added swear word.

Sheryl uncrossed her legs and readjusted her position in the chair. "I'd like to know more about Lily's involvement in your post-rehab life. You mentioned being angry about her moving your home. Tell me more about that." A question I had not been prepared to answer.

"Well—I guess it just felt like she was planning my new life for me . . . like I was her charity case and I wouldn't succeed without her help." A weight lifted from my shoulders. Thoughts I had never said out loud were now laid in the open for anyone to see. I didn't want to come off as unappreciative and bitchy. I averted my eyes.

Sheryl pressed the edge of her pen against her lower lip. She furrowed a brow, but her gaze remained still and focused.

"I'm an ungrateful bitch, I know," I said.

Sheryl shook her head and set her pen down. "I think Lily is a great friend, Prudence. But I have seen patterns of her trying to micromanage you. You have every right to be annoyed."

"But that doesn't excuse me kissing her husband. I'm a bad friend."

"You're right, it doesn't," she said.

I looked down at the couch, observing the tiny scratches in the beige leather.

"But—maybe you kissing Binky was a way of subconsciously rebelling against Lily. She's held you on a tight leash for a while now."

I looked back up at Sheryl. Perhaps she was right. Of course I was jealous, but Lily was jealous of me too. A best friendship was never absent of some competition. It relieved me that my actions were not completely abnormal.

Sheryl squared her body to face mine before continuing. "Only you can answer why you did this. You more than likely already know but don't want to accept what you understand to be your truth."

I remained silent. Inside, I was plagued with disgust over everything I had done, disgust over my bizarre way of coping with Lily's controlling behavior.

"I acted on impulse without thinking about the ramifications of my actions." I was trying to convince myself as much as Sheryl.

She scratched her nose. "Your behavior is not ideal. The tapes playing in your head need to change. Take some time to regroup. Think about the positive things you took away from rehab. There is a process. You will not be fixed overnight, or over five weeks. This is why every inpatient treatment program encourages aftercare, which you opted not to do. The twelve steps only work if you work them."

It was the end-all-be-all one-liner on every wall at Serenity Hills. I sighed like an impatient child then gazed out the window, weighed down by the pressure to unload all my troubles in under an hour.

"The same illicit texts are clogging up my phone. I've deleted every single person I'm not interested in, but the dick pics keep coming. I can't stop the dick train."

"You can block the numbers as well."

A rocket-scientist therapist.

"I didn't think of that," I replied, distracted by the threads in my ripped jeans.

"Do you enjoy receiving the messages?" she asked as though she wasn't asking about photos of penises.

I rolled it around in my head while scrolling an array of images. "I mean, I would say I'm sickened by them. A reminder of how desperate I used to be. Yet a small piece of me relishes the attention."

I worried about keeping Alistair's number. Where did he fall in the lineup? Was he from my past? Or did he fit in with the new, improved Prue? I avoided mentioning him. Sheryl didn't need to know about the kiss in rehab. That was between me and Mike. But was being in Alistair's life hindering his recovery? The thought that perhaps I could be a part of the problem summoned the guilt and shame, which was never very far away.

I want him to succeed, and I want to as well.

"Something else has caused me a lot of stress," I said, remembering I hadn't told her about Mike. "My counselor at rehab, Mike, the one who led my group, well, I found out he left Serenity." I rubbed my ear.

"Mike has provided you with the skills to transition into a healthy lifestyle. He is not your safety net," she said. "Now that you are out of rehab, come to weekly therapy sessions, regularly attend meetings, work your program."

She's jealous of my relationship with Mike.

I glazed over everything she said. The thought of life without Mike was becoming more than I could bear. It hurt just saying the words.

"I'm freaking out over violating the most basic rule of friendship."

My sticky armpits glued together, my breath shortened, and the parqueted floor seemed farther away. A tangled cord of emotions choked me.

"Let's take this one step at a time and work on applying what you learned in rehab. Continue to work on creating spaces between thought, feeling, and action. You need that space to evaluate before succumbing to your impulsive behavior." Sheryl locked her gaze on me. "This is a setback."

Like my mother when I didn't make an A in calculus. How much I hated disappointing people, letting them down in every way. Her expression became stern. The gravity of my behavior occurred to me in a new way. It was about more than a kiss; it was a breach of the commitment I made when I checked out.

"It just happened. I tried to take something that didn't belong to me." I gripped the throw pillow, a life preserver to save a drowning soul.

"I have discussed with you before the concept of associating sex with love. With connecting your vagina to your heart." The pledge-of-allegiance stance with a hand over her heart. I exhaled with relief that she didn't touch her pussy. An inappropriate laugh perched, ready to dump out of my mouth. "The connection of your mind and body is critical, but you crossed some strong boundaries with your actions."

I told her what she wanted to hear. "I can try. All I can do is my best." The Serenity Prayer played on repeat through my head.

She chose her words carefully, each lightly passing over my fragility, moving almost tentatively, all to avoid shattering and sending shards of me all over her office.

"Prue. I need you to listen to me. You exhibit narcissistic tendencies. It would serve you well to put some energy into something other than yourself."

I bet she struggles with focusing like me.

"I already mentioned it would be beneficial for you to get out of your head, stop obsessing over your problems."

I couldn't tell where she was going with this. *Nick is the one who's the narcissist, not me.*

"For homework, think about how you could give back to the community through volunteering. You might find something fulfilling about serving others."

The word *homework* put me in a tailspin, but I agreed. She glanced at the wall clock. Fear struck as my time with her came to a close.

"I am here to help you heal from the past."

Narcissist?

The panic must have bled through the serene mask I slathered on my face because she smiled kindly, her palms pressed together. "Setbacks are natural. They are necessary. They are important for growth."

Growth? I made out with Lily's husband. I missed all the signs around Christian. Hell, I was in the waiting room calling everyone freaks, thinking five weeks was a cure.

There I sat in a never-ending cycle of internal berating. I treated myself worse than anyone had ever treated me, including my mother's second husband, Richard.

Back in my rehab sessions with Mike, he'd taught me to envision *Little Prudence.* "See her sitting on your shoulder. What is she wearing? How old is she?" He would give me a moment to imagine myself as a little girl, beaten down in so many ways—her messy braids, octagonal glasses, mismatched socks, wearing Henry's ill-fitting hand-me-downs. Mike somehow knew when I had the visual and would speak on cue. "Protect your inner child. Take care of her the way you want to be taken care of." He spoke in such a way that even I believed the broken child could be saved, should be saved. "Care for Little Prue. She is worthy. You are worthy."

I tried to conjure up my inner child but instead, the unbearable shame cloaked me in darkness. I stared at the floor with burning eyes. Every counseling session was the same. Each one—a word jumble of emotions, me fighting to focus, struggling to decide how much I wanted to disclose truthfully. They undoubtedly ended just as I landed the rhythm of sharing. And always Sheryl, with her fucking nods of acceptance. Acceptance I didn't deserve.

"That's all we have time for today."

Glass pieces everywhere.

On the drive home, I stopped at 7-Eleven to buy a pack of Twizzlers, which I hoovered in my car.

Chapter Seventeen: Prue Past

Mitch and I went straight to the smoking veranda. Neither of us wanted to wait in line for food. We decided to sit it out until the mobs of recovering addicts schlepped their trays along the metal track, picked over the salad bar, made their choices, got their drinks, and claimed their usual seats. Over the past few weeks, the two of us had been hanging out and sharing a lot of personal stuff. People were accustomed to seeing us together.

"Hey, aren't you guys going to lunch?" Gloria stood at the edge of the two steps that led to our smoker's paradise, where we could be ourselves and speak freely.

"We're waiting for the line to thin out. Plus, Mitch needed a cig." The Arizona heat thawed my air-conditioned body.

"Will you wait for me to have a smoke?" My sweet and childlike friend. I struggled to not let the horrors of her life play like a film running through my head.

"For sure." I patted the seat next to me. We had painted each other's nails the night before, and hers were already chipped.

"How did you and John meet, anyway?" she asked while popping off a few smoke rings.

"Grinder, a dating app." Mitch seemed amused. "I'm using the word *date* loosely. It's more for hooking up."

"And was it love at first sight?" I asked, wondering what they both had been wearing. He nodded.

"So cute," Gloria said.

"If you call blowing someone behind a dumpster cute, then yes, it was." I could relate to the way he said outrageous things to create a reaction. I shared the tendency. "The cop almost catching us added to the thrill."

"Whoa," I said. "That would have been a ticket for indecent exposure."

"Oh, well," Mitch said. "One hundred percent worth it."

"Naughty boys," I said, a teensy bit jealous.

"The naughtier the better."

"Prue and I might need to get some pointers from John. He sounds like he's got some talent," Gloria said while jabbing me in the ribs.

I refrained from adding to the conversation. It was far out of the realm of a permissible discussion according to the abstinence contract I'd signed at check-in. I was already acting like a rebel.

"And I thought it was going to be a one-night stand." Mitch smiled. "I'm sure it helped when he found out about my hefty bank account. I suppose what I lacked in a body I made up for in personality."

"You know what I think is sexy?" I rolled out the answer. "Confidence, and you've got it."

A stream of smoke traveled to the peak of the veranda and dissipated. "Fake it 'til you make it," he said.

"You're better at long-term relationships than I am." As usual, I bounced around subjects.

"Because John is the glue. You and Nick had no glue holding you together." His cheeks sucked in as he took a Parliament puff.

"Excellent point." I stood to signal we needed to head out. The last thing I wanted to do was talk about Nick. "We better get food or we're going without."

In the dining room, I refilled my water bottle while avoiding the tray of raspberry jam thumbprint cookies made with some kind of unidentifiable non-sugar sweetener. In a moment of weakness, I went to grab three, settled on two, and shoved them both in my mouth.

"Aren't they yummy?" Gloria took a handful of cookies. She didn't struggle with body issues the way I did. She had an easiness being in her own skin. I prayed for some of that for myself.

I ate faster than Mitch and opted for a cup of tea while he finished eating. Gloria sat beside me with her cookies and a fascination for all the happenings at the surrounding tables.

"What the heck is that guy doing?" She pointed to someone at an adjacent table with his index finger digging for gold.

"Picking his nose. Mitch, would you agree?"

Mitch's post-stomach-stapling-surgery eating proved difficult to watch. My food issues were a living hell, but his hell was far worse.

"One thimbleful at a time, Thumbelina." A spoon with four grains of brown rice entered his mouth.

"Not like there's somewhere pressing I need to be."

"Three more bites," Mitch said." He chewed things like fifty times. I counted. "To think John fell for me despite our twelve-year age difference and being obese." He put another morsel in his mouth.

"I call that unconditional love." I dunked the teabag in the now-lukewarm water, hoping for micrograms of caffeine. "Nick told me it didn't exist."

"Dear Lord." Mitch pulled out his chair. "Nick is a charming fellow."

We discarded our plates while Gloria waited near the door, her eyes still locked on the nose-picker. I took one sip of the bitter tea, grimaced, and left it in the gray plastic bin by the exit. The worker collecting dishes winked at me. I winked back and immediately hated myself for it.

"I saw that." Mitch interlocked his arm in mine, and the three of us headed out the door.

Mike stood by the door, ready for us. I was curious whether he spent his lunchtime making personal calls, or maybe he bantered with the other staff members. Bantering didn't seem to be his style. Sudoku? The curiosities I conjured up over my counselor were boundless. When I couldn't find the answers through clues in his behavior, stories would clamor around as entertainment. There wasn't a lot for me to go on. One oddity I had noted—he never smelled like food. Did he even eat lunch?

He might be the kind of guy who has a huge breakfast and a light dinner when he gets home.

Serenity gave us decaffeinated coffee. We could consume all the caffeine-free java and herbal tea we wanted. I missed a full-bodied, highly caffeinated morning brew. Did Mike drink the same decaf crap they served us? I pictured him rolling through a Starbucks drive-thru and transferring the dark nectar from the to-go cup into his ceramic mug. Throughout our session, he would drink from it with a little too much deliberate disdain. I didn't buy it. The more he sipped and frowned, the less I believed it to be the sludge we drank.

Well, at least someone in the room is catching a buzz.

"Mitch has offered to start the afternoon session." Mike, holding court. "We will continue with the subject of trauma. A reminder, there are five forms of abuse: emotional, physical, spiritual, verbal, and sexual. All have a negative impact on us. The important takeaway from today is that we can heal and move forward with healthy adult relationships and self-love." His voice leveled with a balance of soft yet powerful, never yelling but compelling us to listen. Compelling me to listen.

"The point is, regardless of whatever form of abuse you experienced as children, we're here to support you. Speaking things out loud is the first step to taking away the power the past abuse has over our adult lives."

Mitch took the floor. My chair felt a lot cozier whenever someone else was the focus. He pressed his black-framed Pradas higher on his face. He hadn't mentioned that he volunteered to start.

No wonder he wanted a cigarette.

"I stuffed my emotions with food." Mitch locked his hands together and lay them delicately on his lap. "Since my stomach surgery, I can't eat very much. I don't know where to put my feelings, or rather, I don't know how to express them."

The tidiness of his clothes matched the manner in which he spoke—clean and succinct.

"I was preoccupied with thoughts about what I would do when I got thin, how fabulous my life would be." He wiped his glasses on his shirt. "You know, like the fat cells represented my problems and when they were gone, my problems would be, too."

I raised my hand. "I completely get what you're saying." Every woman in the room agreed with me. "I obsess over my weight and believe things will be better when I hit that magic number." I loathed weighing myself yet I couldn't stop. "Who knows how I came up with the number, but I believed, and sort of still do, that weight is the key to my happiness."

"Ditto. The trouble is, I hit well below my goal weight, and I'm still not content." I obsessed over the elasticity of his creped, loose skin and how it might flap over his belt. "Fucking sucks, because I didn't understand how the basic chemistry of my body would be dramatically altered after stomach stapling." Mitch breathed in, which I gathered fended off nicotine cravings. "The things John and I once enjoyed together are no longer available to us." A gruff laugh. "We're both foodies and wine connoisseurs. Now a thimble of liquor sends me into a blackout. My personality changed, I raged at him and remembered nothing in the morning."

Rhoda raised her hand. "This is where AA and the twelve steps come to your rescue." Her frosted hair glistened with spray. "Recovered alcoholics have to reinvent themselves. Everything I loved to do circled back to alcohol. I get it, and it's hard to imagine my life without it, but living with it is unbearable." She turned toward Mitch. "I can't speak for you, but I assume you can relate." He nodded and unlocked his hands.

"Good stuff," Mike said. "When we work the steps, we learn we are not alone and our stories are not unique."

Heat radiated from the sidewalk outside the window. A gecko bobbed his head on the windowsill then darted away.

"At the end of your five weeks, you will find a sponsor in your local AA chapter. There is a system in place to help you settle into a sober life." Mike pointed to the poster on every wall at Serenity. "Memorize the steps," he said. "Know them like the back of your hand. Work them and humble yourself."

My heart bounced in my chest like a tennis ball in the dryer when he said the word *memorize.*

"Let's say the first step out loud right now." Mike waited a beat for us to gather our breath.

"We admitted we were powerless over alcohol—that our lives had become unmanageable." As our voices melted together in unison, I silently added "sex" when everyone else said "alcohol."

Mike assured us it would all work out. A painted rosy picture of rainbows and unicorns, but we knew better.

"I'm not saying it will be a cakewalk. It won't be. Take it one day at a time." He bowed his head toward Mitch. I was curious about Mike's life, his happiness factor, and if he convinced himself he was happy along with the rest of us.

"I sure hope so, because that's all I have," Mitch said. I braced for the tales that unraveled my protective donkey skin. "At the age of ten, my father found out that I was gay." He picked some lint from his pants and flicked it on the floor. "I don't even know what was the tipping point. From that moment on, he started calling me a sicko, a queer, a faggot."

A knot wedged itself in my throat. My earlobe heated over my incessant rubbing.

"He called me filthy—the most filthy little faggot on earth."

We gave a moment of silence for Mitch and his harrowing past.

"That's awful." Gloria's shoulders sagged. "Sorry." She fidgeted with the stack of black rubber bracelets on her delicate wrist.

"Thanks." Mitch acted as though he were recapping a work project instead of a sad story from his childhood.

I wanted to cry.

"Continue." Mike tapped his fingertips together.

"So when my dad started name-calling me, I thought my mom would defend me, but she didn't, and I grew to hate her, too. Even the kids at school called me gay, so if no one cared about me, I didn't care either, and I ate everything in sight. While my parents slept, I pigged out in the kitchen. I thought it would be better to be a fat pig than a faggot."

The more vulnerable he got, the quieter he became.

"How did you come to peace with your mom?" I failed to raise a hand. "Are you still angry with her?" A small chunk of hair rolled around my finger, a habit my mother used to say in jest made me appear highly intelligent.

"She never said the word sorry, but I saw no point in harboring resentment over a small-minded ignorant woman I call Mom."

"Your dad might have threatened and coerced her into taking his side." Perhaps if Mitch and I could fill in the missing pieces of his childhood and his maternal relationship in the puzzle, I might be able to do the same and forgive my mother too.

"Possibly, but you're a mom. You wouldn't do that to your kid no matter what, gay, straight, trans, or whatever. You know?"

The sickening thought of some other version of me name-calling Christian invaded my mind. Me, verbally beating him down and looking the other way when someone teased him.

"My mother didn't protect me. I'm still trying to figure out how to wrap my head around it so I can forgive her. I appreciate your honesty." My palms glued together in prayer.

"The difference between us is that your mom may not have been privy to what was going on. My mother witnessed everything and said nothing." An evil twin took over his body. "After I ate myself into oblivion, I became promiscuous and screwed around. I stuck with all the guys who lived straight in public and were gay in private. Just knowing their secrets, knowing I could mess with them and ruin them, gave me this newfound confidence."

He redirected his eyes down toward the floor. "If that makes sense," he added.

Mike was ready for battle. I imagined him riding a dragon like the ones in my son's video games, fighting our abusers, his sword drawn as he flew through the air.

"Revenge is a concept we will discuss in more detail," Mike said, "but as adults, it is not healthy or productive. It's something children fantasize about and act out on, which typically does not end with a positive result."

Mitch continued without pause. "Ah, but it's so sweet." We all nodded. "Sorry, I got sidetracked. Imagine being a Black kid from Chicago with a dad who's a cop. To be a fag on top of that? A death sentence." He had a nervous habit of adjusting his untidy shirtsleeves over and over. "My real honest-to-goodness revenge has been in the form of financial success."

"Let me interject here." Our fearless ring leader. "A healthier way to frame your success might be to say your hard work has paid off."

"Started in the mailroom and worked my way up to creative director." Mitch puffed out his chest. "Then I bought the company, and my dad can't steal that from me even though he thought he could beat the gay out of me."

He laughed the way I do when things get too damned painful.

"Excellent share," Mike said. "One of my fascinations since becoming a therapist is the resilience and strength of the human spirit. Mitch is an example of someone who has risen up from a difficult past and is trying to rewrite the story of his life."

He propped himself against the desk.

"Everyone in this room has lived through something that could have broken you, but you refused to allow it to. You are stronger than you think, and the power to change is inside of you."

He pressed his palm against his heart while his left arm hung by his side.

"You all should be proud you took the first step by coming to rehab. Most people don't make it that far." He sipped from the water he kept next to his computer. "Every day, I am deeply moved by your stories and inspired by your strength. Do not give up. You are worthy."

Gloria cried. Dierdre and Rhoda followed. A tissue box landed on Gloria's lap. The simple gesture brought me to tears.

"That means a lot to me," Mitch said. "Anyway, I think that covers how I ended up in rehab."

"Alright," Mike said, "let's go around the room for comments."

He signaled for me to go first. I wanted to say something impactful, but no words came. A tightness remained in my throat. The pain bore down on me, Mitch's and mine.

"Mitch, thank you for sharing your story with us," Deirdre said. "I totally get what you said. My father hated me too, but for different reasons. You've come so far, and you inspire me."

After the rest gave their input, Gloria raised her hand. "Can I share next?"

The plan was for Alistair to return to the limelight, but she asked so genuinely that there was no chance Mike could tell her anything but yes. She held an innocence that contradicted her experiences. He commented quite early in one of our sessions that adults who had been abused as children were often stunted in their maturity, which culminated in different ways, in different aspects, but was entirely consistent.

"I already told everyone that Tom paid for me to be here so I could deal with my pill addiction. What I didn't understand until I got here was that I had a gnarly childhood." Gloria spoke in an easy, casual cadence. "My father was a sick, twisted man."

We were dutifully listening, but I wasn't sure how much more I could take.

"I want to talk about my relationship with Tom and how I ended up in rehab. I'm not blaming him for my addiction, but what I'm trying to understand is why I started using."

I twirled my hair.

"My boyfriend was the one who first gave me the Xanax. He said I would scream in my sleep if he touched me. I didn't doubt that, after what my dad did to me." The memories walled off and buried interred at a safe depth. "Bars had always done the trick. They calmed me, but what I realized is I took Xanax to block out everything that had happened to me."

Snow White. Her poison apple, Xanax.

Rather than absorb her painful story, I studied the way she hooked and unhooked her hoop earring. There was a disturbance beneath her every move. The way she pulled knots out of her hair or dug into her cuticles. There were some small scars on her wrist that she had attempted to cover up with foundation, stacks of bracelets, and hairties.

"You're safe here," Mike said.

The room became cloaked in silence. I rubbed my ear until it swelled to twice its normal size. The truth about her horrific past had been hard to hear when she shared her timeline. It would be agonizing to sit through it again.

"My father molested me." Gloria destroyed the last remnants of her black polish. Dark, snowy flecks tumbled to the floor around her chair. "I'm pretty sure my mother knew, but she never stopped him."

The way she delivered her earth-shattering experiences never ceased to astound me. My mouth hung open and became parched. I flipped the top of my water bottle and took a swig.

Gloria continued. "I slept in the cold, hard bathtub. That's where he abused me, always in the bathroom."

I swallowed a few times to stop myself from barfing.

"Tom saved me, but he also kept me in a sort of prison."

I thought about Lily and how I had sometimes felt the same way about her. I detested my toxic habit of always trying to find the bad in the good people and the good in the bad.

"How so?" Hearing Mike's voice provided a sense of peace, but it was fleeting.

"He said he planned to leave his wife. I trusted him." Her words trailed off. "I'm not sure now if he was appeasing me." A bird rested on a branch, looked at me, and flew away. "I love him. He's a great deal older than me, which some people find weird." I forced a smile. "He is nothing like my father." She might have been trying to convince herself as much as all of us. "And he held me prisoner with the Xanax and the money he gave me to live in an apartment big enough for me and my little brother." She turned her attention to our leader. "Tom helped me get my bro out of the House of Horrors too." She doodled a heart on her notepad then filled it with ink.

I raised a clammy hand. "May I please excuse myself?"

Gloria touched my knee. "I'm sorry. I'm so sorry."

I stood, light-headed and unsteady. The door seemed a mile away. Mike sounded as though he was six feet beneath the ground. Two hands grabbed me from behind.

"I have you." Mike gently gripped my shoulders. He then addressed the group. "Let's take a twenty-minute break."

A whoosh of cool air hit the room when the door opened. Gloria hovered above me. My vision turned blurry. I didn't want to be the cause of her concern or hurting her feelings.

"I'm fine." Mike passed me my water. "Thank you."

"Oh, Prue." Gloria knelt by my feet and sobbed into my knees. "We both had it rough. Dammit, I wish I knew what we did wrong to deserve what we got."

Mike pulled Gloria from the floor like picking up a piece of paper. He put her in the chair next to me then crouched in front of us.

"You did nothing wrong." Frustration came to the forefront of his voice. "You were both innocent children. Victims."

He walked over to his desk drawer and pulled out a doll wearing a white gingham dress. It lifted my spirits to witness such a strong symbol of manhood carrying a baby doll.

"I want you to bring her with you everywhere you go." He put the baby in Gloria's arms. "Care for it the way you wished your parents had cared for you."

A twinge of envy poisoned my insides. *Why wasn't I given a baby to carry around?*

Gloria adjusted the little dress over its chubby thighs and kissed its pink cheek. When she did, the baby blinked. Gloria's eyes lit up, and a warm joy washed over me.

Chapter Eighteen: Prue Present

Since the incident with Binky, I obsessed over all the times I had let Lily down. The first summer we spent together, I stuffed the spinnaker wrong for the end-of-season regatta. She had instructed me, but somehow I still screwed up. I couldn't wrap my arms around messing up on something so important to Lily. Had I done it on purpose? I sabotaged relationships with the people I loved most. We all held a dark side, but mine erred on the side of evil.

Throughout middle school, Lily was teased for being skinny. A pack of mean, popular girls became relentless with their teasing, and I was too weak to defend my friend.

When the crew included me in a movie night, I accepted. It was the ultimate betrayal. They had invited me to make her feel bad. I didn't care. I craved the in-crowd and I shit-talked her behind her back to pump myself up. I remember Lily asking me about it in the locker room at the Sound Club.

"Did you tell Carolyn that I didn't need a training bra and call my boobs mosquito bites?" Lily stepped out of the rolled-up swimsuit and wrapped herself in a towel. I had wedged myself in the corner of the tiny dressing room, my suit dripping on the concrete beneath my feet. I remember how tightly I gripped my ponytail to wring it out.

"What?" I feigned disbelief. "I never said that." I wrung out my hair, hoping I could wring out the fear of my lie coming to light along with the excess water and the envy of her life being infinitely better than mine.

When my demons weren't getting the best of me and I was being a worthy friend, Lily and I more resembled an old married couple than a couple of teenagers. Most women remember what the love of their lives was wearing on the day they met. I remembered what Lily had on—a sky-blue t-shirt the color of her eyes.

*   *   *

I couldn't help but think of the negatives as I walked through every room of the house waving a tied-up bunch of burning sage. I continued recapping all the shitty things I'd done to Lily over a lifetime. And when I got tired of that, I recapped the highlights of my problems that led me and Nick to break apart. For good measure, I folded Gloria's death into the playlist like some twisted punctuation point. So there I was, sage smoke trails following me from room to room as consistently as my past. I needed to scrub myself of all the negativity.

Afterward, while waiting for the air to clear, I sat outside on the porch, craving a cigarette despite having broken the habit in my twenties. I missed the camaraderie at Serenity Hills. The smoking veranda had brought so much positivity. Mitch, Gloria, Rhoda, and I often gathered there to share, laugh, and bond. I needed some of that love just then.

I gazed at the sky. *It's so damned hard to appreciate what's happening until everything is behind us.* Rehab reminded me a lot of the time I spent doing Outward Bound. Mom had sent me between graduating college and landing my first job, just me and seven guys in the wilderness for three weeks. The group started with ten, but two girls dropped out the first few days—one from a twisted ankle and the other from some seriously awful blisters. Green flies swarmed and bit my flesh. The shoddy issued tarp gave minimal coverage to the elements. One morning, I woke up to see some wild animal had snacked on my boots the previous night.

There were things about the experience that hadn't been intolerable. We read maps, set up camp, cooked our meals, and talked together in our tents until our eyes grew heavy with sleep. Most days, though, I dreamed of nothing more than going home to a hot shower and my bed. After it was over, all said and done, the lessons percolated in me like the slow drip of the coffeemaker I'd used as a kid to make my mother's morning cup.

I remember the guide wondering why I preferred walking in the back of the line. It was because I worried about the underdog, the weak links. It seemed wrong to leave them behind. What mattered to me was that they were safe and looked after. The guy said I exhibited leadership qualities. He then recounted a book he'd read once on wolves—how when they traveled distances, they put the elderly between the weakest in the front and the strongest, who took up the rear. So often I just erased the positive and focused on everything wrong. Perhaps I needed to rediscover my inner wolf who had unknowingly led the pack.

The waves crashed inside my head. I pushed myself to the surface, fighting for breath.

"Hey." I hadn't even heard Lily approaching. "We have never gone this long without talking." There was a crack in her tempo. "I don't know about you, but this has been an agonizing few days. I also can't help but wonder if you're alright, even though I'm not remotely over this."

"Classic." I wiped a sleeve across my nose. "I kiss your husband and you're asking me if I'm okay."

Lily held a bottle of chardonnay and two cups. She moved a lawn chair next to me and sat down. A royal-blue pashmina fell from her shoulders as she unscrewed the wine. There I sat, the same old Prudence, the one who ruined everything. *The Saboteur.*

"Binky confessed about the kiss as soon as he walked in the door, which was a relief." Lily ran her fingers through her poker-straight hair. "I told him you texted me about what happened. In all honesty, I still can't fucking believe you didn't drive straight to my house and tell me in person. Completely fucking shocking." She gripped her knees into her chest. The most curse words Lily had ever said. "In so many ways, you expressed to me loud and clear that I don't matter to you the way you matter to me." Lily's eyes welled up. She turned away.

"You do matter," I spoke through the fingers that covered my face. "So much that I sabotaged our friendship because I still feel unworthy."

"Bullshit." Her voice raised three octaves. I tightened into as small a ball as my body could muster. "Stop making excuses for your shitty behavior. Newsflash, the world doesn't revolve around you. We all have problems, unhealed wounds from our past, but we can't go around kissing our friend's husbands now, can we?" Her jawline moved as she clenched her teeth. I braced for the hits I deserved. "Your selfish actions have permanently altered the foundation of our friendship. You tore the rock out from under us."

The moon shone on her face. Nowhere near enough stars in the sky for me to wish away the damage I had done.

"You're right," I said. "Everything you said is true."

The shame oozes from me and poisons everyone in my path.

Lily sipped her wine and looked at me. "But I know you, Prue. Sometimes better than you do. I want to believe you wouldn't hurt me on purpose. It goes against who I am to see the worst in people. I'm not saying you're off the hook, but in order for me to process this, I can't make it about me. I didn't do anything wrong. You did, and I want to help you never do this to me or anyone else again. I shudder to think what would have happened if Binky took your bait. How far would it have gone? But I'm not going to play that mind game. It will only drive me insane." She took a huge swig and refilled her glass. "This is about us, two women, besties since second fucking grade."

I chugged and poured another cup. "I'm a messed-up person who doesn't deserve friends or any blessings in my life." I was cloaked in a load of hopelessness. "I can only imagine how you're feeling. You give and give to me, and this is what I do in return. I'm a great friend."

The truth unfolded as I spoke. *The broken child believes she is undeserving of anything wonderful.* Things never worked out for me. I may as well screw them up now rather than wait for everything to unravel later. They were bound to. The same story played on repeat.

"Do me a favor." Lily's tone was cold and sharp. "Stop the fucking pity party. I'm over it. Your excuses, your negative self-talk. Move on. Everyone experiences hard times. Don't make that an excuse for your bad behavior."

"All I can think is that I'm jealous of your life."

"Well, don't be drinking the hate-or-ade, because I worked to build a strong foundation in my marriage." I'd rarely seen this side of Lily. It scared the shit out of me. "You need to take the lessons you learned at Serenity Hills and hold them tight. Life is hard. When things become stressful, you can't go around kissing other people's husbands."

I wanted to drink to excess, but it was time to face things head-on.

"I've let your bad behavior slide in the past, but not this time." Lily stared into the darkness, the darkness I feared would engulf me. "Like when you talked shit about me to those popular girls and denied it. I knew, but I let it go. That pales in comparison to what you did with Binky." She drank her wine and pulled the shawl tighter over her shoulders. "It has always been in the back of my mind that you and my husband dated in eighth grade. He was drawn to you from the get-go when he moved to Goose Neck Harbor. He told me once by the lockers how he thought you were so pretty. I have to live with that, and it has, at times, eaten away at me."

Fear loomed like a dark shadow. She vented, and I waited until a window opened for me to speak. I slumped in the chair, knowing she perpetually lived with the idea that Binky had wanted me first. We were so young then. It didn't matter now. They were the perfect couple. I was the crazy friend.

"I hope you can forgive me. Nothing can justify what I've done. I love you, I'm sorry."

She leaned toward me and wrapped her hands around my neck, planting a kiss right on my lips. It caught me off guard, something completely unexpected and far removed from Lily's character.

"Don't do it again. You will not receive a second chance," she said with a grin. Her hands were still around my neck, and her face looked directly at mine. She released her grasp and I stared at the ground, completely thrown off by the kiss. Was it a sign of endearment or a tactic of manipulation? Either way, the action left me feeling uneasy and confused.

Lily looked away. "I want to put this behind us. Nothing worse than harping on crap from our past. If we can't move forward, then the bad guy wins. You let your sick stepfather win. Fight through this."

"I'm trying," I said.

Crickets chirped from the rosemary bush. My scalp prickled.

"For the record, Binky said kissing you was like making out with his sister."

The hit stung for a moment, and then I asked myself why? Why would I want her husband to like kissing me? It was the addict talking, the person who needed every man to want her. The person I was trying to ditch.

I wondered what had prompted Lily to kiss me, why she had acted like it was no big deal. Maybe it wasn't a big deal; perhaps I was focusing on the wrong things. Either way, I couldn't help but wonder. Was kissing me a way for Lily to gain back her control or get even with Binky?

I watched the sky darken among the curving blue air. After Lily and I shared a few moments of silence, she touched my knee.

"Everything is going to work out for you," she said. "I promise."

As I sat there, I couldn't help but compare the kiss that Lily had just planted on my lips with the one I had received from Gloria. The two of them couldn't have been more polar opposite in personality or in the way they kissed. Gloria's were soft, sensual, and unassuming, while Lily's felt rough and controlling. If I had to choose between the two of them, it would be Gloria.

*   *   *

I searched for the silver lining. The underlying blessings in every emotion. All I had to do was find them. I filled my time with outer-circle activities and rediscovered my joy for reading.

With the intent to read more, I tried to find the perfect spot in my house to settle in with a book. When I read in bed, I ended up falling asleep. The living room felt awkward, too fancy for leggings and an oversized sweater. The family room sofa became my sanctuary. A standing lamp illuminated the room. I stacked coffee table books underneath lamps and boxes, the colorful binders facing out with titles that told the world who lived in this house: a designer, fashionista wannabe.

I lined an end table with my favorite things: a pair of brown-and-white Staffordshire dogs I inherited from Gram, a jade figurine my father collected on a dive trip to Palau, a photo of a young Henry and me right after he gave me a special haircut. My jagged bangs half sticking up, his face beaming with pride over his artistic creation.

Patrick Dunn bequeathed me the sofa before he went into semi-retirement. It was the day he had told me that I was his protégé, the designer in his group with "the gift." His words rolled off like water on a duck's back when he chose Sam to run the company.

The Himalayan salt lamp was my newest addition. It came with a promise to cleanse negative ions from the air. I lit a Diptyque candle in a scent called Baies, the latest obsession purchased at cost with my credentials. I settled in wrapped in a cashmere throw with a book. After five pages, my phone rang. I lazily checked who it was, figuring I would ignore it. Alistair's name popped up. I answered.

"Hey." I tucked a bookmark on the page. "Thank you for the beautiful flowers. That was so thoughtful of you."

"Glad you liked them. I'm excited to see you in LA." Alistair sounded light and airy. "Aftercare is turning out to be a nice transition from rehab to the real world." Something was off. I determined it was a combination of reality hitting him and leaving the safety net of Serenity Hills. "Can I forward your personal information to Mitch so he can connect with you regarding Gloria's funeral?"

"I actually was invited. It went to Lily's house. I forgot that I gave her address to everyone when I left rehab since I didn't know exactly where I would be living."

"Glad that got sorted out." Another call was coming through. I pulled the phone from my ear to see who it was.

"Nick is calling me on the other line. I better run. He is supposed to drop off Christian any second."

"I'll call you when I arrive," he said.

I switched the call to Nick. "What's up?"

"That doesn't sound very friendly," he said. "I'm calling for a few reasons." Nick cleared a frog from his throat while I endured one of his stall tactics.

"Fine." Not wanting to give him any leeway.

"I'm sorry for walking out when you asked for a divorce. It was immature."

"Thanks. That means a lot."

"Are you sure you want to go through with this?"

"Yes, I'm sure. I found a mediator if you're interested in trying to negotiate."

"This is such a flip from everything you said in rehab. And yes, email me the contact information. Better yet, make an appointment for any Wednesday in the next month. That's the only day I can possibly leave work early."

"I'll handle it."

"One more thing, my car isn't working. Can you pick up Christian? If you're not doing anything . . ."

"I'll be there in a few."

As I drove out of Nick's driveway with Christian, another car was pulling in. I strained to see past the headlights. The driver waved. It took a moment to register whether my mind was playing tricks on me. I slowed and glanced in the rearview. There was Naomi, getting out of her car and into my soon-to-be ex-husband's arms. To calm my nerves, I admired her outfit—a white miniskirt and beige sandals.

I promised myself I wouldn't allow a bad mood to radiate into Christian's day. The decision to divorce was not one I had taken lightly. Nick's vacillation had me questioning my choice. But I found it fulfilling to know that he was well aware I saw Naomi at his house. It was over. The cards had been laid out. From that moment forward, my relationship with my ex would be like a business transaction. I needed to disconnect from him emotionally. I could no longer afford the day-to-day drama of life with Nick.

*   *   *

The awkwardness of Naomi pulling into the driveway gave way to the normalcy of Christian's anecdotes from school and work.

"Any idea about what you want to do for your community service hours?" I took my aggression out on the steering wheel and crushed Naomi. "Clearly you are bored. Now is a fantastic time for us to start."

My therapist's words jumped into the frame. *Give back to others.* Maybe my son and I could do something together. Christian fidgeted with the lacrosse team pin on his backpack. "Something to help the homeless," he said.

My thoughts centered more around battered women's resources, mentoring, and supporting Planned Parenthood.

"I love that idea," I said.

*   *   *

After searching for various organizations that provided aid to the homeless, I called Lily to see if she wanted Charlie to volunteer with Christian. I was afraid of hurting her feelings if I didn't include them.

"I'd love to. I haven't exactly been my usual organized self." *And it's my fault.* A pan crashed on the floor. "Sorry, I'm baking cookies for the soccer team. Don't worry, the cookie sheet was empty. What were you thinking?"

"A nonprofit called Lunches with Love gives away bag lunches in downtown LA a few Sundays a month, and a soup kitchen in Hawthorne that needs volunteers."

"Let's do both. Has Christian volunteered before?"

"No, this will be his first time," I said.

"Aw. Well, you know what they say, better late than never! Charlie has been volunteering since he was a little kid, so he can show Christian the ropes."

Lily's tone was condescending, and I could feel her competitiveness radiate through the phone. We'd never had this type of friendship before. Why was she suddenly trying to act better than me? I chose to ignore it, convincing myself it was simply Lily's way of coping with what had happened between me and Binky.

"Looking forward to it. Want to come over to make the lunches on Saturday?"

After some back and forth with emails and texting, Lily and I got the lunch supplies. Lunches with Love posted details about what needed to be included in each bag on their website. They also told us where to meet on Sunday so we could take them to be given away. The four of us got together at my house to assemble the bags with all the specified items. It took more than half the day to make over a hundred lunches. After we finished, the boys disappeared to Christian's room while Lily and I cleaned up.

The next day, my alarm went off at five with the sort of anticipation I usually reserved for certain holidays. I made coffee before waking up Christian, which I poured into my favorite mug and added a generous amount of sweetened creamer. As I took the first sip, I decided this would be a blessing for both of us. I could have handled the weed situation in a multitude of ways. Rather than turning it into a battle, I managed to focus his energy on helping others.

Christian popped into the kitchen wearing a beanie, soft blue flannel, and jeans. "You ready?" He scanned the food. "I hope we made enough."

"I was thinking the same." The coffee warmed my insides and alerted the sensors in my brain. "I guess we'll have a better idea when we get there." I checked the time. "I'm going to dress. They will be here any minute."

By the time I finished dressing, Lily and Charlie were at the back door. The four of us loaded up my car. The boys were surrounded by a sea of lunches in the back seat.

I printed out an instruction sheet from the Lunches with Love website. We were to meet in Manhattan Beach in a grocery store parking lot. There, we would connect with other volunteers. Apparently, not everyone wanted to deliver food, but many offered to prepare the bag lunches and bring them to the meeting spot. A liaison greeted us with a clipboard. She inspected how much room we had left in our vehicle and instructed three lunch-making volunteer groups to load their bags into our car.

"Any questions?" the woman asked as she leaned into the window. Lily shook her head. She handed me a piece of paper. "This will take you to the Los Angeles Mission. You can park nearby and pass out the meals." She walked to another car to give them their instructions. Lily pulled the paper from my lap and typed the address into Waze.

It was a blue-ribbon day, a perfect California morning, the kind from which an entire genre of sunny music was born. The boys laughed in the back, sharing memes and discussing YouTube videos they'd discovered, but when we got to the edge of Skid Row, they became quiet. I flipped off the tunes and slowed down when we found a street with layers of tents two and three deep.

"What do we do?" There was a bit of fear in Christian's voice.

"Roll down the window with a bag in your hand and see if anyone takes it."

The kids opened their windows. I pulled over but kept the engine running.

Christian spoke to a guy passing by on a bike. "Would you like a free lunch?"

The man stood beside our car. "Can I have one with a Coke?"

"Sure." Christian chose a lunch containing the soda of choice. "Here you go."

"Can I grab another for my friend?" He pointed to a tent. "He's in there and can't walk." Christian gave him another lunch. "God bless you," the man said. He walked the food across the street, lifted open a flap, and passed it to someone inside.

Charlie was passing out lunches so fast that Lily got out to reload from the supplies stashed in the way back. Within minutes, we had a steady stream of people along both sides of the car who were needing food.

"God bless."

"Got any with Doritos?"

We did everything we could to accommodate the choices. "You got anything but peanut butter?"

"Nothing but peanut butter."

"Alright, bless you."

We witnessed humanity and the incredible grace, gratitude, and kindness of those in need. Everyone said thank you, they all blessed us. The supply ran out in less than an hour. A few stopped to ask about lunch. Perhaps the word had spread about the free food.

"We're all out," Christian said. "We'll be back in two weeks."

And there it was. Christian decided this would be our community service project. The boys rolled up their windows. An ominous cloud hung in the air. I prayed as I drove until I pulled the car over. A thickness laid across my chest. We hadn't put a dent in filling the bellies of the hungry, but we had filled our souls. The simple act of giving back was what I needed to get out of my head and out of my own way.

"How's everyone doing?" I asked.

"I'm just trying to process it all," Lily said.

"We did good, Mom," Christian said. "But we must do more."

I nodded in agreement. And I thought about how those nights I went hungry as a kid didn't begin to compare.

"None of us are better than anyone else. That could be us." I held a hand out for Christian. "We are blessed to have a roof over our head.

So many things to be grateful for."

Lily knew I was referring to her and what she'd done for us. We probably would have wound up in a one-bedroom or studio in San Pedro, but it was about the support system of people who helped us along the way that made all the difference.

"I loved how everyone watched out for each other. You know, like that guy who took the lunch to his friend in the tent," Charlie said, staring out the window.

"Me too."

Chapter Nineteen: Prue Past

I didn't feel like partaking in movie night. The idea of sitting in a dark makeshift theatre with a bunch of recovering addicts seemed as fun as putting a sharp stick in my eye. Mike encouraged me to go. He said I needed a night off from homework and worrying about things I couldn't control. He might have thought that if I went to the movies, I wouldn't have time to call Nick. Every conversation I had with my ex during rehab put me in anxiety overdrive.

Gloria clapped when I mentioned movie night. I couldn't figure out the hype about going to a film in our general meeting room, but she was excited, so I worked at feeling the same. She said something about Alistair and Bo, which inflicted panic over what I was going to wear to the non-movie. When I picked up Gloria, she was carrying a pillow and wearing fuzzy pajama pants with a pale pink tee that might have also fit her baby doll.

"You look adorable." I cursed myself for not wearing something cuter and more flattering.

"Why, thank you, Prudence."

She did a little curtsy while I embedded the way she said my name into my eardrum. I often hated having such a weird, unusual, old-fashioned name, but when Gloria said it, it was as though I had the greatest name in the world.

"Everyone on campus will probably be there," I said, attempting to downplay the Alistair comment. "Not like there's anything better to do."

"You're right." She swiped a wand of gloss on her lips. "You know, since Alistair switched to our group, he and Bo hang out. Isn't that so cute?" She pushed me out of the room and closed the door behind us. We strolled down the sidewalk to where we would be gathering. "I'll share my pillow with you." She put her head on my shoulder. "I love my Prudence."

"I love you too."

I was preoccupied with the Alistair and Bo show. More than that, I detested my outfit. My confidence rested somewhere near the gutter, or someplace even lower than that. I pulled up my hoodie as we entered the brightly lit room. Gloria bolted ahead to scope out the real estate. Bo, with his sly, thousand-watt smile, had a thing for my friend. Anyone who denied that was a total liar. Perhaps it wasn't completely unrequited.

I found the idea of Bo and Alistair hanging out amusing. Bo proclaimed to be a redneck from a yeehaw town where the men were men and the sheep were scared. What could they possibly have in common beyond both being addicts who had tons of sex with a lot of women? Maybe that was enough for men.

Their friendship was odd. Their backgrounds couldn't have been more different; Bo and all his "ah shucks-like" quaint aphorisms, Alistair and his dry, distant, very British charm. Still, they shared similar addictions—a good bump often followed by a good pump. I laughed at my thoughts but refrained from saying them out loud.

Whenever someone went out of their way to mention Alistair, I wondered how many people heard about the kiss. Then, I remembered that gossip flew through the campus like a California wildfire.

He didn't appear to be the type to participate in the Serenity Hills extracurricular activities, so I figured Bo asked him because he needed a wingman. Everyone saw how the cowboy looked at Gloria. And Bo's best play might have been trying to sweeten the deal for Alistair with the prospect of me being at the movie too.

The funniest part was that Mike was the person who convinced me I should go. He'd been worried about me withdrawing after the last few tough sessions. Mike also was the one who made me promise not to talk to Alistair anymore. Now here I was, about to be sitting next to the British charmer in an unsupervised activity.

I waited at the edge of the room while Gloria located the perfect spot and waved me over. A moment before the lights dimmed, I spotted Alistair, looking like a true American in a basic navy-blue shirt with well-worn khakis. Bo stood beside him, craning his neck through the crowd. I edged my pancake ass closer to Gloria while saying a prayer of gratitude for the darkness. Bo maneuvered around the scattered bodies. Most people brought pillows. I was the only fool who hadn't.

Gloria twisted around and squealed when she saw Bo. I turned to see Alistair shadowing him, who, somehow despite the light, strolled directly toward us.

"Bo, get your sweet booty over here," Gloria said. Bo sat and straddled her with his legs. His scuffed boots blocked others from getting close. Gloria dropped her head on his chest.

"Welcome to cowboy country," Bo said.

Alistair stood behind them. At first, he didn't notice me due to my face being buried in my sweatshirt.

I pulled off the hood. Our eyes met. He smiled.

It seemed wrong to encourage him by patting the floor with a come-hither look, so I remained still and he sat beside me anyway.

His timeline revealed he was accustomed to being chased by women. I decided to act aloof, especially after the indiscretion. The more aloof I became, the more attention he gave me. I justified everything with a pack of lies I told myself about trying to be an agreeable patient and following the rules of rehab. Alistair sat in the small piece of available carpet between me and the person next to me.

"You made it," I said.

"I've never seen this movie." Alistair put his hand next to mine, inching it along like a small animal searching for warmth.

"One of my all-time favorites." After the film started, my voice lowered to a whisper. "I never get sick of it."

He smelled fresh and clean. Goosebumps ran down my arms. Even though we shouldn't have been touching at all, I kept my hand resting next to his. When I moved to tap Gloria or gasp over one of my favorite scenes, I put it back where it was, skin to skin.

Alistair didn't give me the impression he cared much about the movie. I felt his eyes bore into me several times but avoided catching him in the act. Maybe he was the type who lacked the attention span to sit through a full movie. I prayed that wasn't the case. Nothing better than a bucket of corn and a great movie. As the lights went up after the credits rolled, I made my move and ushered Gloria out of the room with me.

Chapter Twenty: Alistair Present

Alistair sat in his hotel room, file folder stacked on the table, post-it notes with scrawled writing smattered haphazardly around the pages. Inscrutable. An opened MacBook rested on the corner with papers wedged underneath. He had gotten in a solid thirty minutes of productive work until his mind began to wander. Once, the old Alistair blared music, watched TV, and held a phone conversation while remaining on task. Now he needed total silence, and even then he failed to maintain focus. The television stayed on but muted while he gazed at the screen. It was a listing of the movies they offered at the hotel. All it took was one glimpse of the title *Pretty Woman* and he went right back to thinking about Prue.

He dialed George. "Hey, old chap, looking forward to your arrival in LA."

Alistair nodded in agreement as he listened to his friend. The familiar accent brought the UK across the pond if only for the duration of this conversation.

"Tesla is being delivered tomorrow night. Thank you for making that happen. You never let me down." He crossed an ankle over his knee and leaned back on the sofa. "Things are moving along smoothly. Your first job is on Sunday. I secured three tickets to the Rams game, VIP box, pregaming. You'll be picking up a friend from my little stint in Arizona." He straightened his shirt cuff, running his fingers down the monogram. "We'll need to do some shopping. See if you can set up a stylist appointment for Friday. I haven't a clue what I'm supposed to wear to a football game."

He laughed.

"Yes, Georgie, not soccer. I've got to embrace the LA lifestyle. I'm sticking out with my monogrammed shirts and such." He unbuttoned his sleeve and began rolling it up. "Right, mate, sleep on the plane. Me? No. No rest for the weary . . . or the wicked, true enough."

He hung up and glanced at his sleeve as he rolled his cuff back down. He removed a rubber band from a tube of tightly rolled papers. The sheets curled, refusing to lay flat. He picked them up and set them on the dining table. He looked over the blueprints for his office remodel and new residence, all the while hoping that Prue would forgive him for all the lies. He was sure she'd understand after he explained himself. Alistair anchored it with a few glasses from the bar. He shrugged off the lingering doubt weighing on his shoulders.

In tight letters in the upper right corner was the architect's name. Below, it said *Patrick Dunn Interiors, Designer: Prudence Aldrich*. He tapped his finger on her name. The thought of Prue made him giddy, but the underlying foreboding feeling he could do without. It was just there, hovering above the excitement, ready to ruin everything, so he did his best to slam it with his imaginary sledgehammer.

Nothing was going to stop him, nothing and no one.

His phone buzzed. He hesitated, then picked it up.

"Hello." He leaned against the dining room table. "Goddammit, my clients have been waiting on this for months. Their patience is growing thin."

He grabbed a tissue from the bathroom and wiped his nose.

"Tell the Chinese to come up with the two million. I don't care how. We aren't turning over the bonds without the security keys in our hands. I need the funds to get them ordered."

He threw the phone down and opened the minibar fridge. Nothing but sodas and juice. He cracked open a Coke and paced around the room. A line would do wonders for his focus right about now. It would only take a few calls. He dropped to his knees.

Dear God, please help me. I'm begging You for mercy. I'm losing my mind.

He rattled off the Serenity Prayer, took a piece of paper from the coffee table, crumpled it into a ball, and threw it against the wall. He grabbed his briefcase from the sofa and put it on the dining room table. The leather shoulder bag had been a gift from Eleanor. Alistair laughed at the irony of it all as he slid out his ThinkPad and a small box that was tucked in the side pocket.

A bunch of emails dumped into his inbox. He left the blueprints where he'd arranged them. It was far preferable to gaze at them and live in a fantasy than face the realities of his everyday life. When he picked up his cell, his elbow swiped one of the glasses that had been anchoring the blueprint. The glass flew to the floor and bounced.

"Dammit," he said under his breath.

Inside the box was a device that looked similar to a calculator. He punched a code on the keypad. A number appeared, which he inputted into his computer. Another screen gained him access to the Henkle Global email system.

He sighed as he began to draft an out-and-out lie. They had to come up with the cash. There wasn't another way.

Alistair ran on gut instinct, and so far it had always worked in his favor.

Dear Client,

We are excited to share that the standoff we mentioned last week has accomplished its goal and the expense money has been released. We are now able to order the backlog of security keys. Please remember, you cannot access your money without a security key. We are doing our part to start the process of disbursement as soon as possible.

The initial deposit of two hundred and fifty thousand is a non-recourse, interest-free loan, collateralized and justified by assets that have been submitted, verified, and marked non-reassignable. The funds will be non-returnable once you accept the loan, at least until the account balance with your individual paymaster portal has been debited, satisfying the loan. We are banking on our ability to perform so we can pay the advance and that you agree with the redemption values of the bonds.

Should you agree to the terms and conditions and proceed to the execution of the loan document, it will require electronic signing via the security key. The only issue holding us back at the moment is the unrest in Hong Kong. The financial district has been closed for several days due to the anti-government protests. They have wreaked havoc on the city and disrupted all services throughout the region.

We hope to share good news soon. Please be patient.

Regards,

Alistair and the Henkle Global Team

He closed the window and logged out of the Henkle site. There was no way in hell he could get anyone in China or Germany on the phone. He moved to his MacBook resting on the bed, took off his pants, and put a stack of pillows behind his back.

After a fleeting effort to google Prue and find a photo of her, he resorted to porn. The one thing he never did was pay for it. That would gum up his computer. He typed in "MILF redheads on MILF redheads" in the Google search bar. A few sites popped up.

With a sufficient lesbian scene on the screen, he stroked himself until he came. The orgasm only satisfied him fleetingly. He continued to tug and rub but was not able to come again. Frustrated and agitated, he got dressed and headed down to the lobby bar.

Alistair drank a vodka soda with extra limes at the bar while he reviewed the menu. A blonde sitting on the far corner eyed him. The bartender took his dinner order—NY strip steak with steamed vegetables and a side of fries.

"Put whatever she's drinking on my tab." He said it loud enough to tempt the blonde with his accent, which he followed up with a tip of his head in her direction. In his experience, the British accent proved to be a sure way to gain attention with American ladies. The woman picked up her clutch and cocktail and sat next to him.

"Thank you for the drink." She held up her glass and clinked it on Alistair's.

"You're entirely welcome."

"Are you from Australia?"

"No. But if you want me to be, I am."

The woman laughed. "England?"

"Yes!"

Alistair engaged in fodder with the blonde, who disappointed upon closer inspection. The cravings for a bump hit harder than expected while perched at the bar. He eyed the bartender. The woman prattled on. Disappointing as she might be, Blondie could make for a convenient distraction from what he truly wanted.

Chapter Twenty-One: Prue Present

I stood in front of my closet and scrolled through every possible outfit option for a Sunday afternoon Rams game. Nothing inspired me. I wanted to wear something special for my first visit with Alistair outside the confines of rehab. At the same time, I was anxious over how much time we'd be spending together. He had told me to dress casually, which was so nondescript. It could run the gamut from workout pants to jeans to something I would wear to meet with a client. I opted to turn casual into chic, which made me feel a ton better. The only problem was that there was nothing with that description anywhere in my closet.

The hardest part about choosing what to wear to meet Alistair was that Mike kept jumping into the frame in front of him. Imaginary Mike rested on my shoulder, playing the role of fun police.

I put on fitted dark jeans, high heels, and a low-cut silk top with the idea that I would wear sneakers to the game and change into heels for dinner. Then I worried that might be weird. My phone dinged on the bedside table. With one shoe on, I stepped over the other shoe to grab my phone.

"Hey, Mitch," I said. "Your timing is perfect." I shimmied a bare foot into the other black stiletto. "I'm in the middle of choosing an outfit to wear to a football game and dinner on Sunday with Alistair. He just got to LA after two weeks of aftercare, which means I haven't seen him in what—three weeks since I checked out?" The phone was propped under my chin. I pulled the sleeve of my leather jacket over one arm and switched shoulders to slip in the other. "Can we Facetime so you can help me decide?"

Mitch agreed. I hung up and waited for his face to pop up. When he did, I answered and flipped the camera so he could see the whole getup.

"Outfit number one," I said.

"Looks amazing," Mitch said. "Did I hear you correctly when you said Alistair just got to LA?"

"Yeah," I said, pulling off the leather jacket. "Ready for outfit number two?"

"Darling," Mitch said. "I don't want to burst your bubble, but Alistair has been in LA for over a week."

I dropped into the club chair beside my bed. "What do you mean?"

"You're not going to like my answer," he said.

"Jesus," I said, my patience growing thinner by the second. "Spit it out. You're killing me, Gladys."

"Fine. You don't have to shoot the messenger." He smiled into the screen.

"Sorry," I said. "I'm a little stressed out."

"I saw him at Bare Elegance," he said. "It's a strip club. And for the record, I was there with a client."

"I know it's a strip club." I gazed at my reflection in the mirrored closet door. "Are you one hundred percent sure it was him?" I twirled a clump of hair between my thumb and index finger.

"Yes," he said. His dark, sultry eyes magnified through his glasses. "I even spoke to him."

"You talked to him?" My voice screeched to an unrecognizable decibel like the bad witch in *The Wizard of Oz*. "Why didn't you tell me?"

"I got so busy with work I must have forgotten. Sorry. I also assumed Alistair would have mentioned it."

Mitch pushed his wire-rimmed glasses up his nose. It took me a minute to register what he was saying because it meant Alistair had lied about being in aftercare last week when we spoke on the phone, and when he texted to invite me to the game.

"I flew in and out in one day," he said. "More on that later."

"What did you two talk about?" I held the phone with one hand and ripped the knot out of my hair with the other. "It's weird that he led me to believe he was still in aftercare."

I wasn't sure who I was more immediately pissed at—Alistair for lying or Mitch for failing to inform me. It was definitely Alistair, but he wasn't the one who was on the phone with me.

"Brace yourself for this one," Mitch said. His face soured. Even he looked nervous over what he was about to tell me.

"I can't imagine how this could get any worse."

The rest spilled out of him like a run-on sentence. "When I walked into the private room, a stripper caught me checking out her Cartier watch and then asked me if I wanted to buy it right off her wrist. I didn't put two and two together until I spotted Alistair in the far corner. The stripper was wearing a watch that looked an awful lot like yours. You know, the one you gave Alistair the day you checked out of Serenity Hills."

"For Christ's sake, I know what watch you're talking about." I panted like I had sprinted a mile while frantically chewing my cuticles. "What the fuck is going on?"

"Maybe it's nothing," Mitch said in an unconvincing voice. "I wouldn't worry about it. I'm sure there is a reasonable explanation." His uneasiness with my distress was obvious. "The ... umm, outfit ... er, that outfit is a winner. I wouldn't change a thing. It's perfect for taking in a game."

"Thanks," I said. "I'm going to have to spend some time processing this." I smiled into the screen.

"The reason why I called was to discuss Gloria's memorial service. I'm trying to finalize the details. I wish Mike could be there, but no telling where he is these days," Mitch mused.

"What I would give to talk to Mike right now."

Chapter Twenty-Two: Alistair Present

Alistair hit a dead end with the blonde. Discouraged, he headed back to his suite with a fresh cocktail in hand. The minute he entered the room, he dialed Prue. Maybe a chat with her would lift his spirits.

"Hi," she said.

Alistair's mood brightened at the sound of her voice. "I was sitting here trying to work and thinking about you," he said. "I'm excited to see you on Sunday."

"Yeah," she said. "It'll be fun." There was an iciness to her tone.

"Did you get my texts with the details about the game?" he asked. "I wanted you to make the final decision about whether we should do some pregaming in the tailgate area or enjoy the VIP section with its open bar and appetizers."

"Why don't you pick," she replied. "It doesn't matter to me whether we go early or not."

"You know," Alistair said in an attempt to reset the tone of the conversation, "I had planned on staying on the West Coast for only a short time, but I found out today that my business deal is moving forward. Looks as though I will have to be here for a while." He waited for her to express the kind of joy he had fantasized about when he played the scene in his head. "I have a broker looking at properties."

"Awesome," Prue said. "I'm happy for you." There was a long pause. "So, I'll see you Sunday. If you want me to choose, I'd rather go to the VIP section to pregame rather than to the tailgate area."

The tone of the conversation was confusing him. Just as he was about to inquire about it, he realized she'd already hung up. Alistair replayed the call in his head, wondering what he might have said wrong.

He paced for a half hour in his room before opening the minibar, which had been restocked by someone who hadn't received the memo about no alcohol in the room. Perhaps another drink would help. Then he decided he shouldn't use alcohol as a crutch for his emotions. Besides, George was arriving early the next morning, and Alistair didn't need a hangover.

His alarm went off at six. Alistair showered and dressed before picking up the house line next to his bed.

"Can you please call for the hotel car? I'm ready to be dropped at the airport." He grabbed a coat and headed out the door. The thought of seeing George made him feel better.

By the time he got to the main waiting area at Bradley International, George was walking through the security doors. He was dragging two large suitcases. Alistair nearly cheered when he saw him, edging his way through the opening to greet his friend.

"Great to see you, you old codger," Alistair said. They embraced, and he stepped back to take all of George in. "You look leaner. I'm a fat, bloated mess."

"Not at all," George said. "You're healthy as a horse."

Alistair grabbed one of his roller bags. "It just occurred to me we have no ride back to the hotel." He stood in the crowd of people, wondering where his brain had disappeared to and when it would return.

"Not to worry," George said. "I've ordered us a car service. It will take us straight to Tesla, where your chariot awaits."

Alistair smiled. As he turned to wheel the luggage to who knows where, he noticed a driver holding up a sign with his name. "Brilliant," Alistair said. "Absolutely brilliant."

In the car, George caught Alistair up on the news of their hometown. Alistair inquired about the well-being of a few certain ladies who George assured him would be waiting for his return, regardless of how long it took.

"I figured it would be easier to get the car at Tesla on our way rather than have them deliver it to the hotel. Plus, I wanted to make sure you were happy with everything."

"Whatever you think is best," Alistair said. "I'm incredibly relieved to have my mate back by my side. I hope you're happy here in La-La Land because we have a lot of business to do, and it's going to take a while."

"I'm sure I will be," George said. "I've no doubt."

When they arrived at Tesla, the car was ready and waiting. Alistair approved of every detail, especially the nubuck seats with navy piping. After touring around LA in the new ride, they headed to the Peninsula, where Alistair had booked an adjoining suite so the two of them could be close but have privacy. Alistair held on to the hope that Prue might be spending the night with him on Sunday, and he wouldn't want George to hear any of the fun that he imagined they would be having.

The two old friends ordered room service and drank a few beers. The next morning, a stylist arrived. George kept Alistair entertained with his complaints about American football. Alistair half-heartedly defended the game as the stylist thrust a panoply of outfits to try on.

When George eventually left Alistair to his own devices, Alistair found himself once again contending with his thoughts. Doubt harangued him. He had failed to attend any AA meetings and failed to meet most of the commitments he had made at Serenity Hills.

There was also the issue of how he'd left things with Eleanor. Had he been wrong not to tell her where he was going when he disappeared? She hadn't known about his cocaine habit. After reassessing the situation, Alistair figured it was better to leave Eleanor out of it. This was especially true since he wasn't sure how he felt about her, whether he truly loved her or wanted an eventual future with her. He remembered he had told Prue he was going to call Eleanor and inform her he was in rehab. Yet another thing he failed to follow through on.

Oh, well, he thought to himself. *Just another little white lie.*

The therapy sessions at Serenity had prescribed a path of rigorous honesty. Since checking out, he had told nothing but a pack of lies, all of which he easily justified. But honesty for honesty's sake was cruel. Even selfish. Wasn't it?

Alistair wondered if he'd ever actually been honest with a woman, whether he even had experienced a healthy relationship beyond Georgie.

Chapter Twenty-Three: Prue Present

After I spoke to Mitch and learned that Alistair had been in LA far longer than he had let on, I didn't get too worked up over going to the game with him. He texted me a few times after our quick phone conversation during which I was aloof. Borderline cold bitch, really. Eventually, game day came. Alistair messaged he was sending a car to pick me up. That way, I could enjoy some drinks and not worry about driving home. I felt vulnerable not having my car. An easy exit strategy should things take a horrific turn.

He will have some sort of explanation as to why he lied. Right? Of course he will.

The driver texted when he was a few minutes out. I locked my front door and waited in the driveway. Lily loaned me the required clear plastic purse so I could get into the stadium without any issues. I held a tote bag with a cashmere shawl, leather biker jacket, and a pair of heels in case we went out for dinner. What a difference five weeks makes. These days when I walked in heels, I looked more like a baby giraffe than a sexy babe. I prayed that wherever we ended up dining, I wouldn't have to walk too far.

While I felt indignant and wanted answers, I felt vulnerable more. It crashed in on me in waves. I struggled to find meaning in what happened between us at Serenity Hills.

The answers would help me decide whether to pursue a relationship with Alistair or cut it off in its tracks.

Stop future-tripping.

Anyone who was in recovery and working the program knew that relationships in the first year of sobriety were a no-no. We both understood this, and yet here I was, waiting to go on a date with Alistair.

But is it even a date?

Once in the back seat of the car, paranoia knifed me in my gut. The driver introduced himself as George with the same accent as Alistair. The car interior had that distinctly new scent. I kept our conversation shallow and small, fearful he would repeat every word I said to Alistair.

When we pulled up to the Peninsula, Alistair was standing out front. I wondered if the driver had communicated with him even though I hadn't seen the man use his phone. The whole thing had an espionage vibe.

My heart played ping-pong when I laid eyes on him. Thankfully, the car windows were tinted so he couldn't see my overly excited expression. It was important not to appear too eager. This was a guy, I imagined, who landed any woman he wanted. Alistair looked like the hunks I'd see on the jumbotron when I went to Lakers' games with Nick. He had on sleek sneakers which also looked new, well-fitted jeans, a softly faded red tee, and a leather jacket that nearly matched the one resting in my bag in the trunk. His thick, dark hair had an effortless James Dean style without any product residue.

"Hello, gorgeous," he said as he opened the door and slid into the seat next to me. He leaned over and gave me a peck on the cheek.

I realized this was the first time we had been together without Big Brother watching. Then again, there was the driver beaming at us through the rearview, so we weren't exactly alone.

"Have you met George?" Alistair laughed. "Well, of course you met him. This is my best mate. Flew all the way from London to be by my side and help get my sorry ass around this crazy town. Bonus, we bought a car for the carpool lane without realizing we would have already qualified with the both of us in the car."

He and George laughed with absolute synchronicity. The rhythm was almost identical, and I couldn't help but burst out laughing too.

"Well, it's wonderful you bought an electric car," I said. "I'm a huge fan of protecting our environment and keeping the carbon footprint to a minimum." I walked my fingers through the air for effect.

"Thank you for joining me," he said, reaching for my hand and placing it on his lap. "It's great to see you. I mean it. You look more beautiful than I remembered."

I smiled even though I wanted to punch him in the arm. His eyes sparkled so genuinely that it melted a few feet off the iceberg I had built since discovering his deceit.

"After seeing you every day for so many weeks, a month felt like forever," he said.

I seethed while maintaining my poker face. With George in the car, I had no real opportunity to confront him. If George was his best friend, then he must have known when Alistair arrived in LA.

Alistair asked George to hand him an envelope that was resting on the front seat. "Georgie, put this on the dash," Alistair said. "My client said this will get us directed to the VIP parking." He passed me a lanyard and noticed a see-through bag resting on the seat beside me. "Awesome," he said. "I forgot to tell you about the clear-bag policy. You're like an old pro. Do you go to a lot of football games?" He turned to face me, his seatbelt unbuckled.

"Not really," I said. "I don't know anything about football. Lily lent me the bag. She told me it was required." I glanced at the hideous plastic tote. "I brought another purse and heels in case we go out to eat."

Alistair glanced at my sneakers. "You are adorable. Don't change a thing." That was the first time I had heard anyone refer to size nine Adidas sneakers as adorable.

We moved through the mess of cars trying to enter the stadium. Alistair stirred with nervous energy, and I shadowed it dutifully like the codependent woman I was before checking into Serenity.

Alistair handed George a pass and told him he'd meet us in the box. We were ushered through security and up an elevator to an open area that bustled with people, all of them wearing VIP lanyards. Alistair led me to a seating area with a reserved sign near a fountain and asked me what I wanted to drink. I wondered if he was drinking, and whether I should. Alcohol might impede my judgment, and there were still things we needed to discuss. Serious things. I caved in a nanosecond.

"I'll have whatever you're having," I said.

Within moments, Alistair was heading toward me with two drinks and a small plate of food. "I got us the signature cocktail, a Moscow Mule, and a few sliders."

He set the drinks and plate on the table in front of us. The fountain drowned out the noise of the people bustling around. Alistair picked up the plate of food and offered me one before taking his.

"No thanks," I said.

"You're not hungry?" he asked.

"I don't eat meat," I said. "It's no big deal. I'll eat something in the box if I get hungry."

"Well I won't eat until you eat, then," he said, putting the plate back down on the table.

I shrugged, not in the mood to create a fuss. "So you're moving to LA?" I asked. It was the easiest way to get on the subject that was bugging me beyond belief.

"Yes," Alistair replied.

Impeccable manners topped my list of requirements when searching for long-term potential. I re-geared my brain to not picture him as a partner but rather a friend. In person, it proved to be far more difficult than I had hoped. There was still this little girl living inside me who wanted to be saved, the princess wrapped in the donkey skin who needed a prince to sweep her off her feet.

"I had planned to open an office here," he said. "Things are moving along faster than I expected. I'm signing a lease next week." His gaze met mine, anticipating, I assumed, some sort of over-the-moon reaction.

All I wanted to do was be the genuine, real Prue, not the fake "I crave male attention" Prue, the desperate chick I had hated before I left her sorry ass at rehab.

While Alistair spoke, I took in his face, and the evident warmth of a friendship made between two recovering addicts. I hoped to never meet the addict side of him. The thought of cocaine turned my stomach, a reminder of my father's demise. That white powder had stolen a piece of my childhood. The image of Alistair snorting lines kept my heart in check.

I cannot go there again. The codependent Prudence is not someone whose company I enjoy.

We finished our drinks and headed to the box to watch the game. When we came to the more crowded area, he took my hand

and held it tight. I noticed women checking him out, sizing us up as a couple.

When we arrived, George was waiting with a bottle of champagne on ice, a veggie platter, chips, guacamole, popcorn, and veggie burgers. It fascinated me how Alistair could shift gears so quickly. Clearly, he hadn't known I wasn't a meat-eater, yet he was able to have all this ready and waiting between him finding out and us taking our seats.

It amused me that neither Alistair nor George knew a thing about football. "I'd vote to leave after the halftime show," I said. Alistair snapped his fingers. When the cheerleaders were doing their moves right in front of our seats, Alistair feigned indifference.

The champagne warmed, and my laughs came easier. Alistair entertained me with stories of London, his clients, and their quirky money habits. How some would call him in a panic when anything happened in the news, ready to sell everything, while others needed constant hand-holding. As he spoke, I found him wiser than I had remembered. Time moved easily, and before I knew it, the halftime show was ending.

About five minutes into the second half, Alistair looked at me. "Want to go?" He smiled, and his hand grazed my knee. "We could grab a drink in Beverly Hills. I made a few reservations and thought you could choose."

"Sounds great."

I stood, and Alistair followed. George waited for me to pass. He and Alistair exchanged words, but I couldn't catch what they were saying. George came across as more of a bodyguard than a driver. It made me wonder what Alistair needed to be guarded against. Maybe he was the cocaine patrol, but then it occurred to me he may have been the one to score his drugs in the past. Thoughts bounced around until I felt as though I might explode. When we were sealed in the car, I turned to him.

"Thank you," I said. "It was amazing, all of it."

"My pleasure," he replied. He grasped my hand with so much purpose it nearly threw me off-balance. "There's something I need to talk to you about."

Alistair removed his hand but remained silent. George and I exchanged glances in the rearview mirror.

"I know you didn't just arrive in LA. I also know you only went to aftercare for a week." My mouth went dry. I cracked open a bottle of Fiji water that was resting in the cup holder.

"I hate plastic bottles," I continued, stalling. "One more thing." I shifted an inch farther from him. The seat belt tightened on my shoulder. "Mitch told me he saw you at Bare Elegance. He also said one of the dancers was wearing a Cartier watch that looked an awful lot like the one I gave you. When the stripper noticed him admiring it, she offered to sell it to Mitch." I started breathing so hard I was nearly hyperventilating. "George," I said, "Can you please take me home?"

"Wait," Alistair said. "George, take us to the Peninsula." He turned toward me. "I can explain. I was worried Mitch would have mentioned it and perhaps that was why you were a bit cold on the phone, but when you didn't bring it up, I figured he hadn't."

"Who cares if he did or didn't?" I asked, the volume of my voice matching my growing frustration levels. "This is all a house of cards. Nothing but smoke and mirrors. Let's be real. Every single thing you have told me since leaving rehab has been a complete and total lie."

I crossed my legs, embarrassed to ask George a second time to take me home—furious at Alistair for countermanding my request. I wished I wasn't so far from home. How much would an Uber cost from here? How much from the Peninsula when I made my grand exit? I made a mental note: I had a bag in the trunk I couldn't leave behind. I half wondered if I was about to be cut up into tiny pieces and left for dead. My old fears reemerged, the victim mentality I'd dragged around from my childhood that had landed me in bad situations over and over.

"I don't feel safe," I blurted out. "I'm truly upset. I don't even know who you are, and you certainly aren't who I thought you were."

I was beginning to feel car sick. My mouth watered. The window child lock was on. "May I please roll down the window?" The window opened. Fresh air filled the car, and the nausea subsided slightly.

We drove with the freeway air ripping through the open back window until we pulled into the Peninsula. A bellhop opened the door. George grabbed my bag from the trunk.

"It's me," Alistair said in a smooth, calming tone. "I didn't mean to keep George from driving you home. Nothing bad is going to happen, I just wanted a chance to explain, and when you hear my explanation, you will feel worlds better. Trust me."

I needed out of the car and so I acquiesced. George kept his distance but followed us to the elevator. I fought a battle between calling an Uber right then and there, but the nausea had not entirely passed, and neither had my need for an explanation.

Alistair had the presidential suite; I acted unimpressed. We entered through the living room with an adjoining dining room. A large stack of blueprints was draped on the dining table. He didn't offer me a drink. I sat on the sofa. George dropped my bag next to me and left the suite. Alistair sat across from me in a club chair. I noted it was covered in the same fabric I had used for a client the previous year. It was still pleasing to the eyes.

"Where to begin? I can't tell you everything yet," he said. "I'm superstitious. I've been searching for someone I lost a lifetime ago. Someone who is very important to me."

He sighed and ran his fingers through his thick, wavy hair. A waft of vanilla reached my nose. Its familiarity calmed me, and I almost wanted to smack him for it. He stood and poured some water in a glass from the bar then put it down on the table in front of me. I sipped while he spoke.

"It's someone who I never mentioned in rehab, mainly because I have hired a multitude of private investigators who have failed to find her. Right now, I believe I may have, but the relationship is tenuous and I simply can't share much about it." He paused while I grew impatient.

"Jesus, did you bring me up here for this?" I said. "I feel like you're talking in code. Is this some kind of British communication style? This is impossible to follow, and you haven't said anything yet that has made me feel better."

"Right," he said. "Sorry." The same sad eyes from the day he checked into Serenity Hills when I was giving him a tour of the campus. The day he nearly fainted. I could see the hopelessness that had taken what had been a confident man before whatever had brought him to Serenity. That same expression was looking back at me as I sat across from him.

"I'm sorry," I said. "Imagine how I'm feeling."

I stood, walked over to him, and bent down to give him a hug. His arms remained by his side. "So this person you're looking for," I said. "Is it a she? An ex-girlfriend?"

He shook his head. "No, no, nothing like that. I mean yes, it's a woman, but no, not an ex-girlfriend."

I eased back onto the sofa and made a vow to keep my mouth shut and let him talk.

"I believe she works at Bare Elegance. Again, the person I hired has told me this, so I went there in search of her. It was my bad luck that Mitch saw me and I didn't have a chance to explain. Believe me, I wanted to, but he ran out so fast you would have thought the place was on fire." He smiled. "All I was doing was waiting until she got off her shift so I could speak with her. Nothing more." His mouth turned down. "I am not a fan of strip clubs. Believe me."

I cringed at the thought of how many strip clubs I went to when I was hanging around with that creep, Roger, who I'd sort of dated. The only blessing that came out of my relationship with him was meeting Frankie.

"Do you have any wine in this suite?" I asked. "I could use a drink."

Alistair trotted over to the bar while texting on his phone. Moments later, George appeared with a tray of cheese and crackers, which he put on the coffee table in front of me. Alistair opened up a bottle of Rombauer chardonnay, which somehow magically happened to be in his mini-fridge and also happened to be my favorite wine.

"You ask, and it shall happen," he said, setting the glass in front of me.

"Thank you." I sliced a piece of brie from the platter, put it on a cracker, and shoved it in my mouth. "You were saying."

George stepped out the door, and I wondered about hidden cameras.

"I will tell you more when I can. I'm sure it will be hard to understand, but this is something that has caused me tremendous heartache." He pressed his palms together. "Please forgive me for lying. It was a vulnerable time. I wasn't sure if I had found her, and I refuse to do anything to jeopardize the situation. It was something I needed to do alone and still need to do alone. Now that I believe I found her, I don't want to say anything until I'm sure."

He sipped his wine while I stared at his intense dimples.

"I told no one I was in LA," he continued. "Not even George, until I asked him to come drive me around. Much of my success relies on not saying things until they are one hundred percent done. No deal is discussed or shared until it's in the bag. I suppose this thought process trickled into my real life, as well."

"Fair enough," I said. "I'm still chapped you lied to me, and I don't trust you, but I respect what you're saying. I don't have to agree with how you handled it or even understand. I just have to acknowledge you chose to deal with it the way you did."

His face lit up as though he was off the hook, and I worried I had let him off too easy.

"What are those?" I asked, pointing to the blueprints.

"Well," he said, "that's another surprise."

I moseyed over to the dining room table, wine glass in hand. Since I had my advanced design degree, I was accustomed to reading blueprints. It didn't take more than a second for me to find the surprise.

"Oh, dear God," I said, putting the glass on the table. Alistair stood behind me and pressed his body against mine to turn the blueprints to face us. "Don't bother. I see my name." I stepped away from the table and picked up my bag beside the sofa. "This is not how I roll, Alistair. I have no clue how you thought it was a good idea to hire me through my design firm without telling me first." A scream brewed from deep within my chest. "As things stand right now, I will have no choice but to work with you. But to go behind my back . . . that's simply unfathomable."

"Really?" Alistair stammered, appearing flummoxed by my reaction. "I thought it would be a fun surprise."

"This is my career," I said. "You clearly have no respect for me as a businesswoman. You knew I would decline your invitation to design your office and loft, so you made sure I couldn't say no."

A lump filled my throat. I had zero desire to give him the satisfaction of seeing me cry. I pulled my phone from my bag.

"What are you doing?" he asked.

"Calling an Uber," I said. "I'm leaving."

"George can take you home," he said.

"The last thing I want to do is sit in a car with one of your minions." Now I was shouting.

"I'm sorry. I had no idea this would upset you. I'm at a loss for words." Alistair held his hands in the begging position.

"Upset me?" I shrieked. "If I don't leave right now, I'm going to say something I might regret."

I scanned the room to make sure I hadn't left anything behind, walked through the door, and slammed it behind me.

Chapter Twenty-Four: Prue Present

When I turned the corner from the hallway to the kitchen, Lily was knocking on the door. I smiled as I opened it.

Lily to the rescue, again.

"Thank you so much for coming over," I said, tucking my hair behind my ears. "I totally need to vent over my day with Alistair."

"I'm dying to hear," Lily said. She never showed up empty-handed, so I wasn't surprised to see her put a bag on the counter. "I brought our favorite dinner—wine and cheese. Binky is getting take-out for the kids."

She could have passed for twenty in her ripped jeans, Gucci slides, and half-tucked Fair Isle sweater.

"You look so cute," I said, pulling a plate from the cabinet.

"Thanks," she said. "I'm stoked Fair Isle sweaters are making a comeback."

She followed me to the living room with a plate of cheese and crackers while I carried two glasses of wine. I sliced some cheese before beginning the story. "The thing is, I'm furious with Alistair but I can't stop worrying about whether I hurt his feelings."

"What exactly happened?" she asked, kicking off her shoes and tucking her feet underneath her.

"The day went fairly well until I confronted him about the strip club," I said. "It was all downhill from there."

"Back up," Lily said. "Strip club?"

"Yikes, I must have forgotten to tell you. I found out from Mitch that he had run into Alistair at Bare Elegance."

"What was Mitch doing at a strip club?" Lily asked. "I thought he was gay."

"He was there with a client and saw this stripper who happened to be wearing what I think is my watch. She apparently offered to sell it to Mitch."

"This story keeps getting better," Lily said, putting a slice of Manchego on a cracker. "I feel like I'm hearing about a reality show." She laughed.

"Yeah," I said. "Except it's my life."

"True," she said.

"I learned about all this before going to watch the game with Alistair. I held it in the whole day until I exploded." I threw my hands around as though a bomb was going off. "I confronted him in the car. Oh, I forgot to tell you that his best friend from London was driving us around in a brand-new Tesla."

"Nice," Lily said. "Not sure how he managed to jump to the top of the waiting list. I've been trying to buy one for a year."

"Who knows," I said. "Alistair must have serious connections."

"What happened when you confronted him?" Lily ate three more crackers.

"He told me he was looking for someone from his past. He said it's not a girlfriend but someone he wants to find so badly he hired an investigator to track her down. He literally gave me snippets of information. I felt as though I was cracking a secret code to figure out what he was saying."

"It's actually kind of sad," Lily said.

"I know." Everything softened as I sank into the sofa.

"Do you have any idea or inkling who he's looking for? The whole thing is so weird."

"No clue, but he was adamant it wasn't an ex-lover. Other than that, he wouldn't say. The thing is with that look on his face, I don't actually think he was lying," I said, releasing an exaggerated sigh. "It was all going fine until I noticed the blueprints resting on the table in his suite."

"Oh, Lord," Lily said. "I have a sinking feeling I know what you're about to tell me." Her hand cupped over her mouth.

"Yup," I said. "He's the big client with the British accent who requested a woman from the firm. He went right around my back to hire me." I shook my head. "He acted as though it was some sort of exciting surprise. I was so pissed I called an Uber and stormed out." The next sentence came out muffled due to my face being in my hands. "And the worst part is, I still have a crush on him. I like him. I really, really like him. I'm such an idiot."

"Maybe he believed you'd be excited, or it was fun to surprise you. He doesn't understand how degrading it is to have you find out from your boss and not him first. It might be a cultural thing."

"I don't think so," I said. "It's not like England is a third-world country. They're pretty savvy with equal rights and what not." I sliced two pieces of cheese, propped them both on crackers, and passed one to Lily. "My heart wants to give him the benefit of the doubt. He's been texting and calling nonstop. I have to talk to him because Sam assured me that I can't screw up this project. It means a lot to the firm, but more than that, I want to be kind rather than be all angry and toxic."

"No point in harboring resentment about what he's done," Lily said. She dug food from her back molar. "But to be perfectly honest, other than dealing with the design project, I don't think you should ever talk to this loser again."

I sighed, disappointed Lily hadn't given me the advice I wanted to hear.

"Change of subject, check this out." Lily pressed her phone in my face. "We have to do this together." I snatched it from her hand to take a closer look at what *this* was.

"Churchill Boxing Club?" I gave Lily a perplexed expression.

"Well," she said. "Binky and I decided to take boxing lessons for a little couple's bonding." I quashed the moment of guilt her words sparked in me and redoubled my focus. "We had our first lesson this morning."

All I could think of was that Binky had better watch out because even though Lily was wiry thin, she had solid amounts of muscle. I bet she would pack a serious punch with those toned arms.

"That's awesome," I said, passing Lily back her phone. "Sounds like fun. I'll totally do that with you."

I was curious but a bit confused as to why Lily wanted me to be involved in her newfound form of couple's therapy. Especially after what had gone down between me and her husband.

"Guess who was there as the manager." Lily cocked her head forward while I feigned guessing who she might have seen other than Nick, who was no doubt currently at my old house banging Naomi.

"I have no clue," I said. All I could think about was calling Alistair to apologize for my abrupt exit.

"Mike," she said. "From Serenity Hills."

"What? He's in LA?"

The ear-rubbing began.

"He's here alright," she said. "Chickie, I saw him with my own two eyes."

"I'm dying that you've known this the whole time we've been talking and didn't spill."

"It was the longest morning imaginable for me to wait and tell you in person. Then you were so upset over Alistair I wanted you to get all your frustrations out first." Lily leaned in and touched my shoulders. "How do you feel?"

"Excited, nervous, confused." My brow furled. *How on earth has Mike gone from a therapist in Arizona to running a boxing gym in LA?* There had to be a fascinating story behind this extreme career change. "Did he recognize you?"

"Yes," she said. "He remembered that I visited you during Family Week. He acted a bit nervous when he saw me. It was like his old life merged with his new one. He was sparring with someone when we left. The guy's boxing skills are no joke." She sipped her wine while I clung to her every word. "He looked like a real pro. You wouldn't believe how hot he is when he's boxing. I was out of my mind."

I absorbed everything Lily was saying while picturing the scene. When she was finished talking, I peeled Lily's phone from her hand again and stared at the boxing gym website. I envisioned Mike there, fighting for his life the way I had fought for mine.

Don't let the bastards grind you down.
–Margaret Atwood

Chapter Twenty-Five: Mike Present

The day Mike found Gloria hanging limp and lifeless from a tree branch on the outer edges of the Serenity Hills campus, he feared he might backslide in his recovery. An alcoholic beverage called out to him the way a baby cries for its mother. Five years sober with a five-year AA pin tucked in his pocket to prove it, and Gloria's suicide turned out to be the tipping point that nearly broke him. He questioned his professionalism and the keen insight required to recognize a patient in crisis. The days that followed were inky, like a sky with no stars. Mike agonized over forgiving himself. He wanted to, but could he? Should he? He had failed to save someone who depended on him. He struggled to shake the embedded image of Prue in the nursing center with Gloria's doll clutched to her chest; how she had fallen into his arms, sobbing.

"Who is going to take care of Gloria's baby?" Prudence had asked, her eyes dark with pain and confusion. Mike had let her down, too. He had failed himself, Gloria, Prue—hell, everyone in his group.

After a few sleepless nights, Mike made the decision to seek help. Dr. Howard Livingston, the resident psychiatrist at Serenity Hills, was available for both patients and therapists. Mike knew that most who worked in the industry underwent therapy at one time or another, so he made an appointment after regular hours. It wouldn't be appropriate for Mike to be in the waiting area with other patients. At exactly six o'clock, Mike entered the psychiatric building. With the receptionist long gone, he continued past the front desk. The office door was ajar. Mike pushed up his sleeves and knocked. There was no point in holding back.

"Mike." Dr. Livingston stood. "Come in." He directed him to a chair across from the modern desk. "I was just reviewing your paperwork. Thank you for answering the questionnaire before your appointment. It gives me a chance to prepare and have a better grasp of what to focus on in the session."

"Thanks for fitting me in," Mike said. He fidgeted with his hands, cracking his knuckles before parking his broad body in the leather chair. "I'm struggling with the suicide of one of my patients." Mike dropped his head and fought the thickness in his throat.

"I read the full report, both yours and the one filed by Serenity Hills," Dr. Livingston said.

A folder sat open on his desk. Inside, Mike imagined, were photos of Gloria's lifeless body hanging from a tree. Dr. Livingston slid the tissue box across his desk. Mike pulled a few and pressed them over his eyes.

"Mike, there was no way you could see this coming," Dr. Livingston said. "She was not exhibiting signs of suicidal tendencies. I examined her when she checked in."

Mike listened, his gaze cast to the floor. Livingston continued. "She may have been in denial over her depression." He cleared his throat. "Some patients lie their way through their psychiatric tests." He leaned in toward Mike. "The fact of the matter is no one saw it coming. This facility is full of specialists who were helping this patient heal and work through her recovery. None of us saw the signs. This is not your fault."

Mike shook his head. "I spent the most time with her. She was in my group. I'm not sure how to get through this." He glanced at the doctor. "That general file, does it tell you what my story is?"

*   *   *

It wasn't clear to Mike whether pursuing a career as a boxer was something he dreamed of or if it was something his father pushed him to pursue. The last thing Mike's father had wanted to be was a mail carrier, but after he knocked up his high-school sweetheart, his dream of lacing up his gloves professionally was shattered.

When Mike was three, maybe four, his mother learned she was pregnant again. The old man went into a blinding rage. After a huge screaming match, Mike remembered him hurling his mother down the stairs. His brother never developed beyond a seven-year-old's capacity. They didn't have enough money to hire an aid to assist with Shane's care. Mike did his best to help his mom, but with every new outburst Shane had, Mike grew to fear the day she would lack the strength to control his little brother.

The same few guys had run the boxing gyms in South Boston for generations. The same coaches that trained Mike had trained his father. They saw promise in the kid, maybe even more than they had seen in his old man. Young Mike Sullivan was tough, light-footed, determined, and unafraid. By the time he hit eighteen, he was drawing a crowd at the Saturday night matches. Everyone put their bets on him, and he always won.

A star was emerging from the dregs of South Boston, proof that their little hood could still breed strong, competitive boxers, that the sport hadn't passed them by. The ladies pined for Little Mike, but his dad, Big Mike, served as a cautionary tale, so the young boxer was leery of the trouble women could bring. Mike's one true love was liquor. The kind that muted the wails of his mother, shooting him straight down a well of oblivion and denial.

"Sometimes I wonder who got the more brains between the two of you. You're not a thinking boxer, you're an ape who swings and flails." His father continued while blowing a stream of smoke from the depth of his lungs. A cigarette dangled from his nicotine-stained fingers. "Got the devil's luck, I'll give you that, but that'll run out on ya. It ain't just about hittin' whatever is in front of you as hard as you can." His father paused, turning his attention to the kitchen. "Goddammit woman, where's my beer?"

Mike's mother scampered in. Her shoulders rolled forward while Mike avoided her eyes, fearful he might cry. With a crack of the can snapping open, he redirected his unwanted attention.

"Plus, you got no conditioning. You don't respect the sport like we did in my time. It's just money to you. A means to an end."

All Mike could do was listen. There was no point in arguing with his dad when he was like this.

Mike decided he would take all that fear and anger and wrap it around his fists every time he entered the ring. They would be his cornermen. Fear and anger would make him money. They'd pay for the aids needed to watch after his brother, which would, in turn, save his mother. One day, there would be enough that they could all free themselves.

Mike hadn't been looking for trouble that night when he stumbled out of O'Malley's bar. In his pocket was a fat check written out to him for winning two matches earlier that evening. A rep from the WBA had been in the audience watching and approached Mike right after the fights. They made plans to meet for lunch the next day at a fancy hotel in a part of Boston where Mike had barely ventured.

He was celebrating his good fortune at his favorite bar with his friends, who were newly flush having just bet on him. The bar vibrated with talk about how South Boston had a would-be champion on its hands.

When his friends called it a night at the second bar, Mike intended to as well, but as he made his way home he found himself entering the old Irish pub his father liked to frequent. Despite their strained relationship, Mike still wanted to share the exciting news. Once inside, he caught a glimpse of his father kissing some woman who was not his mother. Mike barreled over to confront his father head-on. All the spoken and unspoken spilled over, and within moments, they were outside.

A blinding rage stole the reasonable Mike, who didn't like to talk about why his brother was disabled. He could only transform into his seven-year-old self, his mind replaying the image of his twisted father pushing his pregnant mom down the stairs until he felt nauseous. His remedy? Alcohol. Lots of it.

For all his father's bluster, the fight was practically over before it began. Mike dropped his father face-down in the snow, which was piled along the road by the city plows. Bits and pieces of details came to him as he sat in a jail cell. It wasn't until his third day inside that he remembered the lunch meeting he had missed. Mike bloodied his fist on the jail wall's cinder block. He couldn't make bail, so his friends and the guys at the gym pooled their money and hired him a lawyer.

His father would never work as a mail carrier again. He went on disability. Mike had left him blind in the left eye and with a lifetime of chronic neck and back issues. At the trial, Mike pleaded self-defense and was acquitted. His mother said six words to him as he exited the courtroom before she turned and walked away: "Get the hell out of Boston."

After the verdict, Mike slept on a cot in the gym's boiler room for a few weeks. He drank all day and most of the night. Eventually, the gym owner's patience ended. Potential champion or not, the owner kicked him out. He even offered to front Mike the cash to go to rehab. With his fees paid, Mike found himself at an Arizona facility called Serenity Hills. After five weeks, Mike remained in Arizona, being hired onto the kitchen staff at the rehab center.

He sent half of every paycheck to his mother. He never heard from her, but the checks were cashed well enough. Mike worked at the facility during the day, and at the encouragement of one of the counselors, he began taking classes at night and on the weekends. All he wanted now was to help people the way he'd been helped.

*   *   *

"When I was first hired at Serenity Hills, I learned there was a promising young man here. A part of the kitchen staff who was attending school for therapy. A hard worker. Driven. He'd been a patient here. I came to know the broad strokes of your situation when I reviewed your patient file after you asked to schedule an appointment with me."

Mike had always found Dr. Livingston nice enough, but quite aloof. Perhaps even a tad pretentious, according to patients who told Mike as much. Whenever Mike had to get a tune-up from another therapist, he'd chosen someone else. Mike just didn't see Livingston as the sort of man who could relate to him, but Scott was on sabbatical and Marcella was overbooked. So here Mike was.

"What I do know is that each of us has many stories, Michael. The overall theme in yours is one you can take pride in. It is about grit and determination. It is about being capable and accountable. The elements of your personality are integral to your story, but they are not the only important part of your narrative. There is another thread of which I'm sure you're aware."

Dr. Livingston paused for a moment to unwrap a hard candy before tossing it into his mouth.

"The question is, do you know what brought you to Serenity Hills? The story thread present from your youth is that you put others before yourself. Certainly not uncommon for those in our profession. Most of us think of this as an asset, especially if we have healthy boundaries. But let me tell you, it will burn you out. Many therapists have gone down that road." Livingston shifted some papers around his desk. "I'm going to suggest you take time off. Balance is key in this business. There's a retreat in Los Angeles where I have sent a few therapists in need of help. The time away can be quite beneficial. The program was started by a colleague of mine and Marcella's." Livingston tapped the desk papers into a perfect square. "The program is four days. Serenity Hills will cover your expenses."

He jotted a few notes on the paper. Mike nodded and glanced at his watch. It was time for him to head to his evening therapy sessions.

"I'll email you the details so you can make your travel arrangements," Dr. Livingston said.

Mike had dealt with fear before, but this was different. It was paralyzing to think someone else might commit suicide under his watch. As he walked out of Dr. Livingston's office, he doubted everything he had once believed in. A sickening thought added to the heaviness in his chest. Perhaps being a therapist might not be his calling after all. He forced himself to punch through and just keep moving forward. There were people waiting to speak to him. But in his head, Mike believed he was the mindless ape his father had once called him. The old man's words kept jabbing at him, ringing in his ears: *"It ain't just about hitting whatever is in front of you as hard as you can."*

*　　*　　*

Mike redoubled his focus on his patients. He owed it to them. He took copious notes during sessions. No room for error. After his last private session was completed, he finished his paperwork and locked his office door for the night. On his way out of the building, he exchanged niceties with the evening nurse.

"See you tomorrow," she said. "Have a great night."

"You do the same."

He jogged at a decent clip across the campus. When he got to his car, he popped the trunk, grabbed his gym bag from inside, and tossed it on the front seat. The smell of his boxing gloves and gear was like coming home. He had continued with boxing while working at Serenity Hills. The dedication kept him quick-footed. If push came to shove, he liked knowing he could put most in a stronghold to calm them down if necessary. During Mike's first year as a therapist, a patient took a swing at him and then a nurse. Before the patient knew it, he'd found himself falling into a pile of chairs.

During the twenty-minute drive to downtown Wickenburg, Mike thoughtfully reviewed the evening sessions, searching for red flags. Inevitably, his mind ended up back with Gloria, chasing what he might have missed.

Arriving at the gym was a relief, even if the parking lot was full. Mike pulled around back in the alley to avoid the crowd. His short-cropped, gray-haired sparring partner leaned against the outside wall. He wore a stained, dark-blue cutoff hoodie with sweat marks streaked across the chest and red satin shorts that hit below the knee.

"I was beginning to think you weren't coming," he said, holding the door for Mike.

"You think I'd miss tonight?" Mike said. He barreled through the door. The guy patted him on the back.

"Better get your gloves on, Donny, it's going to be a rough night," Mike bantered.

"You bet," Donny said, following Mike through the brightly lit gym to the locker room. Mike changed into his boxing gear with purpose. Donny noted Mike's energy. Mike tossed Donny the tape.

"Man on a mission," Donny joked.

Mike responded with something between a grunt and a nod. Donny began Mike's favorite part of the boxing sacrament and proceeded to wrap his hands. That undeniable rhythm, that familiar act between two boxers, somehow deeper with partners who'd sparred together as long as he and Donny had. Mike liked the sound of the tape, the quiet coiling of his body as it was primed, almost like the meditation he put his patients through every day at work.

When the two of them left the locker room, Mike drank in the smells and sounds of the gym. He breathed it in greedily. Even after all this time, his heart still quickened. After some stretches and jump rope, he stepped in front of the speed bag as Donny looked on, commenting and coaching.

"Looking strong," Donny said.

"Not bad for an old man," Mike replied.

He swung a punch at Donny, which the two-time Navy Brigade Boxing champion easily sidestepped.

"You never fall for that. One of these days, I'll get you."

Mike shoved a mouthguard in and entered the ring, and all his worries disappeared.

Chapter Twenty-Six: Prue Past

The word around the smoking veranda at Serenity Hills was that we were all cross-addicted. No one left rehab with one diagnosis. If we were oblivious to our other demons, the experts were there to slap us into reality.

I had checked in with the belief that I was a sex addict. My extra-marital affairs were wreaking havoc on my relationship with Nick. I lived with a tremendous amount of guilt mixed with a solid dose of self-loathing.

As I strolled over to the counseling building, I contemplated the possibility that I might be addicted to Mike. It didn't hurt that he was a buff, sensitive, mysterious guy with a huge heart. But instead of worrying about something I had no control over, I resorted to counting steps, calming my breath, and listening to the creatures who emerged at nightfall.

It had become a habit for me to arrive at the private therapy session early so I could wish upon a star right outside of Mike's door. I figured out the perfect strategy to land the last spot on his evening counseling calendar. That way I wasn't rushed when someone else was lurking outside. I could savor every moment with him and know that I was the last patient he would see before he left for the day.

The entire campus was up in arms over Gloria's suicide. At first, I was shocked. Then I spent several days in complete denial. Out of habit, I would stop by her room to pick her up for the morning meeting. This time she would not greet me with her warm and inviting smile. No, she never would again.

As I stood at Gloria's door, I felt my heart thump and fall. Through the square window, I could see the cookie-cutter furniture, but no sign of Gloria—no beads hanging from the lamp, no colorful t-shirts piled on the chair, and no flip-flops scattered across the floor. I would stand there, my mind picturing her belongings where they should have been as if time had stopped short of her death. And there I'd be, stuck in some sort of limbo land between the past and the harsh realities of the present.

The words of Emily Dickinson came to my mind. "Because I could not stop for death, he kindly stopped for me." The earth had gone cold right under my feet. I kept replaying the scene when the Serenity Hills security staff removed everything from her room, wiping it clean as though Gloria had never existed.

After a few days, I avoided her room altogether and took the long way around the building. I became angry that she left me behind, an anger that turned to rage. Not at Gloria, but at myself for failing to see the signs. She had been my closest friend in rehab, the one who I opened my heart to and shared my deepest secrets with. How could I have missed all that lurked below the surface?

Mike's door opened. Alistair walked out. He smiled as he moved past me and gave me a gentle pat on the shoulder.

"Next victim," he said.

Mike leaned in the frame of the doorway, trying a little too hard to appear relaxed. Ever since Gloria had killed herself, even stoic Mike struggled to hide his sadness. I could already see the dwindling light in his eyes. When he feigned happiness, we could all tell he was forcing it for us. The way I slathered on a smile when Nick would give me the same red Chanel lipstick for Christmas. The color that made me look like a clown.

"Hey," I said as I strolled through the entrance to my happy place. The beautiful part of Mike's office had nothing to do with the furniture, lighting, ambiance, or window treatments. It had to do with Mike. When he left, the room rolled itself in gray. I dropped into the sofa and kicked off my sandals, tucking both feet under my thighs. Mike leaned out the door. His back widened as he breathed in the indigo air.

"Beautiful evening," he said. His shoulders were uncharacteristically slumped forward. I glanced at a bottle of Visine on his desk, which he snapped up and dropped in a drawer.

"It is," I said, shrugging as I fought the urge to hug him, his pain becoming mine due to continued unhealthy boundaries. "How are you?"

Mike sighed, his lips pursed together. Silence consumed the room. "It's been a while since someone asked me that," he said. "I'm still sad. Very sad. Gloria was wonderful. What a tragedy."

His strong hands were clasped in his lap the way my mother's were when we attended Sunday service. That forced peaceful aura we wanted to portray to the world that never convinced anyone, least of all ourselves. He took another sigh, his gaze meeting mine.

"The important question is how are you doing?"

"Dr. Livingston offered to prescribe something to help me deal with the pain. I told him no." Mike, always the adult in the room, allowed me to resort to my usual fidgety survival mechanisms. "I'm one of those people who relishes feeling the pain. I like to wallow and allow it to dig into my very being."

"I told him to offer something to you," Mike said. He smiled in the warmest way, like one would when holding a kitten. I couldn't tell if he'd done it mindfully or if the act was involuntary. "You and Gloria were close." Mike parked his eyes on the floor for a moment. "I'm not surprised you chose not to take anything. You've been white-knuckling through your whole life. I just wanted you to know the option was there."

"When my mother died in a car accident, some doctor offered me Valium. I said no then too." I smiled to let him know I wasn't going to off myself anytime soon. "Don't worry. I'll be alright. I always make it somehow, but the truth is, I am sad." The desk lamp created a merged shadow of our images, as though we had become one person. "I miss her. There's a gaping hole in my heart, and I'm carrying a lot of guilt. I mean how couldn't I have known she was depressed? It's not like I wasn't in her room playing cards nearly every night."

Gloria's face popped into my head. The way she shuffled, flipping and arcing the cards with a lip-gloss smile. Her perpetually chipped polish. It dawned on me that she wasn't just beautiful and sexy, she was humble and innocent and kind. There was so much more to her than others saw at face value. People were threatened, women especially.

I could not fix her. I had failed as a friend. My face dropped into my hands, and as hard as I had tried to be strong, the sobbing began. Mike passed me the tissue box. I yanked out three and pressed the white pile to my face. He gave me a few moments to cry without interrupting.

"It's okay to cry," he said. His voice cracked. Out of respect, I gazed at the tissues and gave him the dignity of letting out his emotions alongside me. "Sorry," he said. "I'm only human."

"I know," I said. "I love that about you." He leaned forward in his chair, and our shadows separated.

"Thanks," he said. "Other than Gloria, how are you doing?"

Professional Mike had reappeared, like the moon in the night sky shoving clouds out of the way. He had composed himself so quickly I'd barely perceived the transformation. Yet I felt lucky to catch a glimpse of his emotional side, if even just for a moment.

"I'm ready for Survivor's Week. It's time for me to put the past behind me. I've heard a lot of things about Survivor's but I'm trying not to anticipate too much and go with an open mind." I tossed the tissue ball in the basket and hit it on the first try. "Ten points."

"Survivor's happens on the last week for a reason," Mike said. "We spend four weeks preparing you for it, but don't expect a miracle."

He turned in his chair. I assessed his outfit, which was always more casual during the evening sessions. Perhaps he kept a spare set of clothes at the office or worked out between the end of the workday and nighttime therapy appointments. He never smelled like cologne, but his scent was clean like soap. His feet weren't oversized, nor were they small. The Adidas sneakers showed little wear and tear, not covered in clay and dust from hiking in the Arizona desert. He had a collection of work sneakers with little to no brand loyalty. Some guys only wore one kind. Not Mike. He was an equal opportunity sneaker wearer.

He gently cleared his throat, casually bringing me back to the session.

"I'm still confused about Nick but not overthinking like I usually do. Maybe the blessing from Gloria's passing is that her suicide helped get my mind off of myself and my problems." I worried that it was too soon to search for meaning in her death. "I'm a bad person, aren't I?"

"Not at all," Mike said. "Everyone mourns differently. There is no right or wrong way."

He smiled. I admired his teeth, all of them a brilliant white, the right eyetooth slightly crooked, which gave character to his smile.

"I believe that the answers you are searching for will come to you in time," he said. "This program packs a lot of information in a short period. You may notice yourself slowly gaining strength and clarity for months after checking out. At least that's how my other patients have described the process."

We went through some meditation and visualization exercises and discussed intentions for Survivor's Week. Before I was quite ready, our session time had come to a close.

"I'm going to miss you," I said, purposefully looking in his eyes. "It's a little scary to think about life without you. You're kind of like my rock."

"Which is why it's preferable you commit to an aftercare program. Patients have far more success if they continue on to at least another month of inpatient treatment to slowly integrate into real life."

"I can't," I said. "Work, my son, life."

"See your therapist at home a minimum of once a week, attend meetings, meditate, and hold yourself accountable. I'll be here if you need me," Mike said.

I stared at him. He blinked. His knees gripped together. Perhaps he was trying to convince me or himself.

"Can I have your cell number?" I laughed.

"I can't give that out, but you can always reach me here," he smiled.

The clock ticked. There were only two more days before I would head to the other side of campus for Survivor's Week, which was led by a different counselor. Then I would be discharged into reality.

"At least I have two more days in group, and hopefully I'll get on your private therapy list," I said.

"If you can't get a spot then I'll add one for you." He stood. I searched the floor for my sandals. When he opened the door, the sound of crickets filled the air. "See you in the morning," he said.

As I walked back to my room, I imagined the night critters were singing about all the opportunities awaiting me after my release from Serenity Hills. My room was painfully quiet. I washed my face and put on a tank top and pajama pants. An open workbook loomed on the desk. I marked the page with a pencil and closed it abruptly. I contemplated praying, but my body craved exercise, to run away as fast as my legs could go and never look back. The sneakers I'd checked in with remained in the closet, never worn since Dr. Livingston had banned me from using the gym. I stared at them for a moment then walked to my door and stepped out, looking right then left. Not a soul around.

I tiptoed to Gloria's room and opened the door. It had been sanitized for the next patient. I dropped onto her bed and curled into a tight ball. It was as though she had never existed; all signs of her gone.

As my eyes began to close, the lamp on her desk flickered on then off. I believed deep in my heart that it was Gloria saying goodbye. I let my tears soak into the comforter the way I did when I cried on my mother's gravestone. Before I realized it, wails emerged from deep within me, easily scaling the well-crafted walls of my heart. I sobbed for my life, for Gloria's pain, for my mother being left for dead on the hood of a car, for my father's dignity stolen by addiction, and for every man who had ever violated me.

They must have been searching for me for a while. The door flew open. Two men barreled in with flashlights, Mike trailing behind. My face was glued to the bedspread, my hair matted and sweaty due to the lack of AC in the room.

"She's here," the man said. It was the same uniformed beefcake orderly who had searched my bag at check-in.

"Oh, thank God," Mike said. He pulled me from the bed. Someone flipped on the light. "Turn it off," he demanded. "We don't want to alarm her."

My heart raced as though I were being pushed off a cliff. I blinked and swiped the drool from my mouth.

"I've got you," Mike said. "You scared me."

Straddling between dream and reality, I pulled myself up to stand. The men watched while Mike walked me to my room. Someone offered me water.

Deirdre stood by her bed. "Holy crap," she said. "Are you trying to kill me?"

I cringed at her insensitive use of the word killed. She stared at my complexion, marked and dented from hours on the bed.

"Sorry," I said. "I wanted to be near Gloria." Even in the dimly lit room, I could see the terror on Mike's face. His pale, clammy skin and wild eyes. He stepped backward toward the door.

"Glad you're safe," he said. "You had us all very worried."

As usual, I had made it about myself. The Prue show. Even subconsciously, I was selfish.

Mike pressed his palms together and touched them on his mouth while bowing his head. The men exchanged words outside my door, faint sounds I could not make out. I rolled myself in the white quilted sheets without a clue of the time or how long I'd been missing.

"Goodnight," I said.

"I miss her too," Deirdre said.

I nodded, knowing I was invisible through the brittle darkness. When I closed my eyes, Gloria was there waiting, a deck of cards in her hand.

Chapter Twenty-Seven: Alistair Present

Alistair flinched when the door slammed. He contemplated chasing after Prue but figured he had already messed up enough. The thought of causing even more damage to their already fragile relationship was unbearable. He leaned over the blueprints draped on the table and let out a laugh. Was it even a relationship? He picked up his phone to check his email. He needed to focus his energy on things he could control.

The German bond deal was tenuous at best. He wiped his nose with the back of his hand. When he did, the cravings for blow hit him like a ballistic missile. What he wanted was to escape from reality and let loose, but that would break his hard-earned sobriety. He picked up the glass of wine he had poured for himself, only a few sips left. Prue's half-full glass was still on the mahogany coffee table. He dumped her wine into his.

"Cheers," he said to himself.

He downed the chardonnay and poured himself another. He was well into reading the first email when his phone rang.

"Hello," Alistair said. He listened without saying a word except for a few acknowledging sounds. "I'll handle it," he said. "This deal will happen. When? I don't know, but these investors need to be patient. The gag order is still active and will be enforced. That includes sending screenshots of emails, forwarding emails, discussing the deal with anyone who is not an investor, and getting on any naysayers' blog sites."

He continued, his tone amplifying as he spoke.

"I won't have it. None of it. I won't tolerate one bit of it. We have ways of knowing who has broken the gag order, and those investors will be cut off at the knees."

He hung up the phone and grabbed his laptop.

Dear Client,

We have been requested to be completely silent for the next two weeks and will be keeping the lowest profile possible. In terms of our transaction, every-thing is going as planned. We will be utilizing the portal payment system to expedite the initial payments. Our portal will automatically generate elec-tronic signatures which will be instantly verified by an attorney making your funds immediately available in the paymaster portal.

We can't say more at this time. Your patience and cooperation are greatly appreciated.

Blessings,

Alistair and the Henkle Global Team

Alistair grinned. At last, two weeks of peace and quiet. He sent Prue an apology text before dialing George to drive him to dinner. Alistair wasn't hungry, not for food at least. These types of moods made him crave the high-energy of swanky, dimly lit hotel bars that swarmed with attractive, desperate women. He liked to eat at restau-rants with a hip vibe and a cool ambiance. If anyone could figure out the hot spots in LA, it would be George, so Alistair didn't bother ask-ing where they were headed. In matters like these, George always took the wheel.

After dinner, Alistair was half in the bag and horny as hell. A few ladies had sidled up to him at the Catch LA bar while they waited for a table, but he found himself bored and uninterested. His mind would not diverge from Prue. Her reddish-brown curls, the way she bit her lip when she focused.

After three large bottles of saké, two martinis, and a hefty order of fresh sushi, he was ready to head back to the hotel. While George drove, he kicked back and admired his new home—the neon lights, chic beautiful women, and the way the palm trees lit up at night. Alistair opened the window and reached out his hand to feel the balmy air. George cued up the song "Dear Prudence" then cranked up the volume. The two friends glanced at each other and they both started laughing.

Back at the hotel, he lay on the bed to call Prue. His vision became increasingly blurry. The light from the chandelier curved and dipped, blinding his eyes as he blinked.

"Please don't pick up," he whispered as he tossed off his Gucci loafers. He didn't want to say something he might regret, or worse, come across as a sloppy drunk.

Prue really got him going, and he wished she didn't have so much power over him. He pictured her body naked, riding him. Within moments, a wave of shame rolled through him. The shared stories of her childhood in rehab dulled his fantasies. An overwhelming urge to protect her the way she needed and deserved fought its way past his sexual desires.

He fell into a restless sleep until a pounding headache woke him up. The sun beamed through the seams of the hotel room curtains he had haphazardly pulled closed. He chugged a bottle of water and then puked in the toilet. A few bumps would have helped his hangover—another reason why he loved blow. Instead, he settled for more pedestrian remedies. After a long, hot shower in the minimalistic, all-metallic bathroom, he wrapped a plush white towel around his waist and called Patrick Dunn Interiors.

The receptionist answered. Alistair kicked himself into work mode with a crisp, firm tone to his voice. "Yes, Sam King please." He cleared his throat as he made himself a coffee and waited for Sam to pick up. "Sam, this is Alistair Prescott." He opened three creamers and poured them into his coffee one by one. "I know it's last-minute, but would it be possible to set up a meeting at the loft this afternoon so Ms. Aldrich can see the space? Now that I've closed on the property, I'm anxious to get the design project underway."

Alistair had learned from experience to allow some silence in a conversation. It gave the person time to think, or squirm, depending on what his end goal happened to be. While Sam blathered on about needing to check Ms. Aldrich's schedule, Alistair sipped his coffee. When he sensed the situation needed a nudge, he moved in with an offer.

"I'll pay any additional fees to have my projects be the designer's top priority." He tapped the thermostat down arrow while he listened. "Yes, the office space is being built right now. A smaller project, but one which also needs to be completed in a timely manner. As you can imagine, I'm anxious to get moved in. There's nothing worse than living and working out of a hotel."

He switched the call to speaker and scanned his emails.

"Sure, I'll hold." Alistair chugged the rest of his coffee. "Perfect," he said. "I'll meet Ms. Aldrich at the loft at noon." Alistair pressed end call twice and rubbed his palms together.

He scanned his closet. His shirts were organized by color, then sleeve length. His pants were folded to ensure there wasn't a seam down the front. There was nothing he hated more than men who creased their pants right down the middle.

The stylist had left Polaroids of outfits to make it easier for him to dress. He put on an effortlessly wrinkled button-down and dark jeans. The stylist had told him he looked best in classic, tailored clothes, and he figured today was the best day to try and work his assets.

He slipped his feet into a pair of low-key sneakers and threw on a sport coat to add a bit of professionalism to his ensemble. Before he stepped out of the dressing room, he spritzed Dior cologne into the air and stepped through the mist.

"Hey, old man," George said when Alistair stepped in the car. "How's the head?"

"Nothing a cup of coffee couldn't cure." Alistair rubbed his nose. "Georgie," he said, fidgeting with the leather band on his wrist. He traced his finger over a small scar. A reminder of the time his friends had dared him to carve his initials into his skin when he was twelve. "I'm not sure I can do this sober thing. There seem to be more and more reasons why I need blow back in my life. Maybe if I keep it to a minimum, you know, only on weekends, it would be alright."

"Whatever you think," George said.

"Right," Alistair said.

As they headed downtown, a war raged in his head. He had skipped out on aftercare, hadn't been to any meetings—he hadn't even done the bare minimum and seen a therapist. He fiddled with the air conditioning in the car, turning the temperature down and the fan up.

"Maybe I should find a therapist. Keep up the stuff I worked on in rehab." He turned toward George, anticipating any kind of unexpected reaction.

"Already have a therapist lined up for you," George said. "I think that's the right strategy. I'll see if I can get you an appointment tomorrow."

"George, do you think I had a problem?"

George tightened his grip on the wheel. "Yeah, Ali," he said, "you had a problem."

"Right," Alistair said. "Quite right."

They rode the rest of the way in silence. Alistair weighed the pros and cons of doing blow, ticking off each valuation like a financial spreadsheet in his head.

* * *

Prue was standing out in front of Alistair's new residence with a Starbucks to-go cup clutched in her hand. She waved as George pulled over to let Alistair out, dark shades covering her eyes.

"I'll wait here. Text me when you're ready to go," George said.

Alistair hopped out without responding. "Are you still chapped with me?" He leaned in to kiss her cheek and take in her scent. Her auburn hair bounced around her shoulders.

Prue sipped her coffee, pulling her tote bag closer to her side. "You have the blueprints, right?" she asked.

"Snap," he said. He pulled his phone from his blazer pocket and called George. The car came roaring around the corner, the blueprints being held out the open driver's side window. "Thanks, Georgie."

Alistair took the blueprints from his hand. Prue smiled and waved at George before he drove away. Alistair noticed a change in her demeanor. He took it as a sign that perhaps she was coming around.

"Now I have the blueprints," he said. The doorman held open the door. "Alistair Prescott, penthouse."

"Yes, Mr. Prescott." The man motioned toward the elevator. Alistair held a fob up to the panel, and the penthouse button lit up. The blueprints tumbled to the floor. Prue tossed her sunglasses in her bag.

"I'll carry them," she said, lifting them from the elevator floor.

"You look beautiful," he said, overwhelmed to be alone with her again.

"Thanks," she said. Adrenaline pulsed through his body. The door opened. He held the button for Prue to leave first. Prue waited while Alistair struggled with the key.

"The view is amazing." As she advanced toward the window, the tap of her heels echoed through the open space. She paused, admiring the beautiful cityscape, the way the palm trees swayed against a breathing air. The loft had been staged to sell.

"Is this your furniture?" she asked.

Alistair was taken aback by her professionalism. Feeling a bit off-balance, he pressed a hand to the window to steady himself.

"It all has to go," he replied. "I haven't done anything. Except hire you, of course."

Prue playfully rolled her eyes before laying the blueprints on the glass table. She reached into her leather tote and pulled out a pencil, measuring tape, and yellow notepad.

"This is a huge space. It will need warming up." She turned to Alistair, whose gaze was fixed on her wide-set green eyes. "Hold this," she said before passing him the end of the measuring tape.

He obeyed while she measured and jotted down notes. "You could do several seating areas in the living room." She tucked the pencil behind her ear and proceeded to the kitchen. "They certainly didn't chintz on appliances."

Alistair opened the Viking fridge and handed her a bottle of Pellegrino, taking one for himself.

"Nice," she said. "Already stocked up." She twisted the cap and took a sip, then shimmied herself up on the Carrera marble island. "You'll need stools on this side, and I think a modern built-in banquette would be a great addition over there."

She motioned to the opposite side of the room. Alistair's gaze was still fixed, this time on her exposed black bra strap. She noticed and quickly covered it with her blouse. "

What kind of vibe do you want to portray?" She dragged the pencil from behind her ear and tapped her lower lip with the eraser.

"Easy yet modern," he said. "I'm a huge reader, so I'll need an area to put books." He wasn't sure if he was lying to please her or himself.

"Oh, I love books," she said.

Her childlike joy overwhelmed him. He moved closer until he was standing in front of her. He noticed her shoulders tense up. She dropped the pencil and slid off the counter, her eyes probing his. The kiss that had happened in rehab lingered in his mind. It seemed like a lifetime had passed since then.

"I'm sorry for everything," Alistair said. "I acted like a fool when I was trying to do the exact opposite. You unravel me, and I'm not sure what to do about it."

Prue remained silent. Her gaze dug into his. He reached a hand behind the nape of her neck and pulled her toward him. Her head dipped back, and she closed her eyes. When their lips met, Alistair felt a warm rush journey through his stomach. Each kiss between them told a story with a beginning, middle, and an end.

Alistair moved his hands up and down her body before finally pulling the blazer from her shoulders. She struggled to release her arms from the sleeves then tossed the jacket to the floor. This was the tallest woman he had ever kissed. It unnerved him to feel so small and powerless.

"I adore you," he whispered between kisses. He lifted her blouse over her head. She wiggled her hands behind her back and unhitched the lace bra, a moment he'd been fantasizing about since the second she walked through the door. His mouth traveled from her neck to her arms. He could taste her goosebumps. With their hands locked together, he led her to the bedroom where the staged bed was waiting with only a coverlet on top of a bare mattress.

"This is a horrid bedspread," she said with a laugh.

"I know," he said, staring down at the bright floral fabric. "Which is why I need you so badly."

When she dropped onto the bed, her breasts bounced. He kicked off his sneakers and scooted himself beside her. "You take my breath away," he said, touching a ringlet that gently rested on her shoulder.

Prue smiled and kissed his cheek. Her green eyes mesmerized while he pulled his shirt over his head. Flashes of negative thoughts began creeping into his head. His stomach twisted in knots. All the women he had played, Eleanor still waiting for him in London, all the lies he had told.

A cloud passed by the bedroom window, casting a shadow over them. Prue ran a hand over his chest. She gently pinched his nipples between her fingertips. Alistair closed his eyes in an attempt to quiet the voices clamoring in his head. His watch suddenly felt heavy on his wrist. The weight of the world dumping down on him in gallons.

Prue knelt beside him while she unzipped his pants. The more vulnerable he felt, the more blood rushed to his cheeks. She peeled off her jeans, keeping her gaze on Alistair, and crawled back up to him.

As they lay together side by side, their naked bodies melted into one. A million thoughts flew through his mind, pressing down on his chest. He breathed in, hoping for some relief. This was a moment he had imagined, yet he was frozen, unsure of what to do next.

Prue moved to her knees and took him in her mouth. Alistair dropped his head on the pillow and closed his eyes. It took all of his focus not to psyche himself out. He forbade his mind from screwing up something he wanted so badly. The more he thought, the worse things became. He went limp within her lips. Alistair weakened.

"I'm sorry," he said. "I'm just incredibly nervous. This has never happened to me before."

Prue lay next to him. Alistair sighed and put a hand over his face in embarrassment.

"It's probably a sign." Prue clutched the comforter, draping it over her exposed breasts. "We're going to be working together." She pushed the hair away from her face. "Let's keep it real. I'm in recovery for sex addiction, you're fresh out of rehab for cocaine." A thick layer of worry grew in her tone. "This is a really bad idea anyway."

"No," Alistair said, "It's not a bad idea." His frustration levels socked him in the gut. "I, I don't know what to say. This is so embarrassing. I'm an idiot."

Prue crawled across the bed, grabbing her panties from the floor. She stood, putting one foot in and then the other while Alistair watched in horror.

"Please don't get dressed," he begged. "Can we start over? It's my head. All these voices bombarded me. It's insanity. I've never had performance anxiety in my life." Alistair dragged his fingers through his hair, catching a glimpse of his limp member draped between his legs. "I'm so frustrated."

"It's fine," she said. "It's probably some kind of an omen." Her hair tumbled around her face as she edged the panties up over her thighs. "The universe is telling us to slow down."

"Please," he said. "I'm begging you." He moved to the edge of the bed and pulled her toward him before she could get on her jeans.

"Stop." She resisted. "Alistair, I said stop."

He continued kissing her as if deaf to her demands, intent on helping her push away the voices in her gut and erasing every bit of reason left inside her. With her eyes closed, Prue breathed in, accepting the part of her that needed to be touched and feel pleasure.

He kissed her belly while tucking his thumbs in each side of her lace panties. When they dropped to the floor, he cupped her ass and kissed her between the legs. This was where he wanted to be. It was right, and he had to prove her wrong. This could only work if he took charge. Prue gripped his shoulders. Her breath turned quick and shallow.

He lifted her to the bed and took her with all he had in him. Prue moved her hips to meet his, the rhythm of their bodies in perfect synchronicity. When his eyes met hers, they were soft and warm.

Alistair kissed her with a hunger that had been aching in him for months. His emotions crashed down on him, and when he came inside of her, his whole body shuddered. He buried his face in her neck. Her body immediately stiffened beneath him. He lifted his gaze. Her eyes had turned dark and cold.

"I better get going," she said, pushing him off of her.

"Are you okay?" he asked tentatively. "Lay here with me." Alistair patted the bed beside him.

With urgency, she slid on her jeans and shoved her belongings into her bag, throwing her blazer over her arm.

"I'm fine, and I can't stay," she said, glancing at her watch. "It's getting late."

Prue opened the door while Alistair stood there in shock. "Oh, and one more thing," she said. Her voice turned from defeated to angry. "I know you gave my mother's Cartier watch to that stripper."

"Prue, I promise I can explai—"

She cut him off. "I don't trust you, Alistair." She stared at him, shaking her head. "I want to understand you. I've given you the benefit of the doubt, time and time again. Now that we've slept together, well, it complicates everything. This is just as much my fault as yours."

He watched her go. When the door closed, he called George to bring around the car. "Were you able to schedule me that therapy appointment for tomorrow?" he asked before hanging up the phone.

Chapter Twenty-Eight:
Mike (Not-So-Distant) Past

Mike lingered in the sauna after his workout. Ever since Gloria's suicide, he had been emotionally drained. He dumped a scoop of water over the heated rocks. Steam billowed from the sputtering stones. With a towel cinched around his waist, Mike lay back and closed his eyes, letting the steam do its work. Sweat dripped from every inch of his body.

He took a cold shower. After a long day working with recovering addicts, he needed to recharge his drained battery. It had never come easy for him to maintain healthy boundaries. And so he used to hold himself aloof when he first started as a therapist. But as he got more complacent, he found he had to work harder not to adopt his patients' pain. The last class of students had been something he had not yet experienced. With Gloria's death, he found himself withdrawing.

His phone buzzed as he opened his locker to get dressed. There were two messages from his girlfriend warning him not to be late. She had gotten tickets to see a cover band at a small venue in Wickenburg. The plans they'd made had slipped his mind. His withdrawal wasn't isolated to work. It had leaked into the personal. His girlfriend, Lauren, had never been the best listener, but she'd only gotten worse over the course of their relationship. Mike couldn't imagine talking in-depth with her about what he had recently endured at work. Nowadays, Lauren had just wanted to stir things up between them. When he pulled up to her apartment, she was waiting out front with her arms crossed over her chest. She marched to the car in a huff. He figured an apology out of the gate would defuse the situation.

"Sorry, been a long day," Mike said. "I got caught up at the gym."

Lauren flipped open the vanity mirror to check her makeup. "That's the thing," she said, "you're always fucking late, and it's always because of the gym." He could already see the hate in her eyes. The car filled with the too-taffy-sweet scent of her perfume, which he had never liked. "What, you think you're going to be a professional boxer or something?" She rolled her deep-set brown eyes. "Give me a break."

"You look pretty." He leaned over to give her a kiss. She scoffed and recoiled. Mike settled back into his seat slowly and put the car in drive. He wasn't in the mood for a fight. "What band are we seeing again?"

"Jesus, I told you ten times. It's that cover band that plays AC/DC and eighties rock. I love these guys, and now we're late for the first set." As soon as the light turned green, Mike gunned it. "Don't fucking kill us getting there."

"I won't," he said.

Lauren fiddled with the radio. Mike tuned out the music and the voice of the woman sitting next to him. What would his life be like if he had gone to two bars instead of three that night? He wondered what it would be like if he hadn't laid his father out on the Boston snow.

*   *   *

Mike felt some measure of peace when the checks he sent his mother cleared his bank account. The guilt would ebb a bit, at least. He was making more now that he was a head therapist at Serenity. By keeping his expenses to a minimum, he was able to help financially with his brother's care, a cost that wasn't insignificant. Money didn't mean that much to Mike. He'd rather send it to his mother than spend it on himself.

He kept the fact that he sent money home to himself. If Lauren knew, it would just be another thing for her to freak out about. Mike tapped the steering wheel. He supposed the red flags had always been there between him and Lauren. If he couldn't be rigorously honest with Lauren, the relationship was destined to fail.

Mike glanced at her and smiled. He reached for her knee. She met his look and her body eased beneath his hand. He knew it wasn't healthy, but the thought of failing at yet another relationship stopped him from breaking up with her and moving on.

By the time they got to the bar, it was standing room only. The band was performing on stage, and the bar area was packed with people three deep waiting to order drinks. Biker types filled the room to hear the metal bands they had playing in their lineup.

Mike pushed his way through the crowd, hoping to get her closer to the front. Once they landed a spot, Lauren's mood began to relax further. Before long, she was belting out the lyrics to every song while she rocked out to the vocals of faux Brian Johnson. Mike maintained a wide stance so she had space to move. Several songs in and people were alive, really throwing themselves into the music.

After the third successive slam into his back, he turned around to see two guys in the beginning stages of a scuffle. The taller of the two grabbed the smaller one's shirt while swinging a wild punch. Mike pushed Lauren, clearing her of the haymaker by shoving her to the side. A full-blown fight broke out. Mike's intent had simply been to help break them up, not get caught in the middle. His instinct had different plans. No sooner did he try to deescalate the situation than the two adversaries turned their attention from each other to him.

"Mind your business, asshole!" they growled before their fists were directed at him.

While he easily evaded the flurry by pinning one guy to the floor, the other one came from behind, striking him in the head. Mike bounced to his feet and squared off in a boxing stance. In one fluid motion, he delivered a flawless feint left to the body, followed by a right-cross combo.

Lauren screamed. The band stopped. Security moved in. Mike was swiftly dragged out by two of the bouncers, leaving the now-dazed instigators behind to contemplate their broken pride and how they'd found themselves ass-to-floor instead of their opponent.

"You're lucky we aren't pressing charges," the bouncer said. "Get the fuck out of here."

There was no point in defending himself.

Mike waited around the corner. Lauren strolled out a few minutes later. "I'm staying. I'll get a ride home," she said. "For the record, you're too broken to date. I can't do this anymore." She turned and walked back into the bar. Mike leaned against the building.

It took him a few minutes to register that Lauren had just dumped him. In truth, his mind was more preoccupied with the fight, replaying his movement and what he could have done better. His assessment was broken by a stranger's approach. He tensed, momentarily unsure if round two was about to pop off.

"You got some moves," the guy congratulated. "Ever box profes-sionally?" He took a drag from a cigarette and blew the smoke out toward the street. "Vince," he said, reaching out his hand, a chunky gold ring wrapped around his pinkie. The handshake came in firm and strong. Vince was shorter and stockier than Mike. His face defi-nitely had taken a few hits. The short guys were quick. Mike kept up his guard.

"Thanks," Mike said. "I was just breaking up a fight. Hadn't planned on getting kicked out."

"So, you're a boxer?" Vince persisted.

Mike recognized the accent. He was one of his own. "I dabble," Mike replied.

"I own a chain of boxing gyms." Vince dropped the cigarette butt and ground it under his shoe. "I'm looking for someone like you to run the place I'm about to open in LA."

"Is that so?" Mike asked. "I train at Iron Gloves."

"I know the owner," Vince said. "He's a buddy of mine."

"You from Boston?" Mike asked, even though he knew.

"Yeah," he said. "Southie." He turned the chunky gold ring around his finger.

"Thought so," Mike said. "Me too."

"Good people," Vince said. He took a card from his pocket and handed it to Mike. "A management-type position. Great opportuni-ty."

"I'm a therapist at Serenity Hills," Mike said. "Got no experience running gyms."

"Doesn't matter," he said. "Think about it."

"I'll do that," Mike said. He shoved the card in his pocket and walked to his car.

*   *   *

Mike examined the card when he got into his car. He turned the ignition and pulled out onto the street. For the first time since Gloria's suicide, he felt at ease. At the red light, he cracked his knuckles and turned up the radio, his hands keeping time with the music the whole ride home.

He unlocked the mailbox and grabbed his mail, flipping through the pile as he walked up the stairs. One envelope caught his eye. He examined it for a moment before opening his door. In black bold letters scrolled across the front, it said *Return to Sender*.

When he opened his apartment door, his tabby jumped out from the shadows. Mike scooped up the meowing cat. "Hey, Marlow," he said, stroking his back. Marlow jumped to the floor and rubbed his body along Mike's legs while Mike opened the envelope. His check usually cleared within days of being mailed. A panic attack was brewing, something he hadn't felt in a long time. He scrolled through his phone, searching for a friend in Boston who might have some information on where his mother moved and if his brother was alright.

He pulled the uncashed check from the envelope and set it on the linoleum counter. Perhaps his mother would reach out to him. She would surely miss the monthly income, wouldn't she? Mike didn't allow himself to spiral and picture the worst-case scenario. There was no point. He would approach this calmly, systematically, the same way he told his patients to approach their troubles.

Wind whipped through the window; it always picked up in the evenings. When he went to close it, the blinds came crashing to the floor. The apartment was supposed to be temporary, a short-term lease until he saved enough to buy a home. It never felt like the right time. In some ways, everything in his life felt temporary, a stopgap. Everything except Serenity Hills.

When Mike began offering free evening counseling, he never imagined it would take off the way it did. Those five thirty-minute therapy sessions were the most fulfilling part of his day. He got to dig into their lives, suture the mental wounds. It was so satisfying, but not this night. Not lately.

Mike dropped the business card onto his coffee table. He glanced at his phone. No messages. He hammered out an apology to Lauren and pressed send. She probably wouldn't respond, but it was the right thing for him to do. When he was in school, he had heard that people became therapists because they couldn't solve their problems. He laughed out loud because he knew firsthand that it was so often true.

*   *   *

The next day, Mike continued to learn about the retreat in Los Angeles that Dr. Livingston had recommended. He appreciated that the program was very discreet. It treated a number of issues common to therapists, and while the language was in no way overt, Mike felt relieved that Livingston had set him on the right course. He pulled the business card he'd received the previous night off his coffee table. The address listed was also in LA. He took a long breath and dialed the number on the card.

"Hello."

"Vince, this is Mike Sullivan. We met outside the club last night."

"Mike," Vince said. "Glad you called."

"I wanted to learn more about the management position you mentioned."

"Since the job is in LA, you'd have to be willing to relocate," he said. "I'd cover all expenses including a six-month temporary apartment." Mike heard him light up a smoke. "These joints are making a killing. Boxing is huge in LA. I need someone with more than just boxing skills. They have to run the place, manage people, keep things up to code."

Mike added a word here and there so Vince knew he was listening.

"I bought Churchill Boxing, and I'm rebranding. I would provide all the training with regards to the ins and outs of running a gym. What I need is someone with a passion for the sport of boxing, but also someone who has a soft touch." He paused. "Celebrity clientele isn't unheard of. The film industry sends big stars there to train for upcoming roles. You gotta be discreet, professional. That therapy degree will be a huge bonus. I'm excited."

"What kind of money are you talking?" Mike asked.

"We'll come up with a number that works for both of us. I'll match what your making, plus some incentives," Vince said. "I asked around about you. Heard nothing but great things. The offer is on the table."

"I appreciate that," Mike said. "What's the timing on this?"

"The sooner the better. It's remodeled and ready to open."

"Let me mull it over, Vince. I'll be back in touch. I appreciate the offer regardless." Mike thanked him again then hung up.

There was nothing stopping him. Mike would always have his degree. His mother used to say that blessings came in threes. This was his third reason to go west—the retreat, Gloria's memorial service, and the job offer. The move felt right to him. He was still young. The job at Serenity Hills would be waiting for him, but as he reviewed his résumé, adjusting it to include his boxing experience, his eye kept returning to how long it had taken him to become a therapist. A year was a long time. What if Serenity Hills didn't take him back after the year? He'd done well there. There was so much at stake. He wished there was someone he truly trusted who could help him make the decision. Marlow weaved between his legs then hopped up on the couch next to him.

"What do you think I should do?" Mike asked.

The cat meowed.

Mike closed his eyes and pressed his palms together in prayer. After a moment of silence, he grabbed his coat, wallet, and keys. When he felt lost, the best thing he could do was to attend an AA meeting. Meetings helped keep him grounded and clear his head.

There were nights when meetings organically formed a theme. The recurring theme for the night revolved around fear and change. While too much change could often be a trigger, stagnancy could be as well. Sometimes taking a step back was the only way to see the whole picture.

When Mike got back to his apartment, he picked up the groggy tabby and brought Marlow eye level.

"Let's go for it."

Chapter Twenty-Nine: Prue Present

The blueprints lay on the passenger seat next to me. Alistair's scent lingered on the paper. I turned off the music and mentally reenacted what had happened. I struggled to pinpoint why I'd changed my mind halfway through the act. The freshly laid woman in me wanted to celebrate, but I squashed the joy with all my might. My sobriety had been broken. I brewed over the glaring fact that I hadn't made it to my goal of ninety days. The tennis game played in my head. Did it matter if I waited? Each red light brought more clarity. I questioned Alistair as a person, and whether the reality of him was not as exciting as the fantasy. The minute I got home, I texted Lily to see if she could meet in the morning for coffee.

As we sat across from each other at Starbucks, I confessed to fucking Alistair. Lily held in her disappointment, reminding me that I wasn't desperate and that Alistair was a pompous asshole.

"Remember the time I lost you at that nightclub in New York City?"

I laughed because I loved this story and appreciated that she did too.

"Yeah, that's right," she said. "I find my best friend in line for the ladies' room, and who is standing next to her? Mick fucking Jagger."

"Truth," I said. "If you hadn't been a witness, no one would have believed me. He took one look at me in the bathroom line and said this line looks like way more fun than the men's room line."

"Yup," Lily said. "That's my Chickie. He was a foot shorter than you. I remember it like it was yesterday." She laughed. "My point is, you have something men want. Don't settle for someone who lies, goes to strip clubs, and gives away your mother's watch. So you guys fucked? Separate yourself from him emotionally and do a great job decorating. How was it, anyway?"

"Started out a bit rocky, you know, performance anxiety. But he's super sexy, nice cock, great body, awesome kisser," I said, running the usual recap list.

"So what's bugging you, other than the crap he's pulled since moving here?"

"He was less aggressive than I imagined, more of a tender lover who leaned on the inhibited side. I was all over him like a spider monkey, which may have caused his performance anxiety."

"Jesus," Lily said.

"Yeah, hard, soft, hard," I said. "He was freaking but came around and then performed like a champ."

"Don't get too attached. The setup is not great for a long-term relationship."

"I'll try," I said. "The trouble is, when I'm around him, I lose all judgment."

"Be professional," Lily said. "Don't fuck him again until the job is completed. Get to know him. If you still want to do it after the project is done, then you did the homework."

When she said all of the things he had done in a row, all in one sentence, I had to admit to myself that they sounded pretty bad. Lily advised me not to tell Sam that I had any connection with Alistair prior to him hiring me. There was no plus side in telling him, and it was imperative to keep the anonymity of anyone connected to the AA program. I walked Lily to her car. When she was in the driver's seat, she rolled down the window.

"I'm going to set up a boxing lesson for us with Mike," she said, a smile plastered on her face.

I gave her the thumbs-up and a fake one-two punch as she pulled away. With all the goings-on with Alistair, I hadn't had time to think about Mike and the fact he was in LA running a boxing gym. The only way I could get through the next twenty-four hours was to stay on task, so I marched to my car and thought about Alistair's loft during the drive to work.

I went straight to my desk with the blueprints tucked under one arm. When I began working on a large design project, I broke it down into pieces, which helped me feel less overwhelmed. The moment I stepped into the space he had purchased and saw the way the light hit the room, the textures and colors in the view, I knew what direction I was headed in.

The firm used Autodesk software, so I began to input measurements from the blueprints, focusing on the largest spaces first. Every designer had their go-to showrooms, the lines they preferred to work with. I certainly had mine. My preference was to continue to work with companies who were timely with deliveries and kept their word on stock availability. This project couldn't afford any delays with back-ordered fabrics, furnishings, and wallpaper.

I hit up an Al-Anon meeting at a local church before heading home in time for Christian. The group discussed the issue of codependency with a mix of recovering addicts, family members, and people in relationships with addicts. I still had issues with codependency and listening to my gut. After the meeting, I questioned my ability to judge a person's character, especially pertaining to Alistair. I took a moment in the car to say a prayer. A knock on the window startled me.

"Everything okay?" a man asked.

I rolled down the window. "Yes, fine," I said, figuring that my parking lot linger had triggered an alert that someone who attended the meeting was unraveling.

After he walked away, I looked over my playlist and chose Bob Dylan to take me home, "Simple Twist of Fate." Gloria sat next to me. Her essence and energy sent chills down my spine.

Don't beat yourself up over fucking Alistair. Sex is a normal thing between two adults who care about each other, and you shouldn't feel badly about satisfying your needs.

When she disappeared, I felt the hole she left in my heart the day she took her life.

That night, I was exhausted both physically and emotionally. I could barely go through the motions of washing my face and slathering on the anti-aging products that never worked. I set the alarm on my phone and noticed two text messages. The first one was from an unknown number asking me to come over and have some fun, which I deleted then blocked. The more power I gave to messages from my past, the more I would backslide. The second message was from Lily.

Boxing lesson is set for Wednesday morning. I can't even wait! I'll pick you up with a latte but we'll probably talk twenty times between now and then.

Before my lids dropped, I double-tapped the message and tagged it with a heart.

Every Tuesday, I had a standing appointment with Dr. O'Brien. This fact was the only reason I was able to sleep. It also helped that Sam had promised to be my "bitch" on Alistair's job through completion. Of course he added strings to his promise by making me commit to helping him with an installation.

The minute I showed up at the house, I let Sam know that I absolutely had to leave for a therapy appointment, but if the install wasn't finished, I would come back. He was preoccupied with yelling at the guys unloading the truck and brushed me off with a nod. This was the stuff I lived for, and Sam let me work my magic on the bookshelves, coffee tables, and end tables. My job was to style every last detail of the house so that there was a huge *wow* factor for the homeowners.

The best part about an install was that Sam left me alone. He was too busy dealing with the large items to worry about what I was doing. There was a level of trust between us that I had earned. I was there with all of the knick-knacks, coffee table books, and lamps. We had discussed in detail the schemes, colors, theme, mood, and purchased everything in advance. I always bought fresh flowers and potted plants on the day of the install.

Once I had all of my displays finished, I ran out to buy roses, orchids, bromeliads, succulents, ferns, baskets, and cachepots to stick them in. I had exactly two hours to get it all done.

With clippers in hand, I began putting together the bouquets. Flowers brought me so much joy, and as I arranged them I reminded myself to buy flowers and to depend on myself for happiness.

"Fabulous," Sam said as he passed through the kitchen. "Everything looks perfect." That was all the confirmation I needed to feel okay about leaving for my therapy appointment. Sam's assistant was putting the linens and throw pillows on the master bed while Sam added the decorative pillows to the sofas.

"I'm headed off to my appointment now," I said. My purse hung over my shoulder. "Should I come back?"

He stepped away from the sofa to soak in his work. "Looks fabulous," he said. "If I have a panic attack, I'll text you."

I laughed. "And starting tomorrow," I said, "you're all mine."

"Yes, girl," he said with a sassy hip sway. "We're going to have some fun with that fat budget."

"No doubt," I said. I had gone one whole day without spewing to Sam that I had previously known Alistair and fucked him at his new loft. I tended to be better at keeping secrets for others and splattered my personal business all over the walls. Not anymore.

I arrived at Dr. O'Brien's right on time, which meant I was a little late. Once I got out of my car, I started running. She was waiting for me with the door open. I dropped on the mind-shrinking sofa a little winded but ready to spew all the news of the past week.

"We had an install today, so I was running on a tight schedule. I'm so relieved I made it."

Sheryl gathered her pad and pen. *She is ready for the crazy lady to start talking.*

"Everything has been agreed upon with regard to my pending divorce," I said. Out of habit, I grabbed a tissue from the box. The twisting helped me focus while occupying fidgety hands. "We went to mediation, which was very stressful. I felt sort of alone and wished I had my mother or Gram by my side." I sighed. The last of the winded frenzy exited my lungs. "The odd thing was that I heard their voices in my head—Mom, Gram, and even Gloria. Guiding me and telling me to hold my ground until I got what I felt I rightfully deserved."

"Those voices are yours," she said. "Whether they sound like your mother or grandmother or Gloria, it's you leading the way. That's your gut speaking to you, and you are finally listening."

"Interesting. I hadn't thought about it that way," I said. "Don't worry, I'm still a train wreck. You have job security." A nervous laugh spilled out. "I ended up having sex with that guy, Alistair, the one I kissed in rehab who also hired me to design his home."

Whenever I told Sheryl about something bad I had done, I said it really fast in the hopes she would barely catch it or perhaps it would lessen the blow. Sheryl jotted notes while I squirmed. I wanted to keep talking but decided against it due to the glum expression on her face.

"This is disappointing for the both of you," she said. "You committed to not having sex for ninety days, and neither of you should be starting a relationship this early in your programs. How do you feel about what happened?"

"Conflicted," I said, mangling the tissue with my hand.

"What is the central conflict for you?" Sheryl asked questions she knew the answers to, and I took the bait every time.

"I believe that sex between two consenting adults is a natural step in every relationship. The question is whether we're in a relationship and if I even want to have a relationship with him." My foot nodded up and down as nervous energy coursed through me. "He has told me a bunch of lies recently. Plus, he's a recovering coke addict. I hate using that against him, but it does trigger me from my past experiences."

I crossed and uncrossed my legs. The tremendous urgency to get it all out, cover every subject, was at times overwhelming.

"Do you see potential in the relationship?"

"Yes and no," I replied.

"It's not ideal to begin a romantic relationship and work with them professionally at the same time." Sheryl leaned toward me, which was her go-to move when she wanted me to pay attention. "Especially not two people fresh out of rehab. But I don't want you beating yourself up over it. What's done is done. My advice is to proceed with caution."

Her words cut through me like a knife. "I understand, and I will. There is a history between us, but he's really pompous and has lied to me a lot. I'm honestly trying not to get caught up in the fantasy of him, the money, the lifestyle. All the things that don't matter."

"That's an excellent place to start," she said.

For a moment, my gut said Sheryl might be proud of me.

"Something exciting is happening tomorrow," I said. Rather than wait for her to question what I was referring to, I blurted it out. "My therapist from Serenity Hills, the one who took a leave of absence, Mike, is now running a boxing gym in Santa Monica. Lily found him, and tomorrow we're going to have a private boxing lesson with him." The tone of my voice raised three octaves.

"That is quite a career shift," Sheryl said. I guessed that she was trying not to be cynical, which came across like a lead pipe over my head. "How do you feel about seeing him in a non-therapeutic environment? It may be a bit of a shock." She set the pen down beside her. "I want you to prepare yourself mentally."

"The thing is, I just want to see him. It doesn't matter to me that he's not a therapist anymore." I fiddled with the rolled-up tissue.

"I still want you to think about how you will feel about seeing him in a completely different setting. You are also sensitive to violence, and boxing may be triggering for you."

I hated that she was always looking at reality rather than the fantasy world I preferred to live in. "I guess," I said, relieved Dr. O'Brien hadn't witnessed me hiding under a blanket in rehab when the patients were hitting a chair with a baseball bat during Survivor's Week. The mere sound of plastic striking the metal chair had sent me running for cover.

"I'll be alright," I said. "I've taken kickboxing classes with no incident." I gazed out the window to gather my thoughts. "Something else cool happened. Some of which is thanks to your guidance. My son and I volunteered to distribute food to the homeless."

"I'm proud of you," she said. "That is the kind of thing that will keep you focusing on something other than yourself." She smiled. I shoved the wound-up tissue in my pocket. "If you need to speak with me after you see Mike, I will be available after three tomorrow."

"Thank you," I said. "I'm sure I'll be fine."

But by the time I left Dr. O'Brien's office, the seed of doubt she planted had begun to grow.

*   *   *

I lay in bed, scrolling through my Instagram feed and searching to see if Churchill Boxing had an account. Once I found the account, I hesitated, unsure as to whether I should go in blind or get a feel for the space through the photos they posted. There at the top of the feed was a picture of Mike, the new manager of Churchill Boxing, with a small bio. It was then that I learned a few details about his personal life I didn't know.

Within moments of turning out my light, I fell into a deep sleep. I dreamed I was at Serenity Hills, and instead of using a baseball bat to hit a chair, we were forced to punch each other with giant boxing gloves. I had the gloves on, and Gloria was in the ring, but she didn't have any gloves. She begged me to hit her. I stroked her cheek, and it went right through her.

The alarm jolted me awake. Then I remembered it was boxing-lesson day. I opened my workout clothes drawer and gazed at the worn-out pile of spandex. After some digging, at the very bottom, I struck gold. A newish pair of Lululemons that I had totally forgotten about. I threw them on with a racerback tank top and checked myself in the mirror for bulges.

I earned those rolls.

I dragged around in slow motion. There was barely any time to get my hair into a cute top knot and throw on a teensy bit of makeup before Lily was out front, leaning on the horn. On my way out the door, I grabbed a protein bar to eat in the car.

"Jesus, do you have to honk like that? It completely jangles my nerves." I slid into the black leather seat with white piping. The special edition with all the extra bells and whistles.

"Someone woke up on the wrong side of the bed." Lily handed me a latte. She had on the perfect boxing getup. I fought the urge to bolt into the house to change. "At least you look better than your mood."

Phew.

"Sorry," I said. "I had a bad dream. Sheryl put some weird thoughts in my head about seeing Mike outside of his usual therapeutic environment. Now I'm all discombobulated and shit."

I sipped the coffee. Lily had nailed it: sugar-free cinnamon dolce latte with almond milk, no whip.

"Thanks for the coffee, Lil."

"I can see how she would be concerned, but in my opinion, it's the same Mike. He's just not your therapist anymore. And even if he was still at Serenity Hills, he wouldn't be your therapist because you checked out. I mean, you could have called him a few times right after you left, but in reality that would have ended pretty fast."

"Do you really think I look okay?" The insecure Prue rearing her head, begging for verbal affirmations.

"You look stunning. I wouldn't say it if I didn't mean it." Lily wore her hair pulled back in a ponytail, which looked chic and fresh. Whenever I pulled my mop into a streamlined ponytail, the unruly strands formed bumps and lumps.

Love yourself, stop berating yourself.

Lily drove as though someone was chasing her. She lurched while weaving in and out of traffic, punching the gas. The Santa Monica exit came fast. I wasn't quite ready to face my new boxing coach. Lily veered off the freeway and there was no turning back.

"So you know how we used to go to spinning and you would get freaked by the women who rode too enthusiastically and bounced around on their bikes?" Lily asked.

"Yeah," I said and laughed.

"There's none of that in boxing." Lily smiled.

I admired her profile. At times, I felt privileged to look at her.

*   *   *

A muscular Latina greeted us at the front desk. I figured she could have knocked the both of us out in one punch. Before I began envisioning her beating us up, I admired her smooth, flawless skin. Every single muscle imaginable was on display, with perfect definition. I crossed my noodle arms over my chest and flexed as much as one could with zero muscles.

"Hello. Are you here for a lesson with Mike?" she asked.

We definitely aren't here to fight in a match.

Popeye's girl, Olive Oyl, could beat me in an arm wrestle at this point. Lily moved to the bench along the wall, and I followed.

"Fuck, her arms are amazing," I whispered.

There was a distinct odor I couldn't decipher. *Cleaning fluid, sweat, leather, victory, defeat.*

The woman at the front desk picked up the phone. When she hung up, she turned to us. "Mike will be right out."

My chest tightened. "I feel so nervous," I said. "Like I'm going to cry."

I looked up and there he was, standing in front of me. The same Mike, sturdy body, big smile, soft blue eyes, defined jawline—only he wasn't wearing business casual. He was in sleek sweats and a t-shirt with Churchill Boxing emblazoned across the front.

I don't know whether I stared for a minute or an hour, because time stopped. "It's you," I said. "It's really you."

Then I remembered I wasn't at Serenity Hills and could hug him for as long as I wanted, but the opportunity never appeared.

"Here I am," he said. "You found me." There was a wall of professionalism piled between us. "You ready to try my favorite sport?" He turned and led us to the gym. "Let's get you ladies warmed up."

When I watched Lily take her first lunge, I burst out laughing and couldn't stop. Lily kept going, and I realized that it was my nerves releasing. "Sorry," I said, wiping away laughing tears. "I don't know what my deal is."

"She's happy to see you," Lily said, her knees lifting up and out with each step. I followed close behind.

As I stepped into the next lunge, a little toot came out without warning. I threw a hand over my mouth. Lily snapped around to let me know she'd heard it. Mike left it unacknowledged. I wanted to die a thousand fiery deaths. But I kept moving and pretended the toot that was still ringing in my ears had never happened.

My feelings came in waves like the wind chimes Mike played during meditation sessions at Serenity Hills. He blurted out instructions, every word sounding familiar, yet here we were in a boxing gym and not in the confines of Serenity Hills. The comparison was mind-blowing. It was almost too much for me to handle. I inhaled with each step to find purpose and meaning in this moment. I also clenched my butt cheeks out of fear and the possibility of more embarrassment.

We followed Mike to the speed bag, where he taped up Lily's hands. I stared in unabashed glory and took in his essence and positivity. I may as well have been a teenager staring at a picture of whatever teenage heartthrob I was into that week. Mike was looking hot as hell. His eyes were focused and deliberate as he wrapped my hands, until by chance he glanced up to find me unknowingly studying him. It was the closest I had been to Mike, and I savored it with every bone in my body. He had saved me, healed me, torn me apart, and put me back together so I could work on being a whole person. I owed him everything. I gave myself a gentle reminder that he put his pants on one leg at a time just like the rest of us.

With both of our hands now taped, Mike asked if we'd ever boxed or had lessons. I shook my head no. Lily told him not formally but that she'd come here a couple of times with her husband.

"But don't worry, we're both originally from back east, so fighting should come naturally to us," Lily said.

Mike smiled. It was warm and open. It was new. Not that he hadn't smiled in front of me before, but this wasn't the muted, tailored smile of Serenity Hills. It was free.

"Well, there are a few things we should go over just in case. For

Prue's benefit." He began his lesson by showing us the correct way to throw a punch, how to position the arm and wrist. Even the right way to make a fist. Both Lily and I caught on pretty quickly, Lily slightly faster than I. That might have been due to me being somewhat distracted. "Now for the fun part," he said.

We stepped back while Mike worked the bag, demonstrating what he'd shown us—nimble, light, and giving off the illusion that it was easy and effortless. He moved from the heavy bag to the speed bag a few feet away. The stories I had told myself about him were true. This was Mike in all his glory, and I loved seeing him shine.

His fists moved in smooth circles, conducting the bag in controlled syncopation. I was practically in a trance when he turned to us. "Now it's your turn." He handed Lily Velcro boxing gloves and had her hit the heavy bag, then motioned me toward the speed bag and handed me a set of smaller speed gloves.

I stepped up to the speed bag, wound up, and swung on the ball of leather. It jigged when I jagged. I nearly fell trying to swing with far more effort than was required. Mike stood behind me and coached with his voice. I hit a rhythm and lost it as fast as it came. A few feet over, Lily worked the heavy bag like a champ.

"Don't worry," she said. "I sucked the first time too."

Mike taught us to bob and weave. When he demonstrated something, he moved like a panther; strong, smooth, and graceful. I forced my mouth closed since I figured it was resting on the floor. Instead, I went to brush a hair off of my face and nearly knocked myself out, forgetting it wasn't my hand anymore.

Mike stole the stage from everyone in the room. I had never seen a man move with such grace.

Lily and I practiced our hooks, crosscuts, uppercuts, and jabs. All the while, we did our best to stay quick and light.

Balls of your feet, Prue.

It felt more like I had bricks attached to my ankles and I was moving through deep water.

"Protect your money-shot," Mike said.

"What's the money-shot?" I asked.

"Your face," he said. His red leather glove grazed my cheek. A beam of light flashed between us.

"Can we get in the ring?" I asked. "It looks so fun."

"Alright, I'll let you two spar for a few minutes." Mike put headgear on each of us. "No shots to the face," he said. "Stay on the bounce, keep it light, step into your punches."

We entered the ring. I felt empowered. The strength I had been searching for finally arrived. Mike stayed on the platform but moved to the side. Lily took her stance and began to shift quick steps from one foot to the other, her gloves framing her face. Her ponytail hypnotically bounced in rhythm with her feet. The gym sounds disappeared, and a private bubble surrounded us. Mike belted out verbal cues, but my ears refused to hear. The sounds were muffled like when Henry, Lily, and I would try to talk underwater when we were young.

Lily swung the first punch with more power than I had expected. Instead of stepping in toward her as Mike had instructed, I covered my face with my hands and blinded myself. Lily moved toward me. With each advancing step she took, I moved farther away.

Her punches came at me swift and strong. I wanted to swing, but she was coming in too fast. All of her punches felt angry and violent. A cross-punch hit my chin like a wound-up-tight jack-in-the-box.

I stepped back, letting out a whimper. Lily charged with a right hook, jab, hook, jab. Each punch was accompanied by grunts from deep within her gut. I folded in half, taking the hits.

"C'mon! Harder, harder," I yelled. I held my ground, inching back but taking the blows. An arm wedged between us.

"Break it up," Mike said, muffled and dark.

Lily switched her stance and extended a cross-punch into my shoulder. I tumbled to the mat. Both arms covered my head as I curled into the fetal position. Lily straddled me with her skinny legs, swinging wildly. I wondered if this was her way of letting out her anger over what had happened between me and Binky.

Mike yanked her off of me. When he released Lily, she collapsed. She tore off her headgear. Tears were streaming down her face.

"I'm sorry," Lily said. "I'm so sorry." The gloves covered her eyes. She rolled closer and draped an arm over me. "I don't know what got into me."

Mike crouched beside us. I pulled myself up to a seated position, my legs splayed out in front of me. "I deserved it," I said. "You owed me those punches." I pulled off the headgear, a clump of hair glued to my forehead. "You didn't hurt me. Just a few bruises."

I rolled onto all fours, winded and weak. Once I was standing, I helped Lily up. Her knees trembled. I wrapped my arm around her shoulders as we walked out of the ring. For the first time since we had become friends, I was carrying Lily. We both dripped with sweat. My limbs were wet noodles. Mike handed us towels. Lily covered her head in white terry cloth.

We shifted to a bench at the edge of the gym. My shoulder throbbed, but I kept an arm wrapped around her. "I deserved it, Lil," I said. Her head hung and the towel covered her face. "You know I did."

"That doesn't make it right," she said. "Maybe I have pent-up anger about your stepdad, Richard, and took it out on you." She peeled the towel from her head.

"Why would you take it out on me? I'm not Richard," I said, confused but trying to understand.

"For some reason, I kept seeing his disgusting face when I was punching you."

Mike crouched in front of us.

"I don't know why you would think about Richard, of all people, when you were punching me. I figured it was because I kissed your husband."

"I've moved on from that," Lily said.

I knew better. *Those punches were over the Binky kiss.* I touched her knee. A glove laid like a body on the floor by her feet.

"You both sure got my adrenaline pumping," Mike said, his voice soft and kind. "It took me a minute to register what was happening before I could break you two apart."

"I don't think any of us knew what was happening," I said.

Mike took Lily's wrist and held it up in victory. "I'd say you won that match."

We both laughed. Lily pulled herself from the bench.

"It would be beneficial if we all had a chat in my office," Mike said.

"I was afraid you were going to say that," Lily said.

We followed Mike to his office. A large window provided a view of the main boxing ring. When he closed the door, the office was sealed in silence. Lily took a seat on the sofa.

"Thanks for everything," I said, starting to shiver.

"Here," Mike said, grabbing a hoodie from a hook behind the door. I pulled it over my head, shrinking under the thick, bulky fabric. Both hands disappeared inside the sleeves. I breathed in the scent lingering in the fabric. He moved to a chair by the sofa and raked his fingers through his hair. I took a seat next to Lily.

"I should have broken that up faster. It took me a moment to gain clarity." The ceiling fan turned and clicked. Mike looked at me. "You kissed her husband?"

Lily nodded. My heart began to pound. The disappointment I had caused myself was minor compared to how I felt about disappointing Mike.

"Yes, I violated the most important friendship code," I said. There was no point in denying what I had done. "A few things had happened. I tried to call you at Serenity Hills."

I swiped underneath my eyes to clear any wandering mascara. I may have been stalling, setting the story straight in my head, asking myself if I was justifying my bad behavior.

"They said you had left. Some guy hit on me when I was installing curtains. I decided to leave Nick. It was like a huge snowball gaining power and speed."

I took in the nuances of Mike's office as I spoke: a brick wall on one side, a desk lamp illuminated the room, the overhead lights remained off. His leather jacket hung on a coat rack. Photos of famous boxers lined the wall. A frame rested on Mike's desk, but I couldn't see the image on the other side.

"Prue and I spent some time talking about it and resolved the situation," Lily said, her posture erect and confident. Even after sweating in the ring, she looked fresh and young. My hands fussed with my top. I adjusted my mashed boobs in the sports bra. "Mike, you can tell Prue what we spoke about at Serenity Hills."

Suddenly, I was the odd man out, the one in the dark. A spark ran up my spine. Had they collaborated behind my back? I caught myself before it spiraled. There was no room for jealousy in a friendship. It was my insecurities seeping from the cracks of the part of me that I loathed.

"You should tell her," Mike said, his strong hands clasped in his lap. Even though he was in a different room, wearing boxing attire, and in LA, it was the same Mike. Nothing had changed.

Lily dropped her head in her hands. Her thick ponytail draped over her shoulder. "I went to speak with Mike when I visited you during Family Week." She licked her lips. "There was something I guess I wasn't facing about my childhood, and it came out when I was there."

I wanted to shake her and scream for her to say whatever it was, but instead, I touched her knee.

"When you were living in the gingerbread house," she continued, "I rode my bike over and wanted to surprise you, so I snuck up the stairs without making a peep. You weren't in your room." Her skin turned white. I gasped. "You were in your mom's bedroom with Richard. I peeked through the door." Her voice trailed off. "I saw what he did to you."

"Ohmygod," I said.

"Yeah," she said. "I saw it with my own eyes, then I crawled down the stairs, got on my bike, and rode home."

"Why didn't you tell me?" I wanted to cry for her and the horrific nightmare she had witnessed.

"I couldn't," she said, shaking her head. "I was too embarrassed. Too afraid. All I could do was bury it and never think about it again." She started to cry.

I didn't know what to do, whether to touch her or if she would be repulsed by me because I reminded her of that man.

Lily spoke through her tears, "I hate myself for not telling my parents. For letting it go on."

"Oh, Lily," I said. Scenarios played like movies. Every horror, every violation—which one had she seen? What day had she come by? I yearned for my mother. What I wouldn't have done for the chance to bury myself in the scent of her clothes, to hide in her closet. "This isn't your fault."

"When I visited you for Family Week, the memories came rushing back." My stomach twisted and turned, the same sickening feeling I would get after Richard violated me.

"I'm so sorry." I touched her back, desperate to change the subject and never mention Richard's name again. So desperate to put the past behind me.

"It kills me every day that I didn't do anything." A huge tear rolled down her cheek. "Why didn't I stop him?"

"Richard was a monster," I said. "No one could stand up to him, especially not two knock-kneed, skinny kids like us." Lily laughed. My lungs filled with air. "We don't need to give him any more power and energy than we already have. He's gone. He can't hurt us again."

Mike jumped in. "What did I tell you the day you came to see me, Lily?"

"That I was an innocent child," Lily whispered. "There was nothing I could do."

"You both were," Mike said. "Forgive yourself. You did nothing wrong."

"If anything, you stood up to him more than anyone I knew," I said. "You were always so brave."

"Thanks," Lily said. "It was then that I realized how strong you are, Prue. I'm awed by the resilience of your spirit. You didn't let him break you."

"It all came apart later in my life." I turned to Lily. "You helped me pick up the pieces."

"I've tried. I keep trying. I didn't protect you then, Prue, and I'm going to spend the rest of my life making that up to you."

Mike tipped his head. "You two have a very special friendship. You're blessed."

Lily and I smiled at each other. For the first time since we met, I felt like the strong one. "We're super lucky," I said.

Lily stood. "I'm going to run to the bathroom and let you guys have a few moments to catch up," she said. "I'll meet you in the car." She smiled to let me know everything was going to be alright. After Lily closed the door, I leaned back and stretched my aching legs out in front of me.

"I don't know where to begin." The familiar thickness filled my throat. "So much has happened."

A choir of conflicting voices sung to me. Mike, my therapist. Mike, just a guy, a coach, maybe a friend? I gathered myself together with the last ounce of strength I had left in me.

"It's great to see you," he said. The sound of his voice was easy and welcoming, like stepping through your front door after a long trip.

"How did all this come about?" I asked. I yearned to look at the photo on his desk. Was it a girlfriend or wife? Clues to the mysteries of his life. "Are you happy?"

"I had to take a break from Serenity," he said. "The whole thing with Gloria committing suicide shook me up." He gazed at his hands. "I was out here for a retreat. Before I left Arizona, someone offered me this job." Our eyes met. I couldn't look away. "It felt like the right time to make some changes in my life." My heart pulsed through my chest. "You know, get a fresh start." A thousand questions waited on the sidelines. "And to answer your question, yes, I'm happy." He smiled.

I wanted to stay there all day and talk to him. Soak in everything he knew, all the advice, life lessons, and wisdom, but I had to get back to Lily. Mike couldn't solve my problems anymore.

He smiled. "Don't worry too much about what happened. This is the beautiful thing about boxing. We leave it in the ring."

"I'm worried about Lily," I said.

"That's the interesting thing about emotions," he said. "If we wait too long to let them out, they end up being released, usually in unhealthy ways."

I couldn't bear to talk about Richard anymore. He had done enough damage. "I think I need to process what Lily told me. It's a lot to take in."

"I'm here if you need me," he said. "You handled it well. All you could do was listen, acknowledge, and console."

"It was really shitty of me to kiss her husband, but I have something bigger to tell you," I said.

"I'm here for you." He shifted to face me, ears ready to listen, mouth closed. *Therapist Mike.*

"I had sex with Alistair." I laughed, caught myself, stopped. No change in his expression, no judgment, shock, or indifference. It was the face where kindness and understanding lived. "I'm having mixed feelings about it. When it was over, I emotionally shut down just the way I did before rehab."

"Okay, wow," he said. "Is Alistair in LA?"

"Yes," I said. "And he went around my back to hire me as the designer for his new apartment. Well, it's more like a massive penthouse loft. I went over there to see the space, and one thing led to another." The blood rushed to my face.

"You're two consenting adults," he said.

I searched for cracks in his voice, flinches in his body.

"The issue is that you are both fresh out of rehab," he continued. "It's not ideal to start a relationship until both people have been sober for a year. We went over this at Serenity Hills."

"That's the thing," I said. "I don't think I want a relationship with Alistair. There are too many red flags. I worry about his sobriety, his vulnerability. He's trying so hard to be with me, but everything he does falls flat. After we did it, I realized I was enamored by the idea of Alistair, but that's it. I don't believe I actually want a relationship with him."

"Follow your heart and listen to your gut," he said.

"I know."

"Are you seeing a therapist here in LA?"

"Yes," I replied. "She's not like you, but I'm going regularly." I tapped on my legs as though they were a piano. "I'm relieved that I told you about the kiss with Lily's husband and what happened with Alistair."

"Thank you for telling me," he said.

The phone in his office buzzed. I jumped. Mike stepped over to his desk. "Hello?" he answered. "I'll be right out."

I craned my head around to glance at the photo on his desk. The picture was faded, Mike as a teenager. His arm was around a smiling boy with clenched fists, his head dropped back. I guessed it was his brother.

He turned to me. "My next client is here." He stepped toward me. "Keep the sweatshirt."

"It's okay." I dragged the hoodie off and hung it back on the hook.

Mike inspected my arms. "You're going to have some solid bruises," he said.

"I don't mind," I said. "Most of my wounds are the kind you can't see with the naked eye."

"The experiences of our lives shape and mold who we are as people."

I smiled. "True." These were the kind of conversations I craved in rehab. "I forgot to ask if you were planning on attending Gloria's memorial service?"

"I wouldn't miss it," he said.

"Awesome," I said. "Gives me something to look forward to."

He opened his door. Gym sounds cascaded over me. All I could think about was what the car ride back home with Lily would be like.

Chapter Thirty: Alistair Present

After Prue left, Alistair stared at himself in the master bathroom mirror. He touched his nose, leaned in closer, and examined every inch of his face. The silence in the apartment overwhelmed him, and he questioned if living alone was the best idea. He picked up his phone, texted George, and left without turning out the lights.

"Have fun?" George asked once Alistair was seated in the car.

"We shagged," Alistair said. "She cried after. I'll never understand women. They simply baffle me."

"Maybe they were tears of joy," George said as he pulled out into the street.

"I don't believe so," Alistair said, distracted by a new dump of emails in his inbox. He began reading, and a smile stretched across his face. "Georgie, my friend and comrade, I've got some great news. I have just received notice from the bank that the first nine million has dropped into the Henkle Global account." Alistair rubbed his palms together. "I want to celebrate in a big way."

"Got it, Boss," George said. "Do you still want to go to that party your client invited you to in the Hollywood Hills?"

"Hell yes," Alistair said. "I'll need to freshen up a bit. Could you drop me at the hotel, run some errands, and pick me up around seven? We'll grab some food then head over."

Alistair's body pulsed with adrenaline. George dropped him off in front of the hotel, and Alistair stopped at the bar for a celebratory cocktail. His energy was high, and any hesitation he had about what had happened with Prue was a distant memory. He drafted a text to Prue while reaching for the Skittles in his jacket pocket.

You must be my lucky charm because after you left, I received word that the first part of my deal has closed. Thank you for meeting me today. You felt amazing! It was everything I had imagined and more. I'll call you tomorrow.

He added the last line to cover his tracks in case she tried to contact him tonight. He wanted to be free to celebrate the way he wanted. After reading through the text, he pressed backspace until the message disappeared. Then he typed out a new message and pushed send.

Had fun. Let's do it again.

A woman with golden skin and dark, sultry eyes took the seat next to him. She smelled like fresh-baked cinnamon rolls and wore a clanging pile of bangles on her wrist.

"May I buy you a drink?" Alistair said. "I'm celebrating." He raised his glass to the woman. "I'd love you to join me in a toast."

"Tequila on the rocks," she said. When she touched her thick, dark hair, the bracelets flew down her arm. Alistair raised his eyebrows. When her drink arrived, they clinked glasses. She told him she was in LA on business and had no plans for the night. "Are you from Australia?" she asked.

"Yes," Alistair said. "How did you know?"

The two of them stayed at the bar, drinking and flirting. She touched Alistair every chance she could get and laughed at all of his jokes.

She accompanied him to the suite while he showered and changed. Alistair ordered a cheese plate and bottle of champagne, which he dramatically popped while she watched with anticipation.

By the second glass, they were kissing, and Alistair canceled dinner plans. He ordered room service, then texted George to deliver the stuff to his room. When George knocked, the woman squealed and ran to the bathroom to cover up her breasts. After George left, she stepped out.

"I'm married," she said. "I don't normally do this. No idea what's come over me."

Alistair was beginning to feel the effects of the alcohol as well. He poured her another glass of champagne. "To living in the moment," he said.

He moved over to the coffee table. She followed. He opened the packet George had brought and removed a credit card and hundred-dollar bill from his wallet. He turned to her and smiled, a pulse check on whether she was partaking or not.

"Yay," she said. "It's going to be a fun night."

Alistair began to sweat. He stood and adjusted the air conditioning then dimmed the lights. When he returned to the table, she had formed two perfect lines for him. "Be my guest," Alistair said, handing her the rolled-up bill. "Ladies first."

"Don't mind if I do," she said. Alistair's heart pumped. Adrenaline blasted through him like a freight train. "Are you alright?" the woman asked. "You haven't even had a line yet."

She laughed. Her expression was judgmental with a hint of playfulness, which showed in her crooked-toothed smile. He settled next to her; his hand stroked her thigh. She leaned in with her eyes closed, and Alistair kissed her. They made out for a few minutes while the coke screamed at him from the table.

He pulled away from her kisses and refocused his attention on the blow. With his face hovering over the cocaine and the bill tucked in his nostril, he turned to her. "I'm happy we met. You made my night." In one long sniff, the line disappeared. Alistair leaned back on the sofa and closed his eyes. The rush hit him hard.

They bantered about life, her kids, and how she hated living in Joplin, Missouri. Her husband was the head of a bank. She was Persian, an anomaly in Joplin.

"My husband bait-and-switched me," she said. "We met at UCLA and were supposed to live here. Then he took this job as the head of the bank. My only break is the few times a year I come to LA on business. Other than that, I'm stuck in Joplin."

Her jaw moved wildly as she talked. When Alistair started fucking her, he remembered what he hated about blow—he couldn't come when he was high.

"Don't I turn you on?" she asked.

"Of course," he said. "It's just not going to happen, but I'm having a great time. You're a very enthusiastic lover."

After she left, Alistair continued snorting lines alone. He smelled her all over him. He picked up the shirt he had been wearing when he met Prue at his loft and inhaled. A porn movie he hadn't remembered turning on was blaring on the television. Alistair shut it off and stepped toward the window. Even at four in the morning, the streets were alive with people walking and cars honking. He moved to the coffee table and chopped up the rest of his supply.

After he snorted the last of the white powder, he dragged his finger along the table and rubbed the remnants on his gums. He began to tug at his eyebrows then crossed his arms over his chest. Without warning, he began to sob. He rolled to the floor and curled into the fetal position, tears streaming down his face. In between his wails, a stream of snot dripped from his nose.

After a few minutes, he composed himself. He washed his face, purposefully avoiding his ghastly complexion in the mirror. He had a few hours to try and calm down before George would come looking for him. He drew the blinds and settled in bed, wild-eyed and restless.

Chapter Thirty-One: Prue Present

There was an unexpected lightness between Lily and me on the drive home from the boxing lesson. The sun was shining. We rolled the windows down, and the wind wrapped around us with its life force. We belted out an old song that Lily found called "The Oogum Boogum Song."

The music therapist at Serenity Hills was right. Music is like tilling. It loosens up the soil and aerates the emotions we neglected from other seasons or didn't know existed. I would forever associate that song with this moment. Happiness was fleeting. We had to grab it and hold on tight. Without bad days, we couldn't appreciate these moments. Without bad days, we couldn't feel this high. The fight between us was in the rearview mirror. The future was ahead of us and looking bright.

As Lily turned to enter my driveway, she found it was blocked by Binky's car. A huge truck was parked on the street smack in front of my house. I cursed under my breath.

"I probably ordered furniture for a client and inadvertently put my address. Ugh, what a nightmare."

Lily parked on the street. I hopped out and ran toward the house, hoping I could turn the truck around and change the delivery address.

Binky stepped out of the back door. "Hey," he said. "There's a surprise for you in the house."

"I actually need to tell the delivery guys to stop unloading," I said. "This is a mistake. I'll tip them dearly."

"It's not a mistake," Lily said as she came up behind me. I picked up the pace as I moved through the kitchen. When I swung around the corner, I froze. Lily stood beside me. "The piano had gone to auction, and the serial number was registered to the person who purchased it. Your old landlord, Mrs. Sutton."

"She gave me that piano as a graduation gift from Edith Woodson," I said. "Remember? She paid my tuition, but the school told me I had a scholarship."

"The auction house contacted her to see if she wanted to buy it back." Lily moved to the piano.

"How did it get here?" I asked.

"Mrs. Sutton called me. I told her about how Nick sold your piano without your permission." She savored dissing on Nick—her smile and tone told the story all on their own. "She insisted she buy it back from the auction house and pay to have it returned to the rightful owner."

"Mrs. Sutton has literally always been my guardian angel," I said, swiping a sleeve over the fingerprints left in the black lacquered wood. "She never wants recognition or asks for anything in return." I filled the hole left in her heart after her daughter's death.

A hole I know all too well.

"There's a letter." Lily passed me a pale-blue envelope.

I pulled out the bench and sat down. With the note resting on my lap, I faced the keys, moving hands along the ivory in scales. They slipped and hesitated. I restarted. It would take some time to get smooth again. I would have to practice the way I had when I was young in Mrs. Sutton's library.

"Open the envelope," Lily said.

Lost in the beauty of the baby grand, I edged a finger under the thick paper flap embossed with the name of the finest stationery store in New York. A single word was written in navy-blue block letters at the top of the pale-blue folded note: Harewood, the name of the Suttons' estate.

Dear Prudence,

I couldn't bear the thought of you not having your piano, so I took the liberty of purchasing it back from the auction house your ex-husband had sold it to. You are and always have been like a daughter to me. I cherish the memories of our days together on Long Island. Your music filling our library, the long trail rides, mornings eating breakfast together before you headed off to school. Thank you for being such a joy in my life. You came when I needed it most and helped me heal from the loss of my beloved daughter Gwyneth.

It is with a heavy heart that I have to tell you I have cancer. My time here is coming to an end. Please don't be sad for me. And I beg of you, don't come visit, because I don't want you to see me like this. I have lived a full life with no regrets. You will receive some money from my estate after I pass. I am incredibly proud of you. Remember your roots. You are a strong woman from Goose Neck Harbor. Hold your head high, don't settle. Love yourself. Then, and only then, will you find a meaningful partnership with someone who deserves a woman of your caliber.

We shall meet again in Heaven, dear Prue.

Love always,

Alexandra

(Mrs. Sutton)

After Lily and Binky left, I played for a few more minutes and then closed the key cover. I stepped back from the piano to admire my old friend. It was a bittersweet reunion with the news of Mrs. Sutton becoming ill. The piano represented more to me than a musical instrument. It had become a safe haven in the storm of my life. I leaned against the back of the sofa, the silence of the house providing space for my thoughts.

At Serenity Hills, I had vowed to tell Mrs. Sutton about my mother's affair with Mr. Sutton, but as clarity set in, I realized it didn't matter anymore. What mattered was telling her that I loved her and thanking her for making a broken little girl feel special. I never belonged in Mrs. Sutton's world, but she believed I did.

I stared at the piano. There was more there than I had realized. As I soaked in its presence, I saw a different narrative in my life. One I didn't acknowledge nearly as frequently. When bad people wanted to break me, another person undoubtedly came along to uplift me. So many bad people, bad situations, but always juxtaposed by the good. Never once had I been truly left without someone there to help lift me up. It had become clear why I adored Mike so much, why he got under my skin. He was my present-day Mrs. Sutton, the person who believed in me and saw the best in me even when I didn't believe in myself. As I passed the piano, I patted it and whispered, "Thank you."

I grabbed my phone from the gym bag where I had left it. There were fifteen messages from a text chain Mitch had put together about the details of Gloria's memorial service, and a message from Alistair. The service would be held on a boat, but everyone was to meet at the Four Seasons, rooms paid for by Gloria's lover, Tom. Mitch put in quotes, "Tom is picking up the tab, you won't need to bring one penny." I had mixed feelings about the man who had sent her to rehab yet failed to show up for Family Week. The kind of man who made false promises, a man much like my father.

I pictured the Serenity Hills feelings chart. *I feel love, joy, and passion.* The situation with Alistair was not urgent. It could wait. He could wait. He was likely freaking about my abrupt exit from his loft and mentioning the watch, his anxiety steeping like strong English tea. I had to admit I found the idea somewhat gratifying. Then guilt pried my heart open. He had come indefinitely stateside fresh out of rehab. No doubt his brain wasn't properly working. *Forgive, Prudence. You aren't perfect.*

Christian came barreling in with his lacrosse bag slung over his shoulder. "Your piano!" I grabbed his stinky lax bag and threw it in the kitchen.

"Mrs. Sutton sent it to me," I said. "Isn't that sweet?"

"So nice of her." He lifted the cover and admired the keys. "I feel like we have our family back together."

"Yeah," I said. "I agree."

He grabbed his backpack and headed to his room. "I have a shit-ton of homework."

"Don't curse," I replied, knowing damn well he had learned every swear word witnessing my fights with Nick. "I'll let you know when dinner is ready."

After helping Christian organize his science notebook for two hours and finally getting him to bed, I stood in my cluttered room. Clothes were piled on the chair, the closet door half open. Sneakers had tumbled out onto the rug. I left everything as it was and lit a candle on my bedside table.

My body had reawakened since having sex again. The physical activity of boxing helped ease my desires, but the warmth had returned.

Sex was one of those things that always left me wanting more, like craving sweets after I ate them. The longer I went without sex, the less it occupied my thoughts. Still, the act with Alistair wasn't replaying like when I had sex with other men. I wanted something else, someone else.

I drew a bath and stepped into the water, my impatience for an orgasm growing by the minute. My foot flicked open the drain. I moved closer to the spigot and turned on the water. I lay down in the tub, my legs straddling the stream. Mike's strong hands, his lips on mine, tearing off each other's clothes. The way I imagined he would look at me when he was inside of me. Within moments, my whole body shuddered.

*   *   *

Friday morning, I drove Christian to school and dropped a bag of his things for the weekend at Nick's.

"Mom," Christian said. I turned down the volume on Drake. "I can't deal with the random drug testing and all that stress."

He stared straight ahead while I pressed my tongue to the roof of my mouth. *Silence*, I told myself. *Now is not the time to interject.*

He swallowed, I imagined, carefully choosing his words. "So, I guess I won't smoke this year."

"Thank you," I said as we pulled into the school turnaround. "Love you."

He was quiet when he got out of the car. Charlie was there, waiting with a few other guys carrying lacrosse bags. I exhaled. Perhaps he was a good kid despite the mistakes I had made raising him. Whatever the reason, in that moment, a sense of gratitude engulfed me.

When I got home, rather than keep fussing and loading more crap in the roller bag outer pockets for the funeral weekend at the Four Seasons, I waited in the driveway for Lily. When she pulled up, she yelled out the window, "You look gorgeous and ready for the swanky Four Seasons, Chickie."

I sighed, certain it was the biggest one of my life. There was an underlying twang to her compliment. I had witnessed those insecure moments when Lily compared herself to me many times before. It was more about her wishing she could let go of control the way I could. That free-spirited part of me made her envious. It seeped out at odd times, but I always knew where it stemmed from and that there was nothing I could do to fix it.

"Thanks. You look great too," I said, scanning Lil in the driver's seat.

She looked me over, raised her eyebrows, frowned skeptically, and turned down Norah Jones. "Spill. You're holding out on me. And don't leave out any details."

Something had altered my feelings. Maybe it was the out-of-character lie—or more accurately, lies—or maybe that Alistair had backdoored his way around my career. *Boundaries Man.* I wondered if he embraced women in the workplace, or maybe he was stuck in some stupid eighties boilerplate stereotype like my boss, Sam.

"When I first laid eyes on him in rehab, I was like a giddy school-girl who couldn't keep her feet on the ground. But lately, the harsh reality is that even his admirable qualities come across as two-faced. You know when you see a person's flaws and ask yourself if they are worth the trouble?"

"That's a positive sign," Lily said. "Your gut is speaking to you."

"But my platinum vagina has a booming voice and sometimes

drowns out the chatter in my gut." I laughed, and so did Lily.

When I replayed my words, they sounded sad and pathetic. I needed to do better. The fact that I had an animalistic attraction to Alistair should not derail any level-headed thinking.

I need to be careful with this one.

"When I think about it with a clear head, I remind myself that we met in rehab when we were both exceptionally broken and vulnerable. It's not an ideal setup for a healthy relationship, to say the least."

Lily nodded in agreement.

The entrance to the Four Seasons was flanked with two uniformed bellhops. I recapped what I had packed. A rush of anxiety hit. I was someplace fancier than I belonged.

As Lily and I walked toward the door, I noticed two attractive women in the window reflection. Before I could acknowledge it was us, the door flew open. I leaned in to take a whiff of the magnificent floral arrangement displayed on a table in the lobby. A distinguished-looking man with steel-gray hair approached us. He wore a tailored suit, no tie, and soft loafers. I had seen the exact same pair on one of the wealthy guys I had dated.

"I'm Tom," he said. "You must be Prue."

"Hi, Tom," I said. "This is my best friend, Lily." I shook his hand and looked into his eyes. The same eyes that Gloria had gazed into. I wanted to know him. I couldn't help but want to weigh the man who'd been the center of Gloria's grief, feel his energy and measure his worth. The handshake was firm. And in those eyes, I could see what she might have seen in him.

"Thank you for coming," he said.

It took me a moment to stop staring. I pictured Gloria and Tom doing the nasty. We stood eye to eye. Gloria was five-one in flip-flops. I supposed he was tall enough for her, but I felt like an oversized lummox standing next to him.

"Here are your keys," he said. "Please charge everything to the room." He was trying a little too hard. *Guilty conscience.*

"Thank you for planning this for Gloria," I said.

I stepped back from him and let Lily review the agenda in detail. Within moments, Mitch and his partner, John, blew through the revolving doors, both of them looking exceptionally dapper.

"Princess," Mitch said as he lifted me off the ground. Since we spoke so often on the phone, we didn't need much time to catch up. With our room keys in hand, we headed to the elevators. On our ride up, we agreed to meet in the lobby bar, get some food, and wait for Mike and Alistair to arrive.

Tom put all of us on the same floor. I wheeled my bag silently, following Lily, who commandeered the room key. Still, I wondered which of these rooms would belong to Alistair.

Tom had booked a mini-suite for those who had two people to a room. We had a separate seating area with a television, a powder room, and another room with two queen beds, a full bathroom, and another television. The moment the door closed behind us, I did what I always did when I checked into a hotel: I unpacked my bags. Lily hooked up her speaker so we could listen to some tunes. It took us a while to notice the cheese platter, fruit basket, box of chocolates, champagne bucket, and two goodie bags resting on the bed.

"Damn, Tom went all-out," I said. "I hope he knows not to leave champagne in the rooms occupied by sober folks."

I wiggled the cork from the bottle until it popped and bubbled out of the top. Since I sucked at pouring champagne, I passed the bottle to Lily while I dug through the gift bags. Lily filled the glasses then scooped a piece of brie from the wedge. We parked ourselves on the sofa.

"Cheers," we said in unison.

"To Gloria, may she rest in peace," I said.

Chills ran down my spine. It was as though she were sitting right there with us in her beat-up leggings and a faded pink t-shirt from the Mirage. I could practically see her smile, hear her contagious giggle and the way she said "Prudence"—all cute, overly enunciated like it was the fanciest name she had ever heard.

Someone knocked on the door. The knock made me jump, forgetting for a moment that we were in a hotel occupied by some of my rehab friends. I ran over and answered it.

"Hey," Alistair said. "Can we join the party?"

I twisted my mouth and cocked my head. "Frankie?" I said, even though I knew it was her. "Wait, what are you doing here?"

It took Frankie a moment to speak. She turned to Alistair. "How do you know Prue?"

The two of them were still standing in the hallway. I ushered them into the room but remained by the door.

"How do you know Alistair?" I asked. "This is so bizarre. You're the last person I expected to see at the door."

"I'm shocked to see you too," Frankie said.

We stood facing each other, but neither of us made a move.

"Let me get this straight," Alistair said. "You two know each other?"

"We know each other." I threw both hands on my hips. Lily turned down the music. "Now you explain how you know her."

"This is simply uncanny." Alistair released a nervous laugh.

"Alistair is my brother," Frankie said.

"What?" I inched over to the sofa. My head was spinning as I processed what was happening.

"This is the person I told you I've been searching for." Alistair's eyes begged forgiveness for all the lies he had told. "Allow me to introduce you to my sister, Susie."

"Okay, wait," I said. "Her name is Frankie."

"That's my stage name," she said. "You met me when I was on a job. My real name is Susie."

"Which is why it was so hard to find her," Alistair said, draping an arm over Susie's shoulders.

"Frankie's your sister?" I started laughing. "This is like a scene from a movie."

"I know, right?" Susie wiggled out from under Alistair's arm. "We don't know each other, really. It's all sort of new and unknown territory."

"Wow," I said.

"I knew I had a brother but never expected in a million years that he would try to find me." Susie threw her hands around the air.

"So you were put up for adoption?" I looked at Susie, then turned to Alistair. "Why didn't you mention any of this in rehab?"

Alistair leaned against the desk. "I was getting close to finding Susie and didn't want to jinx it by talking about it."

"I think rehab would be a good spot to talk about your past, but who am I to judge?"

Lily nudged me in the leg. Her signal that I was taking it a little too far.

"Alistair thinks everything is hunky-dory and he's going to 'save me,'" Susie said, adding air quotations for effect. "I was kind of shocked when he found me." She poked a finger through the ring she wore around her neck.

"That ring," Alistair said, pointing to the chain. "Belonged to my mother's grandmother. That's how I knew it was Susie."

I glanced at her arm. The watch I had given Alistair was clasped around her wrist. Betrayal crept in, but I fought it. It wasn't Frankie . . . Susie's fault.

"I have a present for you," Alistair said. He passed me my watch.

"But she's wearing the same watch," I said, looking at the watch he handed me, then the one on Frankie's wrist.

"He bought me the same Cartier watch as yours when he took yours back." Susie moved the band around her wrist. "I call him Cartier now, as a nickname."

I belted out a laugh while a veil of guilt weighed me down. I hadn't trusted anything Alistair had said. And now, to find out he was searching for his long-lost sister, made me feel even worse. "I'm sorry I didn't give you the benefit of the doubt. I had no idea . . ." Something had changed in Alistair's face. I couldn't pinpoint exactly what other than the dark circles and pale complexion.

"It all looked really bad," he said. "I couldn't blame you at all."

"Alistair told me that the guy I offered to sell it to was a friend of his from rehab. I was only joking around, but honestly, how small can this world get?" Susie eyed our champagne.

Lil grabbed two lowball glasses from beside the minibar and poured Alistair and Susie some bubbly. We lifted our glasses.

"To Alistair and Susie reuniting," I said.

Alistair came across as more excited about finding Susie than Susie was about being found. It occurred to me that I did not really know all that much about Alistair. All I knew was what I had seen in rehab, the deep, spiritual Alistair. The party-man stories, the socialite, the man about town, and they were always in relation to his addiction. It was never simply who he was day-to-day. It had been difficult for me not to future-trip over Alistair in rehab, but my fantasies had been clobbered with a strong dose of reality.

When we opened our hotel room door to head down to the restaurant, Mitch was standing there, his hand lifted in the knock position. "Princess," he said. "We were just coming to pick you and Lily up." He craned his neck to see in the room. Mitch exchanged an inscrutable look with me. "Well, this little scene made my night. Who might the lovely lady be?" He blinked a few too many times.

"That is Alistair's sister," I said quickly. "I believe you may have met her while she was at work." I avoided including "stripper" and "strip club" out of respect for Susie.

He strolled past me. "It's wonderful to meet you," he said, "with clothes on."

"The face looks familiar," Susie said. She took the hit like a champ.

"Are we ready to dine at the Fucking Four Seasons in Beverly Hills?" Mitch asked. "Wouldn't Gloria be proud? Damn, I miss that little nugget of love."

"Anyone know where Mike is?" I asked. "I thought he was going to be here."

"He's coming after work, so I'm guessing any minute," Mitch said.

I ushered Lily, Alistair, and Susie from the room. Before closing the door, I wished Gloria could have been there to witness this crazy scene unfold because I was certain she would have gotten a kick out of it.

When we got off the elevator, I pulled Alistair aside. "I have to ask you something, and I want a direct answer. Why did you go around my back to hire me as your designer?"

"You weren't returning my calls or texts, so I went forward with hiring your firm." He moved his hands as though smoothing out a crinkled sheet of paper. "You were the only designer I knew in LA, and honestly, I wanted to see you." Every word came across as though he had rehearsed what he was going to say. I waited for him to say something else, something that gave a better explanation. "Are you angry?"

"Let me paint a picture for you," I said. "I hire your firm to manage my finances, go around your back but request you be my broker. Wouldn't you wonder why I didn't go directly to you?"

He glanced at the ceiling. "This could be a cultural thing," he said. "I do see your point and hope you accept my apology."

"That's the thing, Alistair," I said, my voice heating up. "You keep doing crap that you have to apologize for. Maybe think about things before you make a move. So yes, to answer your question, yes, I'm upset. It feels—I think it's very odd the way you do things. The way you keep secrets."

"I'll work on it, try to do better," he said, begging with his eyes.

"If it were my decision, I wouldn't do this project, but Sam is making me. I'm not sure it's the best plan for us to be working together. Not right now, fresh out of rehab. Especially now, after having sex."

"Very well," he said. "I will call Sam and tell him that he can design the loft. I was hoping to work with you."

"You don't need to do that, but you should have asked me," I said. Frustrated. Irritated. Actually fuming. He backed down so easily. Never put up a fight. It would be different if he were learning something, but I wasn't sure he was capable. I had seen the same thing with my father.

"I will make things right," he said. "Please forgive me. There has been a lot going on between finding my sister, leaving rehab, work.

I'm probably not thinking straight."

"It's alright," I said, pulling him in for a hug. Hurting someone was not my preference, but standing up for myself was imperative. "I'm flattered that you believed in my talents, but I wish you would have talked to me about it first." The idea that he simply wanted to get in my pants through all of this manipulation rolled through my mind. When I was close enough to his ear, I whispered, "What happened the other day, neither of us are ready for that. I'm not saying never, I'm just saying that right now, I can't."

I wanted to know him better, but on my terms. And my terms needed to involve caution and patience. My desire to move fast had always been a problem for me in the past.

Chapter Thirty-Two: Prue Present

Tom chose soft drinks and sparkling water to serve with dinner, which left a zero chance of drunken misconduct. Bouquets of yellow roses, white tulips, and bright-pink Gerber daisies decorated the long, narrow table. He claimed they were Gloria's favorite. I found his display of generosity mixed with this sticky-sweet thoughtfulness to be curious, even off-putting.

Would he ever meet another woman like Gloria?

I couldn't help but wonder about his wife, and if she was at all relieved about Gloria passing. Relationships were complex. An affair was simply the result of something already broken. I knew that first hand.

Tom saved us from playing musical chairs with name cards at each seat. Perhaps he anticipated drama or secret agendas. He was smarter than he appeared, more thoughtful, deeper, and even controlling. A man like that would put me right in the grave. My soul needed freedom and trust.

When I'm not being controlled, I can be trusted; when I'm not being trusted, I can't be controlled. Exhibit A: Nick.

Lily jabbed me in the ribs. Mike headed toward our table. I jumped up. "You're here."

"Bloody hell." Alistair shook Mike's hand. "Great to see you. After you left Serenity, things just weren't the same. You are irreplaceable.

That gym is damned blessed to have you." There was an unsteadiness to Alistair, as if he needed something solid underneath his feet to act as a ballast.

"Thanks, great to see everyone again," Mike said.

It was the first time I had seen Mike in jeans. They were well-worn, faded, and fit him in a way that made my scalp prickly. He wore sneakers and a polo shirt I had seen him wear in rehab.

Tom showed Mike his seat. "Michael, glad you could make it. I'm Tom, here's your key. Charge whatever you want to the room."

"Please, call me Mike, and wow." Mike held the plastic room key card like it was the holy grail. "Thank you. This means a lot to me, the opportunity for closure around Gloria's passing." He tapped the card on his palm.

Tom whispered something to Mike. They both nodded. Mike looked toward the floor. The realization that he was deeply hurt over Gloria hit me in the gut. Time for me to focus more on others and less on myself. The narcissist needed to go.

I sat between Lily and Susie, with Mike to her right. Mitch, his partner, and Alistair settled across from us while Tom held court at the head of the table.

I related to Gloria's attraction to Tom. Money had lured me in as well. The idea of never struggling again, moving beyond a poverty-stricken childhood, was quite appealing to people like us.

The banter that evening had a lively, positive, hopeful energy. Susie and Mike talked mostly to each other. I fought pangs of envy. After the laughter from one of Mitch's funny stories subsided, Tom tapped his water glass with a spoon and stood.

"Thank you all for being here for Gloria." He commanded our attention with his powerful presence. "Her bright light burned out far too soon." His Adam's apple punctuated the sentiment before he continued.

"I felt alone before I met Gloria. The truth is, she saved me. She taught me how to find joy in the small victories of life and to not take things too seriously."

I fought back tears. As the honesty in his speech intensified, Tom's voice began to soften and shrink. His pain became evident and contagious, opening the hearts of nearly everyone present.

He cleared his throat before continuing. "I'm sorry that I couldn't save you from your demons. Goddammit, I wanted to."

He began to sob, and so did every single person at the table. The waiter passed around napkins and filled water glasses. We wept for the dark places hidden within our hearts, for our told and untold stories, for the depth of pain from loved ones lost, for the tight spaces that held us captive. Up until this moment, we had expressed our emotions in our own unique ways. We had built separate walls, each one fortified and closed off from the other. But in this moment, it was as if Gloria had snuck in through the window to plant a kiss on our cheeks. The tea light candles on the table twinkled with a heavenly, celestial feeling that circulated through the room. And just like that, we became one.

*   *   *

True to his word, Tom graciously picked up the tab. Every once in a while, Mitch stepped outside for a smoke. Lily patted her stomach and complained about being too full. I avoided berating myself over food and made a promise not to pour salt on the next dessert that landed in front of me. All a part of my healing journey.

Tom took the chair beside me. The ice ball clinked rhythmically in his Scotch glass. Lily, Susie, and Alistair sat in a line on the sofa. Susie molded well with everyone, being a misfit like the rest of us. Alistair focused on her. A welcomed reprieve. The body language screamed of someone who was trying super hard: small laughs, nods, and a gentle head tilt. The casual way his leg crossed in her direction. I respected the value of family, especially now that mine only consisted of my brother, Christian, and me. Mrs. Sutton would be gone soon, too.

Alistair's sudden burst of energy kept me from my impending slow descent. He wove a new yarn to entertain us with, dry and a bit bawdy, but perfect to stave off the inevitable moroseness intent on setting in at such gatherings. Yet something seemed off. He was never one to force his emotions, but he was clearly attempting to convince everyone of his happiness.

"Would either of you like a drink? An aperitif?" Tom, the quintessential host.

Lily put her phone down and provided us with her undivided attention. "A glass of chardonnay. Prue, you want one?"

"I would like a Coke," Alistair said. He looked over to me, expecting some type of reassurance.

"Chardonnay, please." I gave Alistair's knee a pat. "And a Coke. There, I decided for you."

"Thank you for saving me the stress of such a huge decision." The easiness between old friends concealed the unspoken.

We both remained guarded. I was still struggling over everything being unresolved. All the odd lies told I assumed were out of habit or fear or something worse. I was disappointed that I lacked the discipline and wherewithal to say no to his sexual advances. When I had first returned home from rehab and saw Christian, the guilt I left at Serenity Hills had come rushing back. I needed to do better. More disciplined. Christian deserved a mother who was present. The walls of Serenity Hills were not surrounding me and Alistair. The only thing stopping us now was ourselves—or rather, myself.

The waitress delivered a round of drinks. I admired my mother's watch. Sometimes grace comes to you, a moment when you realize you hold in your hands everything you want in the world. Small and fragile, like crystal, because what we desire moment to moment is so mutable.

Joy filled me. Friends that I adored all together, laughing and sharing. My sister and bestie, Lily, sitting next to me. Nick, cloudy in the rearview mirror. I asserted myself and took my time with what could be someone to share my life with. I worked in a fulfilling career with a truly amazing son. *What would my mother say?* I gazed at the floor and said a prayer of gratitude for my unsurmountable blessings.

"Where are you from, Tom?" I heard Lily ask.

Alistair's thigh pressed against mine. I slid mine away.

"I grew up in the DC area." Tom made eye contact as he spoke. "Moved to LA when I started my firm in nineteen-ninety." He sipped his cocktail and crossed an ankle over a knee to reveal red-and-blue striped socks. I found him to be pleasant, perhaps even attractive.

Alistair's light touch ignited memories of our tryst, but I pushed them down. A contented silence grew inside me as the elevated spirits of our Serenity Hills group bounced off one another.

Tom's aura was unassuming. I could picture Gloria and him at dinner, or in a retro record shop, but I struggled to envision them banging it out.

Sweating, pumping, moaning.

I caught myself.

Stop, Prue.

As I sank in the habitual sexualizing, a bruising, sickening fear entered, and flashes of me and Tom instead of Gloria and Tom.

You meet Gloria's man tonight, at her fucking memorial, and you're fucking him in your mind!

I fought to shake it loose. Entirely sick of the social niceties. I wanted to ask how Tom started cheating on his wife and screwing Gloria. I turned to Tom. "Do you still go to strip clubs?"

"Filter!" Lily nearly threw her hand over my mouth. "I'm so sorry, my friend has an issue with boundaries. Please disregard the question."

"All good." Tom spoke in an easy manner like I had known him forever. He picked up the chair, the one strategically placed by the interior designer for the Four Seasons, and moved it closer to us.

"I prefer not to yell this across the lobby." Tom went on to say that he had endured a sexless marriage for ten years before Gloria. He'd slowly begun to lose his mind. On a business trip to Vegas, he overindulged in alcohol and found himself in a strip club. His intention was to merely observe the women, then go to his room. "That night, I met Gloria."

I could feel myself quieting, the anger and shame giving ground to my curiosity.

"What captivated you about her?" She had cast a spell on me, too.

"Her beauty." He held a distant look in his eyes. "She was super sweet and kind."

"I agree."

"Gloria was a warm-hearted woman who will be missed." The generic, neutral description, not the norm for Alistair. "When I heard about that father of hers, well, I'm not surprised she carried around a bag full of demons." The comment put a cloud over our little group, so profound that we couldn't work our way back from it.

"We're going to sleep." John laid a chin on Mitch's shoulder. "We're exhausted. See you all in the morning. We'll be at breakfast, whoever wants to join us." They walked to the elevator. I stood. Lily followed.

"Tom," I said, "thank you for a lovely dinner."

There were far too many snares for my drained mind to navigate in the same room with Alistair and Mike. All the excitement left me edgy and sexually frustrated. My nervous tics were making a grand entrance.

"I'll come up with you guys." I worried about leaving Mike, but most of us were inches away from a spiral. We had to be up early to get on the boat when the seas were calm. Back in the room, Lily took off her shoes and made herself comfortable.

"Many unanswered questions, but I need to let them go." I rubbed the tension from my shoulders. "Gloria loved him, and after what he did tonight, he clearly loved her too."

Lily nodded. Billie Holiday sang to us as we finished our wine. We brushed our teeth side by side, pulled back the sumptuous covers of each of our respective beds, and crawled underneath. Within a moment of my head hitting the pillow, I began to drift off to sleep.

Lily's phone dinged. "Hey, babe." She moved to the other room, closing the French doors behind her. I honored the respect she gave her relationship, the sanctity of privacy that I'd blatantly disregarded in my marriage. I needed to learn from my mistakes, to do better, and improve as a person.

My phone buzzed.

Good night, Prudence. I'm laying my head down on my pillow full of hope. One of them is the chance to know more about you and see what the future might hold for us. xo A

Lily settled back in her bed.

"Night. I love you," I said.

"I know."

*   *   *

The hotel phone rang and jolted me awake.

"Hello?" Lily mouthed, "It's Mike." Her eyes lit up. I took the receiver from her.

"Hey." I wrapped the cord around my finger.

"I'm sorry to call so late, just wondering if you might want to meet in the restaurant." Everything inside me tingled when I heard his voice. "Grab a cup of coffee or something."

"Yes, I would love to meet you for a coffee." I hung up and shot Lily a look of excitement. After digging through my clothes, I put on ripped jeans and a black t-shirt. I sat on an adjacent chair to lace up my sneakers.

"Aren't you proud I remembered this?" I held up the room key. "Don't wait up, no clue how long we'll talk."

Lily smiled in a supportive way, but around its edges lingered some concern.

When the door opened, it took a moment to register my whereabouts. I passed the giant bouquet and leaned in to smell the flowers again.

As I turned into the restaurant, I slowed my pace. I didn't want to miss finding Mike or appear too eager. I scanned the dimly lit room.

A hand waved from the far corner. I waved back. My mouth went dry.

"Hey." He stood to pull out the chair beside him, which made it less awkward for me to decide where to sit. A black coffee rested in front of him. The waitress delivered a small silver creamer pitcher. On the saucer were two lumps of dark brown sugar and a biscotti.

"This is probably the most expensive coffee I've had in my life."

"Welcome to the Four Seasons. Cha-ching." My finger waved through the air. "Would you mind if I ordered a glass of wine?" Not holding back from being myself. "I'm a little nervous." Heat radiated through my cheeks. "I'm also a horrible sleeper." My hands flew around as I spoke like in an Italian movie. "The teensiest bit of caffeine will keep me up all night staring at the ceiling."

Commence with the garlic milkshake. Was he analyzing my every word? How could he not? That was his job. *He can't just turn that switch off.*

"Order whatever you'd like." Our server showed off her sexy figure in a fitted, plunging top. I acutely regretted my frumpy outfit choice. *What am I thinking? I'm at the Four Seasons in Beverly Hills.*

Mike wore the same clothes he had on earlier. I sat close enough to catch a faint whiff of cologne or fresh soap I couldn't decide which.

How big do stomach butterflies get?

"A glass of chardonnay, please, something buttery."

"Can we see a menu?" When the waitress walked away, Mike turned to me. "I'm a little nervous too. When I feel that way, I eat." He smiled, and so did his eyes, super warm and genuine.

"Why are you nervous?" I kept my hands quiet and avoided incessant fidgeting. The server brought my wine, two menus, and three small bowls with nuts, olives, and sesame sticks. I grabbed a few of each and popped them in my mouth.

"I have some difficult news." The sugar lumps sank to the bottom. His hand appeared oversized by the tiny spoon. The cream swirled through the dark liquid. The guy made coffee look so epic that I craved one for myself. The biscotti flipped off the dish when he set the cup back in the saucer. "Do you want this? The darned thing is wreaking havoc on my drink situation." I accepted the cookie and ate it in one bite.

I felt as though I might be dreaming, sitting next to my therapist and group leader from Serenity Hills. He knew every gory detail of my life and still talked to me.

He tapped his fingertips on the rim. "Thank you for coming down to see me." Our eyes met. My heart beat like a high-school marching band.

"I'm dying. What do you need to tell me?" I turned into a pool of melted butter. A voice told me to say something outrageous so he would start laughing. That might have worked for someone else. The old Prue who filled emotional voids with humor couldn't fly through these woods. She would hit a tree.

"I first want to say that I have permission to share this with you."

He took a sip of coffee while I assessed every inch of his face. I folded the cocktail napkin around the base of my glass. The glow of the candle flickered against his skin. At Serenity, he kept his face clean-shaven, but a shadow of a beard gave him a tough edge. It suited him. I wanted to tell him as much, and more. I was hard-pressed not to spew a line of compliments all over him. The space between us became charged with nervous energy. I retreated to the menu, a stall tactic I had learned from the best, Nick.

Perhaps I didn't want to hear whatever he had to tell me. What if it was bad news? I pretended to ponder what I wanted even though I already knew. "For some reason, the fries are calling my name."

"Me too!" Common ground brought us unity.

The server with all her telepathic skills came by with her pad and pen in the ready position. The room now bustled with chic, elegant people probably post-partying after some swanky event.

"An order of fries, please." The waitress took my menu. "We might get something else, so is it alright if we keep the menus?" Mike held on as she tried to take it from him.

The respect a person shows for service workers told me a lot about their character. *Rude to someone who serves you, a definite deal-breaker.* She probably wondered why such an attractive guy dined with a slouch like me. I self-consciously adjusted my posture. Mike waited until she had walked a safe distance away before he began talking again. Discretion must be like breathing to him, and something that I frankly could have used a little more of in my life.

"Susie came to me regarding something about Alistair."

"Really?" I was confused and mildly irritated that Susie was Mike's new BFF and confidant. "When?"

Mike dragged his hand along his jawline. "Well, we spoke during dinner and a moment after, while everyone moved to the lobby."

I wound the napkin around my finger. "I did see you two having a quiet conversation and was curious about what you were talking about."

The French fries were truffled and arrived with a dish of mayonnaise, aioli, and catsup. "They don't do anything half-assed in here." An overwhelming display of fries. I took the initiative and dragged a crispy fry through the mayo, then the catsup. *A party in my mouth.* He followed my lead.

"I've never mixed mayo with fries." I watched his evaluation face, much milder when assessing starch versus psychological states. "Not bad."

"I got into it while traveling in Europe." *You know, blowing Roger all over London and Milan.* Everything I said had a story attached to it, and he knew them all. "You were saying something about Alistair?" I couldn't wait another minute to hear the reveal. Equal parts curious and terrified.

"Susie told me that Alistair relapsed and is using cocaine again." He stared into his coffee as though the liquid held the answers to all our problems.

My stomach twisted in a knot. "Are you sure? I can't believe it. I'm sickened and saddened."

Had I been responsible for his relapse? Was it my fault? I wanted to cry and run to Alistair's room to confront him, or maybe tell him I was sorry for everything. I feigned shock, even though Alistair's relapse was something I had subconsciously expected. His lies were the first clue.

Mike continued. "From what I gather, he hasn't been attending meetings. The program only works if you work it. This is not your fault. He set himself up to fail."

"What can I do to help?" The napkin slid to the floor. I leaned over and picked it up. With the napkin back in hand, I continued twisting away.

"I'm glad you asked." A plan had been under construction. "We need to face this head-on. We're going to pick up Susie, and the three of us are going to talk to him."

"Won't that be ganging up?" I was not entirely sure I wanted to be a part of this confrontation. I didn't love the idea of Alistair associating me with something so traumatic.

"We're not confronting him. We are approaching this with care and concern for his well-being. Tell him we're here for him and that we are aware he has relapsed. The secrets are as toxic as the relapse. He needs to understand with an open, caring heart."

Mike flagged the waitress while I searched for the nearest exit. I could run away and never come back. This was not my first time facing an addict. I remembered the time my father left me and Henry after one of his all-night benders. His drugged-out girlfriend tore his house apart while two kids watched in horror. The intervention with my father had not gone well. He needed to hit his own form of rock bottom before checking himself into rehab.

I chewed my cuticles. "Shouldn't people come to this on their own? I mean, I'm not an expert, but my dad didn't do shit when my brother and I confronted him. He kept using for six more months before he sought treatment."

"Alistair needs us." Mike spoke with confidence and wanted me to buy in. "He is in a life-threatening situation and has already hit bottom. I want to get a pulse check on his emotional well-being and tell him he has options."

The bill was left on the table between us. "I've got this," I said, half-joking since Tom was paying our room bills and told us to charge whatever we wanted. Mike stood, and I reluctantly followed. The elevator took forever. I wanted to jump out of my skin. The only thing keeping my head on straight was self-assured, stoic Mike.

He slid a paper from his back pocket, the room listing Tom gave us when we checked in. "She's in 1021." After a few false turns, we stood at the door. Mike lightly knocked.

"Hey." Susie popped out. "I've been waiting for you guys." She could have passed for fifteen in her leggings, hoodie, and Vans.

"Let's chat in your room," Mike said. We huddled like a football team before the snap. I fought the urge to slip under the bed and hide. I began to shake the way I had when my dad snorted lines.

"I'm scared," I said. My fight-or-flight kicked in.

"No doubt." Mike kept us on task no matter what. "But you're here, and that speaks volumes." He gave me an encouraging smile before continuing. "The most important thing we can do is assure him that we are concerned about him. He has a support system he can lean on." Mike, back to the role of the therapist. "Are you committed to being there for him, to take his calls when he's weak?" We both gave a delicate nod. "Alright, let's head over."

Mike knocked on Alistair's door. It took a moment for him to answer. Long enough for me to picture every scenario I could possibly imagine. Alistair saw my face first. He greeted us with a smile that quickly turned. "What's going on?"

"May we come in?" The envisioned barnstorm didn't happen. Instead, Mike waited for permission.

"Sure." The television was on, the volume barely audible. There was an open laptop on the desk and a file folder with neatly stacked papers resting beside it. "Just getting some work done." His confusion lasted a few seconds. "Oh, Lord, I know what this is about." As he fell onto the sofa, he dropped his head into his hands.

Susie settled next to him. Mike and I took the adjacent chairs. The coffee table provided a buffer between us. He had taught us not to overpower someone when dealing with a difficult subject.

The silence killed me, agonizing silence. I wanted to scream and knock him into reality. The only thing I could do was rub my ear.

I was no better. I had relapsed as well, failed to wait ninety days before fucking someone.

Susie put a hand on his knee. "I had to tell them. I'm sorry."

"I understand," Alistair spoke to the floor, shaking his head.

I pushed back the brewing tears until I couldn't anymore. My words came out scratchy. "I'm so sad for you and feel responsible."

Alistair glanced over at me. "Looks like someone is still codependent."

I crossed my legs under me to make myself small. "Clearly still codependent," I said.

"We're here because we care about you." Mike spoke with the same tone as when someone was having a meltdown in group therapy, commanding yet nonjudgmental. "Want to tell us what happened?"

"Not really." An unnatural laugh spilled out. "But I suspect that you won't leave until I do."

Mike took the remote and turned off the TV.

"Bloody fucking hell." Alistair pressed his palms in his eye sockets. A group passed by with post-party voices and laughter. "I guess I didn't deal with my emotions appropriately, and everything piled up until I imploded." It appeared as though he wasn't sure if we were buying his story.

"What happened?" We had no choice but to respond when Mike asked us a question.

"I relapsed. Is that what you want me to say?" Alistair's tone screamed with defensiveness while I cringed from the sidelines.

"When? How many times?" The same uneasy sensations I had from rehab emerged when someone else confessed in therapy and I lived their pain.

"The day Prue and I went over to my loft, my deal closed. I decided to celebrate. In hindsight, I realize it wasn't the most stellar idea." We all stayed quiet. I made a point to keep my expression soft. "George purchased the blow at my request. For the record, I also asked him to make a therapy appointment."

"Have you been working the program?" Mike leaned in. "Going to meetings and securing a sponsor?"

I squirmed. How would I react to being bombarded with questions? This tough-love approach would have snapped me in half by now.

"I haven't." Fresh yet brutal honesty. "After I did blow again, everything ached. My head pounded and my stomach burned like hell. When I checked out of rehab, I failed to appropriately handle the stressors of everyday life. The curveballs that I glossed over with a coating of cocaine. The strip club when I was there trying to find my sister became a trigger. The triggers came out of the woodwork." To witness his sense of defeat was both painful and an honor. "I didn't know myself anymore, who I was before, and how to handle things without this crutch I had depended on for so long. Then my business started causing me trouble. I had severe issues communicating with Prue. Everything I did was misinterpreted. The downward spiral began, and I couldn't stop it. When the deal went through, I crumbled."

"Were you alone?" Non-threatening yet firm. "The more details you can give, the better I can understand."

"Yes and no." His cheeks turned red and blotchy. He glanced at me. I looked away. "When George went to get the drugs, I visited the lobby bar at my hotel. I met someone. She joined me in the room." I unwillingly moaned. "I'm sorry, Prue."

"Is George aware that you were in rehab?" Mike shoved his hands in his pockets.

"Yes, and when I asked him if I had a problem before rehab, he said yes."

"Yet he was still willing to go out and buy drugs for you." Mike stating the obvious—for effect, I supposed.

"Well, he works for me." I played marble statue while Alistair spilled.

"I'm not placing blame, but the idea is to set you up to succeed, and George must be a part of your sober team." Mike checked off his list of co-conspirators. "Would it be alright if I had a word with him?"

"He won't have any issue with being told not to buy me blow." The color left his face. I worried he might faint.

"Let's regroup. None of this is George's fault. You can score drugs anytime you want. No one can police you, but we can be there for you. Take a call day or night, be your sobriety team. All three of us are committed to doing that for you." Susie and I agreed in unison. "Getting George on board will only add to the strength of the group." And before Alistair could answer, Mike continued. "I would like to extend an offer to be your sponsor."

"Really." He looked hopeful. "You would do that for me?"

"Of course." Mike struck the yin and yang of business with soul. "Be prepared to work the steps, attend meetings, see a therapist, and check in with me every single day." Mike may as well have been at Serenity the way he leaned against the desk. "If you dive down the rabbit hole into another relapse, I would like you to commit to living in an aftercare facility for one year."

Alistair took a moment. My stress levels dropped. If anyone could help keep Alistair on the program, it would be Mike. "I'm ready to start my new life. I didn't like anything about the next morning. The whole experience gave me a rude awakening."

"I'm so relieved." The pain of the situation eased from Susie's face. "You had me worried."

"It makes me feel good to know that you care." Alistair's eyes glistened. Susie wrapped her arms around him while he sobbed on her shoulders.

Mike tapped my arm and ushered me from the room. Susie and I waited outside the door while he and Alistair had a word alone. I strained to grasp what was being discussed between them. Susie was scanning her Instagram while I focused on listening. It seemed as though she couldn't deal with the harsh reality of finding her long-lost brother and dealing with his drug problem all at the same time.

As my ears grew accustomed to their soft voices, I began catching a word here and there. I for sure heard my name mentioned a few times. When Alistair began talking, his tone increased enough for me to hear.

"I see the way you look at her, Mike."

Mike attempted to interject, but Alistair stopped him.

"I'm not stupid," Alistair said. "There's something between you and Prue that is undeniable."

Mike said something in response, but he spoke so softly I couldn't make out his words. The door opened and the two of them walked out into the hallway. Alistair gave me an encouraging smile, which hit me in the gut considering he was the one about to check back into rehab. Mike followed with rosy, flushed cheeks. I had never seen Mike blush before and wondered if the heat in his face had something to do with me, or if it was about getting Alistair situated in rehab.

*   *   *

Lily had a book propped in front of her face when I got back to the room. I peeled off my clothes, put on pajamas, and slid into bed. "What a night." The pillow-dance ritual began. "I'll tell you everything tomorrow. Sorry, I'm just fried."

"Good night." Lily put the book on the bedside table and turned off the lamp.

I replayed the course of events like a movie I had seen at the theatre but not actually lived. The time alone with Mike, the way he took charge of handling Alistair's relapse, how he gathered the troops. The ambient sounds of chattering people and clinking china drowned out the intensity of our conversation. Alistair had worked to garner my attention, and everything he did fell flat. Perhaps I had been too hard on him and hadn't considered all he was handling and how much he white-knuckled his recovery.

As I relaxed in the sheets, the clarity I craved overcame me like a deity handing me a gift. My body relaxed with a floating sensation. I could not and must not pursue a relationship with Alistair.

Chapter Thirty-Three: Prue Present

I was confident Lily wouldn't mention to anyone that I had rendez-voused with Mike the night before in the lobby bar. We jockeyed for mirror space to get ready for the boat ride where we would say our goodbyes to Gloria. I wondered if she'd sprinkled her angel dust over us the entire weekend.

Lily checked out my outfit and gave the stamp of approval: "Ohmygod, you look amazing."

When Lily and I took our coffee to the living room, I told her everything that had happened the previous night. She listened, and the only thing she said was that I could not date Alistair.

"I know." The old me, always needing advice and validation. "It all became clear last night. He said he would call Sam and request him to be the lead designer on his project, but I don't want to bail on him when he's down. This is when I have to put my agenda aside and be available for him."

"You are evolving, and it makes me so proud. I'm shocked that you aren't freaking out that the exact same day you banged him, he was doing blow in a hotel room with another woman. I mean, that's just too much." The story of disgust was plain to see on Lily's face.

"I turned into my old self the moment we finished the act. You know, my habit of shutting down emotionally and turning to stone. I'm obviously not ready for real intimacy. What matters now is that he gets better. All I can do is look ahead. No point in harping on the past."

"True." Never short on words, but this time, she was.

"While I'm here, I want to focus on Gloria."

Gloria would never plan a wedding or bear a child. The darkness had taken over any remaining light. Some days I wished my life would end, but as I sat next to Lily, I was filled with hope. Lily teared up. I wrapped my arms around her. "I feel so blessed to have you as a friend."

Lily sighed. "I don't know what I'd do without you," she said. We crossed pinkies the way we had when we were kids to make a pinkie promise. But this time, we were promising to always care for each other, no matter what, and to never take our friendship for granted.

We delivered our bags to the bellhop, ordered two fresh to-go coffees, and walked out front. A shuttle was waiting to transport us to Marina Del Rey. Mike was already seated in the back. He was timely like that.

"Morning." I raised my cup. "How did you sleep?"

"The best in that soft, fluffy bed." A clean-shaven face with smooth, luminous skin. His eyes complemented the shirt. The perfect backdrop for the sea. Lily turned and said hello. She took in his expression, assessed him, captured his vibe, and then smiled.

"I slept like a baby too," I said.

Tom arrived next. He waved with a somber smile and unrested eyes. Mitch and John zipped up the steps and sat in the row across from us. They were wearing tonally complementary outfits, the way I envisioned every in-sync couple dressed.

"You guys are so adorable." I enjoyed seeing how everyone had rallied.

"We wanted to go all-out for Gloria." A waft of spicy cologne hit me as Mitch passed.

I gave him a nod. "She would have loved everything."

Alistair and Susie arrived last. Susie wore a pink miniskirt that matched her pink-tipped hair. Alistair coordinated in a navy sport coat with a hot-pink pocket square and a pink-and-white-striped button-down.

Once everyone boarded the bus, Tom stood and gave a small speech from the front. My sadness rose to my throat. Funerals weren't just attended by those who remained but also brought memories of the ones who left us too soon: Gram, my mother, my daughter. The guardian angels flew around with their soft white wings.

Anticipation equaled expectations. Everything had dragged us down. We couldn't top the previous evening's events. The addicts became restless, each of them preoccupied with thoughts of reality, of how they would endure another day without their drug of choice.

We moved along the dock to where the boat was waiting for us. The seagulls sang overhead, flags moved in the breeze, halyard lines clanged and chimed. Tom led us, carrying Gloria's ashes.

Everyone was in tears, even Alistair. Susie took his elbow. We removed our shoes as we boarded. My feet grounded me on the deck. Mitch took my hand. We headed to the bow as the boat pulled out of the harbor. Mike and Lily followed while we hid behind the safety net of dark sunglasses. Tom, Alistair, and Susie sat inside. The wind whipped around, so we huddled together.

Mitch dropped his chin to his chest. "God bless you, sweet angel." He wiped the tears that were pooling under his glasses.

Mike looked ahead, his hands clasped in his lap. We came around the jetty and headed out to sea. We passed a regatta of small sailboats.

Lily watched with eagle eyes as they rounded a mark. I looked over and smiled, remembering the day I had stuffed the spinnaker wrong, the day she forgave me.

The sound of the anchor dropping informed us of our arrival at Gloria's final resting place.

Tom emerged from the cabin. The others followed close behind. "It's time."

He carried Gloria. We gathered at the stern, holding hands like when we recited the Serenity Prayer at the end of a meeting. A bouquet of flowers, a basket of rose petals, and a Holy Bible were laid out on a small table. Tom put the box down and picked up the Bible. He pulled his reading glasses from his pocket then opened a page marked with a satin ribbon.

"Though I walk through the valley of the shadow of death, I will fear no evil; for

Thou art with me; Thy rod and Thy staff, they comfort me.

And if I go and prepare a place for you, I will come back and take you to be with me that you also may be where I am

A time to be born and a time to die, a time to plant and a time to uproot, a time to kill and a time to heal, a time to tear down and a time to build, a time to weep and a time to laugh, a time to mourn and a time to dance . . ."

Alistair began to sob. I lost it. We must forgive ourselves. It was time to look ahead and open our hearts to those who needed us the most. I wrapped an arm around him.

"You will get through this, and I am here for you."

"I'm so sorry for everything." The agony on Alistair's face stabbed me in the chest.

"It's alright." No point in beating him up any more than he was probably already doing to himself.

We all crumbled. Mitch leaned heavily into John's arms. The many hardships endured from his alcoholism created a bond. A testament to the power of love and forgiveness. John consoled him, whispering in his ear. I imagined the magic that Gloria spread with her spirit.

"Let's bow our heads in prayer." If I didn't know better, I might have mistaken Tom for a preacher. "May you rest in peace, my darling. I will miss your sweet, bright smile and the way you made everything more fun. Thank you for all the blessings you brought to me and so many others."

Mike dropped his face in his hands. His shoulders rolled forward as he wept. I stepped over to him and held him. The tissues were plucked from the box then passed along. I absorbed the irony of our roles being reversed. I glanced up to the sky.

Tom picked up the box holding Gloria's remains and moved to the edge of the boat. A pelican circled above. With one sweep, he released her ashes.

Lily passed around the basket of rose petals. Gloria's remains swirled around the ocean. Tom tossed the flowers then turned to us. "You may take a moment to say your goodbyes."

I released a handful of petals. "So long, sweet friend." I wiped my running nose with a crumpled tissue. "I will never forget you." I moved away for the others.

We said our farewells, uniquely tailored to our respective personalities or relationships with her. Mike waited to go last. The sea captivated with a magnificence about it as the sun danced and sparkled on the surface. He stepped closer to the water, the petals clutched in his palm. He bowed his head. Tom stood beside him, and they wept. Mitch moved closer and reached for my hand. Tears streamed down Susie's face. I imagined that she cried for us, for our loss, and for those she had lost herself.

The two men exchanged words inaudibly. Tom consoled Mike, his arm braced around his shoulder. The group moved toward them and held each other up. A ball of energy moved through me. The sea ebbed and flowed. It reminded me of life. We never predicted what direction it would take. All we could do was our best. I turned toward the floating petals one last time.

The anchor pulled up and the engine started. As the boat headed back to the harbor, I waved goodbye. Mike pressed his hands in prayer as the roses slowly disappeared. I stood, ready to help him the way he had helped me. We walked together to the bow. Those who had not been to Serenity Hills would never understand how close we had all become in such a short amount of time. Time moved faster than dog years in rehab. Each week equaled seven-plus years.

Alistair and Susie joined us as we motored home. "That was beautiful." Susie, the outsider, had stitched herself seamlessly into the group.

"I'm glad you were here," I said. Mike and I broke apart to let Alistair and his sister come between us.

"Susie and I have been talking about what happened last night." Alistair was not his usual, confident self. It was hard to witness him breaking down. "It was tough for me. Been in a bit of shock over the whole thing, but in the end, I understand why you did it that way. An intervention before the intervention."

"We needed to take the tough-love approach," Mike said. "Things appeared to be taking a turn. The best decision was to handle the situation head-on."

"Right." Alistair nodded, it seemed, to believe it himself.

I encouraged everyone to sit down where the wind wouldn't be whipping around us.

"How are you processing everything today?" Mike dug into Alistair while we all listened. "Are you ready to take everything you learned at Serenity Hills and make it work for you?"

"I don't know," Alistair said. "For a while, I thought I could drink and not do blow. Then I believed I could do a little. You know, on the weekends, or when I was celebrating something." He focused on the horizon. "Now I'm not sure I can do either. I guess having you confront me was a reality check."

I crushed the urge to save him. "We care about you, Alistair."

"I haven't had any real family. My friend works for me, and almost everyone has done what I told them to do, agreed with whatever I said. I've always been the one in control."

"No one is always in control," Mike said. "We all struggle. We all deal with daily life stress and troubles."

Alistair laughed. "You don't."

"I have plenty of problems. No one is trouble-free."

I leaned in, interested but more curious. "Yeah, I don't think I need to say that I have my fair share."

"I don't." Susie lightened the mood.

"I'm not sure I can do this on my own," Alistair said. "Cocaine preoccupies my thoughts. The addiction consumes me. I'm craving it as we sit here, especially with the emotions stirred up from this whole weekend and putting Gloria to rest."

"How about we head straight to a meeting from here?" Even though Mike made it sound like a question, we all knew it wasn't. "One hour at a time, one day at a time. Don't worry about using tomorrow, try to stay sober today."

Alistair leaned back and closed his eyes. "Tell me about your problems and I'll go with you."

"Fair enough," Mike said. "But not here. We're about to pull into the harbor. Let's regroup back at the hotel."

Chapter Thirty-Four: Prue Present

Mike took an Uber back to the hotel rather than ride with us on the bus. I figured he wanted to be alone. "Whatever you do," Mike instructed as I boarded the bus. "Don't let Alistair out of your sight." I nodded while the weight of this responsibility pressed on my shoulders.

On the shuttle back, Lily told me that I should stay to help with the Alistair situation. She offered to pick up Christian at lacrosse practice and bring him to her house.

"You seemed a little distant on the boat," I said. "Are you alright?"

What I wanted to say was that I knew she was ignoring me, icing me and giving me the cold shoulder. Lily refused to look me in the eye on the boat and had her nose high in the air. After being married to Nick, I knew when someone was giving me the silent treatment.

"Well," Lily said, "I was thinking about what you did, and you know what I realized?"

I tightened the cross of my legs. The last thing I wanted was to keep rehashing what I'd done, but I had to let Lily speak her piece. I had to allow her to be angry and handle it her way.

"Your motivation was to push me away because you struggle with feeling worthy of love." She paused. I kept my mouth zipped shut. "I believe that by me being there for you, especially when you're down, it freaks you out, so you will do anything to push me away and try to break what we have. This time more than any other."

There was still a part of me that hated confrontation, hated any sort of disagreement and strife, but this was my fault. The drama was all on me. I had to own it, every bit of it.

"There is a heaviness inside me. A fear of being a burden, like an albatross around your neck," I said.

"Sometimes, I think you're just a selfish bitch."

Lily shifted in her seat to create space between us. I cringed at the stab in my gut. A stab I wholeheartedly deserved. The rumble of the bus engine drowned out our conversation from the rest of the group.

"I don't do anything I don't want to do." Lily needed to be heard, to vent, and even though the timing of this was less than ideal, I had to let her express her feelings. "Everything I do for you is because I love you." Her lower lip began to tremble. "It's been hard for me to imagine that you would violate the foundation of our friendship and try to meddle with my marriage at the same time. It was a double whammy, Prue. It is truly unfathomable that you're so damned self-centered."

My adrenaline pumped. The name-calling hit my imaginary shield, bouncing to the floor. Evil Richard had done so much damage to my psyche with his sharp tongue and never-ending barrage of verbal abuse. I dug into my library of skills from Serenity and asked myself what part of this was mine to own and fix, what was hers. Sure, I had done something horrible, but this new reaction seemed, extreme so I held my tongue to avoid gaslighting an already volatile situation.

"I'm sorry," I said. "This will take time to get through, but I value our friendship and want to make things right." I exhaled through the nausea stirring around my gut.

"You have to do better," Lily said. "Think before you do something like that again, because I won't forgive you next time."

Her hands formed fists. I braced myself for another punch but instead, she broke down. I touched her knee while she cried, fearful some of this had to do with Richard and what she had seen. Lily's silence created a wedge between us, one I wasn't entirely sure how to work through.

"I'm sorry you had to deal with Evil Richard when we were kids," I said. A poisonous snake wound its way through my stomach. "Mike helped me with processing what happened, even in that short time."

Lily shook her head. "I've been thinking about why I punched you when I got in the ring." She stretched out her fingers. "That fucker stole my childhood, too." Her face twisted in pain.

"Yes, he did," I said. "I'm sorry." A chill ran through me. I pulled my sweater higher on my shoulders.

"Don't apologize for something you didn't do," she said. "Women need to stop apologizing."

"You're right," I said, catching myself before the words "I'm sorry" spilled out again.

I prayed this would be the last time my stepfather would have any power over us. There more than likely would be more conversations. Lily wasn't one to let go of a bone that easily, but as we pulled into the Four Seasons, I refocused my attention on Alistair.

"Thanks for getting Christian for me," I said. "I'll text you when I'm on the way to pick him up."

Lily nodded but refused to smile as she stepped off the bus and headed to her car. I breathed in with purpose, gathering my composure so I could deal with helping Alistair.

Mitch and John headed straight to the airport to fly back to Atlanta. Susie had to go to work at Bare Elegance. That left me, Mike, and

Alistair alone to deal with everything Alistair had told us on the boat. We expressed our gratitude to Tom for putting the event together. A thickness coated our goodbyes since we were well aware that he was heading home to be with his wife.

Alistair dipped out like a stealth bomber. George waited out front of the hotel in the idling car. I ran to stop him, but he wouldn't listen and said he needed to do some work. "Whenever you guys want me, you can find me."

Mike pulled up in time for him to put a kibosh on the situation. He leaned in the window to speak to George. "Alistair will be with me this afternoon," Mike said. It sounded more like a command than an ask. "I'll make sure he gets back to his hotel."

George appeared nervous and dodgy. Alistair gave him a nod, and his friend drove away.

The three of us were hungry, so we headed to the restaurant to grab lunch and map out a plan. We tailed Mike like children following a parent. Alistair and I exchanged a few words, but this was more serious than anything we'd had on our past agendas. I craved a glass of wine but knew better than to order alcohol during a time like this.

"You wanted to hear about my problems." Mike never gave up on us, not ever.

"I was half-joking." Alistair kept his face in the menu. "You do seem superhuman. Nothing permeates the Mike barrier."

I laughed, mostly out of nervousness. I was curious and had to agree with Alistair about the Great Oz.

"I'm happy to share some personal struggles with you, but I want some answers first." Mike rolled up his sleeves. Alistair nodded. I was nothing more than a voyeur watching the scene unfold, not participating but thrilled to be included. "How did you feel the morning after using? You had been clean over ninety days, and your sobriety was broken."

"I have been drinking far too much, so my sobriety was brimming on sketchy." Alistair laughed, but no one laughed with him. "I'm angry at myself, repulsed at how weak I am, and depressed, which is normal with cocaine."

"Did you do anything else that night that you normally wouldn't have done had you not been high?" Alistair squirmed. I thought about going to the bathroom and staying there for about an hour.

"For Christ's sake. I told you I had a woman in the room with me." Alistair pushed his plate to the side. "I can't even eat. This conversation is making me sick. Quite painful to reenact that night."

"Do you understand where I'm heading with this?" Mike's voice softened, which complemented his non-threatening body language.

"That I become someone else when I'm high. Someone I loathe, someone who has no morals and no scruples." Alistair propped his chin in his hands.

"What I would like to do today is take you straight from here to a sober-living facility." Mike dropped the news without pause. "I made a few phone calls on my way back from the boat. A room became available in Malibu, and they are holding it for you. The facility is discreet with a strong track record. I pulled a favor to score you a spot. The waitlist is a mile long, and you were bumped up to the top." Mike faced Alistair head-on. "If you don't check into a facility, you are going to die."

My hand jumped. The spoon sailed to the floor. I froze. Alistair slid back his chair and stood. "No fucking way." Every head turned. "You can't do this to me." He began to shake.

Mike eased him back to seated then crouched next to him. "Listen to me," Mike said. "You can't white-knuckle through this, you won't make it."

Alistair started to cry. Not regular tears, but snotty, blubbering tears. That made me want to cry with him. I inched closer and rubbed his back, helpless yet devastated for him.

"Don't you think I know?" He slid the napkin from his lap and blew his nose. "I hate who I am, who I've become." He shook his head. His hands trembled. "So much to lose, but blow wins time and time again."

"Don't let it win anymore," Mike commanded. "This is your chance to take everything you learned at Serenity Hills and make it work for you. Invest in yourself. Gain strength, because while you are sober, the addict is doing push-ups and sit-ups—gaining strength to break you down. You must be in tip-top shape to fight your inner demons."

"I'll bring anything you need," I said, "and will visit you every week." I was the perpetual codependent cheerleader. "When you check out of sober living, your loft will be all decorated."

Alistair stared at me, his eyes glassy and glazed over. He nodded, his body folded in defeat. Mike lifted him from the chair. His car was waiting out front. I was in awe of his powers, his magic, the way he genuinely cared. I took the back seat and Alistair sat in front, our roller bags stacked in the back of his SUV. Mike drove us out of the Four Seasons parking lot and called the sober-living facility. "We're on the way." He checked the navigation. "Catch you in about an hour."

I leaned back in the seat, drained and devoid of emotion. I gazed out the window. It occurred to me that the psychic Madam Beatriz had been right all along. Every word she said washed over. She predicted smooth seas ahead. All I had to do was listen to my gut. I looked at Mike's profile as he drove. My whole body felt alive.

My Ace of Cups.

"Alistair," Mike said, "I promised to tell you some of my troubles, and I think now is the time for me to share them with you."

I held my breath, afraid to break the beautiful rhythm.

Alistair stared at the road, his posture stiff and erect. "I'm ready. Got nothing but time on my hands."

I loosened the seatbelt and leaned closer to the front. Once he started sharing, neither of us said a word. I didn't want Mike to stop, and I figured Alistair didn't either. While we sat as witnesses, he broke the barriers between us, changing the parameters of our relationship from patient and therapist to peers, perhaps even friends.

We rode along the Pacific Coast Highway as we passed through Santa Monica and entered Malibu. The traffic was moving well. After we flew through two green lights, the cars slowed and we came to a screeching halt.

"For a moment," Alistair said, "I forgot about my problems. It was such a fucking relief."

"I'm glad," Mike said. "You're going to be alright. Embrace the process, do the work, follow the rules. You will come out on top." He smiled at Alistair while I sat quietly in the back. The cars began to move again.

"Bloody hell," Alistair said, running his hands through his already tousled hair. He twisted in the car seat to address me. "I've done one more thing behind your back. Well, I was trying to do something nice, but now that I'm a bit more clear-headed, I think it was sort of presumptuous."

I gripped the edge of the seat, bracing for what could possibly happen next. "What did you do?"

"Well," Alistair said, and a deep exhale followed. "I booked a casita for us at San Ysidro Ranch for this weekend. It's a hotel in Santa Barbara. Thought it might be nice for us to get away together. Was going to surprise you." His eyes were void of emotion, dark, cavernous holes.

"Oh, Alistair." I reached a hand to touch his shoulder. "Your heart is in the right place, but yeah, that would have not been the best plan for us. Not right now, at least." It was important to come across as grateful and kind. No point in continuing to punch someone on the ground. "I've heard about that hotel but have never been." I glanced out the window, a bit sad that I would probably never get to go, at least not on my budget. "Why don't you call right now and see if you can cancel?"

Alistair typed something into his phone. "You should go, take Christian and get away for a few days. I just emailed you the reservation information." My mind scrolled through my calendar, trying to remember if there would be anything important—lacrosse practice, a game, or if we had committed to volunteer. "Everything is paid for. Breakfast, dinner, and two spa treatments. I bought the weekend getaway package."

"I'm sorry we couldn't make it work between us, but we are focusing on what matters, you and your sobriety." I gave him a genuine smile. "I don't feel comfortable accepting such a generous gift."

"Please, go," he begged. "Do it for me. It will make me happy to know you're there with your son. Truly, it will." His frustration level rose as he gripped the phone tighter in his hand.

"Are you one hundred percent sure you want me to go?" I clicked on his forwarded email to confirm I had received the information. "It's so expensive, and you can probably just cancel the reservation."

"Yes," he replied, "I've never been more sure in my life." He turned back to face the road ahead while I began planning what I would pack and how I would convince Christian to go with me.

"I'm glad we got that settled," Mike said. "That's super nice of you, Alistair, and I'm glad Prue accepted your generous gift." He glanced at me in the mirror. "So, to change the subject, I contacted a few buddies back in Boston. They're figuring out where my mom moved to, and if my brother is alright."

"Where's your father?" I asked, curiosity getting the better of me.

"He died last year," Mike said. "I found out from a friend."

I opened the window, overwhelmed with sadness for him.

"You alright?" Mike asked.

"Yes, still have some boundary issues," I replied. "That must have been hard to find out your dad passed away from a friend."

"It is what it is. My father and I had our issues, but yeah, I was devastated when I found out," Mike said.

A thickness filled the car, and I was desperate to get out.

"Alistair, we are about five minutes away from the treatment facility," Mike said. "We won't be spending any time with you. Someone meets us in the driveway, you will be escorted in, and then the usual protocol—drug-tested, bags searched, paperwork, a physical, and then you will be issued your room. No visitors allowed during the first month, but we can deliver whatever you need to the front office. They will communicate everything when you check in."

"Oh, Lord," Alistair said. "Here we go again."

"This time you'll do it," I said. Helpless, I kept feeding him words of encouragement. "I believe in you." I tried to act cheery and excited for him. "Mike and I will see you in exactly one month."

Guilt weighed on me over the excitement I was feeling about getting away and staying at such a gorgeous hotel, one which I had dreamed about seeing someday.

"After three weeks, the rules lighten immensely, and you will be able to leave the facility to work, but you must report back by a certain time and check in every hour," Mike added. "It will be quite doable for you, and won't disrupt your life too terribly much. The most important thing is you hold yourself accountable."

"Right." Alistair's voice flattened.

We turned into a beautiful home on the ocean side of the street. No signs out front that screamed *treatment facility for drug addicts!*

Mike entered the parking area while making a call. "We're pulling in," he said.

Within moments, a large man wearing scrubs came out to greet us. He opened the passenger door. Alistair got out. Mike and I followed. I wrapped my arms around him.

"I'm so proud of you," I said. "I will be praying for you every day."

"Thanks," Alistair said. "See you in a month."

I got back in the car and closed the door. It seemed right to give Mike a chance to talk to Alistair before he disappeared behind the healing walls of rehab.

Mike gave the aid who greeted them a hug then turned to hug Alistair. The aid stepped back to allow a moment for Mike and Alistair to talk alone.

"Thanks for everything," Alistair said. "You've gone above and beyond."

"I care about you," Mike said.

I leaned back in the seat, feeling like a voyeur but unable to stop myself.

"Listen," Alistair said. "If there's one thing I know about, it's love, and I see a spark between you and Prue." Alistair patted Mike on the arm. "You have my full blessing."

"You're relentless," Mike said. "I appreciate your insight."

When he turned to get the suitcase from the back of the car, I pretended to be looking at my phone. Mike handed the roller bag to the man in scrubs. Before Alistair disappeared inside the treatment facility, he turned and waved. Mike waited a few moments before returning to the car.

"We did it," he said.

"Do you think he'll be okay?" I asked.

"He's going to learn to live a sober life and will become far better than before he checked in." Mike put the car in drive and began pulling out onto the Pacific Coast Highway. "You skip the steps, you're setting yourself up to fail. When I found out Alistair had left aftercare early, I had a deep concern for his well-being. Knowing he's in rehab will help me sleep at night."

While we drove, the horizon turned vibrant orange with bursts of pink. We flew down the PCH as the moon began to rise.

"Looks like it might be a full moon tonight," I said.

"I think you're right." Mike glanced toward the sky. "The same color as this dress my mother used to wear. I remember it like it was yesterday."

"That sounds like a beautiful dress."

"Yeah, like from the fairy tale *Donkeyskin* you told me about at Serenity Hills."

"Yes." I was honored and touched he remembered.

Mike's phone rang. The name Liam lit up on the screen. "Hello." The Bluetooth connected.

"Mikey boy." A thick Boston accent. "Got some information for ya. Not the best news, so I want to say I'm sorry to be the one delivering it."

The thought of more bad news made me want to fall out the car window.

"I appreciate you doing some sleuth work for me. What did you find out?" Mike asked.

"Your mom passed away from cancer last month." Liam paused a moment to allow his words to sink in. "I'm sorry, man." Mike swallowed, and his head dropped to his chest. "Apparently the house sold, and the proceeds went to your brother."

I reached for his knee. "Any word on where my brother might be?" Mike asked, his voice cracking. I tried to respect his privacy with no choice but to get involved. He swiped away a tear with his hand.

"He's been allocated to the state, so my best guess is he's in some kind of home or something."

"Thanks so much, Liam."

"Anytime, buddy. I miss you, man, and hate that you're finding out this way." His tone lifted. "I gotta come out to LA and check out the gym. All the guys are talking about Churchill Boxing and how Mike Sullivan is making his big comeback."

"Not true, but you should spar with me. I'll kick your ass." The more Mike said, the thicker his Boston accent emerged. "We'll have some fun."

"Yeah, we will."

"Listen, if you find out anything else, let me know," Mike said.

"Will do." Liam paused. "Come back home to Boston. No one is telling you not to. Get back to your roots."

"I'll think about that. Talk soon." Mike hung up.

"I'm sorry," I said. My words seemed stupid and small.

"Thanks," he said. "I lost my mother a long time ago." His hands held the wheel with purpose. "I appreciate your sentiment. Now I want to focus on finding my brother."

"I want to help." I imagined putting my hand at the nape of his neck, running my fingers through his hair. "You were amazing today with Alistair. The way you handled everything. I'm super impressed."

"I do what I can." His hands were on the wheel at ten and two. "So, are you excited to stay at San Ysidro Ranch?"

"I mean, I guess, but I feel sort of guilty having fun when Alistair is going through hell in rehab." I reached for the ear that wasn't facing Mike and began rubbing. "It seems sort of selfish and wrong."

"You should go," he said. "Alistair told you to, and when you're there, write him a letter and tell him all about it. That would be really nice."

"That's a great idea," I said. "It sounds like you know about the hotel. Have you been?"

"Me? No." He laughed. "I've heard of it."

"I mean, how have you heard of it?" I backpedaled. "Not that you aren't the type to stay at a fancy hotel, but it doesn't seem like something you'd know about." I figured I'd better stop while I was ahead.

"The Kennedys honeymooned there." He glanced over with a smile. "I'm from Boston. The Kennedys are royalty. Always wanted to check it out and walk on the same paths that were graced by Jack and Jacqueline."

As we drove along the PCH, there was nowhere I'd rather be in the world than sitting next to Mike. For the first time in my life, I relaxed about tomorrow or what the future might hold. This moment was all that mattered. This moment with him by my side.

"I'm going to go," I said with conviction. "I need to."

"Yes." Mike tapped the steering wheel. "I'm glad."

A peaceful silence filled the car. I figured he was thinking about the turn of events—the news of his mother's passing and making plans to find his brother.

I stared at the road ahead with newfound clarity. Everything happened for a reason. All the experiences of my life had brought me here. I vowed to help Alistair. Then I made a promise to myself to embrace the power and independence of paddling my canoe alone.

"Can I play DJ?" I scrolled through my Spotify playlists.

Mike nodded, pleased with my offer. While I connected my phone, he began to laugh. It was a contagious kind that got me going too.

"What's so funny?" I asked, queueing up Frank Sinatra's "Fly Me to the Moon."

"Life." His smile lines deepened. "The way we all move through this world, one day we're on top, the next day we're down. It all goes back to boxing."

"Yeah. I totally relate to what you're saying." I tucked a foot under my leg and twisted toward the driver's side.

"When you knock an opponent down in the ring, you reach out a hand to help them up. That's one of the things I love most about the sport." He glanced over at me. "You uplifted me today. I didn't want to forget to tell you."

"So what was making you laugh?" I asked.

"Picturing the two of us boxing." He burst out laughing again.

"Ohmygod, hilarious! Olive Oyl and Popeye."

"In all truth, you're stronger than you think."

A wave of guilt moved across my chest as I thought about Alistair and what he was enduring. I wondered whether he was afraid, ashamed, or feeling depressed. My thoughts went straight back to the moment I checked into Serenity as I tried to tap into the emotions I felt that day.

"I'm beginning to realize that I actually am strong and becoming more comfortable with the concept," I said.

"That's good," Mike said. He turned toward me and smiled. "Where should I drop you? Is your car at the hotel?"

"Shit," I said. "I rode with Lily, and she went home. I'm such a ditz. I don't have a car." I grabbed my phone. "Why don't you drop me somewhere convenient for you and I'll call an Uber."

"Absolutely not," Mike said. "I'll take you home. Just need the address."

On the way to my house, Lily messaged that she could drop Christian off at the house.

"I'm ordering takeout, do you want anything?" I asked, a bit nervous by the idea of superhuman Mike coming to my house—the Great Oz. "You can stay and eat before you head home."

"Sure," he said. "That sounds nice."

I immediately messaged Christian that Mike was dropping me off and staying for dinner.

As Mike drove, I recited the menu then ordered food. When we pulled in the driveway, the delivery guy was leaving and Christian was sorting through the food bags in the kitchen.

The three of us sat at the kitchen table like old friends. We spared Christian the gory details of putting Alistair in rehab and focused on the blessings we had taken away from the memorial service. Christian asked Mike about boxing. Mike invited Christian to Churchill's to take a lesson.

"Can I bring a friend?" he asked.

"Sure thing," Mike said. "We'll have fun."

"Cool," Christian said.

Between delivering Alistair, spending time alone with Mike, and witnessing his human side, something inside of me changed. I was no longer seeing him as someone above me but more as an equal. He was a man, a regular human being. I realized that I tended to put people on pedestals, and the only place to go from there was down.

When I put people I admired above me, what I was really doing was putting myself down. All of this, I realized, stemmed from feeling less than as a child. I praised myself for having some insight as to why I did certain things. None of this self-realization would have happened without Mike's help.

Chapter Thirty-Five: Prue Present

I made the executive decision to let Christian skip school on Friday so we could get an early start to San Ysidro Ranch. After some minor whining about leaving for a whole weekend with his mom, Christian began to get excited for an adventure.

While we loaded the car, we blurted out, "Road trip!" as we passed each other with suitcases, snacks, and various electronic devices. By the looks of the car, you would have thought we were going away for a month. With Christian buckled in the front seat, headphones on, his eyelids quickly began to drop due to me making him get up so early. I delivered Lou to Lily's on our way out of town and then sent a dog-sitting payment to Charlie through Venmo.

Once I was on the freeway, I took a deep, long breath. The car was quiet, and I finally had time to think. I rehashed the weekend at the Four Seasons, everything that had happened with Alistair, what I could have done better. When I couldn't clutter my mind with anything else, I attempted to address my feelings for Mike.

As I drove, my mind replayed every interaction Mike and I had shared throughout the past weekend. I fantasized about the possibility that he might be thinking about me the way I was him. Either that or it was all in my head. I remembered the way we locked eyes in the car, the way he grazed my knee when we were discussing Alistair then quickly removed it. Subtle moments that could not leave my mind but I could easily skew to fit the narrative I had so perfectly assembled in my head.

At a stoplight, I glanced at my hand as it gently grazed the leather wheel. My eyes studied the purple veins, which had become prominent with age. The brown sunspots that danced across my wrists and decorated my long, thin fingers reminded me of my mother. Her face popped in my head with her usual coral lipstick and pale, airbrushed complexion. I recalled a time when she cradled my adolescent palms and caressed them with her fingertips.

"I remember when my hands looked young like yours," she would often say, admiring my smooth, youthful skin. The fading memory of her touch brought tears to my eyes.

"It has been so long since you held us," I murmured to myself. My poignant daydream was interrupted by a series of loud honks. "Fuck," I said, pressing my right foot on the gas. I had nearly missed the green light.

What I had realized throughout the long, meditative drive was that I didn't need to sexualize every man in my life the way I had pre-rehab. Some men were meant to be friends, great friends, and some were meant to be lovers. There was a process to falling in love, and I was constantly rushing something that needed time to grow. The answers would come, and what I truly needed to work on was patience and finding peace with being alone.

Christian woke up right when we were pulling off the freeway into Santa Barbara. "I'm hungry," he said, and from experience, I knew that I had only a few moments to get him food before his hunger turned to *hanger*.

"There's a huge wharf in town, and I have a restaurant in mind that has food we both will like."

We got a table outside, and it was one of those perfect blue sky Southern California days. The wharf was bustling with people. The sun was shining, and I was elated by a sense of hope and gratitude. With our bellies full, we headed to check into the hotel.

"This town is pretty cool," Christian said. "Charlie and I need to come up here and go surfing." He craned his neck to check the waves as we drove along the coast.

"If you keep up your grades, you could get into UCSB," I said. "It's a really good school."

"That would be awesome," he said.

There were things Christian would have to figure out on his own, but I could plant the seeds. No one can tell you that the world doesn't begin and end with high school, but when you're in the weeds of those four years, it certainly feels like your whole world. My mother used to remind me that I didn't want to peak in high school.

As we pulled into San Ysidro Ranch, I eased up on the accelerator and loosened my grip on the steering wheel. Vibrant bougainvillea in various shades of magenta wrapped along the drive. A koi pond with blooming lily pads shimmered along the turnaround near the registration desk. The buildings were tucked around the property as though they were part of the land. Wild grasses moved with the breeze alongside wild California sagebrush. A gated flower garden with bursting blooms sat adjacent to the main building.

"Wow," Christian said.

I grew anxious about whether Alistair's room was really paid for even though I had the confirmation number. The thought haunting me was that my credit card might be declined, or worse, we would have to turn back because I couldn't afford to pay for the room. It was the same less-than feelings that plagued me—unworthy of staying at such a beautiful hotel. As we walked into the check-in area, I held my head high and pushed away my self-doubt. Christian held his lacrosse stick, cradling it side to side as the ball sat motionless in the mesh pouch.

"Welcome to San Ysidro Ranch," a man said as he held open the door, the scent of lavender surrounding me from the blooming plants flanking the entrance.

My heart pounded as the woman at the front desk pulled up our reservation. "I have you in the Ocean View Hideaway Bungalow for two nights, breakfast and dinner are included." She smiled. "Will you be needing a cot?"

Christian and I looked at each other. He shrugged.

"Sure," I said. The days of Christian and I sharing a bed had ended when he turned thirteen. "That would be lovely. Thank you."

"We'll have it delivered to your room." She passed us two sets of keys. "Armando will show you around the grounds and explain the amenities to you. Your reservation comes with two complimentary spa services. Would you like to book those now?"

"Would it be alright if I checked out the options and called to schedule?"

"Of course, Mrs. Prescott."

"Oh, I'm not Mrs. Prescott." I laughed while Christian looked confused. "That's my friend, he made the reservation." Guilt laid across my shoulders. "He wasn't able to come."

"Lovely," the woman said. "We're happy to have you. Can I have a credit card for any additional expenses you might incur?"

I passed her the card with the most available balance, figuring she'd only hold a hundred dollars on it, then sighed with relief when she handed it back to me.

"Enjoy your stay."

We followed Armando to our room as he told us some of the history of this special hotel. He pointed out the pool and spa, told us about the tennis courts, wine cellar, various restaurants where we could eat, and pointed out the farm-to-table organic garden.

The minute we got to the room, I unpacked my suitcase. Christian begged me to go to the pool, so we put on our suits and headed over. I filled a bag with a pile of magazines that were resting on the coffee table and the book I'd been trying to finish. The last thing I did before leaving the room was put on a big floppy hat.

We relaxed by the pool until the sun began to set against the horizon. I sipped on a piña colada I had ordered from the bar—my biggest weakness, and something that reminded me of my college spring break trips.

While Christian was in the pool, he began chatting with a cute girl in a tie-dye bikini who appeared to be around the same age. She was pretty in a nerdy way, with straight hair and a freckly, pale complexion. Christian came up to me, his lean frame wrapped in a striped blue towel.

"What are we doing for dinner?" he asked.

"The hotel lobby has a restaurant, so I figured we would go there. When would you like to eat?"

"I'm pretty hungry right now," he said.

"Let's go back to the room, shower, and then we'll head over to the restaurant," I said, putting a bookmark in my novel and shoving it in my pool bag.

Even though I was curious, I decided not to ask him about the girl he had been talking to. As we walked through the pool gate, the girl waved and said, "See you later, Christian."

I nudged him with my elbow and smiled as we walked along the lavender-flanked paths back to our room.

Christian showered first then kept his nose buried in his phone while I got myself ready. I spent some time drying my hair to create the bouncy curls I loved. All the while, I told myself the primping was for me. The chartreuse slip dress was new, one I had saved for a special occasion. So many times I had waited for this or that to wear a dress or use my wedding china. I vowed to celebrate every day in ways that brought me joy. I walked back to the living area, and Christian looked up at me.

"Wow, Mom, you look really pretty," he said. Then he quickly glanced back at his phone to send a text.

"Thank you," I said, slipping my foot into the sandals I had left by the door. "Who are you texting?"

"That girl who was at the pool," he said.

"You guys exchanged phone numbers?" I asked, tightening the backs on my gold hoop earrings.

"Yeah, don't get too excited. We're like just friends."

"I'm not," I said. "I was just thinking it's nice there are kids here your age." I slid the room key from the top of the bureau and tucked it in my purse.

"She wants to meet at the hot tub later, so I'll probably do that if it's okay with you." He said it as nonchalantly as possible for a thirteen-year-old.

"Of course," I said. "Ready?"

Christian pulled himself off the sofa, and we headed over to the restaurant. We were immediately seated at a table under a tree with twinkling lights strung from its branches with a full view of the hotel grounds. A sliver of ocean shimmered in the distance as the sun set.

After we ordered, I asked a few questions about the girl from the pool. "Do you know where she's from?"

"She lives in Marin County," he said, a curious expression on his face.

"Oh," I said. "That's up north near San Francisco."

"Yeah, she said it's like over the Golden Gate Bridge or something. Her dad works in Silicon Valley heading up some kind of dot-com startup. She plays Dungeons and Dragons too."

"Really? That's awesome. What's her name?"

"Her name is Addie. She's like a really cool girl," he spoke as he dug into a sizable piece of ribeye.

Compliments of Alistair, I thought to myself.

"I'm excited for you," I said, not wanting to get too overly inquisitive out of fear he would close up.

As soon as he finished eating, he asked if he could go meet the girl. "Sure," I said. My plate of food was only half-eaten. "We can order dessert to be sent to the room later, maybe watch a movie."

"Are you okay with me leaving you alone?" he asked, already standing in the ready position.

"I'm one hundred percent okay," I said, raising my glass of rosé. "It makes me happy that you're having fun and not bored. That would be my worst nightmare."

"Awesome," he said. "I have my key, so I'll meet you back at the room later."

"Have fun," I said.

Christian walked through the restaurant with a regal gait and a confident posture. As I watched him, I beamed with pride over my handsome son who was becoming a young man.

I ate a few more bites of food while forcing myself to be comfortable with being alone. The waitress came by and asked me if I wanted another glass of wine.

"Sure," I said. "All I have to do is make it back to my room." When I started laughing, the waitress did too.

The sun cooled the air as it dipped in the sky. I wrapped the pale pink pashmina I had tucked in my bag around my shoulders. With the second glass of rosé resting on the table, I shifted my chair to face the colorful cutting garden.

The chattering voices of other diners provided a buffer to my thoughts. I breathed in and closed my eyes to say a silent prayer of gratitude. When I opened them, I scanned the crowd, which consisted of families, groups of friends, and couples. I pushed aside any negative thoughts that crept into my head about eating alone, sitting by myself in such a romantic and beautiful setting.

The wine warmed my insides and lightened my mood. A sense of hope filled me. I couldn't think of anything I had to worry about and embraced this moment, believing that everything I had endured in my life had brought me to this place. I considered taking a detour by the pool on the walk back to my room but decided to give Christian a chance to be a full-fledged teen. If he needed me, he would let me know.

The waitress delivered the second glass of rosé and set the dinner tab on the table in a leather folder. "Please sign and add your room number," she said. "Gratuity is already included."

I waited for her to step away before inspecting the bill. The food had been delicious, the service impeccable, with a price tag to match. I scribbled my name and room number on the check then gathered my things. With my wine glass in hand, I strolled along the hallway of the main building where there was a display of old photos. Some of the black-and-white images were of movie stars with small typed snippets below for viewers to learn more about who had stayed at this historic hotel.

When I came to the images of the Kennedys on their honeymoon, I put my bag on the floor, drew out my phone, and took some photos. I was careful to make sure they were focused well and included the writeups below. After a few more minutes of admiring the display of images, I strolled back to my room.

Halfway to the bungalow, my phone dinged with a message from Christian.

I'm heading back to the room. Can Addie watch the movie with us?

Yes! I texted back.

Cool, see you in a minute.

A light breeze blew, and the air filled with the scent of night-blooming jasmine. I paused to appreciate the magnificent floral scent while the crickets chirped from the surrounding bushes. When I arrived, the front door was open, and Christian and Addie were sitting on the living room sofa scanning the movie options.

"This is Addie," Christian said from the sofa. "This is my mom."

"Nice to meet you," Addie said. She wore cutoff shorts and a cropped, sleeveless tee. A small tote rested on the floor with a bikini balled up on top. Her braids were damp on the ends. "I hope it's alright if I stay to watch a movie."

"Absolutely," I said. "I'm actually going to sit outside and let you guys hang out." I dropped my things on the chair near the bed, keeping the wineglass and phone with me.

I opened the double doors that led out to the patio. There was a candle on an outdoor table, which I lit with the complimentary pack of matches they had conveniently left next to the container. I sat on the green cushion of the twinned wooden lawn chairs without a worry that no one was with me to occupy the other seat. A soft breeze rustled the leaves in the canopy of trees above me. I slipped off my shoes and crossed my legs.

While sipping my wine, I scrolled through the photos I had taken of the Kennedys on their honeymoon. After choosing the best ones, I cropped and did some light editing before drafting a message to Mike.

I couldn't help but think of you when I saw these. With the photos added to the message, I pressed send with a giddiness tickling the back of my throat. Within moments of sending, a message chimed on my phone.

Thank you! I hope you and Christian are having fun. These photos are amazing. I must see them in person someday . . .

I studied his text while fighting the urge to message him back. *Less is more,* I thought to myself. After waiting long enough to avoid appearing too eager, I double-tapped his message with a heart.

The thought of Mike brought me straight back to Alistair. I remembered what Mike had told me in the car about sending him a note and figured now was the perfect time. The muffled sounds of Christian and Addy along with the movie playing brought me comfort. After a deep inhale, I typed a heartfelt, thankful, and encouraging email to Alistair. With no clue when he would have permission to use a computer, I wanted this email to put a smile on his face while letting him know that the weekend at San Ysidro Ranch had been picture-perfect. A much-needed getaway for me and my son. I avoided asking him about rehab or mentioning anything about our past. This was a message to thank him and tell him how grateful I was for his generosity and kindness.

After I pressed send, I set the phone on the table next to me and picked up my wine glass. I gazed up at the sky. The golden moon tucked itself amongst the trees, illuminating the branches. Every star I had ever wished on in my life twinkled above me. I felt as though I were floating—soaring, really, above the earth. All the hardships from my past had brought me here, shaped and molded the woman I am, and allowed me to be in this beautiful place in my life.

The patio door opened, and I turned to see who was there.

"Thank you for having me," Addie said with a wave.

"You're leaving so soon?" I asked. Christian stood beside her with an adorable sparkly smile.

"My parents want me to get back to the room," she said. "I think we're going to meet at the pool tomorrow, so I'll probably see you."

"Sounds great," I said.

Rather than stand and walk her out, I gave them privacy. A moment later, Christian joined me outside, settling in the empty chair next to me.

"She's cute," I said.

"Yeah, she's super cool."

"I'm sorry for all the stress that I have caused you over the past few years," I said, grabbing the moment and diving in. "I know the divorce hasn't been easy on you, and then me leaving to go to rehab, well, it was a lot for you to deal with." I turned to my son without saying another word. It was important to give him space to think and express his feelings.

"Honestly, it hasn't been that bad." He propped his elbows on his knees. "But I hope I never get a divorce."

"You won't if you listen to your gut. It will always guide you in the right direction."

"I'll try," he said. "I am a lot happier since you've been home and not with Dad. Even being with Dad has been way more fun than ever before."

Relief washed over me. The tension I had held in my shoulders softened. My work was not done; there was still more healing that needed to happen, and I had to watch myself. The bad habits could creep back in if I got too cocky.

He stood, signaling that the deep talk was over. "Want to watch a movie and order dessert?"

"Yes," I said. "Pick out whatever you want to watch, then call room service and order two hot fudge sundaes. I'm going to finish this last sip of wine and I'll be right there."

"Okay," he said. "I'll pick out a rom-com since I know you love those movies."

"That's sweet," I said. He stepped into the room and closed the door.

I finished the wine and put the glass on the table. With the shawl wrapped around my shoulders, I stepped to the edge of the patio. The anchor that had been holding me back released, setting me free. I became untethered. No longer swimming upstream—battling the demons of my past.

My canoe moved effortlessly across the glassy water. I turned to look behind me. Christian was there, helping me paddle.

About the Author

Jennifer Irwin's debut novel, *A Dress the Color of the Sky*, was published in 2017 and has received rave reviews, won seven book awards, and was optioned for a feature film. Jennifer's short stories have appeared in numerous literary publications including *California's Emerging Writers: An Anthology of Fiction*. Jennifer is represented by Prentis Literary and currently resides in Los Angeles.

CPSIA information can be obtained
at www.ICGtesting.com
Printed in the USA
BVHW071450251021
619820BV00007B/69

9 781736 776278